THE LIVING-DEAD

THE LIVING-DEAD

ABHIJEET INGLE

PARTRIDGE
A Penguin Random House Company

ISBN: Softcover   978-1-4828-1552-8
               Ebook   978-1-4828-1551-1

To order additional copies of this book, contact
Partridge India
000 800 10062 62
www.partridgepublishing.com/india
orders.india@partridgepublishing.com

To my wife Sudha and family, for all the motivation, love and endurance to make this book happen. To my friends Dhananjay and Shashikant, for the help they rendered during the vital stages in the writing of this book. To Ranajoy Mukherjee for the cover design and author portrait of this novel.

CHAPTER 1

▼

In the summer of two thousand and four, the sun gasped as it loomed over the cotton fields of Vidharbh. The heat emitted from below scalded the sun, which dreaded to hang in here. The sun wished to circumvent this circuit, but protocol prevented it. The world over temperatures soared above normal, and nations wrangled over the Kyoto Protocol, but in Vidharbh, the sun scorched, because farmers committed suicides in huge numbers, and their corpses burnt like forest fires. India spanned a decade of liberalization, and boasted about a robust economy, but somehow the mood in this part of the country remained dispirited. The country debated the phenomenon, and the government alleged it took measures to break the trend; yet, the cotton farms of Vidharbh identified as the killing fields of India. A few villages, which ducked the trend in Vidharbh, lay scattered across the region. One such village was Ramwadi.

Ramwadi stands on the borders of Maharashtra and Andhra Pradesh, in the district of Yavatmal, in Vidharbh. It contains a cluster of rectangular tin huts and few houses built from mud. The lanes in front of these houses meet in the village square, while the other ends dissipate into the surrounding fields. A temple of Lord Hanuman stands in the centre of the village square, encircled by a peepul, neem and tamarind tree. Shacks that serve tea, snacks and operate as gambling dens lay below the peepul tree. The men of the village gather here to socialize in the mornings and evenings.

A tar road leads into Ramwadi, and ends at the footsteps of the Hanuman temple. Parked opposite the temple and in front of the tamarind tree auto-rickshaws, tempos and trucks ferry passengers and goods in and out of Ramwadi. Behind the rickshaw stand, sits a Veteneriary hospital and a Co-operative bank, and between these a tin shed, which sells seeds, fertilizers and pesticides. The neem tree at the other end of the square shelters blacksmiths, carpenters, pan stalls, kirana shops, a tailor's shop, a tyre and water pump repairing shack.

A Government Primary Health Centre and common village well occupy the space between the neem and tamarind tree. The village school stands at a distance of two kilometers from the village square along the main road that merges into the state highway that leads to Yavatmal. Two mansions called waada encircled by a courtyard, and fenced with a wall of brick and cement, stand near the village square. These pacca houses belong to the moneylenders of Ramwadi. The one next to the seed and fertilizer shop belongs to Seth Dhanichand or Sahukar as addressed by the villagers. The other waada stands at a distance from the peepul tree and belongs to the Sarpanch of Ramwadi(Abba Deshmukh), who runs the village and the Fair Price shop (ration) situated in a corner of his courtyard.

Life in Ramwadi revolves around agriculture. In April, the farmers apply animal dung manure to the fields. They cart loads of manure from open pits owned by big farmers, who have cattle on their farms. The dung gathered from cattle sheds, and farm waste dumped into these pits rots there the whole year. Men, women and children help to load and cart the manure from the pits to the fields. They slog whole day, heaving loads of manure into bullock carts or tractors. Their bodies sweat, but their callous hands and feet continue to labour, while the animals yoked to the carts cower as the load piles up. The loaded carts then plod through the village square along bumpy roads, which jab the wheels that squeak, groan, and spill the manure along the village lanes. Children scamper after the wobbling carts, hurtling down the tracks, and try to sneak in from behind, while the riders struggle to control the reins and shoo away the trailers. Sometimes, the carts break down and carpenters and blacksmiths repair wooden planks and broken metal rims of the carts. The village square echoes with the holler of wheels, hammers and saws.

In May, the temperatures soar, while animals bake and stagger as they tow the plough under the sun. The farmers donned in skimpy outfits lumber behind the animals, striving to keep pace, panting and mopping the sweat off their foreheads. The women sit at home or under trees, preparing pickles, papads and masalas for the year, while the children run around the village in groups undeterred. They pelt stones at mango trees, fight over the dropped kairis, bite, and suck on the juicy green flesh to savor the sour taste, which lingers on the teeth. They then dart around the village lanes, playing marbles or touch and go games or rolling wasted tyres and chasing them down the battered tracks, ramming into walls, trees and other tyres. They smile, chuckle, grin, scowl, or cry and then heave their bruised bodies and continue to vault down the lanes, until the shrieks of the ice-cream vendor resonate in the hot air. The games cease and the children scurry back home, where they grovel, rant, crib, and harass their mothers and nannies for golas. The women relent, and then the delighted children pick up tumblers and race to the ice-cream vendor, where the crowd gathers to hanker before the vendor. After an intense struggle, they suck at the golas, and lick their forearms right down to their elbows. They then continue their pranks with red, blue, pink and green stains dotted on their bodies and clothes.

At sunset, the men in the fields unhitch the bullocks, and fasten them to stakes hammered into the ground. They fill up the animal troughs with water, and chop up fodder for the hungry animals that dig in for a bite, while the farmers wash and return home. Back home, the women light the chullahs, and knead the dough to cook the evening meal. A delicious aroma of charred wood and baked dough wafts through the village, arousing hunger in the childrens bellies. The games seize and the children lumber back home with wounded bodies, and pester the women for a meal. The families dine, and then the men saunter to the village square to smoke, chew tobacco, play cards and gossip. They argue and crib over crop failure, pest menace, broken hedges, unpaid debts, corrupt government officers, political parties, thekedari, bataidari and other agrarian issues. A few of them get drunk, pick up fights and collapse in the temples or sprawl on the lanes or slump in hotels and under trees. The lucky ones may wake up in their homes, but the habitual end up, where they crashed. By ten in the night, the village sleeps.

In June, black clouds unwrap and trickle down on the fields. The parched lands gulp the water and let out an exotic fragrance of wet earth that pervades the atmosphere. A cool wet breeze drifts through the air, and the farmers breathe a sigh of relief. Grass unfolds over the dry land and patches of muddy water scatter across the fields. The village square bustles as the farmers throng the input dealers for seeds and fertilizers. The families gather in the wet fields to sow seeds for the kharif season. The bulls plod through the mud, while farmers trudge behind crooning ballads and tossing seeds into the funnels of the dibblers. The village then anxiously waits for the next bout of heavy showers to fill the fields, rivers, wells and reservoirs.

Diwali beckons harvest. The flowers ripe with grains bloom, sway in the wind and dangle as if to kiss the earth. The farmers hopes soar at the sight of the luscious green fields tucked under the early morning mist and covered in dewdrops that thaw as the sun unfolds over the horizon. A sweet fragrance of moist pollen and wet earth lingers in the air as the white veil of early morning mist unfolds over the fields to reveal the abundance of nature. The murmur of the wind in the meadows drowns in the din of the village square, where the holler of the hagglers for threshing teams and machines resonates. The rich hire threshing machines, while the others settle for threshing teams. The threshing teams comprise families and communities, who pool in their labor to reap more profits. The barns with threshing teams' bustle, with the cackle of people, who gossip while they cut, bundle, and stack the harvest on the open fields. The air smells of grain dust, human sweat, animal dung and cacophony of children that run around the barn after school. The mechanized barns chime with the raucous sound of machines that rip the soft rhythm of the meadows and drown the human voices. Puffs of black smoke emitted by engines smothers the atmosphere and the air reeks of gasoline, which subdues the sweet fragrance of human labor. The people yell, scream, and shriek for an audience that drowns in the din of threshing machines.

At night the farmers sleep in the barns to guard the grain stacks from robber bands that prowl in the dark. The fear of erratic rain haunts their minds and they want to sell off their yield to traders. Engines putter, horns blare, tyres screech, trolleys rattle and dust clouds envelop the air, when trucks and tempos of the grain merchants race into the village square to transport the harvest to market yards. After an intense haggle with the merchants, the produce leaves the village square. The farmers spend on Diwali and save money for the Rabi season. The colony of shops in the village square, witness a sudden spurt in sales. The gamblers pitch higher and the bootleggers sell more spirits. The kirana shops stock disappears and appears in the kitchens of the village, where women prepare delicacies for the festival. A crisp aroma of rice flakes, groundnuts and masala wafts through the air as it sizzles over the tawa. The women dab sweetened bundi on the flat of their palms, and shape it into small round balls of ladoos, while ants shuffle around on the kitchen floor to grab drops of liquid sugar that dribbles down the back of their palms. Children dash in and out of the kitchen to feast on the delicacies, while the women sit in circles and gossip.

In the village square, people cram into rickshaws that ferry them to the towns, where they shop for Diwali. When the day arrives, the families get up early in the mornings for a bath, offer worship and then invite others for a feast. Children run around the lanes, with tickli guns and burst crackers, while the village square becomes a riot of colors as people gather to greet each other in their colorful attires. After Diwali, the village prepares for the Rabi season that ends in May. The life and culture of Ramwadi revolves around agriculture and the spirit depends on the monsoon. They have lived it for years, but all that will change for a few families from April 2004.

CHAPTER 2

▼

On April 2, 2004, a hot and dry afternoon, a jeep raced down the tar road into Ramwadi. It displayed a colourful logo painted on its body: SANTANO Bt COTTON SEEDS. The jeep screeched to a halt outside the Sahukar's seed and fertilizer shop: Rashmi Enterprises. A young clean-shaven suave well-dressed man opened the front door and stepped out. He stretched out, tidied his hair, arranged his tie and pulled out a leather bag from inside the jeep. He tossed it over his shoulder and ambled towards the shop.

Inside his home, the Sahukar reclined for siesta. His servant boy dashed in and broke his sleep, "Sahukar," he gasped, and then pointed out. "He says he's a salesman and wants to meet you."

"Damn these salesmen! They come in the afternoon," snapped the Sahukar, sitting up on his charpoy. "Tell him I'll come in a minute."

He put on his shirt and shambled to his shop.

The salesperson stood up, and then thrust his hand forward, "Sir, I'm Joy Gupta. The distribution head of this area for Santano seeds," he smiled, waiting for the Sahukar to shake his hand.

The Sahukar folded his hands and greeted him, "Namaskar. Please sit down," he said, drawing a chair for him.

The tin shed that appeared a virtual oven reeked of seeds, fertilizers and pesticides stacked on wooden planks, against the wall behind the counter.

"Yeah," murmured the salesperson, slumping in his chair. He opened his leather bag and rummaged through for something.

"I'm sorry about the heat in here. The power cuts bug," the Sahukar apologized, shrugging his shoulders. He pointed to a small table fan, with blades of dust, perched on the cranky table, which served as the counter.

"No problem. I'm used to the heat," the salesperson admitted, with a nod, and then rummaged through his bag. "It's a lot hotter in my hometown Kota in Rajasthan. Heat, cold or rain; I have to visit input dealers," he submitted, yanking out a brochure and tossing it on the table. The Sahukar stared at the colored canvas slack-jawed, while the salesperson grinned and continued his rabble. "A multinational company called, 'Santano,' based in America," he paused, looking at Sahukar, who still gawked at the brochure, as if an alien showed from somewhere. The salesperson beamed at the sight and stiffened his back. "With an annual turnover of $15 billion and the best research laboratory in the world," he stopped for the figures to sink into the Sahukar's head. The Sahukar raised his eyebrows and reclined in his chair. The salesperson inhaled a deep breath, straightened his tie, leaned forward and rambled on. "We," he exhaled, thumping his chest, as if he owned the company, "have developed a new high yield variety of cotton called Bt 25."

The Sahukar sat up and interjected, "Bt Cotton! I'm aware of it!" he exclaimed, scouring the cover, He scratched his head, and then slumped back in his chair. "This variety looks expensive," he assumed, dropping his eyes, and then whispered. "Speak slowly I'm not fluent in English."

A smile dangled on the corner of the salesperson's lips as if his appearance and fluency in English exhibited an impression. In a country steeped in colonial mentality, a few words in English often maul the vernacular. It does not declare the English educated more intelligent, though, most will think that way.

"Sirji, this foreign variety is jhakas!" he exclaimed, slapping the table and persisted. "I need to explain it in English."

The Sahukar squirmed in his seat and yielded. "Yeah, speak in English," he stuttered, not sure, whether he yielded under pressure; he clinched his jaw and conceded. "I understand the language, though; I'm not fluent, although, I graduated in English from Regional University."

It seemed as if the word English crashed, like a ton of iron on his head and split his resolve to remain rooted to his native language.

"Ah," the salesperson sighed; it seemed he wished to lash his customer with his English tongue. He grabbed the opportunity and parroted. "The Bacillus Thurengienesis cotton varieties in the Indian market cannot protect the flowered plant against the lethal pest, 'Bollworm,' as a study conducted by the Universal Institute for Cotton Research in Nagpur showed."

The Sahukar mopped his forehead and interjected, "What's this Baci Thur?" he inquired, unable to pronounce the words that the salesperson spurted for an added impact to seal the deal.

"Its abbreviation for Bt—Bacillus Thurengiensis; a botanical name," the salesperson grinned and his eyes widened. He elbowed the table, leaned forward, cocked a wry smile and inquired. "Haven't you studied Biology or Agricultural Science?"

"No. I told you I'm an English graduate," replied the Sahukar, half-aloud. "I studied for a degree, took admission but never attended college, because I am more interested in business. You see this," he reiterated, spreading his hands in the air to display his hard-earned asset; he arched a sly brow. "After all, I'm a Marwari and like most of my community I'm interested in the money," he pinched his fingers, and then flicked them and stated. "We don't value education unless it pays."

The Sahukar affirmed the Governments policy to manufacture graduates, precisely, what thousands of universities, which have sprouted like weeds of grass across the country produce. So it didn't matter, for the Sahukar remained another census oriented English graduate, who operated a seed and fertiliser shop in Ramwadi, because capital remained the sole criteria, to offer a license to run a Krishi Kendra (Agricultural shop) in Maharashtra. Knowledge of the technicalities of agriculture or a basic graduation in agricultural science seemed taboo. He appeared one of the many non-technical graduates, selling agricultural inputs to illiterate farmers in Ramwadi.

The salesperson laughed and conceded. "It doesn't matter, because in India things stay fine, as long as you have the money to get them done," he winked, and then carried on his prattle. "Our company in America developed this unique variety of Bt Cotton," he bragged, pointing to a picture on the brochure and plunking down his finger on the cotton bud. "This Bt25 variety carries a foreign gene that expresses the protein, CryAC, to kill the bollworm, Helicoverpa Armigera," he declared with aplomb, straightening his tie. "This will help the farmers save on the costs of pesticides. Presently, farmers spray pesticides fifteen to twenty times. They will save on the amount, which will reduce their cost of production and increase their yields," he boasted, drumming his fingers on the table.

The Sahukar's brows knitted in a frown. "Who will buy my pesticides? I'll loose my commission on pesticides," he lamented.

The salesperson raised his palm to assure his customer. "Don't worry. The Company knows your grievance. It will offer you a fifty percent margin for each packet you sell. A packet of 450 Gms of seeds costs two thousand rupees and no other company pays such huge margins. But this American company does," he insisted, yanking out a packet from his leather bag and dangling it in the air.

The input dealer stretched his hands out, grabbed the packet and looked at it. The cover contained information printed in English with certain terms and conditions scribbled in the tiniest of fonts. The Government never deems it necessary to make most terms and conditions readable and written in vernacular, perhaps, the reason why most Companies continue to hoodwink consumers. The Sahukar strained his eyes to read the terms and conditions; his eyes ached and popped out as if they would fall off the sockets. He brushed the packet aside and complained. "I can't read the terms and conditions."

The salesperson snatched the packet. "Don't bother. I'll tell you all," he replied; he dug his hand into his leather bag and drew out a bundle of posters. "These contain real stories of farmers, who used the Bt25 variety and reaped rich yields. This variety of cotton gives a yield of ten to twelve quintals per acre. Our company policy demands that you stick these posters on the walls of your shop," he asserted, springing to his feet and rolling his eyes around to survey the shop.

"That's not an issue. I'll pin them up," the Sahukar nodded in agreement and accepted the posters.

The salesperson stomped out of the shed and studied the rectangular tin box nailed to the ground. The weathered tin sheets revealed a patchwork of holes interspersed with a wafer thin rusted coat, which stuck out in places. He scowled and plodded back into the shop.

"Sirji," he said; he nodded his head in disdain, picked up the brochure perched on the table, flicked through a few pages and pointed to a well-painted structure. "Your shop must look like this," he demanded, hunkering down on his chair. "Our Company will bear the expenses. We will use high quality oil paint and paint your shop. All the four sides of your shop must bear this logo, like the one on the jeep," he twisted to one side, and then pointed to the jeep stationed opposite the shop.

"Hmm," nodded the Sahukar;he grinned and mulled over the offer.

It appeared the Sahukar never renovated his shop for the past ten years. When he started, the shop resembled a shed, except for the tin roof; the walls remained a bundle of dry stalks hedged between the ceiling and earth. Within a year, he made a fortune. One of his customers, like most of them over the years, failed to pay the credit and interest borrowed for inputs. The moneylender razed the poor peasant's tin house to the ground and ordered his henchmen to gather the tin sheets. The same sheets adorned the walls of his shop.

"Your company spends a great deal to promote its product," suggested the Sahukar.

"We have to spend to market our product."

"Hamara bhi dhanda hai, par thanda hai," grumbled the Sahukar. Like a typical Marwari; he refused to admit that he made loads of money in the countryside. It shielded him from greedy Government officials, helped stifle competition, because the people who heard his woes would not dare take up the venture.

"Don't worry Sirji. Sell these seeds and make loads of money," the salesperson replied; he smacked his lips and dropped his hands on his knees. "This American company pays well. Take my case, earlier; I worked for an Indian seed company. They did not pay me enough and paid the travel allowances at the end of the month. This company offered me an AC jeep with a driver. I'm happy," he grinned, stretching his legs out and taking a deep breath. "I've paid a fortune for my management degree. I need to recover the expenses," he exhaled slowly, nodding his head.

"I expect credit," the Sahukar demanded, elbowing the table and casting a sly look at the salesperson. "An American company can indeed give me goods on credit. I do not have capital, because the villagers fail to pay on time. It all depends on the rains."

"We will give you the seeds on credit and not charge interest. Pay us, as and when you make money. But you must sell our seeds," replied the salesperson.

"I'll sell your seeds. Tell Santano ki yeh Marwari baitha hai. Dhanda hai par thanda hai," declared the input-dealer. He slumped back and cocked a wry smile. "Aapko bhi commission milta hoga?"

The salesperson gave a wry smile and tilted his head to his right. "Yeah, the company pays me a commission on each packet, much more than what the Indian companies paid me. America knows the value of hard work. I'm happy."

"It's a good thing if both of us make money," the Sahukar suggested. He ruminated for a while and creased his forehead. "What if the farmers buy our seeds, reuse them and sell the surplus to their neigbours. Hamara dhanda to thuk jayega, pehle si hi thanda hai," complained the input dealer.

The salesperson waved off the apprehension. "Don't worry. American Company knows all. The gene will prohibit a second germination so the farmers will buy new seeds from Santano, which means more sales and more commissions," explained the salesperson, with a gleam of deviltry in his eyes.

The input dealer's face lit up and he smiled with glee.

"Think over it. Such offers don't come often," suggested the salesperson. He stood up and showed his little finger. "Excuse me," he said, and then stomped out to relieve himself.

It appeared as if the multinational companies patented everything under the sun. Santano charged royalty from Mother Nature. It meddled with the genetic matrix, claimed an invention and then charged the poor farmers a royalty, similar to a few that have patented neem, haldi and basmati rice. Someday, they will patent human semen, charge a royalty from all the women and proclaim—a baby that never falls ill, and most women may fall for the bait: Why not? This baby will not need medical insurance.

This latest form of colonialism unlike Lord Macaulay's education policy that kept the body intact and subjugated the mind aspires to own the body, mind and soul—Genetically Modified Colonialism (GMC). The terms and conditions will state that each woman can have only one baby at a time: no twins, triplets and the like. If you want another baby, pay another royalty because each vial of semen will come with a brochure, which will inform you about the following: How will you nurture the baby? What will you feed the baby? What can you expect from the baby? The Indian Government will endorse this product, as a means to save on health care.

In most cases, the Government's health care budget does not reach the people, like most other budgets. This new invention can appear as an alternate solution to the corruption woes of India. So, import this MNC policy, like most other policies imported from MNC's, because MNC policies never go wrong. An aberration to this remains; MNC economic policies run through the World Bank and International Monetary Fund that knock down most of the economies the world over and ruin the environment. However, because the policies named MNC and backed by firepower, they stay good and democratic. This GMC policy, too, will help control the Indian population. The rich class that can afford the royalty will claim the privilege and own babies, since, the World Bank and IMF does not finance subsidies, the poor will never get to possess a baby. This new form of, "GM induced legalized extinction," of the meek will endorse what unbridled capitalism preaches: survival of the richest. It appears the world will remain for the rich people and not the poor. Real egalitarianism promoted by GMC.

The salesperson returned and jigged his head. "What did you decide?" he asked, with a broad smile. He knew the offer appeared too tempting to resist.

"Hmm," murmured Sahukar, nodding his head in agreement.

The salesperson smiled wryly. "I told you these multinational companies pay well," he bragged; he gathered the packet of seeds lying on the table, tossed it in his bag, looked up at the input dealer and winked. "Dhanda hai, Par thanda nahi, Sirf chanda hai," he thrust his hand out.

Sahukar beamed and shook the salesperson's hand, "Badiya hai, tell Santano that this Marwari will sell their seeds," he stated with aplomb, pointing at himself, and then stood up.

He walked the salesperson to his jeep, opened the door, bowed humbly, motioned the salesperson to climb in, and asked. "What about the oil paint?"

The salesperson twisted and settled down in his seat. "I'll send the painter tomorrow, along with your first installment of Santano seeds. You get started," he replied, with a thumb up gesture, and then slammed the door shut.

The jeep puttered and then hit the road.

CHAPTER 3

▼

Except for one Brahmin and Marwari family, Ramwadi comprises of Kunbis, Marathas, Dhangars, Dalits, Banjaras, Kolis and other Hindu castes. All castes live within the bounds of the village square, except the Dalits, who live a little further from the village, next to a seasonal riverbed. Ramwadi possesses rich dark cotton soil, which stretches from the fringes of the village for hundreds of acres and beyond this appears a vast expanse of dry and rocky land called the dry patta of the village. A water tank or talav sits in the middle of the dry patta, and at a distance of two kilometers from this tank appears a taanda, comprising of a cluster of ragged canvas tents, which shelters cane harvesters, bootleggers and gambling dens.

At noon on the same day, a peasant couple cleared their patch of land, which stood on the dry patta by the talav. The elevated land overlooked the water tank, about five hundred metres from the state highway that led to Yavatmal. The couple removed the big stones that lay scattered on their land. The afternoon sun scorched the parched land and burnt the faint breeze that blew across the dry patta. The rocky terrain stretched for miles with sparse vegetation that comprised of an odd acacia (babul), neem or mango tree, which managed to survive on this ruthless terrain. The peasant couples' land appeared hemmed in between the water tank and a sugar plantation, which bordered the dry patta.

"Mangala, do you think it will rain this year?" asked Vasu, hunching over and grabbing a big stone lying on the land.

His wife shot a glance upwards at the sky and scowled. "It depends on the mood of the monsoon," she replied, watching the clouds drift under the blue sky; she looked down and nodded her head.

"I hope it rains," said Vasu, flinging the stone on a heap of rubble stacked on the wayside. He unwrapped the scarf tied around his head, wiped the sweat trickling down his forehead and lumbered towards the neem tree perched in the middle of his land. "I'm hungry let's have lunch."

Mangala followed him and they walked to the neem tree. A claypot and lunch basket lay under the tree. They sat down and Mangala opened the lunch basket. "I hope Abba gives us our quota of wheat and rice. We have little jowar in our house. If it doesn't rain, we will have no grains this season," admitted Mangala, unwrapping the lunch basket.

"What's for lunch?" asked Vasu.

"Bhakri and chutney," replied Mangala; she unfolded the bhakri (Roti) and showed it to Vasu. A lump of red chutni mixed with oil stuck on the surface of the bhakri.

Vasu's jaws stiffened and he slammed his eyes shut. "Damn it! The same old crap."

"The rich eat when they feel hungry. We eat if we have something to eat. We're lucky to have this," said Mangala, with a lackluster smile. She tried to soothe her husband's frustration and stretched out to hand Vasu his lunch.

Vasu dropped his head and accepted his lunch. "I'm fed up of chewing this stuff. Farmers till the land and raise the crops. We feed an entire population and for all our labour and toil. What do we get?" he grumbled; his nose wrinkled as he showed Mangala the bhakri. "Do you call this a meal?" he asked, shrugging his shoulders. "The tiller gets nothing to eat," his face stiffened. He ripped the bhakri, crammed a portion in his mouth and chomped on it. His eyes reddened like tomatoes when he dispatched it in his stomach. "Do you at least have an onion?" he begged.

Mangala shook her head in disagreement. "I told you, we have only some jowar. This house runs on credit."

Vasu shook his head. "Continue to run the show on credit. I don't have a penny on me," declared Vasu. "Huh! Huh!" he coughed to clear the lump of food stuck in his throat. He grabbed the clay pot, heaved it over his mouth and gulped down the water to wash down the clog

"For the past six months we lived on credit. Whenever, the rations arrive we don't have a penny," complained Mangala.

Vasu's eyes reddened and water trickled down his chin, while he guzzled the water. He finished and swiped the drops off his chin. "How much more can we do? Last year we borrowed and sowed. The rains delayed so we sowed again and managed to harvest only three sacks of jowar on this rocky land. This year we will have to borrow again. The rains deceive and our loans and interests mount. Sahukar badgers me for the money I owe him. It's a pain to walk past that input shop, because he pesters me for the money, and to make matters worse, I'll need more this season," Vasu narrated his woes.

"Why do you walk past that shop? You must take the route behind the temple. It annoys me when people insult you," Mangala remarked, with tears streaming down her face.

"Why do you take it to your heart when people say things to me?" fretted Vasu, edging closer to her. "It seems the world has the right to trample and kill us, because we remain poor," moaned Vasu, wiping the tears under her eyes. "Don't cry. I'll work out something."

"We remain worse than animals, because the Gods won't bring down the rains. You should have skipped the pilgrimage to Pandharpur. Lord Vithal sits there, accepts our meager offerings with delight and gives us nothing," riled Mangala, with her voice caught in her throat.

"We can't do that, because our family tradition demands that we visit Pandharpur. My father, despite all odds, never missed a pilgrimage all his life. Lord Vithal will work out something for us," asserted Vasu, trying to infuse confidence in Mangala. He tried his level best to give her hope, though it looked like he wielded a candle light in a storm.

"What good did all the penance do him? We remain worse off then when we began. My father promised me that my new home would give me all the joy in the world. What did I get? Not even a decent saree to wear. Look at this," Mangala sneered, pointing at her tattered attire. It looked like a shoddy patchwork of rags. "Twenty years since we married, yet, I haven't bought a new saree," she regretted, slapping her forehead in disgust.

Vasu shut his eyes, buried his face in his palms and deliberated about his fate.

As most Indian girls bound for marriage, Mangala's father promised her the sky, but the eighteen years of marriage heaped misery. Each year, unfolded for the worse, while she mothered a sixteen-year-old daughter and a ten-year-old son. Both went to the local school in the village. Shobha, the girl, dropped school after the tenth standard, because her parents could not afford higher studies. She now helped make ends meet. Mangala's physical features betrayed her age. Although, in the late forties, she looked older and despite a fair complexion, the regular toil in the open fields dried and tanned her skin. The grind of poverty showed on her coarse hands and heels. Before marriage, her father informed her that Vasu owned three acres of land, but the land carried little value. It yielded a pittance and each year the moneylender edged closer to snatch it away from them.

She never desired a second child, but Vasu insisted otherwise. "We need a son to bring us luck and care for us in our old days," he argued. Mangala protested on grounds of poverty, but her heart raced and craved for another child. "Poverty may remain, but who carries all the wealth to heaven," she concluded. The poor desired children despite poverty because it helped them pull through the grind. Her husband may not give her the wealth and luxury, but she too belonged to a poor family. Deep down in her heart, she knew that Vasu performed his best, and if the rains betrayed, he remained helpless, though, it occurred harmless to pull and nag him for more affection, so like most Indian women, she decided to badger her husband to avenge her marital woes.

Vasu's mind regained poise; he looked up. "Don't bother about sarees. You wait and watch. There'll come a day when I'll buy you a dozen," he promised, with a smile across his face, tugging her hand.

"The same empty promises for the past twenty years—vanvas. Instead of twelve sarees give me one and I'll stay happy," Mangala joked and then grinned. The tears dried up and it seemed she wanted to squabble.

"I've big plans for your sarees," said Vasu, sprawling on his back and tucking his palms under his head.

"Do you plan to rob a bank or break a house?" taunted Mangala.

Vasu shook his head, smacked his lips and cocked a smile.

"What then?" Mangala questioned, with a toothy smile.

Vasu fixed his gaze on her but said nothing.

"Do you wish to work for Abba again? I'll rejoice, if you choose to."

Vasu's jaws dropped, his brows bumped together in a scowl and his mind raced down memory lane.

Vasu exhibited courage and hard work, but remained short of luck. He happened to slog on Abba's farm for ten years, to provide for his parents and younger brother, Gunwant, a spiritualist and devotee of Lord Vithal. In fact, the family remained Varkaris—a sect that worships Lord Vithal and Rukmini. The sect worships Lord Vishnu and his avatar Lord Vithal. Each year in August, the Varkaris visit Pandharpur on the banks of the river Chandrabhaga, to pay obeisance to their God. The family never missed an annual pilgrimage to Pandharpur and Gunwant paid with his life: trampled to death in a stampede in the temple. His death shattered the family. Vasu's mother lost her will to live and died within a short time, while his father, though heartbroken, continued to till the land. However, their six acres of dry land that depended on the rains could produce just enough, to feed them for an entire year.

This forced Vasu to work for Abba, the Sarpanch, who demanded much work and exploited his workers. Vasu toiled on the fields the entire day and at night; he slept in Abba's house to keep guard. He swept, mopped, dusted, milked the cows, ran door to door to recover the money Abba lent and then rushed to the fields to channel water for the crops. The irregular power cuts made matters worse and forced Vasu to water the crops late in the night. He tried hard to grab some sleep, but it seemed impossible. One afternoon, while he channeled water for the sugarcane crop, his tired eyes forced him to take a nap. He rested under the neem tree and soon fell fast asleep. The water overflowed and spilled over the baandh (hedge), but Vasu slept like a log. The motor pump drained out half the well. Abba happened to visit the field. "Damn it! You filthy swine, you have wasted all the water. Who the hell will pay for it?" shouted Abba; he kicked Vasu in the stomach. Vasu squeaked like a rat that grovels under the paw of a cat. He apologized, agreed to compensate the damage and forfeited half his annual pay. The incident convinced Vasu about the hidden dangers of a job. He could have invested the money he lost in his land, so he vowed never to work for others again.

But his father fell ill and the medical expenses soared. His father advised him not to spend on the treatment, because he manifested no interest to live further. Vasu refused and admitted his father in a private hospital in Yavatmal. He borrowed money from Abba and cleared the medical bills, but his father died within a month of the treatment. Vasu piled up a huge debt of over fifty thousand rupees and worked again for Abba to clear the loan. This year he gained freedom to run his life on his terms and conditions. The memories that came back to mind frightened him. "No. I will never work for Abba. I've paid a heavy price," snapped Vasu.

Mangala twisted her nose. "Then what will you do? Money will not rain down here," she snapped, dusting the rag and tossing it in the basket.

"I've decided to dig a well and sow soyabean. I am sure Lord Vitthal will change our fortune. We have seen so much misery. I've faith in him, this time he'll deliver," asserted Vasu, drawing his legs up and curling his knees.

Mangala looked aghast. "Have you lost your head? We just paid back all we borrowed and managed an entire year on credit. This year we have to think of Shoba's marriage and you mention this new investment. Oof," she complained, slapping her forehead.

"Soya will give us the money to fight poverty. The prices of other food grains diminish in the market. How much will three acres of jowar give us, if the rains fail us again? We will not manage to pay back the interest on the money we borrow. How do we manage the year and Shobha's marriage expenses? Better to take a chance and drill a tube well," Vasu argued.

"If we fail to tap water under the rocky land then we loose all our money and the loans will pile up. I feel it's better to sow jowar. The seeds cost little and if we have to sow, again, it will not cost much. We will have enough to feed ourselves, because we cannot depend on the ration shop. The rations come once in two months and if we have to take it on credit it will cost us more," reasoned Mangala.

"Damn the jowar! It hardly pays. Soya bean sells a thousand rupees and more per quintal. Imagine the money we can make if we have water," declared Vasu. He picked up a stone and flung it away in anger. Suddenly, he smiled and his anger melted, while his mind conjured about his plans coming alive. "The whole village will look up to us. I'll buy sarees for you, dresses for Shobha and a silver pendant for Bapu," he blabbered, as if in a trance.

"Oof!" gasped Mangala; she slapped her forehead, wary about her husband's dreams. She dug her hand into the rocky land and scooped out a little soil. She showed the stones to Vasu. "Look at this!" she exclaimed. "All stones and you expect to manage a good yield. Huh," she scoffed, throwing away the soil. "I doubt this land has water underneath."

"Don't worry about the soil. We can dig out the silt from the talav and spread it over this soil. Many have done it and reaped good yields. Remember water stored in that talav sinks right beneath this land," he pointed to the talav. "The water table below our land seems high. You see that borewell that Abba sunk next to our dry patta," said Vasu, pointing in the direction of the sugarcane plot. "It contains loads of water. I have toiled on that sugarcane and channeled water from the tube well. It pumps water the whole year. I know that water exists down under."

Mangala smiled at Vasu and admired his grit, which helped him push through the rough and tumble of a peasant life. He bore an earthy tenacity, the kind the land posseses, the power to endure the pounding from the sun, wind and rain. The risks and stakes in agriculture remained high, but Vasu knew that a family depended on it. There existed no chance for the slightest margin of error, because if it failed, it would uproot a family out of this world. All big dreams come with a price and Vasu agreed to pay for it. The sun descended and the heat dissipated, while a cool breeze blew over the rocky terrain. It appeared as if the horizon sounded the bugle. The couple gathered their belongings and headed for Ramwadi.

CHAPTER 4

▼

Abba, the Sarpanch (headman) of Ramwadi, owned the largest chunk of fertile land (three hundred acres) in the black patta. His family included a wife, a son named Vinod and four married daughters. His four daughters married similar landowning gentry within sixty kilometers of Ramwadi, while Vinod also addressed as "Tatya," in the village married a landlord's daughter, who gave birth to a son and daughter. The family owned the legacy of political control over Ramwadi. In nineteen sixty-two, the family circumvented the Land Ceiling Act of Maharashtra, and conveyed their surplus fertile land in the names of their bonded labourers. The village rumored of how: Kanha, the cowherd; Ganpat, the water carrier; Limba, the chamar and Vani, the dhobi carried land titles. All these servants worked for this family, since, generations. Abba looked after their basic needs, and gave them money for marriages and festivals. In return, he expected them to meekly obey and work for him.

Abba also owned the fair price shop (ration) in Ramwadi, which made him an absolute ruler. He decided how much ration to distribute to the people. He never gave the people their ration cards. They remained with him and he made good use of them. He fudged entries and during elections, he got twice the number of ration cards issued, so that he could include the Taanda to vote for him. Most of the rations he sold in the open market and, whatever, little remained he distributed within a day. The district supply officer, inspector and the Tehsildar remained on his pay roll. He bribed and kept them happy so that he could run Ramwadi like a fiefdom.

The only concession his father made included that of gifting a stretch of seventy acres of dry and rocky land to the Government, in the presence of Acharya Vinobha Bhave, when the bhoodan movement reached Ramwadi. The government distributed this stretch of land amongst the poor and landless peasants of Ramwadi. The village called this stretch the dry patta, which once served as "gairaan" or "milch pasture" of Ramwadi. In the famine of nineteen seventy-three, the government dug a huge water tank (talav) in the dry patta, as part of its water harvesting scheme. The storage tank worked as a means to increase the groundwater level and store water for the Rabi season.

Most of the farmers, who got land from the Government never cultivated the land. They did not have the capital so it remained largely a gairaan. A few attempted to cultivate it, but managed a poor yield of jowar and tur in the Kharif season. They could not cultivate the land in the Rabi season, because they did not have the capital to lay pipelines and draw water from the talav. Over the years, the dry patta witnessed a few changes. Most of the beneficiaries, belonging to the Dalit community, sold off their lands to the small and marginal farmers, while others leased it out on theka and a few settled for bataidari; it operated as a fruitful venture for these poor owners. They managed two crops and if the rains failed, they worked as wage labourers to provide for their families.

Abba hated his father's benevolent gesture and opposed it tooth and nail. Like a true aristocrat, he hated the socialist ideals of equitable distribution of wealth. "If someone has wealth; destiny desired it, so why feel ashamed of it," he had argued, with his father. The old man, steeped in experience saw things differently, "this largesse will help strengthen our political control over Ramwadi. In a democracy, power lies in numbers and what have we forfeited? A dry patta worth nothing," he had reasoned, with his son. Yet, Abba remained adamant, "if every one in the village owns land and cultivates the same. Who will work in our fields? If people do not owe us, they will neither fear nor respect us. Even a rag tag peasant may stand up and challenge our hegemony," he had riled. His father, a seasoned politician persisted, "mere ownership will not make them rich, because agriculture needs capital and the peasants have none. We will take back the land," he had boasted. The argument ended, but not the vengeance. Abba vowed to take back the entire seventy acres of land: "to hell with socialism. I'll bulldoze these peasants out of my land."

Over the years, the old guard gave way to new. His father expired and mother followed soon. He gained an easy ascendancy, because he remained the only son. He contested the Zilla Parishad elections and completed three terms. He coveted positions in the political set up of Yavatmal. He operated as the director of the District Co-operative Bank, the sugar mill and served on the board of the Cotton Federation. In short, he displayed a successful political career. These positions added to his stranglehold in and around Ramwadi.

Each morning he sat in his hall known as, "the peoples contact chamber," and attended to people from in and around the constituency, who approached him with their grievances. They came to settle petty disputes; family feuds over baandhs, disputes over the share of mango and tamarind trees, and petty quarrels between bataidars and thekedars. Many suffered at the hands of the state administration. The women came to have their alcoholic husbands and gamblers released from lock ups. Farmers wanted credit in the sowing season and money for weddings and festivals. The sugarcane and cotton farmers wanted the sugar mill and cotton federation to buy their produce. A few wanted loans from the co-operative banks. There lay complaints against MSEDC officials, who snapped electricity connections, for the non-payment of dues. It remained tough, to survive as a people's representative, because there existed bouquets and brickbats; Abba lay trapped in a chakravyah, which his legacy pushed him in and he longed to get out. Yet, his tradition demanded that Abba must stay and so Abba sat in his chamber, each morning, ready to go through the grind.

The first thing in the morning, he read the newspaper, named, "Lok andolan samachar." This morning the headlines read, "Cotton mess—the graveyard of Vidharbh." Abba creased his forehead and scoured the inside story: "Maharashtra contained a State Co-operative Cotton growers Marketing Federation, from nineteen seventy two to two thousand and two, whose purpose remained to procure cotton from farmers at reasonable prices and sell it to the mills and traders. However, it occurred that this body never included a farmer's representative and lay riddled in corruption. The appointments made on the basis of political affiliations damaged the purpose of the federation: to buy cotton at a Minimum Support Price (MSP) and distribute the profits to farmers as advance bonus in April and May, so that the farmers possessed money for pre-sowing activities.

'In nineteen ninety-four, the ruling government integrated the MSP and advance bonus scheme to form a, 'Minimum Guaranteed Price,' to pay the farmers irrespective of profit and loss. This election year, the ruling party wanted to lure the farmers. The world over the prices of cotton fluctuated, due to liberalization and the federation wanted to procure cotton at cheap prices. At the same time, there remained a huge influx of cheap cotton into the Indian market. The prices of cotton fell, and the federation could not sell the cotton; it procured at higher prices, and incurred heavy losses. To make matters worse, the opposition, which came to power further raised the procurement price of the federation in order to strengthen its vote bank in Vidharbh. The procurement price stayed at rupees twenty one hundred per quintal from the earlier seventeen hundred rupees. The hike happened without the federations consent and until two thousand and four, the federation procured cotton from the farmers at prices that ranged between seventeen hundred to twenty five hundred rupees. The price per quintal depended on the grade of cotton. Many times the federation indulged in corrupt practices, while it sorted the cotton. The government officials took money from farmers to grade the cotton. Those who could pay received higher grades. The procurement monopoly and rampant corruption, threw the federation in financial difficulties, but things did not stop there.

'The federation also deducted three percent of money from payments made to farmers to create a corpus fund. Co-operatives set up claimed that they wanted to develop a cotton-to-cloth infrastructure to gin, press and manufacture yarn. The farmers would own all the mills and it would run like the sugar co-operatives in Maharashtra, but that never happened because corrupt political leaders, siphoned off the funds and the loot continued until kisan sanghatna, the farmers' organization protested and forced the government to stop deducting the money. The Government under pressure stopped this practice in nineteen ninety-four, but over seven hundred crores of farmers money, remained with the federation.

'Throughout the nineties, with the liberalization of the markets, the prices of fertilizers, seeds and pesticides skyrocketed. These new hybrid seed varieties encouraged by the Government increased the input costs of agriculture, which skyrocketed and forced farmers to take loans from private moneylenders, but due to the mess in the federation and low cotton prices, the farmers could never recover the costs of production. At the same time, the Union Government's policies on import duty also hurt the farmers. The import duty on cotton continued at a mere ten percent as against the import duty on sugar, which rose to near hundred percent. Most of the political leaders that belonged to Western Maharashtra lobbied hard for sugar, but neglected the cotton farmers of Vidharbh. The inevitable happened and in nineteen ninety-seven, the markets crashed for the first time. Since, that year the number of suicides started to climb.

'The State Government took the decision to end procurement monopoly and open the market for private players. In the year two thousand three and four, the procurement monopoly ended, but the federation remained to compete with other private entities. The same year, the cotton produce in the international market plummeted and pumped up demand for the Indian cotton. The bania and marwari traders of Vidharbh made a kill. They procured cotton from the farmers directly, through kheda kharidi, at rupees twenty eight hundred to thirty two hundred, and sold it at two times the price in the international markets. Many of these traders, who made a windfall, also joined the money lending business. The farmers preferred to sell the cotton to private traders, because they owed them money and because they paid them quickly. The federation sunk in further trouble with little cotton to procure and entrapped itself," concluded the story.

Abba's eyes stayed glued to the newspaper, though his mind appeared distraught. "Damn the news reporters! They will always blame the federation," he thought, flicking over the page for a better news story.

A man in a safari suit and with a leather pouch stood at the door for an audience. Tired of the wait, he summoned the courage and greeted Abba. "Namaskar Abba."

Abba pulled down the newspaper, "Maske," he said, with a smile across his face. He shot a glance at the clock on the wall. "You've come after a long time. I wanted to see you," said Abba, motioning him inside. "Come take your seat."

The man walked in and sat down before Abba. "I waited for a long time, but you seemed engrossed in your newspaper. What is in the news: anything catchy?"

"You should have come in and sat down. You are not new to my place anymore. The news stays the same; the suicides grow in numbers each day. We sound like the suicide belt of the world," replied Abba. He ordered tea for the agricultural extension officer.

"The government remains under constant pressure from the media and it vents its anger on us. It fires and orders us to prevent suicides in the villages. Why blame the agricultural extension officers?" fumed the official, crossing his leg over his thigh and reclining in his chair.

"No! No! The Government cannot shift the blame. It is the climate and without rains and proper irrigation facilities. How do you expect the crops to grow? The costs of inputs rise and the market prices of produce crash. What can you do about that: do not worry? Go ahead and drink your tea, it'll get cold," suggested Abba, pointing at the teacup lying on the table. "Would you like some nasta (snacks)?"

"No, thank-you," replied the officer, sipping his tea. "I'm in a hurry. Last night I stayed at Chikli and today I head for Borgaon. I wanted to meet you earlier, but the summer schedule remains hectic, and includes agro tours to educate the farmers and escort the fact-finding committees that tour the area. The Courts appoint one, the State Government appoints another, the Central Government appoints a third and then thousands of NGO's tour the countryside to search for answers. I do not know what facts they gather. But the government wants to run down our necks and warns us of suspensions and terminations."

Abba laughed. "Despite all these fact finding committees, the suicides haven't abated. They multiply by the day and it sounds like a joke."

"Hmm," nodded Maske. He finished his tea, hunched over and put the cup down on the table. "I've worked with the Government for over a decade. The Government first told us to propagate the tenets of the green revolution. Then the Government changed course mid-way when it realized that the fertilizers and pesticides damaged the environment. The Central Government came up with the concept of sustainable development. Now it wants us to propagate organic culture. First, you draw people away from organic culture and then you push them back

25

to organic culture. It sounds stupid! It takes years to convince the villagers about change and if they agree to change, they do not have the capital for hi-tech agriculture. In most cases, they will want others to experiment and then they will try things. That is the reason we have to convince the rich and educated farmers like you. So the village will follow," confessed Maske. with a wry smile. He removed his spectacles, wiped them and slumped in his chair.

Abba scowled at the admission. "So, we remain guinea pigs for experimenting new agri policies. It sounds good, if the experiment turns out fine, but if your new varieties fail, we burn our fingers and your Government does not compensate us for the losses. Always the small and marginal farmers get subsidies and loan waivers. Your Government presumes that we have all the wealth in the world and our loss seems a mere prick in the pockets. Yet, the fact remains that agriculture entails expenses. The input prices and labour costs have sky rocketed. The luckiest lot in the villages remains the wage labourers. They earn a cool one hundred rupees per day for the least effort. They come at eleven; get started at twelve, dismiss for lunch at two, resume work at three and and wait for the sun to set. By five o'clock, they pack to leave. Moreover, they get food grains from the ration shop at subsidized rates. They do not need to spend. The Government's labour oriented policies have pampered them," riled Abba; he shook his head and took a deep breath and exhaled slowly.

"I agree," added Maske, with a smirk.

"Big farmers who own the land spend heavy and risk more. The Government restricts us from selling our produce freely in the markets, because it wants to control the price rise of food and fears a backlash from the urban middle class constituency. It is sheer hypocrisy!" exclaimed Abba, slapping the arms of his chair. "The middle class can't pay an extra rupee for milk, vegetables, grains and sugar, but they remain free to buy luxury items. They never question the electronic goods and automobile companies when they hike prices, and cite production costs. Farmers have no choice but to kill themselves, because they cannot recover the production costs. I do not live off farming rather I live off politics. Otherwise I'll have to jump in a well, drink pesticide or hang myself to death."

"I agree with you," Maske reiterated and then laughed. He looked around slyly liked an inquisitive bureaucrat wanting to fish out information and hunched over. "Abba," he hesitated in a soft voice; his mind wondering whether to proceed.

Abba waved at him. "Go on I wish to hear more," he encouraged the officer.

Maske widened his lips slightly as a programmed bureaucratic half-hearted smile that can disappear if the boss frowns. He rolled his eyes sidewards and spoke. "You sound like the opposition," he stated.

"Ha! Ha! Ha!" Abba laughed.

Maske gained confidence; he scratched his head and proceeded. "I wanted to ask you out of curiosity, because rumors fly thick and thin in the Zilla Parishad that you wish to contest this election as an independent candidate."

Abba shrugged his shoulders. "I have no choice. My entire life I toiled for the party in Government and they offered me a few irrelevant offices. I want more. After all politics remains an investment. I have slogged day and night to take the party to the villages, and this time, again, they want me to wait. 'We'll give you the ticket for the next election,' they say. It has happened the second time. I'm frustrated," grumbled Abba, looking away in disgust.

Maske put on a grim look to please his boss. He grabbed the opportunity to assuage and flatter Abba. "I must say that you've made the right choice, because when I travel the length and breadth of our constituency, I find the people seethe with anger against the Government. It is not just the suicides and cotton prices, but the abject neglect of Vidharbh's development that bothers them. The erratic power cuts, delayed irrigation projects, bad roads, price rise and corrupt co-operative banks add to their worries. They feel cheated and want a separate State. They remain annoyed with the opposition alliance, for their communal overtones and disastrous first term in office. The electorate wants change and they will embrace you. What's your agenda?"

Abba smiled and his ego puffed up. "I want Statehood for Vidharbh; if Chattisgarh, Jharkhand and Uttarakhand have achieved Statehood. Why does Vidharbh have to wait? We have a genuine demand. Nagpur loomed as the capital of the erstwhile Central Provinces and Berar, from eighteen hundred and sixty one to nineteen fifty. Then it stayed capital of Madhya Pradesh for the next ten years. In nineteen hundred and sixty, we signed the Nagpur Pact that made it the second capital of Maharashtra, on condition that the winter session of Maharashtra's legislative assembly takes place at Nagpur each year. The pact wanted the Government to address the grievances of the people of Vidharbh, but what happened since decades thereafter manifests a mere ritual?

'The legislative sessions exhibit contempt and deliberate disruption. All legislations pass in a moment without deliberation, when the legislative assembly implies a forum for the people to express themselves. It seems the Government does not wish to hear us. How long will we continue at the mercy of leaders of Western Maharashtra? They look more interested in the plight of the sugarcane farmers and not us. The government continues to increase the import duty on sugar over the years to protect the interests of the sugar lobby. Yet, the same never happens with cotton imports. The leaders take all the funds to Western Maharashtra and siphon off the funds meant for Vidharbh. It is high time the Central Government concedes to our demand," fumed Abba. He pointed his finger at his chest. "I moved several resolutions for Statehood at the ruling party's Conventions," he boasted, dropping his hand. "In fact, all the representatives of Vidharbh supported it, but the leaders of Western Maharashtra forced me to withdraw, because they see Vidharbh as a milking cow. They want our cotton for their cotton mills in Ichalkaranji, our coal to generate electricity to run their sugar mills and bamboo for their paper mills, and so they oppose our Statehood. I will take these matters to the electorate. Give us Statehood and the suicides will stop."

Maske clapped his hands and applauded Abba. "Fantastic stuff!" he exclaimed.

Abba blushed and nodded his head.

"It'll go down well with the electorate. No wonder, Abba condemned the Government. Ha! Ha!" cackled Maske.

"I have to get used to it. I have lived with the Government for decades and lost aggression. The usual answers we gave remained: 'We will conduct an inquiry'; 'Situation though tense, remains under control'; 'Our party remains secular'; 'The high command will decide'; 'Our leaders sacrificed their lives for the unity and integrity of India'; 'Garibi hatao'; 'Hume dekhna hai,'" joked Abba.

"Ha! Ha! Ha!" the men cackled.

"Abba, I wish you all the luck," said Maske; he looked at his watch and stood up. "I must leave. I have a hectic schedule. Abba, do not forget about the fact finding committees. They will come any moment. Your lucky Ramwadi hasn't seen a suicide, but you never know."

"Don't worry, I'll take care of that," said Abba. "If you happen upon any new money spinning scheme of the Government then let me know."

"Sure," said the official; he bowed before Abba with folded hands and walked out of the contact chamber.

CHAPTER 5

▼

Senator, Sam Strosberg, from Texas carried German lineage; his ancestors migrated from Germany, in the early twentieth century, and sailed to America, because they hated the Europeans penchant for war over colonies and internecine conflicts, to dominate the world. The Strosbergs identified as pure business minds, lapping up anything that made money, so the discovery of oil forced them into this new venture. They knew that oil stood out as a commodity that would dominate world trade in the twentieth century. It displayed the potential to drive economic growth and human development. Yet, Europe with war clouds, looming over the continent exhibited danger for entrepreneurial activities. Europe struggled to wriggle out of the grasp of narrow sectarianism, laissez faire and communism, because each of these ideologies fought to govern the continent.

The left movement, which followed the Bolshevik Revolution, loomed like a shadow over Europe and threatened to gobble up capitalism. It swept away everything that came in its way, and paved the way for the creation of a, "Welfare State." The growth of pro-labour laws reduced the profit margins of the Capitalists, and battered business ventures. In Germany, the Communists grew from strength to strength, because of Germany's debacle in the First World War coupled with the disgrace, which the Treaty of Versailles heaped on it. These twin factors shattered the German economy and pauperized it. These developments influenced the Strosbergs decision to migrate to

America—the land of dreams, because America embraced people like them: ambitious, bold and innovative.

The Strosbergs soon made money, in the land of their dreams, and "Strosberg Incorporation," popped up. Their business interests remained oil and minerals. The Gulf of Mexico proved a veritable gold mine, and the Company dug deeper and deeper and sucked out oil from the ocean bed. The Strosbergs backed business acumen with foresight, and understood the importance of political connections to bag contracts, so the second generation of the family, joined the Republican Party, and entered American politics. They preferred the nationalist party, because it remained hawkish and hard core patriotic. Unlike the Democrats, the Republicans manifested a larger degree of love for their homeland. If the Democrats claimed to love America and the world, the Republicans claimed: You love America and the world, but we love America and America alone. For starters, this remained the distinct ideological difference between the two political parties that ran America and nothing else. The political acumen of the Strosbergs seemed as good as their business acumen, because the family wrested the Governorship of Texas, endorsed a seat in the US Congress, and at last Sam Strosberg hoisted the family fortunes into the Senate. The sole political office that appeared unconquered remained the American Presidency, and Sam Strosberg schemed day and night to make it the family home. It looked like Strosberg Incorporation blessed this family with wealth, power and influence.

Like most Americans, the Strosbergs simmered in the American melting pot long enough to suffer family woes. Sam's father, "Sandy," built his marriages on sand. Sam's mother remained Sandy's fifth wife, and considered herself lucky to have survived the snap. Sam's family contained three stepsisters, from his father's earlier marital ventures. He grew up with his lucky mother and errant father. Windsurfing stayed his passion and it helped him, ride over many a storm, and surf into the Senate. He studied Business Management, at the, "Rock and Roll University," in California, where he indulged in rock music, sex and drug abuse. He beat down anti-Veitnam war protestors in the campus and suffered punishment on several occasions for drunk driving. He loved movies and his favourite film remained, "Godfather," because it preached: behind every fortune, there is a crime.

Like many Americans, the film helped Sam absolve his guilt, whenever he read history, which reminded him that America first belonged to the Red Indian tribes. The, "Godfather," salvaged his guilt, indeed, most American sins. Most Americans, who sneered at the Roman Catholic Church, displayed their dislike for an orthodox faith. They wished for a, "God Of Big Things," who represented American values until Mario Puzo baptized them with a, "Godfather," which redeemed them of their sins, each time they invaded and bombed innocent civilians, to further their national interests: behind every fortune, there is a crime.

Senator, Sam Strosberg hated green activists like the early Capitalists hated Communists. Capitalism survived the wrath of the, "Trade Union Movement," in America and weathered the bite of the Cold War; but the collapse of the Berlin Wall, opened the floodgates for many new age movements that suffered confinement during America's war against Communism. These movements, like many, which wriggled under the notorious Mc Arthur era, broke loose and threatened the, "Great American Elitist Democracy," governed so far by two major political parties, which claimed to represent the labyrinth of multi-cultural America. Many political scientists foresaw the decline of the influence of the two major political parties, because America wielded too many activists. There existed: "green activists," "organic food activists," "gay rights activists," "feminist activists," "civil rights activists," "child rights activists," "black activsits," "anti-obesity activists," "AIDS activists," "anti-nuclear activists,' "anti-war activists," "Khalistan activists," "Kashmir activists," "Palestine activists," "Zionist activists," "neo-nazi activists," "anti-dragon activists," "anti-Castro activists," and so an and so forth. The American people seemed to grow more and more politically active, and America stayed dotted with all kinds of activists. It seemed that every American stayed active, except the political parties.

Sam Strosberg agreed to accept all kinds of activists, but not the green activists. The, "Green Peace Movement," that created a political space in the German polity, remained Sam's biggest headache. He chided the Germans, who offered space to the green activists. Like a true corporate, he accused the green activists, whom he claimed stalled the economic growth and development of Capitalist America. He called the green activists, "terrorists," and mocked their efforts against ecological degradation. Like most typical Republicans, he termed every adversary a, "terrorist," and their cause, "a war against American National Interest." He hated the green activists, because they made their presence felt in his constituency (Texas), where they persisted with their efforts to close down every oil refinery that threatened the fragile eco-life of the Gulf of Mexico.

His fears came alive in the year, nineteen ninety-two. Sam disliked this number, because it flagged the Earth Summit, in Rio de Janeiro, Brazil. It happened that the UN Convention on Climate change, agreed to cut back green house gas emissions to restore the ecological balance in the atmosphere. The same year, also, proved unlucky for Strosberg, because his only son Michael Strosberg—heir to the Strosberg Empire, converted to the green faith. Michael renounced his allegiance to the American Godfather, declared himself a green activist, and vowed to preserve the environment for future generations. This initiation and Michael's decision to marry Linda Kohl, a green peace activist from Germany irked Sam, who declared him a prodigal son. Michael and Linda studied anthropology at the, "Green faith University," in California and presently pursued a Doctorate in, "tiger and human conflicts for habitat." The lovers backpacked the world to study tigers, and ecological degradation. Sam seemed to hate Michael's apathy for business, and hoped that some day his son would give up his romanticism, and pursue serious business.

The events that followed the Earth Summit further angered Sam. In Kyoto (Japan), in nineteen ninety seven, a conference of parties to the UN Convention on Climate change, agreed that green house emissions (GHE) required a cut back by 5.2% of the nineteen ninety levels, which must happen between the years two thousand and eight and two thousand and twelve. The KP provided a forum for the, Governments of over one hundred and eighty countries, NGO's, scientists and other organizations of countries to deal with anthropogenic climate change, which affected livelihoods, public health, and threatened the planet. It appeared the KP would manifest into law in February two thousand and five, on condition that countries that emitted fifty five percent of green house gases must ratify it.

Senator, Sam Strosberg, hated this condition and perceived this as a conspiracy against the United States, by those who could not come to terms with America's economic growth. Further, to add to his woes, the conspirators also alleged that the US remained the biggest polluter, and that a US citizen emitted twenty times more carbon dioxide than a citizen of the less developed world emitted. This in a way forced the US to endorse the KP to help reverse global warming, because it appeared that without the ratification of the US, the KP would not come alive. Sam Strosberg took up this challenge on a war footing, and vowed to defeat the KP on the floor of the Senate to save the US from this biased law. He received support from Corporate America, and agreed to help them, because he needed funds for his Presidential campaign.

CHAPTER 6

▼

Days passed on and the month of May sizzled, while the farmers ploughed their lands. Most farmers in the dry patta borrowed bullocks and ploughs from their bataidars and thekedars to plough their lands. Vasu entered into an agreement with his neighbour Gangaram, who owned six acres of land, and shared a baandh (hedge) with Vasu. Vasu's land lay between Gangaram's land and Abba's sugarcane plantation. Gangaram, a sixty-year-old man, owned bullocks that he lent Vasu in return for fodder, which Vasu offered Gangaram. The deal existed for years, while Gangaram rotated his six acres of land amongst his three sons (Shrinivas, Mohan and Pandurang) for cultivation. One of them cultivated the land, while the others took up jobs as farm labourers in and around Ramwadi. This year, it occurred that Pandurang alias Pandu would till the land. Shrinivas and Mohan left for Nagpur to find work, though their wives stayed back home.

Vasu happened to convince Pandu that together they dig, haul and smear the tank silt, from the talav to their lands, and Pandu agreed because his land resembled Vasu's land. Pandu came across as a tall, slim and swarthy youth. He remained a good hand—tough and earthy. Though unmarried, he seemed unlike the spoilt youth of Ramwadi, who loitered around the village square and wiled away their time on cards and drinks. Vasu knew Pandu ever since both worked for Abba. They understood each other well and this complimented their efforts.

The task stayed difficult. They needed more hands, but neither could afford to hire wage labourers. In any case, to hire wage labourers required more money; also, the labourers came late, complained, dodged work and waited for the sun to set and left. Vasu and Pandu divided the task of hauling the silt between their families. Vasu's family helped unload and spread the tank silt on the fields, while Pandu's bhabhis and Vasu, dug and loaded the silt into the bullock cart at the talav. The tasks rotated each day.

At the break of dawn, the families went to the talav and worked until noon. They rested until three in the afternoon, and resumed work, until six in the evening. Before noon, the cart unloaded for the last time, then went to the talav to collect the folks, working there, and drove them back to the fields for lunch. Pandu unhitched the bullocks, tied them to the stakes under the tree, poured water into the trough, and served them fodder. The families then opened their lunch baskets and shared their meals. They gathered drinking water from the tube well in Abba's sugarcane plot.

Pandu seemed a good storyteller, and the group listened in rapt attention. Shoba, in particular fancied his anecdotes. Both studied together until the fifth standard, when Pandu dropped out. Shobha continued until the tenth standard, and then abandoned her school in Ramwadi, because her parents could not afford to send her to the town for higher studies. She still accomplished a lot, because her mother never went to school, and Vasu never studied beyond class five. Pandu on the other hand led an adventurous life; he spent three years in the jungles of Gadchiroli, and trained like a revolutionary. After he dropped out of school, he joined his mama (maternal uncle), who worked for a timber contractor in Gadchiroli. The timber contractor paid the revolutionaries to enter the jungles and take the timber. The revolutionaries believed in the ideology of Mao, and fought against the State for the rights of the tribes. They belonged to an organization called the Liberation of Forests Army (LOFA).

One night it so happened that the group of labourers, who worked for the timber contractor, lay stuck in the forests, because the truck that carried them in and out of the jungles broke down. The revolutionaries offered them food, shelter, and propagated their ideology. Pandu listened in rapt attention, as the dalam (squad) leader gave an entire discourse on class struggle. The leader appealed to the workers to join the revolution to uproot the feudal system, which exploited them, because the landlords would never give the poor and landless peasants their rights.

Pandu still in his nascent years sat mesmerized. The dalam leader; also, gave them the choice to join the LOFA, and train for a few months. Besides food and clothing, the volunteers would receive a monthly stipend. Pandu wanted adventure and carried no responsibility. He made a little amount, because he worked with the contractor, and resided with his mama; but, at times, he felt he burdened his mama's family. This offered him an opportunity to venture out, and learn the ways of life. He decided to give it a shot. He approached the leader, along with four others, and volunteered to train with them. Pandu seemed fascinated by the gun that the leader shouldered; an interest, he carried since he stayed in Ramwadi, because he desired to join the Indian Army. There stayed one jawan, called Gopal fauji in the village, who worked with the Indian Army. Pandu made it a point to visit him, whenever, he came to Ramwadi. Gopal fauji told him stories of life in the Indian Army. He impressed Pandu, who longed to join the Indian Army, but his economic conditions never permitted.

This early desire reignited, when he saw the guerrillas in olive green uniform, with guns slung around their shoulders. Pandu trained hard in the jungles of Gadchiroli and worked with the dalam for three years. He learnt the use of weapons, how to lay mines and make bombs, but the jungle life remained tough. The revolutionaries walked for miles and miles with their backpacks and always kept guard. They battled mosquitoes, scorpions and snakes. Pandu suffered from malaria and dysentery on a number of occasions. He struggled hard with the guerillas, which fought the police and para-military forces. Then one day, Pandu decided to leave. The village failed to reason why; but speculated that Pandu surrendered to the police. Pandu never revealed his operations to the villagers.

On his return, he worked for Abba for a year and did odd jobs for sometime. Gangaram remained wary that his son would disappear anytime in the jungles, so he did not badger him to marry. He feared that if the inevitable happened, he would have to shoulder the responsibilities and look after Pandu's family. Pandu, who remained in his early twenties lead a carefree life; and yet, when he saw his brothers

Shrinivas and Mohan married and settled in life, he too craved to settle down, so he requested his father to find him a match, but Gangaram wanted to test his resolve. Pandu took up the responsibility to prove himself, and agreed to cultivate the land.

The afternoon sun blazed and baked the dry patta. A hot breeze, like the loo whistled as it gathered the dust in circles and blew over the land. The team sat under the neem tree on Vasu's land after lunch for a short respite. Vasu sat opposite Pandu, who sat next to Shoba and Bapu. Mangala and the other women—Kamala and Jija, sat next to Pandu.

"Pandu what follows this Pao guy that you talked of yesterday?" Vasu asked, with his back to the trunk of the neem tree.

Pandu interjected to correct him, "it's not Pao its Mao," he demonstrated.

"Ha! Ha! Ha!" the group laughed.

"Say Ma and then ao," said Pandu, stretching his mouth to demonstrate the pronunciation.

"Whatever, it sounds like get to the point," Vasu demanded, embarrassed with the correction.

Pandu smiled then explained. "Mao's ideology propogates that those who contol the means of production, also control the system. In simple words, the stomach controls the mind, because it feeds the body. You cannot think on an empty stomach. Take the case of a farmer. He produces the food but he lacks the skills to control the food supply in the market. If all the farmers unite and refuse to sell their produce in the market, an entire population will starve; and yet, it never happens that way, because the enemies of the farmers will not let them unite. In our case, it means the moneylenders, which control our fate. They lend us the money and force us to oblige.

'We borrow money on interest for the inputs. The interest that Sahukar charges in this village is atrocious. He lends us money at five to fifteen percent of interest per month; and yet, the money we make after selling our produce remains insignificant. In the market, the trader controls the prices. These traders come together and make sure that the prices paid to us stay low. This class of the moneylenders and traders controls the means of production.

'We only labour like donkeys, and bear the risks and losses, but they have the capital. The same capital funds the politicians' election expenses. In this way, the capital class ensures that they control the police, courts and administration. We continue to suffer and blame our fates. In short, it means that unless the present system changes, our fate will never change. This appears the reason why Maovadis kill moneylenders, political leaders and don't believe in democracy."

Vasu's heart jumped in his mouth; his eyes blinked and he appeared apprehensive. He looked at Pandu with suspicion. "Do you mean the guerrillas actually kill the moneylenders? Did you see it happen?"

Pandu nodded his head. "Yeah," he replied; his eyes widened at the sight of the audience staring down at him.

"Did you shoot down any?" inquired Vasu.

Pandu smacked his lips and shook his head. "No not me, but I witnessed the revolutionaries kill many. On one occasion, the commander ordered me to drag a moneylender out of his house and he shot him in his head. Right here," said Pandu, pointing in the middle at the back of his head. "I can see it happen before my eyes. They call it justice for the poor—the cold-blooded massacre of the bourgeoisie. The adivasis in the jungle swear by them. The police don't dare to enter these villages, because its LOFA territory."

Vasu stared in disbelief. "You mean they don't fear the police. I can't believe it."

"Why don't you call them to Ramwadi and shoot down Sahukar?" asked Mangala.

"She's right! He's sitting on our necks," added Kamala.

Pandu looked around and put his finger to his lips, "Sssh," he shooed. "I don't mind doing that. I am not in contact with them. They remain far away in the jungles."

"Why don't they come to Ramwadi?" asked Kamala, softly.

"I told you, its jungle warfare. They need forest cover to launch their attacks and retreat. They declare an area a liberated zone, then spread out further, and try to capture more territory. They will reach here someday," replied Pandu.

"Do the revolutionaries have families?" asked Jija.

"No," snapped Pandu; he dangled his index finger. "It's a strict no. One can marry a revolutionary, but one cannot have children. The men have to undergo a nasbandi."

"Oh! My God! It sounds ridiculous!" exclaimed Jija, putting her hand to her heart. She smiled mischievously. "Is that the reason, you ran away from them?"

The audience giggled.

Pandu interjected. "No! No! I told you, that life in the jungles stays tough. I got bored, and remained homesick, but remember this; the revolutionaries appear brave and committed."

"So, when do you plan to marry?" asked Kamala.

Pandu blushed and shrugged his shoulders. "God knows," he replied. He cast a glance at Shobha and observed her looking at him. "When the time comes, it will happen. One calls it yog, and I don't know when my time will come."

Jija turned to Mangala, "When will they come to see Shoba?" she asked. She referred to the proposal that Vasu pursued for Shobha.

"We don't know. Everybody remains busy. We sent word through my brother, 'Angad.' He'll let us know, if they show interest," replied Mangala, whose brother lived in Borgaon, a village thirty kilometers from Yavatmal.

"I heard the boy's educated and has a job," added Jija.

Vasu's heart puffed up. "He works as a peon at the Zilla Parishad. He took up the job a few months ago," he answered with an air of dignity.

Kamala added. "I hope things work out well. Good he has a job—"

"Sarkari job," Vasu interrupted with pride.

Pandu looked away and giggled.

"Good if he has a sarkari job. The life of a farmer appears uncertain and debt ridden," Kamala remarked.

"We hope for the same, but it doesn't end there. It all depends on the dowry. If they demand too much, then it may not work out. Angad says that the folks seem good. They'll not pester much, if the boy likes Shoba," said Mangala.

Pandu wrinkled his face and looked at Shobha. "Make sure they don't bother you for money. I have heard of plenty that demand more and more. The more you pamper them, the more they crave."

Shoba added to what Pandu suggested, "He's right. It appears pointless, giving them money, and pampering their demands. My husband must love me, and look after me. That's what matters to me," she said.

"She's right," added Jija.

Vasu shook his head, looked at Pandu and smiled wryly. "It sounds fine, but you need money to run a family. Marriage is a responsibility. Not the same as, fighting in the jungles."

Pandu felt the jibe; his face stiffened at the remark. "Damn the jungles! He must not pester for money. If he has a sarkari job," he sneered, uttering the last two words with contempt. "I don't understand, why he asks for dowry? You said that he works in the Zilla Parishad, and we all know the sipahis there, make money throughout the year. They will not let you in, if you do not pay them their share."

Vasu's blood boiled at the sneer; his face reddened. "Why single him out for corruption? Everyone makes money, when given an opportunity."

Pandu grinned at the provocation. He raised his eyebrows. "I'm surprised to hear these words," he commented, with a tinge of sarcasm. "We complain about corruption, and how the rich fleece us; and yet, we defend our kith and kin, when they indulge in corruption? 'Every body does it, so why single him out,'" Pandu mocked Vasu; he looked him in the eyes. "I suppose you don't mind, indulging in corruption, if given an oppurtunity," he proposed with contempt.

Vasu's face dropped; he waved his hand to brush off the barb. "When you marry, and have responsibilities, you will know," he stated, to avoid an answer.

Pandu twisted his nose. "Huh," he scoffed at Vasu. "Everyone in this village wants to marry his daughter to a Sarkari naukar, and they will go to any length to make it happen. They will sell their land, and borrow at an exorbitant rate of interest to pay for the dowry, and they do it with an air of dignity, as if they conquered the world."

Vasu cocked a wry smile. "It's the way the world runs," he prattled with delight. He flicked his fingers, "money runs a family and all parents want the best for their daughters. You will know it, when you have one. If you do not pay dowry, your daughter remains home all her life. The government may pass any legislation to ban it, but it'll continue—"

Pandu interrupted him. "Don't give me that excuse! I'll tell you a way out," suggested Vasu.

"No! Thank-you, I do not wish to hear your jungle talk. We live here, where the traditions and conventions of Ramwadi matter. Now go and fetch water. We have to get back to work," snapped Vasu, sprawling on his back and shutting his eyes.

Pandu shook his head, grabbed the pitcher, stood up in a huff, and sauntered down the track.

"Wait for me. I'm coming," yelled Shobha.

Pandu halted and turned around. "Make it fast," he snapped, shouldering the pitcher.

Shobha put on her chappals and followed him.

"Shoba stay alert! This greedy lot can be dangerous," warned Pandu, kicking a lump of dirt on the ground.

"I know, but what do I do? It seems difficult to choose between money and trust," replied Shoba, who remained in a state of confusion. She caught up and walked besides Pandu.

"I'd settle for trust and not money. You don't carry the money with you after death."

"You talk intelligently, but how do you run a family? You need money to help make ends meet," said Shoba, pointing at herself. "Look at me! I dropped out of school, because my parents didn't have the money."

"What if the man you marry, chooses to have a second, third or fourth wife, because he has loads of money? Will you stay happy, and put up with so many women in the same house?"

Shoba halted in her track. Pandu hit a woman, where it hurts the most; he tickled her jealousy.

Pandu stopped, and then twisted about. "What happened? Let us move. I know it hurts, but I've stated the truth."

"I won't put up in the same house. I'll leave him, and come back to where I belong," fumed Shoba, with her hands on her hips. She dropped her hands and walked ahead.

Pandu laughed and joined her. "It's easier said than done. The village will gossip, about, how he left you for another woman, and you will add another burden on your parent's shoulders. You will loose both, money and trust, and remain worse off then, when you started," prodded Pandu. He made a point, which happens with thousands of girls in India. Shoba knew of such instances in the village. All parents condemned it, but when the time came, they fell in the same trap.

They crossed the baandh that separated Vasu's field from Abba's and entered the sugarcane plot. The soil looked dark and healthy, and the sugarcane rippled on both sides of the track, which lead to the tube well. Shoba did not say a word. She silently followed Pandu.

"Why don't you say something? You haven't answered my question," insisted Pandu.

"What can I say? If my fate appears bad; I can't help it," replied Shoba, helplessly. "I only prayer, nothing of this sort happens."

They reached the tube well. Pandu bent down and lifted the pipe that pumped water into the channel. Shoba placed the pitcher under it. Pandu scooped out water and splashed it on his face. "Oooh—" he snorted, when the water dampened his skin.

Shoba joined him and washed her face. She collected some water in her hands, and threw it on Pandu.

"Damn it! Don't get sore with me!"

"You seem more interested in my marriage, than my parents."

"I think I can help you get a good match," replied Pandu, throwing scoops of water back at Shoba.

"Stop it! I sense there seems more to it than that."

"What do you sense, besides what I have said?"

"The same as you sense. You know it."

"I wish to know. What do you sense?"

"A girl never makes the first confession. You'll have to work hard."

"I can work hard. I'm a peasant and it runs in my blood," said Pandu, looking into Shoba's eyes.

Shoba pushed Pandu, who fell in the pool and splashed water all over the place.

"Damn it! That's rude of you!" he said, gathering him-self and standing up drenched.

"I told you that you'll need to work hard," Shoba reiterated, in an imperious tone, hauling the pitcher on her hip.

Pandu caught her hand.

"Leave me! How dare you hold my hand?" she cribbed, trying to wriggle out of Pandu's grasp.

"I'll hold the pitcher. Let me carry it. Your hips seem delicate," said Pandu; he smiled mischievously.

Shoba handed over the pitcher to Pandu, who shouldered it and they walked back.

"First; you show interest in my marriage, and now my hips. What else fascinates you?" queried Shoba. She enjoyed the attention Pandu gave her—a welcome change from the regular grind.

"Everything you have interests me," declared Pandu, winking at her.

"I told you, you have to work hard to get it. Boys say the same things to all the girls. You have traveled a lot and must have met many girls. How do I trust you?"

"There you go; a typical girl. You've just confirmed, what I said.'

"Don't put words into my mouth. I have not said a thing. You seem interested in me."

"You just mentioned the word, 'trust'. That's the point I made,' reiterated Pandu, halting in his track. He turned around to face Shoba, who blushed and then both of them giggled.

"You sound mischievous," grumbled Shoba.

"You love the mischief. I don't think, you want things to remain normal," taunted Pandu, grinning. He turned around and walked.

"I don't wish to talk to you anymore," cribbed Shoba.

The duet reached the baandh and crossed over.

"Stop acting fussy. You know, you love to talk to me," insisted Pandu.

They reached the team, sitting in the shade of the neem tree. Pandu hitched the bullocks to the cart, while Vasu, Kamala and Jija boarded it, and the cart rattled down the rocky terrain towards the talav.

CHAPTER 7

▼

In June, the entire village waited for the rains. In the last week of May, a few sporadic showers fell and disappeared. These mango showers, created by intense heat failed to excite the farmers, who awaited the monsoon. In India, the monsoon first hits Kerala, on the first of June and then travels upwards to the Deccan plateau, and reaches Vidharbh by the end of the first week of June. Vasu and Pandu worked round the clock to prepare their patch of land for sowing. The rains continued to play truant and did not fall, until the twentieth of June.

This period of uncertainty forced Vasu's mind to waiver upon the course of action. Whether, to drill the well or not, and whom to approach for the money? He conjured up various permutations and combinations that appeared before him. First, he thought of the Co-operative bank; but the buzz remained that the banks could not offer loans. The government declared the banks would offer loans, but it depended on the financial condition of each bank. In Maharashtra, scams after scams occurred, and most of the banks run by politicians stayed neck deep in corruption. The banks pleaded before the Central government for a bail out, but the government remained reluctant to salvage the banks, so the Co-operative banks found themselves in the lurch. The few that managed to run well, offered a pittance to the farmers in Vidharbh. While a farmer in Western Maharashtra, who owned three acres of land, received a loan up to three lakh rupees. In Vidharbh, the same farmer received up to ten thousand rupees, besides, the procedures remained lengthy and cumbersome, which forced Vasu to seek other options.

Vasu thought of approaching Abba for a loan; but remained hesitant, because he took rations on credit and owed Abba money; also, he may need to borrow from Abba for Shobha's wedding, and if he borrowed now he may not get the money for the wedding. His last option remained Sahukar, from whom he borrowed for the last sowing season, and piled up liabilities of over twenty thousand rupees. Vasu's poor yield of jowar made it impossible to pay back the amount he borrowed, but his redeeming feature appeared his six acres of land with a clean title. He could always persuade Sahukar for more money, and Sahukar would not refuse, because other borrowers also defaulted. In fact, half the village that took loans last year suffered the same fate, so Vasu did not mind, approaching Sahukar for money for sowing, but the problem of getting a loan for the tubewell persisted. He remained unsure about Sahukar's willingness to offer him a loan and decided to test the waters. He figured if he could convince Sahukar for a loan for the well, and if he succeeded in tapping water, Sahukar may give a loan for Shoba's wedding, which may happen anytime.

So far, his first gamble failed, because he relied on the monsoon to fall on time to postpone, drilling a well. If that happened, he could sow soya bean, reap a rich yield, clear the debt he owed Sahukar, and then borrow a little for the tubewell. But; because the rains delayed, the chances of a good Kharif crop receded, and despite the delay, if the monsoon remained good he would also have a Rabi crop. These thoughts criss crossed Vasu's mind, when he approached Sahukar for a loan. He took the flight of stairs to the hall, and met Raghu, the servant boy.

"What do you want?" asked Raghu, coming out of the hall.

"I want to meet Sahukar," replied Vasu.

The servant told him to sit down, and went in to call his master. Sahukar barely stretched himself on his charpoy, when he received the message. He decided to come over and walked into the hall.

"Namaskar Sahukar," Vasu greeted him, with folded hands.

"What's the matter?" inquired the moneylender haughtily, motioning Vasu to sit down.

"I need seeds to sow," said Vasu, nervously. He continued to stand.

"Hmm," murmured the Sahukar. "You owe me over twenty thousand rupees."

"I know—but what can I do? The rains deceived me last year, and I don't work anymore."

"The whole village says the same thing, as if, I dole out charity. You know the rules; you'll have to settle the earlier amount, if you want a crop loan this season."

"Sahukar please have mercy!" begged Vasu, with folded hands. "What do I do?"

The Sahukar interjected angrily, "you can't till that dry patch of land! You should not have quit your job. I would consider, giving you some money, if you worked for someone."

"I'll pay you back your money," implored Vasu.

"How can you?" asked Sahukar. He scratched his head, and his brows bumped together in a scowl. "Money lending is tough business. You must consider yourself fortunate that I lent you money. Even the Co-operative banks have stopped, lending farmers' money, because they could never recover the money lent. Farming remains the most risky business in this world, just imagine what happens to me? If the entire village raises their hands, and declares, they have no money. They will blame the rains, but I take the hit. What am I to do? Even, I have a family to tend."

"I understand Sahukar, but I don't wish to depend on the rains anymore," stated Vasu; his heart fluttered, while he wondered, how to get to the point.

"What do you mean?" said the Sahukar, shocked to hear Vasu. "You don't have a drop of water on your land! One needs water to grow crops. Do you imply you wish to become a bataidar or thekedar?"

"No! No! I wish to drill a tube well," replied Vasu, nervously. He looked at the moneylender from the corner of his eyes to study his reaction.

The moneylender's eyes rolled skywards. "Do you know what it takes to drill a tubewell?" he asked. A smile dangled on the corner of his lips. "Your dry patta doesn't have a drop of water. What do you expect—the machine to pump out air? Even if you tap water, you will still need to spend on the motor. It costs money. Who will lend you the money?"

Vasu's face paled, and his forehead puckered. He felt his hopes shrinking. It seemed the Sahukar appeared apathetic to lend him money, but he hung on, "Sahukar, give me a chance," he pleaded; his brows knitted in a frown. "You know, my land stands, on the fringes of the black patta, and next to Abba's sugarcane plot. If Abba's tube well has water so can mine. If you'll lend me money for the tube well, I'll stay obliged."

The Sahukar gave an unrelenting stare. "I don't say you cannot tap water," he conceded, shrugging his shoulders. "And yet, I wonder, what keeps you rag-tag peasants going? You borrow again, and again, and expect the impossible. Why do you keep farming? Go to the cities and find a job! You'll at least pay me back my money," he advised, arching a sly brow. He may have said what he did, but he did not mean it. If all the peasants started to leave Ramwadi, he will have no business to run. Yet, the Sahukar's, sermonizing to debtors never stopped, because he knew, they listened to all he said.

"We have tilled land for generations. We cannot do anything else, because we remain uneducated. Our hopes depend on the rains. I promise to give you back your money. I swear!" implored Vasu, pinching his throat.

"The tube well costs money. What can you mortgage for the loan? Your land values nothing!" the Sahukar sneered; he smacked his lips. He lied and knew it. The land, on the fringes of the black patta, valued more than one lakh rupees per acre. He waited for Vasu to respond.

"Sahukar!" pleaded Vasu, "you know my land values enough to repay what I borrow. I agree to mortgage one acre of my land against the loan."

"One acre!" the Sahukar mocked at the offer, slamming his eyes shut. He pointed his index finger at Vasu, and then jeered, "one acre! Stop joking!" he exclaimed, with his hand on his heart.

Vasu clinched his jaw, and his gaze dipped.

"Come on! Answer me!" prodded the Sahukar. "I have other business to attend. I'm not free the whole day."

"What do I say?" replied Vasu; his eyes bleared, and his face shriveled.

"Don't pretend! You know what to say?" snapped the Sahukar; he gnashed his teeth, glared at Vasu, and shook his head vigorously. "You bloody swines!" he blurted with contempt; his eyes narrowed to crinkled slits. "Stay thick and stingy!" he yelled; his eyes burned with hatred. "You want all the money in the world; and yet, you never care to look at yourselves in the mirror, and see your worth. I hate this obsession of tilling a dry patch of land. Why not consider, working for someone? Take up a job!"

"I want freedom, I cannot work under anyone," said Vasu softly; his eyes dropped.

"Ha! Ha! Ha!" the Sahukar roared with laughter. "Freedom!" he smirked, rubbing his hand over his head. "The most deceptive, yet, desired word in the world. What do you think, happened on fifteenth of August, nineteen forty seven? The nation won freedom from colonial tyranny. Do you know the price our country paid to free itself, from the clutches of the firangees? Thousands laid down their lives, and it took decades to push out the British. An entire generation sacrificed themselves for freedom; and you want freedom, mortgaging just one acre of land. Freedom does not come so cheap! Let us assess your capacity to break free. You, owe me, over twenty thousand rupees, which will touch thirty thousand, by the end of the year. Then, you want money for a tube well, which may cost you close to one and a half lakhs. Add ten percent of interest per month to this amount, and it works out to one hundred and twenty percent per year. It means you owe me, over three lakhs rupees. If you fail to pay up this year, it will keep adding. Besides, you also need money for seeds, fertilizers and pesticides, which will cost you another thirty thousand rupees without interest. Add interest, and the money you owe me, reaches more than four lakhs—"

Vasu interjected. "Why do you charge, ten percent interest per month? It is unfair! The charges must stay at three percent per month—"

"Shut up! You filthy swine!" shouted the Sahukar. "You don't tell me what to charge? I decide! Either, you take it or leave it; and for all this arrogance, what does your land yield? No one will pay you more than twenty thousand rupees per acre. Your entire stretch values not more than one lakh and twenty thousand rupees, and you owe me over four lakh rupees. You still want freedom! You should have thought over it, before begging for money," chided the Sahukar. "Speak out!"

Vasu shivered and looked down worried. He knew Sahukar cheated, but he must submit. The Sahukar cheated the whole village. It seemed the moneylender possessed the fundamental right to cheat, while the peasants remained helpless. Vasu only virtually lived, in the largest democracy in the world; whose Constituion guaranteed all the rights—human, fundamental, natural and legal, to its citizens.

Yet, the truth remained that most villages in Vidharbh, including Ramwadi existed as Republics with their own rules and conventions. In Ramwadi, Abba and Sahukar created the law. The RBI (Reserve Bank of India) never regulated banking in this village, because it looked as if the apex bank lacked jurisdiction over Ramwadi. Ramwadi appeared alien to Indian laws, and the peasants possessed no rights over here. The nationalized and private banks charged a pittance to the middle class for home, vehicle and personal loans. Ramwadi charged a hundred and twenty percent annual interest for the amount borrowed. Assuming the rains fell on time and the markets paid the farmers the right prices for their produce; it remained impossible to repay the loan. This business model forced upon the borrowers, bonded them for life, and compelled them to live for the moneylenders. It appeared, as if, even the world's best entrepreneurs, who made it to the Forbes magazine, will not break even in Ramwadi. In Ramwadi, if you borrow, you stay indebted for generations.

Vasu dropped on his knees, and touched his forehead to the floor, "sorry Sahukar," he apologized, with tears in his eyes. "I made a mistake coming here," he admitted, standing up.

"Where do you think you can go?" asked the moneylender, with a toothy smile.

"I cannot afford so much," confessed Vasu, wiping his tears.

"Go to hell! I give a damn! But pay me back the money you owe me," demanded the Sahukar, smacking his lips. "You cannot leave without clearing my dues."

Vasu's legs felt heavy, as if chained to iron balls, and he found himself trapped in, "Abhimanyu's Chakrayvuh." Once one entered, one never came out. Vasu remained penniless, besides, he needed seeds to sow, and Sahukar remained the sole input dealer in Ramwadi. Vasu lacked a choice; he must accept Sahukar's terms and conditions.

"I'll pay back your amount this year," Vasu said, softly; though, he knew his commitment stayed in the hands of nature.

The Sahukar's eyes arched a sly brow and a lackluster smile dangled on his lips, having cornered his prey for the kill the time to unleash the terms and conditions looked ripe. His eyes squinted in a furtive manner, because if he remained adamant, Vasu would go to Abba, who would agree to the deal. He mellowed his voice, and a gleam of deviltry showed in his eyes.

"Vasu, now you must understand, I need to buy inputs from Companies. They want the money immediately. If, I take goods on credit, they charge me an interest. If you don't pay me the money, how do I pay the companies?" he asked, shrugging his shoulders. "Business appears easy, but remains difficult because, if, all the customers take credit and no one pays back, I will run into losses, and will have to shut down my business. But, because you belong to Ramwadi, I cannot refuse you. If it were anybody else, I would not give a damn. I will give you a loan, with certain terms and conditions. First, you register three acres of your land in my name, and then I will lend you money for your tubewell. Next, I want you to sow cotton on your land, because the cash crop will guarantee me my money. I have a new variety of American cottonseeds—Bt25, which yield twelve to fifteen quintals per acre. Your six acres will yield, more than ninety quintals of cotton. The prices of cotton will remain good. Last year, I bought organic cotton from farmers, at seventeen hundred rupees a quintal. This year, the prices will climb higher, and assuming you grow the Bt25 variety, you will make five hundred rupees more per quintal, because of the demand for this grade in the international market. At two thousand rupees a quintal, you will make close to two lakh rupees. You can pay back my loan, and take back your land," suggested the Sahukar, with a wry smile that surfaced on his lips.

Vasu's eyes gawked, his head reeled, and heart pounded with excitement. The sum that seemed beyond his reach beckoned him. He could not believe what he heard. He pinched his forearm to come to terms with the reality, because he had his reservations.

"I wished to sow soya bean and jowar; I need grains to feed my family, and fodder for bullocks," he urged.

"How much will soya fetch?" asked the Sahukar, fixing his eyes on Vasu. "The problem with peasants lies in their inability to think wisely. Soya will fetch you about a thousand rupees per quintal, depending on the market. You know that over half this village sows soya, which means that the supply will outstrip the demand, and lower the prices. But this will not happen with Bt25, which guarantees a fixed amount, because of the demand in the international market. I see no point in growing jowar. You can buy food grains, from the ration shop, at subsidized rates. If, you want money for the food grains, then I will give you credit at three percent interest per month. Think over it."

Vasu did not have a choice, anyways. He could not exercise his right to choose. The debt burden had snatched away his freedom. He lived in a virtual democracy that offered freedom of choice on paper, like many Indians, whom democracy has little to offer. The Government complains it has no money for rural credit; that farming remains a loss making enterprise; that farmers drain the exchequer, demanding subsidies; that farmers display stupidity, lack business acumen; because they don't follow government advice, which propagates that farmers take to capital intensive agriculture, and adopt inorganic farming of cash crops to increase, purchasing power parity in villages. Where will the capital for this recommendation come from? What will be the interest on the capital amount borrowed? In Ramwadi, it is a staggering one hundred and twenty percent per year.

Vasu finally nodded his head in agreement. "I agree," he concluded.

CHAPTER 8

▼

At the end of June, the clouds suddenly gathered, and burst into the first downpour of the season. The farmers breathed a sigh of relief. Vasu and Pandu harrowed their fields twice, while other farmers' decided to sow seeds. The farmers rushed to Sahukar for seeds and fertilizers, and the Sahukar forced the creditors to buy Santano cottonseeds. Half of Ramwadi sowed cotton this season, and the interest rates spiraled with demand. Sahukar now charged eight percent interest on credit for a month. The farmers agreed because, if, they wanted to sow they needed to borrow.

After harrowing his farm, Vasu collected, "Santano Bt25 cottonseeds," from Sahukar. The six packets cost him a whooping twelve thousand rupees, and the interest soared to five percent per month. Pandu protested against the deal, but Vasu had no choice. Pandu insisted they sow soya bean, but Vasu sealed the deal. Pandu sowed soyabean, and Vasu sowed cotton. Within a week, since the showers, the village finished sowing, and waited for more rains. The skies cleared, and as the days passed, it seemed as if the monsoon hesitated to drop over Ramwadi.

By the fifteenth of July, the rains still remained elusive, and the seeds that germinated dried up, and evoked anxiety amongst farmers. The draught like conditions spurred the media, which started to beam news of the possibility of a draught. Because of the coming elections, the ruling alliance made false promises to the electorate, and a clamour ensued between the political parties to win the electorate. The opposition questioned the Government's intent, and demanded that the government declare a draught and deliver a special package to the farmers. But, the Government dilly-dallied, because it wished to intervene, when it felt the time ripe to deny the opposition any credit.

Abba canvassed hard, and succeded in building support for his candidature. This made Dada anxious, who made repeated attempts to reconcile differences with Abba, but the efforts failed. Dada desperately wanted Abba to withdraw from the electoral arena, but Abba stayed adamant. This defiance forced Dada to take strong measures against Abba, and he retaliated. A few Dalit villagers from the village Tembari, complained to the Tehsildar about irregularities in the ration shop run by Abba's son Tatya, who denied them their monthly quota of rations.

It seemed a regular practice in majority of the ration shops run by political bigwigs in Maharashtra, without any action taken against them. Abba had managed the Tehsil office, and considering his political clout, the Tehsildar dare not question Abba. But the equations changed, after Abba decided to contest the elections against the official nominee of the ruling party. He automatically forfeited the privileges that accrued to ruling party members, which meant he remained liable to prosecution like a common person. Dada decided to take on Abba and the fact that the complainants comprised Dalits helped his cause.

The ration shop at Ramwadi catered to five other villages, within the vicinity of Ramwadi. On the fifteenth of July, the supply inspector visited Ramwadi, and found Abba had violated the rules under the PDS control order. He discovered that the stock display board, registers and sealed samples never existed. Besides, the beneficiaries never signed the sales register at the time of issuance of foodgrains. Moreover, the beneficiaries failed to recieve ration cards for months. These irregularities, though, the norm in most of the shops across Maharashtra appeared serious, because Abba challenged the ruling party. The supply inspector sent the report to the district supply officer, who suspended Abba's license.

The manouvre created the required effect with the "Lok Andolan Samachar," carrying the news on its front page. Abba's image took a beating, and added to his resolve to hit back, because Dada tried to malign his image, which did not go down well with Abba. If Dada targeted his fair price shop, and created an anti-dalit image, Abba would have to target Dada to even the situation.

"Tatya!" shouted Abba.

Ganpat, the water carrier, who attended to the peoples' chamber, appeared on hearing the call. "Tatya has left for the village square," he said, softly.

"Damn the idiot! He is never here when I want him! What does he do at the village square? Go and get Hira! Tell him that I wish to talk to him. Run!" ordered Abba.

"Yeah-Tatya-Hira" stuttered Ganpat; he looked confused.

Abba stared down at him with a stiff face. "Thickhead! Get Tatya and Hira immediately!" he shouted, snapping his fingers. "Get going!"

Ganpat raced away.

"Lakshmi!" Abba called his wife.

A woman appeared at the door in a silk saree, with gold bangles dangling on her wrists. She bore a fair complexion, with sharp features, and looked healthy and much younger for a fifty-year-old woman. "What is it?" she asked, standing at the door that separated the peoples' chamber from the house.

"Why don't you put some sense into your son's head?" lambasted Abba.

"Isn't he your son? You should discipline him. A mother has her limitations," grumbled his wife.

"Look at this!" said Abba, holding up the newspaper, and pointing at the headlines: ABBA STARVES DALITS—THE RATION SCAM.

"Hmm," murmured his wife.

"I've worked for the ruling party all my life. And the party has this to offer me. First; they deny me my ticket, and now they plant anti-dalit stories in the newspapers," moaned Abba.

"In politics, you must prepare to face all," added his wife.

"I know and I will face it! But the message sounds clear—stay alert. A warning, which your son fails to heed, because he has got things easy in life," complained Abba, flinging the paper on the floor. "He must give up that affair, with the nurse in the Primary Health Centre. The village keeps talking about it. It's risky in these vulnerable times."

"I've told him an umpteen number of times. Even his wife—Radha, left this house in disgust. Her parents refuse to send her over, until Tatya mends his ways. It's humiliating to hear that he sleeps with a Chamar girl," said Lakshmi, indignantly.

"Today the newspapers allege that I starve Dalits! Tomorrow they will scream that my family rapes them! The idiot fails to understand the nuances of politics. The entire ruling brass guns for me, because I challenged Dada."

"Why don't you withdraw from the contest? What's the point, fighting against the system?" suggested his wife, sitting on the chair opposite Abba.

"It's easier said than done. You need to wear my shoes to understand my woes. I deserve much more than what they offer me. We have to think of rehabilitating Tatya. The time has come for him to contest the Zilla Parishad elections. I wish to make space for him, and seek a larger role for me. But the idiot doesn't understand a thing," said Abba; his eyes peering angrily through slits in his puffy cheeks. "If he wants to join politics, then he must give up his lecherous ways. Times have changed!"

"Why don't you send him to the farm to supervise activities there? The ration shop kept him occupied so far, but now he needs to keep busy. Otherwise, he'll wile away his time in the village square and keep visiting that wench," suggested his wife.

"I want him to help out with the election activities. But, I fear he may mess up things. He remains irresponsible and immature and I fear, if, he comes in the limelight, he will stay easy game for my opponents. You talk to him and put some sense in his head."

"Yeah," replied Lakshmi.

"Namaskar Abba," said Hira, standing at the door.

"Come in and sit down," Abba beckoned.

His wife stood up and left the hall.

Hira entered with a tall, dark and muscular physique. He proudly wore a walrus moustache, and copper rings dangled from his ears. One of his eyes, which he damaged while working on the fields, stayed tucked under an eye patch. He wore a dhoti and kurta, and carried a wooden pole. He reached Abba; bowed, touched Abba's feet and squatted on the floor.

"How are things at the taanda?" asked Abba.

"We get along with your blessings. The draught remains our concern; I do not think we will have a good harvest this year. It means no work and no food. We have not received our wages, which the sugar mill owes us, since two years. If, not for your blessings, we would have starved to death," replied the nomad.

"This time we'll protest against the unpaid wages. I will join you in a rally. You gather your entire team of harvesters. I will foot the expenses. We'll make Dada pay the wages. Remember you are elected the President of the cane harvesters union this year," said the headman.

The nomad looked stunned, because, since the last two years, Abba objected to the strike. But now, Abba wanted to join the protest. "Abba, do you mean what you say?" asked Hira, nervously. He failed to believe what he heard.

Abba saw the surprise on his face and interjected, "I know what you think! But, I cannot see you suffer anymore. This remains our best moment to negotiate. The elections come once in five years. If we don't protest now, we'll stay exploited," said the wily politician.

Hira kept quiet, and tried to get over the shock. He failed to discern— how to react? He declared hesitantly, "Abba our rations have dried up."

Abba saw the confusion in his eyes and smiled, "don't worry about the rations. I will send a truckload of grains to the taanda. You gather your people from all around Ramwadi, and prepare for the rally. We need the numbers to threaten Dada. Even the media will cover our rally. Dada will pay the wages," declared Abba.

"Yeah," replied the nomad, nodding his head.

"Have your tea," said Abba.

Hira took the tea offered to him, and spluttered, while he drank it.

"Hira you remain my most trusted man for years. Maybe, you wonder; why Abba trusts me and enjoys my company, despite, his riches, name and stature? Abba lives in a mansion, owns three hundred acres of land, and appears happy and free from worries. But this belief needs correction. Politics stays dirty and demanding. All the time you have to please people. They come with their problems, and expect me to settle them, but; I have limitations, unlike the Gods, which occur better off, because they sit in the temples and take offerings. To them it does not matter, whether they answer prayers, because people keep going to them. Unlike us, who have to face the electorate every five years? We do not possess any divine powers like the Gods; we remain human. No matter what we do, the people complain, because it remains impossible to satisfy the needs of all the people all the time. We have; also, to please our bosses in the party hierarchy, who demand money, but outwardly pretend to fight corruption. The truth stays; nothing moves in our system without money.

'You may wonder; why Abba tells me about these things? Perhaps you forget that we all need to bare our hearts. In politics, friends do not exist only interests count. You cannot talk freely, because you may give away your weaknesses that will ruin your career, but; because you remain my most trusted man; I talk to you. I understand the lives of your people, and the conditions they live in. They rise early in the morning to cut cane, stripp off the leaves and bundle the stalks. They barely have clothes to cover their bodies, and the heavy sugarcane stalks damage their skin and hair. You lost an eye working on a plantation. But, despite all odds, your people continue to slog in the bitter cold and scorching heat. Most of your women deliver their babies in open fields. What kind of a life do your people live? I do not think they exist like human beings or come anywhere close to it. Can your people grab proper sleep for their tired bodies? The trucks come late in the night, and your people get up to load them. The poor little babies cry for milk, but your women straddle them in slingss around their bosoms, and continue to toil.

'I often wonder what the future holds for your children. Do they have the time and convenience to attend school? Your people keep shifting from one sugarcane plantation to another, without a permanent home. When they reach a new plantation, they nail tents, and begin all over again, cooking, bathing, eating, sleeping and delivering in the open fields. If they fall ill, the hospitals remain miles away, and the expenses stay unbearable, because they loose their daily wages. They live a harsh life, worse than animals! I feel bad and guilty. I wish to help your people, so I gave them that patch of land. At least, they have a home, a place they can call their own. I gave them ration cards, so they have an identity. I have lobbied hard for your wages. I kept protesting about the unpaid wages in every board meeting, but I had my limitations. I remained a humble and disciplined party cadre, who would not cross the party line.

'I belonged to a party, which professed, 'Gandhian Socialism,' and coined catchy slogans like, 'garibi hatao,' and bragged about its commitment for the upliftment of the poor and downtrodden. It boasted about the policies drafted for the poor and needy, and the money released for the policies, but the policies failed when implemented, because of corruption. Majority of the party workers, want a share of the money allocated for these schemes, because they spend to keep the party alive, and expect compensation. An entire lot of party bearers wait for an opportunity to make money. Politics remains the biggest business in this country. It stays an investment, but poses as social work. I dislike many things, but I cannot do much. A rotten system has established itself firmly. One needs money to contest an election. No matter what the election commission preaches. One needs to spend, and when one spends, one must recover the money spent. The law must declare politics a business, because I will not have to live in guilt. I will know I am doing the right thing. The reason I say you remain better off than me," philosophied Abba.

The poor nomad forced to listen to his mentor's woes cried. "I thought only the poor endured and suffered, but it seems that the rich, also, have their woes," moaned Hira, wiping the tears streaming down his cheeks.

"You call us rich! A disgrace!" exclaimed Abba, slamming his foot on the floor. "I can understand the poor, who do anything to feed their stomachs, because, it entails an effort to stay alive. But the rich have no such excuses. Once they make money, they indulge in hedonism—a senseless satiation of craving, which remains worse than animals. They vent their animal instincts, buried under the pile of norms and values. Their suppressed demonic behaviour pops up, and they crave for God-like reverence. So they spend to achieve fame, because they wish to stand out, amongst the multitude and proclaim their presence to the world. They strive to bestow favours upon their fellow beings to make them look small.

'It stays worse when bequeathed a legacy, because society expects the legatee to pile more and more on the mound of inheritance or labels the legatee a waste. In most cases, the norms and taboos force indulgence. The poor have a legitimate excuse—food. But, what excuse do the rich have? Your people sleep in peace, despite the harsh conditions, but the rich have to swallow pills, and battle all kinds of diseases, which range from hypertension to blood pressure. They cannot sleep well in their cozy mansions. And when death strikes, they burn, like the poor on a funeral pyre. They carry nothing with them, when they leave. It all stays here. Many times, I feel like renouncing all, and going to the Himalayas. I yearn for peace, but I stay helpless against a corrupt system. The poor crave for food, and the rich crave for peace. I often doubt the creator's emblematic perfection, because the creation manifests imperfection—"

"Abba did you send for me?" a voice interrupted abruptly.

Abba looked up, and then nodded his head in disgust. Tatya stood at the door. Abba turned to Hira, "go and prepare for our rally," he ordered.

Hira having listened to his mentor with rapt attention, felt jolted at the sudden outburst. He gathered his wooden pole, stood up, bowed humbly and walked away.

CHAPTER 9

▼

The debate on the Kyoto Protocol grew shriller, as the deadline for its enforcement (Feb, 16th 2005) came closer. Scientists, environmental conservationists and political leaders in America continued to voice their views on; whether America must ratify the Kyoto Protocol or not? On the twelfth of June, nineteen ninety-two, America signed the United Nations Framework Convention on Climate Change (UNFCCC), in which; the parties stated their determination: to protect the climate system, for present and future generations. The problem for America lay in its economic model, which remained energy driven, and dependent on fossil fuels. The use of fossil fuels, as an energy source, stayed an essential part of modern consumption and production. The growth of a capitalistic economy bore a heavy dependence upon consumption of energy: more the consumption the more the growth. The reductions of risks to climate change; demands a substantial reduction in the combustion of fossil fuels, which will impinge upon life style and consumption patterns.

Besides, two major issues wobbled, when it came to assessing the cost benefit analysis of regulating climate change. The first: Inter-generation shift of costs, which means those who create the risks, may not bear them, and the bulk of the climatic changes will stay inconsequential for the next fifty years or more, when future generations will occupy the planet, rather than present generations. The second: Intra-generation shift of costs; which, means the benefits of fossil fuel consumption remain domestic, while costs of climate change stay diffused across the world.

These major issues dominated the debates, in the Senate of the United States. Most of the partisan positions in the Kyoto debates continued, because of deep regional differences. Senators representing States, that risked economic loss, found it politically difficult to support a global climate treaty that would result in domestic federal legislation to price carbon emissions. Coal, oil and agricultural States in America, remained opposed to carbon pricing and Kyoto in particular.

Under the US Constitution: the President shall have power, by and with the advice and consent of the Senate to make Treaties, provided two-thirds of the Senators present concur (US Constitution, Article II, Section 2, Clause 2). When the Senate considers a treaty, it may approve it as written, approve it with conditions, reject and return it, or prevent US participation by withholding approval (by not holding a vote in the Foreign Relations Committee or on the Senate floor). The Senate traditionally gives its advice and consent unconditionally to the vast majority of treaties submitted to it; however, it has ratified few environmental treaties in the last 20 years.

The negotiation and conclusion of a treaty remains the President's exclusive prerogative. The President chooses and instructs the negotiators, and decides whether to sign an agreement after the negotiation of its terms. The Senate or House sometimes proposes negotiations and influences them through advice and consultation. Moreover, the executive advises appropriate Congressional leaders and committees of its intention to negotiate significant new agreements and consult them on the form of an agreement. The Senate has sometimes appointed observer groups to negotiations of important treaties, especially treaties on arms control and environmental matters.

In the Kyoto negotiations, Senators stayed engaged, and Congressional observers remained present at international meetings, where they collaborated with the teams that negotiated. At their first Conference of the Parties (COP1) in 1995, the UNFCCC (United Nations Framework Convention on Climate Change) parties agreed on the Berlin Mandate. In which, they stated their intent to agree on quantified emissions limitation targets, emphasized that industrialized countries have a particular responsibility to take the first steps, and confirmed the UNFCCC clause of 'common but differentiated responsibilities'. According to this clause, developing countries would stay exempted from their responsibility to cut or limit their emissions under the new protocol.

The US consent to the Berlin Mandate, went against the advice of several lawmakers, who feared negative consequences for their constituents, if the United States decided to cut emissions, while other large economies stayed exempted. In the Senate, the President's acceptance of the Berlin Mandate caused anger, frustration, and a feeling of going unheard on a major issue. Sam Strosberg stayed infuriated and hell bent on cornering the President. This forced the Republicans to act, and they saw this as a blatant attempt, by the Democrats to bulldoze American national interests. As the Kyoto negotiations progressed, and this sense of apathy continued, the idea of a sense-of-the-Senate resolution developed. Backed by Corporates, Sam Strosberg lobbied hard with Senators for, "a sense-of-the-Senate resolution," which made sure the President, knew about the Senators' concerns, and exhibited a red flag against US acceptance and ratification of Kyoto.

In July nineteen hundred and ninety seven, five months before the Kyoto meeting, Senator Sam Strosberg pushed hard for, "a sense-of-the-Senate resolution," which laid down the framework within which America would work towards climate change. It stated that: "the United States should not be a signatory to any protocol . . . which would (A) mandate new commitments to limit or reduce greenhouse gas emissions for the Annex I parties, unless the protocol . . . also mandates new specific scheduled commitments . . . for Developing Country Parties within the same compliance period, or (B) result in serious harm to the economy of the United States."

This successful manouvre by Sam Strosberg made it difficult for America to ratify the Kyoto Protocol. Though the sense-of-the-Senate resolution remained legally non-binding, it demonstrated the intent of the legislature. While Senate ratification requires a two-thirds majority, the sense-of-the-Senate resolution managed a 95-0 vote. Thus, to achieve ratification, the US administration would require changing the minds of at least 67 senators—a formidable task. This manifested a handy tool for the two thousand Presidential elections, which saw the election of a Republican President.

Sam's tactics earned him great respect, as he remained the President's closest advisor. Many saw this as a master strategy for Sam to acquire nomination from the Republican Party for President in the near future. The newly elected Republican President, when repudiating Kyoto in February 2001, echoed the requirements of the sense-of-the-Senate resolution: 'I oppose the Kyoto Protocol, because it exempts 80 percent of the world, including major population centers, such as China and India, from compliance, and would cause serious harm to the US economy.' The President also referred to this resolution directly, stating: 'the Senate's vote, 95-0, shows that there lay a clear consensus that the Kyoto Protocol remains an unfair and ineffective means of addressing global climate change concerns'.

Sam Strosberg's effort won a major battle for the Corporates in America and snubbed the green activists. However, the international media criticized Sam, and soon developed a campaign to malign his image. The Senate continued to generate acrimonious debates, as the February two thousand and five deadline, for ratification came closer. The international community continued to build pressure on the United States to ratify the Kyoto Protocol. A few Senators started seriously thinking of rebuilding the American credibility that lay shattered, in the aftermath, of the nine-eleven attacks on the World Trade Centre in New York. These and many American intellectuals, lobbied hard for the ratification of the Kyoto Protocol.

One such Senator: Bob Benton; a physicist, environmentalist, green activist and an independent had studied the melting glaciers in the Arctic, and warned the world of the dangers of Global Warming in nineteen hundred and eighty eight. He continued his efforts relentlessly and debated in the Senate to express his concerns for the environment, in this July session of the House.

"Senators, our X-mas spending damages the environment and I would like to draw the attention of this house to a report titled: 'the hidden costs of Christmas,' published by the American Foundation, which meticulously calculated the environment impact of spending on books, clothes, alcohol, electrical appliances and lollies during the festive season. Every dollar, Americans spend on new clothes as a gift consumes sixty litres of water and requires 9.2 square metres of land, in the manufacturing process.

'Last X- mas, Americans spent over three billion dollars on clothes, which required more than 3.6 million acres of land and X– mas drinks, made from barley and grapes, last December consumed water that would approximately fill 1,26,000 Olympic sized swimming pools. The report further states that packed gifts like DVD players and Coffee makers generated 25, 40,000 tons of greenhouse pollution. A third of this pollution occurred, due to fuel consumption during production. Even a box of thirty dollars of chocolate or lollies consumes twenty kilograms of natural materials and nine hundred and forty litres of water.'

'The writer of this report, James Branson, the foundation's executive director, said in a statement and I quote, 'if your bank account is starving under the pressure of Christmas shopping, spare a thought for our environment. It is paying for our Christmas presents with water, land, air and resources. These costs stay hidden in the products we buy.' The report further states, and I quote, 'we can all tread more lightly on the earth this Christmas by eating, drinking and giving gifts in moderation and by giving gifts with a low environmental cost, such as vouchers for services, tickets to entertainment, memberships to gyms, museums or sports clubs and donations to charities—'"

"I object," shouted Sam Strosberg, jumping to his feet, fuming with rage and slamming his fist on the desk. "Senators, pardon me; Bob seems impressed with a report, prepared by a pagan; anti-religious American Conservation Foundation, which dares to tell us that our X-mas," he uttered the word loudly, with sarcasm and continued, "spending damages the environment, and yet, he forgets in a fit of passion that our God created this world and reigns supreme. Our American currency has the holy words, 'IN GOD WE TRUST,' inscribed on it. We retain our most sacred and inalienable natural rights to life, liberty and happiness, which give us the freedom to enjoy the fruits of our God's creation. Our God has created the environment, so that we live off it and prosper.

'The Great American Continent, which comprises of plenty of natural resources, exhibits blessings of God. Let us not forget that our ancestors, who discovered this rich land hundreds of years ago, fought bloody battles against the Red Indians: the most barbaric, heathen, irreligious and uncivilized tribes, civilized them, and built the first church on America's fertile soil. Our great ancestors, out of gratitude dedicated the first church to God and in return, God helped us in all the battles against the pagans to spread God's faith. Our ancestors fought the Red Indians and won. They succeded in driving out the colonial powers, and beat the communists, who remained anti-God. And in every righteous war, God stayed with us. We love our God and God loves us, and as a token of appreciation, we celebrate Christmas. Our faith in God stays reinforced in Christmas and the more we love our God, the more we spend on Christmas.

"X-mas spending damages the environment,' says Bob the pagan and dares to read a flimsy report on the floor of this house. Bob calls our Christmas, 'X-mas,' and conveniently forgets that Christmas symbolizes the celebration of the birth of Christ. I would like to remind such atheists that Christmas remains a faith, which millions of Christians swear by in America. I order him to put, 'Christ,' back into, 'X- mas.' Using the term, 'X- mas,' means celebrating the birth of an unknown person and insults every Christian. I often wonder, whether our battle against the heretical red faith has ended. Because, the new devil in disguise seems the 'green faith,' with Bob as the Devil's Advocate, who remains hell bent on turning this great God loving nation into a pandomine. He may claim it his prerogative to choose a faith, and take umbrage under the First Amendment of the US Constitution. I will not dispute that, but if he chooses to turn this paradise into hell, I will question his right to do so.

'Bob appears a confused man, because he doesn't belong to any of the two national parties that have governed America. As an independent, and bereft of either the Republican or the Democrat values, he professes a value system, which occurs so miniscule or microscopic that it fails to fit into the definition of even a minority opinion, and in his zest for an independent opinion, he ignores the very definition of democracy. A democracy runs on majority opinion, and the Great God loving American electorate, have reposed their faith in the Republican Party to protect Christianity. Because they know that, 'We Republicans,' can take on the, 'clash of civilizations'. I hate, interfering in the personal beliefs of other people, so I refrain from suggesting that Christmas spending stay moderate. I remain not only a staunch Republican, but also a die hard Constitutionalist, and our Constitution clearly states that all citizens of America possess, the right to live life the way they want to best live it. Maybe, Bob needs to read the Constitution or maybe he never read it, and then do some serious self-introspection, and revisit the pagan report, which he shamelessly read aloud on the floor of this house as, 'X-mas,' spending. He needs to ask himself, if he posseses the tyrannical right, to impose his pagan views on the Senate.

'Let me hasten to add that Bob, not only questioned my religious beliefs, but slighted one of Christianities greatest traditions by calling it, 'X-mas'. We Republicans always upheld the American God, and let us not forget that a Republican President has launched a 'war against global terrorism.' The 9/11 attack on our sacred World Trade Centre, the symbol of our wealth and hegemony, by a band of mullahs ensconced in a cave in Afghanistan, appears directed against the citadel of the Christian faith. This war, which; We Republicans wage, resembles the crusades of Medieval Europe, when the Church rescued the Christian faith. Today, the Republicans alone can save the Christian faith. It remains not America alone, but the greatest of all civilizations the, 'American Civilization,' which fights Islamic fundamentalism. And all righteous Christians, who support us in this war on terrorism, fight to save the Christian faith. What more proof do you want to prove that the Republicans, pose as the saviours of the American God? We love the American God, the most, and our actions throughout history have proved it repeatedly.

'But unfortunately, there exist a few pagans in America-traitors, who live off the Great American Civilization, but don't support our war on terrorism. They seem bloody parasites, who fatten on American soil, but betray it. Bob Benton and his bandwagon of, 'green activists,' represent such bunch of traitors. They have joined hands with the uncivilized world, against the Great American Civilization. These 'terrorists,' funded by China and India, masquerade as green activists, and feel jealous of America's wealth and military might, so they have conspired to stall our progress in the name of, 'Clean Development Mechanisms,' (CDM's), by coaxing us into reducing our green house gas emissions, so they can catch up with America, surpass America and then dominate America. Let us not forget the blood, sweat and toil our ancestors sacrificed to build America. Bob and his gang remain ungrateful, because they never read American history. I fear, they never read anything of America's interest, the reason why, they remain ignorant minds—the kind that appears, easily influenced by, 'Conservation Conversation'.

'What's this crap called, 'Kyoto Protocol,' and what does it require? It demands that America cut down its green house gas emissions by 7% of the 1990 levels. What will this cost us? More than five million jobs and billions of dollars. Do we wish to convert America, into an unemployed race of civilization? So that all our jobs, stay outsourced, to India and China. All the innovations and inventions, in the realm of science and technology, happen in America. We spend billions of dollars on research and development, and these thieves steal our expertise, and flood cheap phony goods in the market that compete with our products. Name any one University or research laboratory of international standards in India and China. How much do these countries spend on quality education? They manufacture educated illiterates capable of doing rut call centre jobs that need no critical thinking. They have mastered the art of cut, copy and paste.

'Look at their legal framework. They disrespect intellectual property rights, because they remain incapable of producing any. They lack an effective administrative and judicial mechanism to protect intellectual property rights. How many Noble Laureates have emerged, from their so-called centres of learning?

'The fact remains that America, alone, posseses the capability to innovate, and produce entrepreneurs, who can generate jobs, and wealth in this world. We symbolize the beacon of civilization, and if you blow off the beacon, because it burns fossil fuel, darkness will engulf the world. India and China cannot innovate products, they can only consume products. Their increasing economic growth rates indicate that their populations consume products, and not create products. They symbolize the kinds that consume and pollute the atmosphere. I do not understand, why the Protocol permits them, to continue emitting green house gases in the name of development that consumes, and drains the resources of this planet. And; yet, they allege that an American citizen, emits twenty times more carbon dioxide than a citizen of their nations. It maybe true, but I do not mind an American emitting that much gas, because it will lead to more innovations, than a Chinese or Indian, which will only result in reckless consumption.

'Besides, their economic growth rates increase at the expense of human rights violations. Children below the age of fourteen years work on infrastructure projects that loom as marvels of modern engineering.

They also work in mines and quarries for a pittance to extract minerals from their forest resources. The cheap unorganized labour, without proper labour laws attracts foreign investments. The electronic goods and textiles from these countries, shuts down American electronic and textile sectors, and creates jobless Americans, who strain our social security package. We must prevent such economies that consume the resources of this planet from further consumption and not offer concessions to them.

'The treaty has exemptions that permit for trading emission rights and creating carbon sinks (forests) to reduce global warming. Such conditions will directly impinge upon our national security interests. We must not overlook the fact that America fights a global war on terrorism. We need to upgrade our defence capabilities, to keep ahead of the rogue states that threaten world peace and security. We need aluminium for our defence industry. Where do we get aluminium? It comes from bauxite found in the forests. But the KP does not permit the exploitation of forest resources, because it considers them carbon sinks that soak up the carbon dioxide in the atmosphere. This sounds ridiculous! It undermines our national security interests. There exists no evidence, cogent and reliable; to prove that global warming happens because of green house gas emissions. Many scientists refute the claims of environmental conservationists.

'Frankly speaking, I feel, we cannot compromise our national interests, and the KP threatens our national interests. It resembles the proverbial, 'Trojan Horse,' that destroyed the city of Troy. The sooner we toss it in the garbage bin, the better for American national interests or else this God ordained super power would have to contend, with the ignominy of taking up beggary. I appeal to the Senate to exercise prudence, wisdom and foresight to safeguard American national interests and avoid this rhetoric called, 'Conservation Conversation,' which threatens our national interests. If, the Senate chooses not to heed my warning, then it risks compromising American national interests, which amounts to treason," concluded Sam Strosberg.

The speech received a heavy round of applause from the Senate, as Sam hunkered down. One of Sam's colleagues, whispered into his ears. Sam looked at his watch, nodded, stood up and walked out of the Senate.

CHAPTER 10

▼

The month of July, hung like a Damocles sword over Vasu's family. The initial showers of the monsoon proved a sham, and the intense heat that followed sucked the moisture from the soil and killed the seeds. Vasu's liabilities mounted, as he owed the Sahukar a further twelve thousand rupees plus the interest. He seemed shattered and worried, because the circumstances clogged his mind, and he failed to figure how to go about things. The family's rations wore out, and the suspension of Abba's ration shop further compounded their woes. Vasu must arrange for food.

Pandu's family often helped Vasu, but for how long. They needed to save, because they remained a big family. Vasu did not want to visit old creditors, because the Sahukar laid stiff terms and conditions, and forced Vasu to buy expensive seeds for which he suffered. Vasu had sealed the deal with a longer perspective in mind—the tube well, because he needed water for his land. The rains proved unreliable and, if, they happened to fall again they would entice another sowing and disappear. It looked like Vasu would have to drill the tube well.

Sahukar had agreed to lend Vasu money, and the circumstances fuelled his resolve. "No point waiting any further," he thought, while his stomach craved for food. He could manage the night, but why should Shoba, Bapu and Mangala starve. He shouldered the family burden, and it remained his duty to feed them. But the responsibilities, despite his will, withered in the face of circumstances. He willed to do any kind of work: dig ditches, cut sugarcane, load trucks, plough fields, thresh grains and even clean toilets. But the village offered no work for him to feed his family. He lifted his hands to the skies, "Oh Vitthal! Give me food to feed my family," he begged the heavens, with a voice lost in a flood of tears, while he sat on his doorstep and moaned his fate.

"Vasu," a voice wheezed.

Vasu looked up and saw Hira stomp towards him, with his wooden pole. "Vasu," Hira reiterated, plopping down next to Vasu. He took a deep breath, mopping the beads of sweat, which dripped down his forehead to the ends of his dhoti. "Ah! The heat continues in July," he gasped.

Vasu stayed quiet and looked down.

Hira looked up and then gazed at Vasu intently. He felt the despondent vibes and saw the tears in Vasu's eyes. "Hey!" he exclaimed, putting his hand on Vasu's shoulder. "What's the matter?"

Vasu remained silent.

"Damn the tears! What's the matter?" Hira reiterated, with his forehead puckered, tugging at Vasu's shoulder.

Vasu said nothing.

Hira's eyes squinted in a furtive manner, and his forehead bumped together in scowl. He withdrew his hands, stood up and peeped inside the tinshed. It was empty. "I don't see your folks," he declared, sitting down next to Vasu. He scratched his head. "Did you fight with your wife?"

Vasu shook his head. "They have gone to Pandu's place," replied Vasu; he bit his lips, glimpsed at Hira, and crossed his arms over his chest.

"Hmm," Hira murmured, nodding his head.

Vasu hunched over to look shorter, and sagged against the wall. He dropped his head and thought. "Should I tell him the truth that I don't have food in my house and that they will stay there so they get some food?" he nodded his head in disagreement, tightening the muscles of his face.

"Why the tears? You look depressed!" Hira inquired, edging closer to Vasu. "Can I help you?"

Vasu's gaze dipped, and he inhaled a sharp breath. "Maybe he will help," he thought to himself, while his stomach yearned for some food. "I must keep quiet," his thoughts riveted back and forth.

Hira finally changed the subject. "The heats unbearable, and the rains have failed us again," commented Hira, his eyes rolled skywards.

"I've lost faith in the rains," said Vasu, lifting his shoulders in a shrug.

Hira smacked his lips, and then looked at Vasu. "The village mourns because, if, the rains fail this year. We will not have water to drink," complained Hira.

Vasu's eyes moistened and tears swelled up on the surface.

Hira cast his hand over Vasu's shoulders and consoled him. "Don't cry," he entreated, patting Vasu on his back. "Hope," he said, softly, squeezing Vasu's shoulder. "The only thing that doesn't cost money," he declared, with a smile that dangled on the corner of his lips. He withdrew his hand and stuffed it in his pocket. "Look!" he exclaimed, yanking out a bundle of hundred rupee notes. "I have something to offer you."

Vasu stared in disbelief. His hopes soared and heart galloped at the sight. He straightened his back. "Where did you get this money from?" he asked, with a toothy smile, and cocked his head.

"Take these," said Hira, in an imperious tone. He flicked out five notes and handed them to Vasu.

Vasu's eyes narrowed to crinkled slits at the sudden magnaminity. "I don't want credit," he clucked, looking away, as if he hated the gratitude heaped upon him.

Hira's eyes flashed. "Damn the credit!" he exclaimed, slamming his eyes shut. "The folks in this village seem to be tizzy with credit hangover," he snapped, took a deep breath, and then looked at Vasu in the eye. "The money comes from Abba, and he pays you to attend his rally at Phoolpur, in the first week of August," he declared, fanning the notes before Vasu's eyes, which lit up.

Vasu could not believe his luck. It did not matter, what Abba said and did. Presently, the election commission of India, and the electoral laws did not matter to him, because his stomach yearned for food, and he dare not let this opportunity pass. He cocked a smile, and grabbed the money. "Thanks to the elections," said Vasu, pressing the notes against his forehead. "I hope we have elections more often," he jeered, winking at Hira.

"Ha! Ha! Ha!" the two men cackled.

"In any case what difference will it make? Whether Abba or any other political party in Maharashtra?" snapped Hira, lifting his shoulders in a shrug. "Our fate will remain the same. They will continue to loot," Hira winked, and then stuck his tongue out.

"Elections remain a farce, and more like a ritual that occurs after every five years," taunted Vasu, scoffing at the, 'Great Indian democracy.'

"These are difficult times for farmers. Our village luckily has not witnessed a suicide. And; yet, the countryside resonates with stories of farmers, who jumped in wells, hanged themselves and consumed pesticides. It never happened a decade ago, but the moment inorganic cultivation of crops started. The cost of production killed the farmers," divulged Hira, scratching his head. "What did you sow?"

"I sowed Bt25, on my six acres. But the heat killed the seeds," lamented Vasu, slapping his forehead.

"You have to stay cautious," warned Hira, nodding his head. "It seems risky to grow inorganic varieties, because they suck the soil dry, and damage the fertility of the land. I suggest that you stick to our local crops like tur and jowar. They grow best in these arid conditions and don't cost much."

"I understand what you mean. But we don't decide," admitted Vasu, pursing his lips. "The input dealers decide, because they happen to give credit and dictate crop patterns. Its small farmers like me, who take the hit."

Hira interrupted, "not anymore." He scratched his arm, smacked his lips and hastened to add. "Also the big ones appear to kill themselves. It happened at Khatgaon. I went there to visit my folks, and it surprised me to hear that the biggest landlord in Khatgaon jumped into a well, and killed himself."

Vasu's forehead wrinkled, his face paled while he stared at Hira with cow eyes. "Don't tell me that landlords have joined the suicide spree," Vasu quipped, nodding his head in disbelief.

Hira inhaled a deep breath and broke in, "Bapuji Kharade owned a hundred acres of land, and for generations his family cultivated the desi variety of cotton, jowar and tur. His family remained the most prosperous family, in and around Khatgaon. In fact, people say that Bapuji's family gave away stored seeds of high quality free to those who needed it. The family owned over hundred cattle and never applied chemical fertilizers to their land," Hira paused for a breather, squared an ankle over his knee and continued his narrative. "But things changed, between nineteen ninety and ninety five, when he experimented with inorganic cash crops. First, he took up cotton cultivation and then soyabean. He invested large amounts on HYV seeds, chemical fertilizers and pesticides, but neglected to invest in water resources," divulged Hira, nodding his head.

Vasu edged closer to Hira, who now assumed a regal poise and spoke in an imperial tone. "He delineated from the traditional ways of farming, and stopped storing seeds. In fact, he sold his cattle, bought a tractor and his problems started, when the monopoly cotton procurement scheme ran into a mess. He soon lost out with high input costs and no returns, but persisted with the same pattern, and plunged further into debt. He still thought it unwise to invest in water resources, and managed to cultivate just one crop in the monsoons," disclosed Hira, showing his index finger to Vasu and continued. "To add to his woes the wages of labourers increased, which made it difficult, to sustain hundred acres of land. In nineteen ninety-seven, a draught occurred, and he borrowed for the first time from private moneylenders. He soon entered the debt trap, with less yields, and more interest on loans. In the years that followed, his loans continued to pile up, and in two thousand and two, they reached mammoth proportions. He borrowed more, but his first and second sowings failed, and when he went for the third borrowing, the creditors demanded reimbursement of previous loans. He couldn't take it anymore and that night he jumped into a well, and killed himself," concluded Hira, in a glum tone.

"How come such a big landlord failed to invest in water, which remains the life line of agriculture?" asked Vasu, slack-jawed.

Hira's eyes rolled skywards and he shook his head. "Even, if, he invested in water," replied Hira, propping his knees and curling his arms around them. "He shouldn't have depended completely on inorganic cash crops," argued Hira, gathering his wooden pole. "So I caution you about the pitfalls of inorganic varieties that ruin the soil, and drink gallons of water. They resemble sweet poison. I need to go, because I have to visit many more people,' he requested, standing up.

"Yeah," muttered Vasu, standing up. "When will the rally be held?"

"Someday in the first week of August; I'll inform you, about the day. Make sure you and your family attends the rally. Abba wants the numbers," Hira reiterated, and then hastened down the path.

"I'll come along," affirmed Vasu; he stood on his doorstep, until Hira disappeared round the bend. He stepped inside his tin shed, stretched himself on the charpoy, and pursed the money to his chest. "Thank-you Vitthal, we can manage a few more weeks," he said. He shut his eyes, took a deep breath and pondered. "If, I tap water; this misery will vanish," he murmured to himself and fell asleep.

In the morning, Vasu decided to visit the village square. It seemed like months, since, he last spent time at the square. The square remained typical of every village in India—the focal point of the village grapevine. Vasu silenced Mangala, with the money that Abba offered, and Mangala and Shoba dashed off to the kirana shop to buy the rations. They would stay busy all day, because they needed to sort and grind the grain so Vasu decided to spend some time at the square then come home for lunch, and leave for the farm. He, also, wanted to fix the dibbler, used to sow seeds, at the carpenter's shop, near the neem tree in the square. He shouldered the dibbler to the shop, dropped it there, and came over to the Hanuman temple located at the centre of the square. He went inside, paid his obeisance to the monkey God, and sat with his back against the pillar of the hall, which faced the square. He saw a huge hoarding pinned to the ground opposite the temple: Abba stood with folded hands, imploring the electorate to vote for him, with a slogan inscribed in the background.

"Blood, sweat and toil,

Abba belongs to men of the soil."

To the right of the hoarding, Raghu dusted and tidied the Sahukar's input shop. Behind the hoarding, a group of men sat under the acacia tree and played cards. At a distance from the men, a water tanker poured water into the common village well. Men, women and children, who carried ropes and plastic pots, gathered near the well to collect water. The veteniary hospital; as usual, stayed locked for the whole year. The government seemed reluctant to appoint a doctor to treat the animals of Ramwadi. Opposite the input shop, the tea vendor served tea and snacks to the customers, gathered under the peepul tree. It seemed a normal day at the village square, while the tum-tum's (auto rickshaw taxis) ferried passengers in and out of the village square.

Vasu watched the happenings in the village square and pondered, "God knows when things in Ramwadi will change? I see the same people, doing the same things for years. Their expressions, habits and attire remain the same. The houses and shops stay the same, and I can bet they, also, think the same: 'when will it rain?' This hoarding seems the only change this square has witnessed for years," he thought to himself, as he sprawled his legs on the floor,

"Namaskar Vasu," somebody, greeted him.

Vasu looked up, and saw five men ascend the stairs of the temple.

"Namaskar Munna," Vasu reciprocated to a man, who spread a soiled bedsheet on the floor of the hall.

Munna Yadav owned three acres of land on the dry patta; his family included four people. Munna's wife Lekha, two sons (Rohit and Tillya) and a daughter named Sushma. Munna remained sincere and worked hard; he started as a landless labourer, toiled hard, and purchased the land a few years ago. He too borrowed for the first sowing from Sahukar and suffered the same fate like Vasu.

"It's the same old story; no rains, only loans," snickered Munna, winking at Vasu

"Yeah," nodded Vasu. He drew his legs and curled his arms around them.

"Would you like to join us? We will gamble," asked Munna, sitting down on the bed sheet.

"I don't gamble and even if I wish I don't have the money to gamble," snapped Vasu.

"I'll lend you some, if, you wish to play," offered a bearded middle-aged man, who sat next to Munna.

"No!" replied Vasu.

"Let's get started. He can watch us play. Why bother?" reasoned another, squatting on the bedspread. He squinted in a furtive manner and bantered. "Maybe, Hira never visited Vasu. There's lots of money, doing the rounds in our village."

Munna shuffled the cards. "It happens every election year," he added, distributing the cards amongst the players.

The bearded man cocked a wry smile. "This seems the beginning. The other political parties have, yet, to open their kitties," he sneered, rubbing tobacco on the flat of his palm. He took a pinch of the stimulant, and tossed it in his mouth. "Abba hasn't paid enough. If, he wants our votes, he will have to dish out more. I'll vote for the party, which pays the most."

"Come on Mesba!" retorted Munna; he picked up his cards, turned them over and held them before his eyes. "Abba, only, paid us for the rally. He'll pay us again for our votes."

Mesba giggled and stuck his thumb out, "Lakya needs more than money. He needs this," he opened his mouth, looked upwards, and then turned his thumb over his mouth.

"Damn it! I am not the, only, guy who drinks. Don't sound like a saint," chided Lakya, curling his lips with contempt.

"Hey!" exclaimed Mesba, patting Lakya's shoulder. "Don't get cross," he urged, pointing at the two men sitting opposite him. "Sampat and Bankya need more than liquor and money," he insinuated, with a cocky wink, and stuck his tongue out.

"I hear there is a tamasha; pretty women will dance before us. This election the parties will spend a lot," added Lakya, smacking his lips, and flinging a card in the ring.

Munna studied his cards, picked one and tossed it in the ring. "The political parties will spend on anything to keep the voters happy."

The men nodded and giggled.

"Tumhavar keli mi marji bahal,

Naka sodun jau rang mahaal," sang Munna.

Lakya picked up the lines of the lavni from V. Shantaram's film, "Pinjara," and joined Munna.

"Papanyachi torna bandhun dolyavarti,

Hi nazar uditey kaljatli pirti,

Javal yava mala pusava, gupit majha khusal,

Harhur mahnu ki ood mahnu hi goad,

Ya basa majki, sutlai gulabi code,

Vir jalita mala raat hi pasri mayajaal, hmm, hmm," their voices, tapered to a soft hum.

"Wah! Wah!" cheered the others. They spread their arms out and swayed to the tune of the duet.

Mesba nudged Munna and motioned him to continue singing.

The duet resumed their singing.

"Ladiladi adbina tumha vinivti bai,

Pirtija ugadla pinjara tumchya pai,

Ashich rahavi raat sajana,

Kadhi Na vhavi sakal,

Hmm . . . hmm," the voices, petered to a hum, and then stopped.

"Wah! Wah!" applauded the audience.

Vasu listened to the romantic gamblers and smiled. "You have a sweet voice, Munna."

"You should hear him, when he's on spirits," sneered Mesba, with a wry smile.

"Ha! Ha! Ha!" cackled Lakya.

"Abba need not spend on the tamasha. He can hire Munna to sing," Sampat jeered, winking and sticking his tongue out.

"I have a better idea," interjected Banku. He signaled the group to come closer and then whispered. "We can have Munna sing, and Tatya's, 'keep' will dance for us."

"Ha! Ha! Ha!" the group roared with laughter.

"I must say she has a figure," said Mesba, twirling his moustache.

"Ssh . . . Ssh," Munna shooed. "Even the walls have ears. If, Tatya hears us we will invite trouble."

"Damn the bitch! She'll live a hundred years!" exclaimed Mesba. "Look there she goes!" he pointed in the direction of the Primary Health Centre. The men grinned, and looked wild eyed to where he pointed.

A gorgeous woman, with a buxom figure dawdled sensually on high heels towards the gates of the Primary Health Centre, where a bullet (motorcycle) stood parked inside the compound, under a neem tree. A middle aged man, with sunglasses, and dressed in a well pressed kurta-pyjama sat on the bike, fiddling with a bunch of keys. It appeared, as if he waited on her, and on seeing her, he twirled the pointed ends of his moustache, and disembarked from his bike. He looked into the mirror on the handle, and forked his fingers through his hair.

"He's after her, like a dog on heat," commented Lakya, leering at the sight.

"It's not a big deal. He's rich and political," countered Sampat.

"I swear in the name of Bt25. A good hundred quintal yield, and I'll have the money to lure Kanta. She'll swoon for me," bragged Lakya.

"Love is an expensive sport," added Banku, with a subtle wink, flicking his fingers.

The women drifted along, until she reached the bullet, and blushed at her lover. He followed her into the hospital.

"Damn the hospital! Why did the Government build it?" questioned Mesba, with a mischievous smile.

"A hospital must treat the sick and injured," jeered Lakya.

"Exactly!" exclaimed Ganpat, fiddling with his crotches and smiling wryly. "This hospital treats heart patients," he grabbed his heart, and gasped.

"Ha! Ha! Ha!" the men giggled.

"If, any of you happen to suffer from heartache," Mesba mentioned sarcastically, pointing to the hospital. "Go there for treatment. She'll cure your heartache," he sneered, and then winked.

"Ha! Ha! Ha!" the men chuckled.

"Leave them in peace. We have business to attend," reminded Munna, motioning the men to get back to the task on hand.

Vasu laughed at the comments passed by the gamblers. It seemed Ramwadi brimmed with all kinds of people.

"I must leave; the carpenter must have fixed the dibbler," he murmured to himself. He got up, headed for the carpenter's shop, gathered the dibbler and lumbered home for lunch.

CHAPTER 11

———————— ▼ ————————

On the thirteeth of July, Vasu hired the boring machine to drill the tube well. The family appeared nervous, when the machine arrived and ripped the earth. They clutched their hearts, and watched with baited breath, as the pipes went deep and deeper into the bosom of the dry patta. The machine quivered, while it pierced the heavy stones below the earth. It sunk two hundred and twenty feet below, but failed to strike water. Vasu sat under the neem tree, with his hands over his head and uttered, "Vithal, Vithal." He did not feel hungry and refused to eat lunch. The silence of the rocky terrain appeared lost in the din of the drilling machine. The owner approached Vasu, and asked him if he would like to drill further. It would cost more, because the rocks remained hard, and the engine consumed more fuel. Vasu stayed determined and agreed.

The machine restarted and roared ferociously, as it pulverized the rocks to pieces. It reached three hundred and twenty feet beneath the earth, but failed to strike water. Hot air, which gushed out off the hole broke the machine. It appeared a technical problem, which needed repair. Vasu's heart stayed in his mouth. The owner wanted two more days to fix the problem. The labourers loaded it onto a tractor, and drove it to Yavatmal.

Vasu's palpitations increased, while Mangala threw her tantrums at him, "I told you not to gamble. We have drilled more than Abba drilled, and there seems no trace of water. Don't you know the ways of the Sahukar?" she fumed, curling her lips with contempt. She slapped her forehead and riled. "He wants our land. The rich in this village

80

never care about the poor, and wait to swallow their land. How could you have agreed to mortgage our land? Can't you see through the intentions?"

"Keep quiet! I know what to do. How do you expect to get money to sow?" Vasu replied, slamming his foot on the ground.

Mangala seething with rage needed to vent her frustration. She put her hands on her hips, and inhaled a sharp breath, "why must he tell us to sow cotton?" she demanded, expelling her breath in a whoose. "You know what cotton does to folks around here. Even, if, we ask for money, he charges an interest, which obliges us to pay. How dare he tell us what to sow?" she bellowed; her eyes flashed. "You're too naïve. You should have taken time to reconsider his offer. Why rush into it? Look how much we drilled, and what happens if we fail to tap water. You mortgaged three acres of our land, what happens if he refuses to return our land?"

Vasu clinched his jaw and his body stiffened at the rebuke. He clenched his fists and ranted. "We don't have a penny on us?" he complained, with a voice that sounded stuck in his throat. "Will you lend me an anna?" he questioned, glaring at Mangala, who tossed her hair over her shoulders. Vasu raised his hand, and pointed a finger at her, "if you can't, then mind your tongue," he warned, with a tilted head, and rolled his eyes about. "Will your folks lend me the money?"

"Why will my folks lend you money? You have no right to pester them. They have a family to tend. Our responsibility stays towards our family," replied Mangala, it appeared as if she refused to give in.

"If that's the case, then I've decided how to go about it? You cannot stop me. Everytime I try to help, you disapprove it. What do you want me to do? Who will pay for Shoba's wedding?" rattled Vasu, in an attempt to justify his actions. He knew that Mangala argued against hope. The family's fortune stayed nailed to borrowing, and nothing could change that, because helplessness has a strange equation, it leads to more helplessness.

"You could have refused the offer, and taken up a job. Pandu and I would have tilled the land. We would not have all the eggs in one basket," proposed Mangala, looking at Vasu from the corner of her eyes. The words hit Vasu where it hurts most. He abhorred the idea of working for anyone, because he had suffered enough.

Vasu's body stiffened at the suggestion. "Oh!" he exclaimed, inhaling a sharp breath. "You want me to work, like a bonded labourer, all my life," he jeered, blowing his breath out slowly. "How much does it pay?"

"It pays enough to survive, and that's what matters. At least, we have our land to feel proud about," replied Mangala.

"The other day, you mocked our land, and called it 'dust and rubble.' Now you say you feel proud of it. What value does land hold without water? We reached the end of June, and the rains have disappeared. What do we do, if we do not have water? Assuming, I take up a job, will it be enough to pay for Shoba's wedding. We will need water for our crops," reasoned Vasu, shaking his head.

"Don't you see the results of your reckless adventure," bellowed Mangala. She pointed at the mound of excavated earth. "All dust and rubble," she sighed; her eyes turned moist, and she broke down. "You don't listen to me."

"We still haven't finished with the drilling, and why don't you understand that the rains played taunt. How do you expect to marry off Shoba? It will please me, if, you can suggest a way. It sounds bombastic, when you defend your land. But empty words don't feed stomachs, you need money, and Sahukar has it. We have to borrow from him, unless you want Shoba to remain unmarried. Shoba has grown up, and the village will mock us, if, we don't marry her off."

Mangala regained her poise, and wiped the tears to the ends of her saree. "Why rush through it, when we have no money? I fail to understand. And why bother about the village? They will always call us names, no matter what we do. If we don't have the money, wait till we make some."

"Wait for how long? What will come of it? The prices will shoot up next year, and the year after that. It comes down to the same thing, so marry her off this year. Whoever, lends us money, will ask for a mortgage."

Mangala remained adamant, "mortgaging land and paying interest does not imply that we follow the lenders intent. How dare he tell us what to sow?" grunted Mangala; her nostrils flared, and eyes widened. "The moment we borrow, the world treats us, like a criminal. The lenders charge an interest, but treat us like beggars. They fatten like pigs on our interest, insult us, and make us feel small. When we pay them back, they still keep reminding us that we once borrowed from them, as if they did us a favour. They talk as if; we owe them our lives.

Money lending seems bigger than God does. We keep bowing before it till death—"

Vasu raised his hand, nodded his head and interrupted. "It's pointless getting cross. Things will stay the same for borrowers, who have to endure," said Vasu; he lay down under the neem tree.

The afternoon heat scorched the earth, because the rains remained elusive. The field; a patch of hard rock lay tucked under a blanket of tank silt. The soil waited for the first showers to fall and soak in. The wind continued to whistle, as it blew over the land. Mangala and Vasu lay under the neem tree. Vasu tried to shut his eyes, and grab a nap, but his mind continued to waiver, while he watched the clear blue sky.

"If, the black clouds gathered and bursted?" he thought to himself. "I can sow my seeds, and in six months the cotton crop will be ready for picking. I will make money, pay for the wedding, and then I can think of other things. Maybe construct a concrete surface well to store more water. I can think of having cows and buffaloes for milk. I do not wish for more; just a little, to live a comfortable life. Hey Vithal!" he implored, folding his hands respectfully before the skies.

He sat up and saw Mangala sleeping with her back towards him. He saw the patches on her saree and felt guilty. He promised to look after her, and give her the best that life could offer, when he circled the sacred fire seven times in his wedding. But the poor woman stayed unfortunate. He did his best, but it appeared too little. What more could he do? The rains played truant, and refused to fall. Things grew worse over the years, because the climate patterns changed. Whoever harmed the environment made the farmers pay for it? Things changed with the advent of technology and capital.

He continued to reflect. "Cattle once grazed on the dry patta, which appeared a common milch pasture. The tall grass dettered people from wading through it, and fed thousands of cattle from the village. At sunset, the cowherds gathered the cattle, and drove them in hordes to the village. The hoofs kicked up dust, which engulfed the village, and took over an hour to settle. The cattle produced milk, ghee and buttermilk, which fed the village; no one charged an anna for these, and no one bought inorganic seeds and fertilizers. The women sorted, selected and stored the seeds in kangis (weed baskets), coated with cow dung. The kangis operated like seed banks, and provided seeds in times of distress. People never paid for seeds, as they pay for the thailis (packets) available in the markets today. It did not cost much to farm, and the rains fell on time.

'Today, things have changed with technology. Tractors have reduced the cattle on the farms, and made animal manure redundant, which has forced farmers to buy expensive fertilizers from the markets. Money drives farming, which remains capital intensive, compelling farmers to buy seeds, fertilizers and pesticides from the markets. The chemical fertilizers and hybrid variety of seeds, guzzle gallons of water that damage the soil. The grains remain susceptible to pests, which attack the crops frequently, and need pesticides that contain toxins. The pests develop resistance to these pesticides, and each year, newer and more expensive pesticides enter the market with higher prices. Presently, agriculture appears commercial and market oriented, which has affected cropping patterns that have lured farmers to grow cash crops, because money buys inputs for farming. The kangi, cow dung and cattle have disappeared, making agriculture capital intensive."

Vasu nodded his head in despair, after ruminating, and agreed, with the decision that circumstances forced upon him. The sun settled over the horizon slowly, and the heat in the wind dissipated. The evening appeared, and signalled the time to go home.

Mangala yawned, blinked owlishly and rose. "Let's leave," she said, tying her hair into a bun.

"I don't wish to leave," replied Vasu.

Mangala said nothing. She gathered the lunch basket, heaved it on her head, and walked away.

Vasu lay stretched under the neem tree, gazing at the mound of rubble heaped at a distance. The sun disappeared, while the stillness of the night gradually loomed over the fields. The hours passed by, but Vasu did not move. It seemed he remained disinterested in time, though the chill of the night bit him. He curled his callous knees against his stomach, buried his hands between his thighs, and tried to grab some sleep, but it seemed impossible in the company of the cold wind, which whistled and disturbed the calm of the errie night.

Vasu stared into the darkness; his heart congealed then melted into the horrors of reality, which his mind conjured. There remained the "if's" and "but's" in life. So far, life seemed cruel and harsh to him. In a country where, majority of the population lived off agriculture, it appeared a disgrace to find a peasant, lying in rags on this rocky terrain fighting adversity. He seemed betrayed by the Government, he voted to power, and ignored by a populace that lost the ability to empathize, under the heavy comfort of opulence.

He now played the biggest gamble on earth. Maybe, it appeared too inconspicuous for the billionaires, but for Vasu the risk stayed laudable. All by himself, he fought hard for a simple life of dignity. He did not ask for much; just a little, similar to a speck of dust for his family. He sat up and looked around; not a soul stirred on the land. It suggested Vasu's predicament, he stayed marginalized, as an outsider to the system, which governed India. He slept alone and pondered; his presence dwarfed by the vast expanse of land, which stretched for miles and miles into the darkness.

At a distance, his eyes noticed a rabbit, which tunneled the mound of rubble, and searched for something to munch. Vasu fixed his gaze on the rabbit, which burrowed, nibbled, and squinted in a furtive manner, wary of predators that prowled for an opportunity. It looked, as if, danger loomed over the rabbit's head, while it searched for food. Vasu rubbed a hand over his dark stubble, and gaped at the rabbit. "I hope I lived the life of a rabbit, and depended on nature for food. A rabbit doesn't have to bother about loans and interests to borrow for food, shelter and clothes," he fancied; his eyes bleared. "Look at me!" he mused; his nostrils flared, heart froze, and then melted to tears. "I don't have a decent pair of clothes to cover my body; and yet, I remain a cotton farmer, who worries about food," he reflected, with tears gushing down his cheeks. He nodded his head in disgust and sat up. "I've tried to sleep for over an hour, but my eyes don't shut, because my mind waivers with worry. I do not think a rabbit has a mind to worry. Hey, lucky one," Vasu called out to the rabbit.

The rabbit sprung on its hinds, cocked his head, and looked around furtively. "Sssh," Vasu shooed at it to draw its attention. The puny animal sprang, and bolted like lightning.

"Gone," lamented Vasu, with a wary smile, surfacing on his lips.

From somewhere, Vasu overheard a voice, which blabbered and sounds of footsteps that staggered unsteadily, advance towards him. His forehead scrunched, his eyes narrowed, and he strained his ears to gather the chatter, but the voice remained inscrutable. He straightened his back, and cupped his ear to the wind to catch the words. The tone sounded wistful, but the words remained cluttered. He twisted to his left and continued his effort to track the voice. He jiggled his head, as the voice came closer within earshot.

"I have four mouths to feed—how much? Four . . . a debt of two lakhs—how much? Two-lakhs . . . what can I do? Nothing . . . even a rabbit doesn't fear me . . . it knows that I can't do a thing . . . I'm lost—"

"Damn the debtor!" snapped Vasu; he slapped his hands against his thighs, winced, and waddled his head in disgust; "another debtor drinks himself to death!" he blurted. "Why does Munna wobble on this terrain, late in the night?" he wondered, with his eyes fixed on Munna, who tottered towards him.

Munna faltered nearer to Vasu, but continued to chatter, as if oblivious of Vasu's presence.

"Hey Munna," Vasu called out to him.

The man halted in his track, and almost stumbled over.

"Careful!" warned Vasu.

Munna regained his balance, hunched over with his hands propped on his knees, and stared wide-eyed. "Oh! Vasu!" he sputtered, and then smiled.

His white shirt soiled and tattered, fluttered like a piece of paper against the wind. His face looked bloodied, and eyes black like a boxer's face, after a bout in the ring. His lips oozed with blood, and resembled a lemon slit to rinds with a knife. The chappals under his feet looked worn, and one of them appeared ripped in the middle.

"The taanda! I suppose," hinted Vasu.

"Hmm," nodded Munna, collapsing in a stupor.

Vasu kneeled and helped him sit up. "Why do you drink yourself to death, and loaf around on this patta at this hour of the night?" gasped Vasu, hunkering down next to him. "Can you reach home?"

"What home?" questioned Munna, sprawling his legs on the ground. He propped his hands on the ground and reclined. "Home means a decent place to live in."

"Hmm," Vasu murmured, shaking his head, and curling his hands over his knees.

"A home means peace and privacy," asserted Munna. He tilted his head to one side, and his eyes flashed. "But my home resembles a pressure cooker, which will explode, because I have four mouths to feed," cribbed Munna. He raised one palm, and curled his thumb inwards. "Four!" he flashed his fingers, and then flung his hand back.

"And a debt of two lakh rupees," he paused, and then questioned. "Do you call it a home?"

"We sail in the same boat, but why drink and invite death?" asked Vasu.

"What else can I do?" he queried, hunching over. He lifted his shoulders in a shrug, and his jaws dropped. "I have three kids. The eldest Rohit, who is twenty-one years of age, displayed keen intellect and aspired to do engineering. As a father, I bore the responsibility, because I brought him into this world," admitted Munna, pointing to himself. "Did he have a choice? No! It remains my responsibility to see him through life. So, I borrowed thirty thousand rupees from Sahukar, to have him admitted to an engineering college to fulfill his dream. Is it a crime for a farmer's child to dream? No!" declared Munna; his eyes bleared. "He wanted to study, take up a job and help run the family. But, what happened? Last month, he dropped out of college. Why?" questioned Munna, with tears gushing down his cheeks. "Not because engineering seems difficult. Nah! Nah!" Munna clucked, shaking his head in disagreement. He raised his arm, and wiped the tears, with his tattered sleeves. "He dropped out, because I didn't have the money, to pay his term fees. I killed his dream," Munna cried out in guilt, pointing at himself. "I needed to manage four years for him, but in the very first year, I gave up. This reveals the truth of our lives. We feed and clothe people, but we cannot afford to provide for our children," riled Munna; his face wrinkled and tears continued to stream down his coarse, dark cheeks. "What wrong did I do? It did not rain for the past few years and I could not manage a yield. Whatever happens to the environment, we pay the price for it. I begged the Gods to let Rohit complete his studies. I told them to punish me, if they want, but let Rohit finish his engineering. Please! Please! I begged, but they gave me a damn. Thu!" spat Munna; he wiped his tears.

Vasu edged closer, and then put his arm over Munna's shoulder, "Munna control your emotions," he said.

"Vasu, the last three months remained horrible," complained Munna. He crossed his legs, and hunched over. "My daughter Sushma was hospitalized for typhoid, and my wife Lekha needed an ear surgery. I took them to the civil hospital in Yavatmal. The Government doctor told me to visit him at his private clinic. He said that the Government does not have medicines. This Government, which calls itself the farmers Government, does not provide us with medicines. Thugs and cheats! Thu!" he spat; his eyes burned with fury. "Jail them for treachery! They promise the world to secure votes, and then disappear for five years, condemning us to starve. Have you seen a peasant with a belly?" questioned Munna, pointing at his stomach. "Huh!" he sneered, shaking his head in disgust. "See the Ministers, who fatten like pigs. Why will they care for us? The thugs loot us. They siphon off the money in the co-operative banks, and force us to borrow from private moneylenders. I borrowed at five percent interest per month to pay for the medical expenses. How much can my three acres of land give, if it does not rain? I suffered a series of crop failures, because I do not have water. The Government can provide us with irrigation facilities, and help us build trickle tanks. But it never happens, because of corruption. This year, I need money for Sushma's wedding. Where will I get the money from?" asked Munna, raising his eyebrows.

Vasu remained silent.

"Do we belong to the human race?" Munna queried, shaking his head.

Vasu stayed mute. It seemed Munna wished to pour out his grief, and Vasu posed as the passive listener to help Munna download.

"We appear worse than animals," shouted Munna, clenching his dirty fists, and then pointing ahead, "there sat a rabbit in my path. Somewhere there," he showed, dropping his hand on his knee.

Vasu nodded his head, "hmm," he murmured.

"It refused to give way. There appeared defiance in the puny creature. I shouted, also, slammed my foot. Yet, it sat there, as if I did not matter. It did not care a damn for me!" moaned Munna. He picked up a stone and flung it in the direction. "Even animals damn us because we remain debtors! Perhaps they perceive our helplessness, and know we cannot do a thing. It seems we remain lifeless corpses, who walk around as living dead—"

"What did you do at the taanda?" inquired Vasu.

"What do you think, I went there for? I did not go there to drink. Nah! I swear!" entreated Munna, pinching the skin over his throat. "I went there to gamble. The other day I lost twice, so I changed places for better luck. Again, I lost; I cannot buy seeds for my second sowing. No creditor wants to lend me money. They know that I stand buried, neck deep in debt, so I tried my hand at cards. The truth remains, if, one starts in life; a looser, then one will never end a winner. Debt appears contagious; it spreads defeat and pessimism. It will not let one win. I stay defeated and do not know what to do. The biggest helplessness appears when you can't control your life!" he conceded, trying to heave himself up. He quivered and stumbled down.

Vasu helped him settle down, "where do you plan to go?" he questioned, gripping Munna's shoulders. "Lie down here and leave in the morning. I do not think you can reach home. I'll get you some water."

Munna sprawled on his back, and slammed his eyes shut. Vasu headed for the neem tree, gathered the pitcher, and carried it to where Munna lay. "Munna, get up and drink water," urged Vasu, tugging Munna's shoulder, but Munna seemed lost in sleep.

Vasu stretched out next to Munna and fell asleep.

CHAPTER 12

▼

The next two days, witnessed a reversal in the weather. Thick black clouds hovered over Ramwadi, the heat soared, and late in the evening, the scent of wet earth drifted across the village. It rained heavily, so the drilling machine failed to arrive, and Vasu rightly reasoned that the rains would delay the drilling. The rains forced Vasu to wait until the sun dried the earth. In the village, another, buying spree reignited after the showers, and it appeared the farmers had no choice but to opt for a second crop. The moneylenders and input dealers were on a song.

Vasu joined the bandwagon, and approached Sahukar for another loan. He bought six packets of Santano's Bt25 seeds, which added an additional twelve thousand rupees and the interest to his liabilities. He, also, borrowed an additional five thousand rupees for rations, which forced his debt burden to soar above forty thousand rupees, excluding interest, and the amount borrowed for the tube well. The drilling stayed underway, so the exact amount remained under wraps, but a rough estimate of the expenses showed that his borrowings touched, almost two lakhs, excluding the interest rate on this amount. The family organized and sowed the seeds.

In the month of July, after the peasants finish their sowing activities, they trek to Pandharpur for a pilgrimage, and converge on the banks of the, Chandrabagha river, to worship Lord Vithal and his consort Rukmini. This pilgrimage called, 'vari,' in Marathi dates back to over a thousand years, and legend reveals that Saint Gyaneshwar of

Alandi started this pilgrimage from Alandi near Pune to Pandharpur, way back in the twelfth century A.D.

Peasants from all over Maharashtra, and even Andhra, Karnataka, and Tamil Nadu trek hundreds of kilometers to reach Pandharpur, to pay obeisance to their beloved God on the auspicious day of, "Ashad Ekadashi." The spectacle appears breathtaking, as a sea of humanity, walks barefoot, battling the rains, chanting, "Vithal, Vithal," while accompanying the dindi to Pandharpur. It seems, as if sheer faith, steeped in tradition drives these people to the doors of the, "Vitthal-Rukmini," Mandir in Pandharpur. The devotees or varkaris, trek in groups (dindis) comprising of ten, twenty, fifty people, strutting across highways and dirt tracks, which lead to Pandharpur. The Varkaris remain a Vaisnav sect of Hinduism, who abstain from consuming meat and liquor, and do not believe in the ritualistic and casteist tenets of Hinduism. This sect originated, as a protest against the Brahminical dominance of Hinduism. The tradition stays despite, the fact that the life of most of the peasants remains miserable, neglected, abused, exploited and betrayed; yet, they continue to worship their beloved God, and make meager offerings that they save from a debt-ridden life. Vasu's family belonged to this sect, and every year Vasu went to Pandharpur to pay obeisance to Lord Vithal.

Over the years, the erratic monsoon disturbed the schedule of the varkaris, who usually waited for the rains to fall, sowed seeds and then joined the dindis. However, if the rains delay sowing, the peasants risk, skipping the pilgrimage. Vasu's family never skipped a single pilgrimage to Pandharpur. This year, the rains delayed, but Vasu stayed determined to go to Pandharpur. In his younger days, he walked to Pandharpur on many occasions, but for the past few years, he preferred to go by bus. This election year, all the political parties competed to sponsor this pilgrimage and gain political mileage.

The elections in Maharashtra remain a binge of, "freebies". Most political parties, who looted the public exchequer, now, dole out a part of the loot to the electorate, in lieu for their votes. The grand electoral candidates; the future lawmakers of Maharashtra, offer everything free for votes. This deal of democracy states: "we, the electoral candidates promise to offer the voters everything free, and when they vote us back to power, we'll ensure their doom for the next five years. Long live Democracy! Long live Freedom!" This priceless freedom (read;

free-doom), offered by Indian democracy, has established itself firmly in the system of Maharashtra, and heaped a debt burden of over two lakh crores on Maharashtra (Bola Jai Jai Maharashtra Majha). Nothing seems out of its ambit: money, meat, liquor, rations, air, water, electricity and even God; all offered free, by most political parties. The political parties will go to any length to buy the votes, and the intelligent electorate oblige. During the build up to the 2004 assembly elections, the electoral candidates traversed the length and breadth of their constituencies, announcing through hoardings, posters, pamphlets and loudspeakers, that they would ferry the varkaris to Pandharpur, free of cost. The competition appeared stiff, because each party offered attractive packages to the varkaris, in a bid to win them over.

Most candidates of the opposition alliance that upholds and guards, "Hindutva," offered the pilgrims free travel, food and lodging, and why not? After all, the opposition Hindutva alliance claimed the custody of Hinduism, as if, the thirty three million Hindu Gods chose this alliance to run the show for Hindus on earth. Yet, this alliance remained a contradiction, and more of an arrangement to seek power. One-half of this alliance espoused the cause of, "Marathi Manoos," while the other half vouched for, "Pan-Indian Hindutva."

The party, which loved the Marathi Manoos, evolved in stages propogating, hatred against the South Indians, North Indians and finally targeting Muslims. Its ideology of hate aroused a fear in the minds of the Marathi Manoos that migrants, who swamped Mumbai, will swallow Mumbai and wrest it from the Marathi Manoos. Yet, when the Marathi Manoos, voted this party to power, the same party that crooned for Marathi Manoos, swindled the exchequer of the poor Marathi Manoos, and heaped a debt burden, which still burdens the Marathi Manoos. So much for the love, care, affection and compassion this party nurtures for the Marathi Manoos (Amchi Mumbai-Bola Jai Jai Maharashtra Majha).

The other half of this alliance vouched for Hindutva, and its headquarters (a research laboratory for historical and archaelogical wrongs against Hindus), vowed to avenge all historical wrongs committed against Hindus. It wished to rebuild temples destroyed in the days of yore by bigots and paint the country saffron. This party, which originally remained a, "cow-belt," party with its bastion in

North India, formed an alliance with the Marathi Manoos party in Maharashtra, which disliked North Indians. When confronted with this logical inconsistency, both the parties justified their hunger for power, on the grounds of their common love for Hindus. The opposition alliance thus remains an opportunistic arrangement for power, between a political party that propagates Pan-Indian Hindutva and another, that propagates Marathi Hindutva or Maratitva. Bola Jai Jai Maharashtra Majha! Politics, as someone rightly remarked makes strange bedfellows.

Most candidates of the ruling alliance of Maharashtra offered not just free travel, food and lodging but an additional pilgrimage to the Mahalakshmi temple at Kolhapur, and the Tuljabhavani temple at Tuljapur. It seemed, as if, the packages offered by the electoral candidates in Maharashtra, would shame the best travel companies of the world, because the packages offered a discount on free travel. Its strange economics but let that remain, because political parties in India will defy even the laws of gravity, so why bother about the laws of economics. The grand ruling alliance of Maharashtra, which claims custody of secularism, happened to sponsor a religious event. This alliance like the opposition, stood on stilts, embedded in logical contradictions. The bigger national party in this alliance claims a legacy of over a hundred years, runs on the principle of dynastic politics, and appears a family fiefdom, controlled by a certain dynasty from Delhi.

In Maharashtra, the same party replicates this dynastism, and analogizes a cliché of sugar barons, who remain loyal to the dynasty (high command) in Delhi. This political organization resembles the Mansabdari system of the Mughal era, in which the Mansabdars run their own little fiefdoms on dynastic lines but derive their strength from the Delhi dynasty. Most of these Mansabdars or sugar barons, control majority of the sugar co-operatives in the state, and claim to represent the poor farmers, but over the years they looted and pillored the poor farmers' co-operatives, liquidated them, auctionioned them, and then bought back the same co-operatives at half their prices as private companies. The data confirms the truth: most of the MLA's, MP's and realtors' earlier fuctioned, as directors and chairpersons of the bankrupt co-operatives. Where did the money vanish? Not to the poor farmers, who remain debt ridden and committ suicide. At least, the opposition alliance did not brow beat that they represented the farmers, but the ruling alliance makes tall claims that it represents the men of the soil, when, in reality majority of the leaders and cadres of the ruling alliance comprise of realtors, contractors, bussinessmen and co-operative tycoons, who swindled the farmers.

The biggest joke of this ruling alliance remains the other half: a self-styled ultra-nationalistic party, with a sub-regional (pockets of Western Maharashtra) presence. The prefix ultra represents the origin of this party: a group of disgruntled Mansabdars of the larger party rebelled against the high command in Delhi, which refused to anoint their leader as the Prime Minister. The rebels declared they defected, because they appeared more nationalistic (ultra), and would not serve under a foreign hand that controlled the dynasty in Delhi. They admitted they had differences over the true meaning of nationalism, but set aside this grievance and joined the same parent party as an alliance partner to grab power, declaring they wished to save the state from the clutches of communal forces. This opportunistic secular ruling alliance remained the abode of mostly neo-rich barons, who made a fortune from sugar, education, infrastructure, milk, cotton, poultry, timber, sand, oil and the like and grew richer by the day, at the expense of the poor farmers. All these neo-rich aristocrats (self-styled after the loot) exhibited a mission. They aspired to create dynasties in their bastions of power and drew inspiration from the high command in Delhi, which remains the biggest political dynasty in India. This opportunistic secular ruling party alliance appeared a contradiction, when it rose as a bulwark to defend democracy against communal forces. Bola Jai Jai Maharashtra Majha! Politics, as someone rightly remarked makes strange bedfellows.

Besides, these established mainstream political parties in Maharashtra, the rebels like Abba also offered to sponsor the pilgrimage. Free and fair elections in Maharashtra threw plenty of options for Vasu's pilgrimage to Pandharpur. The only hiccup seemed time, because he wished to finish drilling the well and then leave.

The hot and humid afternoon, with the sun overhead baked the dry patta, which sported patches of green that sprouted due to the rains. The soil retained some moisture, though most of the water drained down the rocky terrain. The family gathered under the neem tree for lunch. Vasu, who stayed hungry for the past few days, sensed rats running in his stomach. It seemed pointless starving, when the machine failed to arrive. Vasu's indefinite fast earned him the wrath of Mangala.

"Do you wish to eat or starve to death?" asked Mangala, with a scowl on her face.

Vasu's body stiffened at the sneer, but he kept quiet. He seemed puffed up, and longed for empathy even though the hunger gnawed at his stomach.

Mangala's eyes flashed and lips smacked. "I see no reason to starve. Whatever, must happen, will happen? You can't change your fate by starving," she mocked, looking at Vasu from the corner of her eyes.

Vasu sat with his hands curled around his knees, and head tilted sideways; his eyes gazing at the ground, as if pondering over his fate.

"Huh!" Mangala scoffed, at the sight; she wrinkled her nose, and nodded her head.

Vasu felt the rebuke and gritted his teeth. He stared at her in anger, "damn the nagging!" he blurted, dropping his knees, hunching over, and snapping his fingers. "Give me my food!"

Mangala rummaged through the lunch basket. "I see no point in going to Pandharpur," she digressed, with a gleam of deviltry in her eyes. It seemed she wished to nag Vasu.

"Leave that to me! I'm not forcing anyone to come along!" Vasu grimaced; he snatched the food from Mangala's hand, ripped out a portion of the roti, crammed it in his mouth and chomped on it.

"Even, if you force me. I won't come along."

"Just keep that aside!" snapped Vasu; his eyes flashed, and it seemed he lost his cool.

Mangala took the cue and decided to keep quiet. Meanwhile, Shoba and Pandu arrived with the pitcher of water, and sat down for lunch.

"The pilgrimage hasn't done us any good. It's only a ritual, which consumes time and money," Mangala continued her tirade with sarcasm, looking at Pandu, as if provoking him.

Vasu nodded his head, dropped it down and munched his food. He decided to ignore Mangala.

Pandu grinned and rattled off. "Religion remains the opium of the masses. The rich have created this institution to control the poor. The rich class creates Gods, builds temples, and establishes trusts, while the poor class makes the offerings. The trusts created by the rich classes grow richer, with the poor man's offerings, while the poor remain wretched," he professed.

Mangala arched a sly brow. "I believe what you say," she endorsed Pandu's view, squinting in a furtive manner.

Vasu squirmed in his seat, and his jaws slackened for a moment.

"Look at the offers, the corrupt political parties make in the name of pilgrimage. They should spend the money on our upliftment," Pandu went on with his tirade against religion.

Vasu continued to look down but his ears stayed hooked to the conversation. He could not avoid it, though; he felt his blood simmering with rage, because he sensed the affront.

Pandu grew bolder "Nothing appears to affect the Brahmins! The Gods and planets never harass them. They skillfully created a complex web of rituals to help them survive. The temple stays the only place where money continues to flow. In fact, people rush to temples more during calamities. Look at the Pandit in our village. He makes money all day. He utters some mantras in Sanskrit like a parrot, which none of us understand, and I doubt he understands it either," Pandu riled.

Mangala and Shobha giggled.

"The pilgrimage resembles a farce. The poor farmers suffer without rains. If the Gods exist, then why do they want us to suffer?" asked Mangala.

"Suffering means loot, which appears the biggest selling point of religion. That explains why Mao advocates the abolition of religion after the revolution. The people must believe that they control their destinies. Religion leads to fatalism; an anti-dote to change," explained Pandu.

"My brother-in-law died in a stampede in the temple at Pandharpur. Do you call it a pilgrimage? It appears a virtual invitation to death," moaned Mangala.

"The worst thing about this holy procession remains the dirt and filth excreted on the banks of the Chandrabagha. People literally shit, bathe and even drink in the river collectively. No wonder many fall ill. The Government stays reluctant to provide for the devotees. I call it an invitation for an epidemic," argued Pandu.

"I don't think Lord Vitthal wants an epidemic. The herd like mentality of the people rooted in tradition drives them to Pandharpur. It appears a dangerous ritual!" gasped Mangala.

"The people who fall ill and suffer include poor peasants. The rich stay away from this ritual. The indebted peasants borrow for the pilgrimage. Does it make sense? Has anyone seen Lord Vitthal for real? When you don't have the money to feed yourself, its pointless feeding God?" remonstrated Pandu, looking at Vasu, who listened to the conversation and raged, but refrained from saying anything, because his hunger prevented him. But now that he had his fill, he regained his energy and thought of silencing his detractors. He relied on his real life experiences to knock down Pandu's argument.

"It's all very easy, when you don't have responsibilities to shoulder. But the moment you marry and have a family, all this talk flies out of the windows," asserted Vasu, looking at Pandu.

"What good did you give me?" asked Mangala, pointing to the patches on her saree. "Responsibility and family," she sneered, and then twisted her lips. "Huh!"

Pandu giggled and forced a frown on Vasu's face. Vasu never anticipated a woman's relentless ability to nag, and found himself in a quandary. He took the charted course to salvage his image. "If you belonged to a Princely family like a Maharani, your accusations would seem sound, and what you said would hold. In any case, marriages happen between equals, so you don't score a point complaining."

Mangala pointed at Shoba, "will you marry her to a beggar?" she asked; her eyes flashed. "It wouldn't cost a dime!" she ridiculed, staring at Vasu with her eyes wide opened. "Why do you worry for her marriage? Because all parents, dream big for their child. They always want the best for their children. And that's what, my father wanted for me," snapped Mangala, curling her lips in contempt.

Vasu remained calm knowing, he succeded in irritating Mangala. He cocked a wry smile and looked away.

Pandu's habit of talking forced him to interrupt. The revolutionary in him showed up. He sprawled his legs and snubbed. "Marriage entails useless expenses that force people to spend beyond their means. Over half the peasant families in Ramwadi grovel in debt, because of marital rituals and conventions. The people who gather to witness a marriage, feast and leave after the ceremony. The couple has to fend for themselves and must save and not spend on the people."

"We live in a society, which means we need to socialize, because we need others to survive. Otherwise people would have gone about doing everything on their own," argued Vasu; he shook his head.

"I don't deny what you say. People may gather, chat and leave. But, why do they expect pomp and show? They know that it costs a fortune," replied Pandu. He seemed to abhor societal traditions.

Vasu sighed and expelled his breath in a whoose. "You marry the way you want, but don't give me your advice. I will witness how you manage what you say. I do not think Gangaram will agree with your line of thinking. If you want, I can bet on that," uttered Vasu; he cast a glance at Shobha.

"We'll see," boasted Pandu.

"Shoba, do you agree with what Pandu says?" Vasu asked Shoba.

"I want to see you happy, when I marry. You did not eat a grain for the past two days, because you worry about the tube well. If my marriage bothers you, then I prefer not to marry," replied Shoba; her eyes turned moist.

"Shoba, don't worry about my fate!" blurted Vasu, putting his hand over her shoulder. "I'll give you in safe hands. I can manage, but I will not let you suffer. I'll do my best for you."

"That's exactly what my father said to me, before my marriage," sneered Mangala, and then smiled wryly.

The rebuke irked Vasu, who seemed tired of the barbs all afternoon. "Shut up!" he exclaimed; his nostrils flared. "Don't compare your fate to Shoba's. Let's hope, we can do a lot better for her."

Mangala cocked a smile at Vasu's tantrums. "My brother sent word yesterday, that we may expect the people to come and see Shoba this week. We better stay prepared," she observed. She referred to the proposal for Shoba, which her brother pursued, and stayed determined to scuttle Vasu's pilgrimage.

"Don't worry!" snapped Vasu, rolling his eyes skywards, as if wary of his wife's dogged attitude. "I'll not leave for Pandharpur, till I see them off," he sighed, sprawling on the ground, and tucking his palms beneath his head. A gentle breeze blew across the terrain, when Vasu slammed his eyes shut for an afternoon nap.

CHAPTER 13

▼

On August 5, Sam Strosberg paced down the corridor, leading to his chamber on Capitol Hill. The lobby of his chamber looked packed with corporate honchos, who wished to have an audience with him. He remained the most sought after Senator, and the President's most trusted man. Like a true Republican, he hobnobbed with the, "decision makers," who wielded influence over the American economy. His arrival sparked a clamour, as the beeline of anxious visitors, beamed and heaved a sigh of relief. They greeted him, as he strided towards the doors of his chamber.

Sam reached the door, gripped the knob and pivoted on his heels to face his supporters. He smacked his lips and nodded his head. "I'm sorry to announce that I have an important meeting; an urgency that will consume time. Besides, I'm also slated to meet the President. There's no point hanging around here," he apologized.

"Huh," sighed the audience, with wrinkled faces.

"Presently, I'm occupied for the day, so cancel all the appointments," he ordered his secretary, who sat at the reception.

"Yeah," she replied.

"I'm sorry," he apologized again to his audience, then whirled about, twisted the knob and entered his chamber.

Sam appeared tired; the morning session in the Senate drained him. He seemed wary of, "Green Bob," and the Democrats, who breathed down his neck. He reached his desk, removed his coat, hung it on the backrest of his chair, loosened the knot of his tie, and then picked up a Havana cigar lying on his table.

"Here light it," proposed a man, sitting on a chair next to the desk. He flicked the lighter for a flame.

Sam lit his cigar, took a puff and squatted on his chair at the desk. "Monty what will you have?" he questioned, blowing out circles of smoke towards the ceiling.

"I'll have coffee," replied Monty Agarwal.

Monty's father came from Uttar Pradesh in India, and his mother belonged to Texas. Monty's parents operated a mining business, since, forty years, which Monty inherited. His company, "Dhatu Private Ltd," remained one of the top mining conglomerates in the world. It acquired mines in Latin America, Africa, Asia, Australia and formed many subsidiaries, when it acquired stakes in the local companies. "Aluminium Private Limited" and "Coal Asia Private Limited," operated as subsidiaries in India, and Sam Strosberg held shares in both these subsidiaries. In India, these companies mined iron-ore, coal and bauxite.

Sam picked up the intercom. "Two mugs of coffee in my study," he ordered, in a gruff voice. "No! I don't want to meet any of my visitors. No . . . No . . . Tell them I'm busy and don't divert any phone calls to me," he urged, and then slammed the receiver.

"Sam, how's the Senate? I can feel the pressure you bear," inquired Monty, reclining in his chair, and fixing his gaze on Sam, who puffed out circles of smoke.

Sam took a puff and nodded. "I'm stressed," he admitted, blowing out the smoke slowly. He straightened his back, dropped his head on the backrest, and gazed at the chandelier, which hung from the ceiling. "It's my second term in the Senate but more taxing."

"Do we sign the Kyoto Protocol?" asked Monty.

"Bull shit!" blurted Sam. He gritted his teeth, lurched forward, clenched his fist, and pounded the table. "We will never sign that crap!" declared Sam; his eyes burned with hatred. "The corporates will burn me alive. Have you lost your mind?"

Monty cocked a wry smile. "The media splashes Green Bob on its cover pages, as if they wish to make a hero out of him," remarked Monty.

"Fuck the media!" exclaimed Sam, stabbing his middle finger in the air. He pursed his lips, shook his head and ranted. "Damn the bubble popularity!"

"What about the Democrats?"

Sam wriggled in his seat, raised his eyebrows, and thrust his palm in the air. "Five million American jobs!" he proclaimed and then paused. He dropped his palm, and reclined in his seat. "Billions of dollars at stake!" he maintained, drumming the desk with his fingers. "The Democrats don't have a choice. They'll create a scene, but finally come around," prophesized Sam; he grinned and slapped the table.

The door swung open and the coffee attendant arrived. "Coffee," she announced.

Sam glanced at her, nodded his head, and turned his attention to Monty. She walked towards the desk with the tray in hand.

"Just one teaspoon of sugar," requested Monty, with his index finger.

The attendant nodded, while Monty looked back at Sam. "If, what you say is true, then, why the hell do the Democrats create a scene?" he questioned, taking his cup of coffee from the attendant. "Thanks," he said, smiling at the attendant. "They did the same over Iraq."

"Your coffee Sam," said the attendant.

"Leave it on the table," replied Sam.

The attendant placed the cup on the table, and then left the study.

Sam waited for his attendant to leave, and then stabbed the cigar in the ashtray. He bent over, propped his elbows on the table, and took a deep breath. A sly smile surfaced on the corner of his lips. He exhaled slowly and answered. "I put it this way. Two guys wished to fuck the same bitch. We did it first, so they cry rape."

"Ha! Ha! Ha!" cackled Monty. "Damn the hypocrisy! It sounds ridiculous!"

"I don't wish to talk about traitors!" snapped Sam, sipping his coffee. He smacked his lips and inquired. How's our venture doing in India?"

Monty sat bestride and looked glum. He crossed his hands over his chest, and shook his head in dismay. "Our venture's jammed," he moaned, tapping his foot on the floor. He released his hands; rested them on the arms of the chair, and gripped the arms hard. He tightened his jaws and spoke with a heavy accent. "Over two billion dollars of investment in shambles," he paused, then gazed at Sam and intoned. "The tribal protests seem to grow louder and louder," he uttered the last three words slowly and emphatically.

Sam gulped his coffee, smacked his lips and placed the cup on his desk. "A major problem when you invest in developing nations."

Monty clenched his fists, and slammed them on the arms of his chair. "The bloody tribal protests!" he exclaimed, nodding his head vigourously. He dropped his head on the backrest, rolled his eyes to the ceiling and pointed to his chest. "I" he said and paused. He straightened his back and spread his arms wide open, "promised them the sky: jobs, hospitals, schools, clean drinking water, roads and concrete houses to live in," he paused, dropped his hands, bit his lips in contempt, and shook his head in disgust. "But they want to continue living in the gutters; like swines. No matter how much you clean them, they will go back and squat in the gutters. We asked for a mountain of bauxite, tucked away in the forests of Orissa. We got the permission, signed a MOU with the Government, and even built our refinery at the foot of the hill. We needed to break down the mountain to transport the bauxite to our refinery," uttered Monty and then paused. He leaned forward, slapped the desk, reeled back in his chair and inhaled a deep breath. "But," he paused; expelling his breath slowly and scratching his forehead. "The tribes which live on the mountains call the mountain their God," he sneered, twisting his lips. "They refuse to vacate the hills and to make matters worse, the bloody Government that first begged us to invest now cringes," he gasped, while he rolled his eyes upwards. "It keeps promising us that it'll arrest the protests, but that's not happening," he fumed, slapping the table. "We loose millions of dollars each day," he declared, with an emphatic tone. He clenched one fist and rammed it on the flat of his palm. "Sam you need to pull strings. We can't keep watching!"

"Hmm," murmured Sam; he straightened his head, which stayed tilted, while he listened to Monty. He leaned forward, elbowed the desk, placed his fingers on the edges of his forehead and rubbed his eyes with his thumbs. "What about our coal venture?" he asked, whirling his neck and cracking his knuckles.

Monty took a deep breath and breathed out slowly. "We suffered a few hiccups initially," he confessed; he stretched his legs, reclined in his chair, and tucked his head beneath his palms on the backrest. "Finally, we managed to get the blocks in the Tadoba-Andhari corridor of Maharashtra. In the beginning, the Gond tribes, who lived near the corridor refused to vacate. They muttered the same old crap: jal, jungle, zameen hamara hai, koi pujipati ki jagir nahi. They use these slogans prodded by some social activists, as if they own the forests. Bloody adivasis!"

Sam crossed his arms over his chest, and reclined in the comfort of his chair. His forehead creased, while he wondered for a moment and then asked. "If, you managed the Gond tribes, and wrested the coal fields," he pointed; he dropped his hands, lifted his shoulders in a shrug and elbowed the table. "You should have handled the tribes on the mountain top."

Monty spread his arms wide open, shrugged his shoulders, dropped them on his knees, and hunched over. "It's complicated," he sighed.

Sam nodded his head, and then rested his chin on his palms.

Monty continued to explain. "Things happened easy around the coal fields, because of a tiger reserve. The Government rehabilitated these tribes for decades in the name of a tiger habitat. The tiger activists lobbied with the Government to rehabilitate the tribes. We joined the bandwagon, funded the tiger activists, and managed to pit the tribes against the tiger activists. However, the bauxite case appears more complicated, because of the absence of a wildlife sanctuary, and assuming we bully the Government into declaring one, we will stay stuck with our foot in our mouth, because, then we cannot bulldoze the mountain. Presently, it appears that we have no option but to wait for the tribal protests to cease."

Sam Strosberg roared with laughter, as he reclined in the comfort of his chair. "Ha! Ha! Ha!

Monty's eyebrows knitted in a frown, and confusion scarred his face. Then in a flash, his eyes widened, and he stared at Sam with cold contempt. "Damn it Sam!" he shouted in frustration. His face turned red with rage, as he clinched his jaw at the sight. "I'm bloody serious and you take it as a joke!"

Sam's guffaw tapered to a giggle. "Cheer up! Monty!" goaded Sam, beaming. "I appreciate your effort and don't deny your intent. I also understand your agony, but what tickled my funny bone in this investment narration is the phony tiger activists, who pose as saviours of the environment and make money out of it. It sounds like the biggest joke! But I must admit that your narration gives me hope. My son Michael appears smitten by this fad, and I have reprimanded Michael for his wildlife craze. But, your narration seems to have faulted me, because I must learn to use his services to expand my business interests the world over. Tiger Activists!" blurted Sam with wide eyes, while he casually flung his hand across the air to signal their insignificance.

"You seem a business mind to the core," remarked Monty.

"Hmm," murmured Sam.

"Where are Michael and Susan? I haven't met them, since our families get together in the Bahamas."

"Presently, in Siberia, Michael backpacks the globe to study tigers. Susan stays in New York, where she muddles in fashion and theatre. I seem unfortunate, because both despise politics and remain disinterested in business. I want Michael to join me so that he can learn quickly," regretted Sam, with a pensive crease that surfaced on his forehead.

"Don't worry he'll join when he understands the ways of the world. You stay lucky to have made a fortune in America. Many people come here with big dreams, only a few succeed in reaching as far as you have. Your family remains one of the richest in America and someday you will be President. I can feel the wind, moving in your favour. Strosberg Incorporation owns the biggest Oil and Gas Empire in the United States and it will benefit more when you move into the White House," disclosed Monty.

Sam's face wrinkled, as he crossed his hands over his chest, and reclined in his chair. "All is not well with the oil and gas business in America," he breathed out the words slowly, and looked pensive. "The climate change has screwed my business in the Gulf of Mexico," he admitted, tilting his head slightly, while he glared at Monty. "The category four and five hurricanes have reduced oil production, by fifty million barrels, over the last six months. These hurricanes have shut down close to sixty percent of, off shore oil and forty percent of natural gas production in America. And Strosberg Incorporation has taken the biggest hit," he spoke the last sentence emphatically, with wide eyes. He flung his hands in the air, hunched over and dug his elbows on the desk. He narrowed his eyes and looked intently at Monty. "We," he went on pointing at himself, "shut down five major oil refineries," he jabbed his palm in the air, exhibited his five fingers, nodded his head in dismay and continued, "which comprise twenty five percent of the US refining capacity. These persisting hurricanes may cause further disruptions. Meteorologists warn that the world will face a cycle of increased hurricane activity that may last another thirty years. The Pentagon has warned that this will pose a major security problem for America. I stay worried of the consequences it will have on my oil and gas empire. In fact, all the Texas oil barons with stakes in the Gulf of Mexico stay concerned. Moreover, this explains why America hangs around in Iraq. America needs the oil and gas that runs our economy."

"I think you need not worry, because we have investments in India and many other developing nations which will help offset the losses. Provided, we settle the Indian imbroglio first," advised Monty, with a twinkle in his eyes.

The arrogant Senator clenched his fist, slithered to the edge of his seat, and pounded the table. "The Iraq imbroglio," he interrupted, with a gruff voice, and then slammed his eyes shut.

Monty's face crumpled like a rotten tomatoe, and the twinkle in his eyes disappeared. He seemed disturbed and wriggled in his seat.

Sam shot an unrelenting stare at Monty, and gritted his teeth. "Iraq remains our bone of contention. We wish to settle the anarchy, restore a stable US friendly government and dig out the oil and gas. But, the insurgency has stalled our plans," he grunted, paused for a breather and continued. "We cannot do business there. It appears like a thirsty person sailing in the ocean, yet, crying: Water! Water!'"

"If you cannot control the post-war damage, why did you go in there?" asked Monty; his brows knitted in a frown.

Sam pondered for a while, then his eyes burned with hatred and his forehead scrunched. "Saddam sold oil coupons to the world, but not America," he complained in an imperious tone, and lifted his shoulders in a shrug. "Did we have a choice? We rescued Kuwait from the clutches of Saddam, capped Iraq's oil production, and curbed the oil flowing into OPEC and the international market. And who gained?" he questioned, and then paused and slapped the table. He leaned across the desk and grunted, "China, France and Russia had a ball. Saddam gave them the contracts and snubbed us. These three nations bagged all the contracts and insisted that we lift the sanctions imposed on Iraq. Saddam played smart and attempted to dodge the sanctions and these three members of the Security Council worked to bail him out. They possessed the veto power to oppose the invasion of Iraq. So we decided to move swiftly but needed some pretext," he paused, clenching the arms of his chairs and grinned. "So, we created the story that Iraq has weapons of mass destruction," he laughed derisively. "All that drama of inspecting Iraq and pressing for Saddam's removal, but things didn't move as we anticipated and then," he paused, snapping his fingers. "9/11 happened and the rest followed."

Monty listened to Sam and empathized. "I understand the problem. It takes time for a nation, reeling under the clutches of a dictator to assimilate democracy. Eventually, things will settle down," he added, crossing his legs, gripping the arms of his chair and lifting his shoulders in a shrug. "But what happens to our Indian investment?" he inquired, with his eyebrows raised. "I need your help."

Sam Strosberg smiled and then hunched over the table. "What can I do for you?" he asked, in an imperious tone.

Monty beamed and the tension on his face vanished. He stood up, unbuttoned his coat, reached for his inner pocket and yanked out a piece of paper. He walked around the desk and halted next to Sam. "We have a plan in mind. I want you to hear me out and give your suggestions. Take a good look at this map," said Monty, unfolding the paper, and then laying it on the table.

Sam frisked around for his spectacles and put them on.

Monty hunched over and navigated his index finger over the map. "This swathe of territory marked red stays out of reach of the Indian Government; called the red corridor, it stays under the iron grip of the Liberation of Forests Army (LOFA) and other militant organizations, which believe in the discredited ideology of Mao Zedong and Marx. These revolutionaries have declared the area a liberated zone and run a parallel Government here. The Indian Government struggles to regain control of this area but has not succeeded. The Indian state literally does not exist in this corridor; although, most of the minerals found in India lay trapped under this corridor, which comprises of Jharkhand, Chattisgarh, Orissa and Madhya Pradesh. Also, parts of Maharashtra, Andhra Pradesh and Karnataka. This corridor stretches from Nepal to Andhra Pradesh and our ventures in India have to deal with this deadly menace," explained Monty; he folded the map, and walked back to his seat. He stuffed the paper into his pocket, buttoned his coat, and hunkered down on his seat. "All the major industries that operate in this area, pay ransom to these organizations. These militant organizations espouse the cause of the tribes and influence their protests. We have, also, to deal with many NGO's, and social activists, who support the tribes and oppose any eviction and rehabilitation. Besides, a few intellectuals and political parties in India sympathize with these organizations. The Indian Government finds it difficult to deal with the guerilla warfare, because of the dense jungles that provide the militants with cover for their operations, and innocent civilians, who may die in the crossfire. The dilemma remains for the Corporates to dig out the minerals from this corridor," narrated Monty.

Sam listened in rapt attention, with his chin resting on his palms. He nodded his head and questioned. "Why not split the unity of the tribes and rattle the LOFA?"

Monty nodded in agreement and explained. "We plan to raise a tribal battalion, and pit it against the militants. We also plan to rehabilitate these tribes along the national highways, and promise them free food, clothing and shelter. We will train those, who join the tribal battalion in combat, and pay them a monthly salary. Initially, the paramilitary forces will back these battalions, and help purge the forests of those tribes, which support the LOFA. At the later stages we wish to engage a section of the armed forces, if, the militants use superior firepower and tactics. The recruitment drive, and training on a pilot basis will commence from June 2005. But—" Monty paused, with his eyes wide open, spread his legs out, hunched over, gripped his knees and leaned forward. "We remain wary of human rights organizations, and fear the internationalization of our operation," he paused, bit his lips in cold contempt and stared at Sam, as if anticipating a question.

Sam stayed silent and rubbed his fingers against his forehead.

Monty declared. "Your services commence," he waited for the words to sink in and continued. "If the Indian defence forces need sophisticated arms or training from America," he paused, uttering the last word slowly and loudly and wenr on. "You convince the American Government and legislatures about selling arms to India and, also, Israel to supply superior intelligence equipments. Besides, you will have to reckon with Pakistan and China's protests, and scuttle any attempt by them to stall the deal. Moreover, we also expect that America help India scuttle any attempt by human rights groups, other nations, or any other organizations from raising the issues of human rights violations or moving resolutions to this effect under the United

Nations Convention. I have spoken with the Indian establishment, which seeks our guaranteed and unwaivering support for this mission. We stand to gain financially by way of investments and through the sale of weapons," he paused, staring at Sam, who had slumped in his chair and questioned. "I put it to you; will you back this proposal?"

Sam straightened his back, crossed his legs, crossed one hand over his chest, tapped his lips with the fingers of the other hand, and gently nodded his head. Silence engulfed the conference for a moment and then Sam spoke. "I support America's national interest. Presently, we have declared a war on global terrorism, and I see your proposal as an extension of our effort to purge terrorism from this world. Capitalism needs at least one enemy to survive and if there is none we have to invent one. I see nothing wrong with this brilliant plan. I will meet the President this evening and talk to him. You go ahead and execute the plan," agreed Sam Strosberg. He looked at his watch and stood up. "I need to leave," he said.

Monty took the cue and stood up. He thrust his hand over the table and then shook Sam's hand firmly. "Good Luck," he said, and then beamed, and walked out of the chamber.

CHAPTER 14

▼

After, the early morning prayers and roll call, the students dismissed for their classes at the, "Vidyamata Vidyalaya," in Ramwadi. Bapu and Tillya chalked out a plan for the afternoon.

"We'll raid the jamun tree this evening," proposed Bapu, with a twinkle in his eyes.

"Yeah," agreed Tillya, hitching his shorts, which appeared loose around the waist. "I'll climb up and beat the jamuns with a stick. You gather them down in a plastic bag and we'll feast."

"What if Kanha, the cowherd appears?" worried Bapu, with his head cocked to one side. He tugged at Tillya's shoulder, as if cautioning him about the danger.

Tillya pressed forward and twisted his lips. "We'll offer him a few and he won't bother us," giggled Tillya, with his hands, tugging his shorts.

"Hmm," wondered Bapu, nodding his head. He conjured the deal and bargained hard. "But I'll have the first pick of jamuns," he demanded, tapping Tillya on his shoulder.

Tillya halted in his track, whirled about to face Bapu, and rolled his eyes skywards. "The rules of our deal, also, suggest that you cannot have all the big ones," he haggled hard, with his hands on his hips and stared at Bapu. "I" he boasted, with his finger pointed to himself, "will climb the tree and you know how difficult it is," he bragged, and then paused for the impact, tilted his head to one side and nodded. "If Kanha asks for more," he spoke slowly and emphatically, while he stabbed his pointed finger into Bapu's chest and insisted. "You part with your share."

Bapu nodded his head in disagreement, and stared wide eyed in disbelief. His face shrunk and he protested, "I will have nothing to eat, you must chip in," he bargained hard to save his share of jamuns.

Tillya shrugged his shoulders and declared. "Fine, if you insist, then you must climb the tree," he sauntered along carelessly, looking at Bapu from the corner of his eyes. He knew Bapu suffered from vertigo, and would not dare accept his proposal, but he wished to show his indispensability.

Bapu scratched his head and frowned. He pondered and dragged his feet alongside Tillya, who reached the classroom humming a tune. They hunkered down together, but Bapu seemed restless. He edged closer to Tillya and whispered. "I'll offer Kanha a few jamuns, but you make sure he doesn't pester for more."

Tillya beamed and bragged. "Leave that to me and make sure, you collect all the jamuns. I don't want to see a single jamun wasted," he ordered, as if making the most of Bapu's meekness.

Bapu nodded in agreement.

The crescendo in the classroom tapered to faint whispers that darted from different corners, suggesting the teacher had arrived. Mr. Kale stared down at the students through his spectacles, perched on the tip of his snout and announced. "It is the tenth of August," he paused, and then continued, "yet, there remain a few students in this classroom who haven't paid the term fees," he stated, with a gaze that swept the classroom. He took a deep breath and pointed his three fingers to the students. "The school gave three customary warnings," he declared, frisking his pant pockets, and then reached for his breast pocket. "But, despite the reminders they haven't paid their fees," he reported, rummaging through his breastpocket, and yanking out a piece of paper. He opened it and read aloud the names of the defaulters. "Ram, Vikram, Sunil, Sameer, Tillya and Bapu," he stopped, folded the paper and put it back in his pocket. "Stand up!" he ordered the defaulters, with a brusque voice.

The six students slowly emerged from the audience sheepishly, and stood with their heads facing the ground.

The teacher assumed a regal poise, and perched his hands over his hips. "The Principal has instructed me to suspend you from school, till you pay your fees," he remonstrated, snapping his fingers. "Out!" he blurted, signalling the defaulters to leave the classroom.

The students obeyed and walked out of the classroom.

"Damn the fees!" shouted Tillya. He drew back his shorts, "it keeps happening with us," he complained, with a cocky smile and gazed at the parking. "We dreamt of cycling to school, on one of those fancy wheels," he said, pointing to a red coloured cycle parked in the cycle stand, and then nodded his head in disgust. "But our parents cannot even pay our school fees," he ranted, hitching his shorts higher.

"I've hitched a ride on that and it runs smooth and fast," bragged Bapu; his eyes glued to the fancy bicycle glazing in the sun. He spread his hands out wide, stooped and glided a few steps. "Just like riding the wind, oooo."

Tillya grimaced, "it doesn't amuse me." He pushed Bapu, who staggered and crashed on the ground.

"Damn it!" blurted Bapu, with a scowl on his face.

Tillya giggled and then asked, "what about the jamuns?"

Bapu's eyes lit up, as he stood up with a toothy smile. "It's too early for the raid," he answered, dusting his buttocks. He mused for a while and suggested. "We'll hang around the Hanuman temple, play a game of marbles and then go for the jamuns," he groped his backpack and confided. "I think I have ten marbles on me."

"I have five on me," added Tillya, yanking out a plastic bag from his side pocket and holding it before Bapu. "We have fifteen marbles between us. We can go on to win many more."

They sauntered along the main road, as if they had all the time in the world to play their game of marbles. It appeared a long trek to the Hanuman temple.

"Tillya look!" exclaimed Bapu, elbowing Tillya and pointing ahead.

Tillya, who kicked around an empty seed packet that littered the road, picked it up, and looked ahead. He twisted his lips at the sight. His brother Rohit happened to shamble towards them. "He will go to the farm as usual," moaned Tillya, in a monotonous tone, and dropped his shoulders. "He goes daily to check whether the Bt cotton seeds have germinated," Tillya spoke with scorn, slapping his forehead. "He's doing the rounds for a week."

"Why?" inquired Bapu, with a tad anxiety on his face.

111

Tillya hitched his shorts, "there's always the fear of duplicate seeds in these packets," replied Tillya, brandishing the empty packet before Bapu.

"Have the seeds germinated?" queried Bapu.

"Don't know," replied Tillya; he lifted his shoulders in a shrug and slackened his jaws. "It hasn't rained for the past one week. Have they germinated on your land?"

"I don't think so, but we have plenty of water, after we drilled the tube well. You can come over someday and we will have a splash in the pool. Why don't we go there after collecting the jamuns?" suggested Bapu, with an air of dignity in his words. It seemed Vasu's endeavours had borne fruit, as his son appeared to invite his friends to play water games.

"I don't mind coming over," retorted Tillya, tugging at his pants. "In any case we have nothing to do, because the school doesn't want us. But I hope your father lets us play?"

"He's gone for the pilgrimage to Pandharpur. He won't come for a week," beamed Bapu, with a twinkle in his eyes.

"Why do you bunk school?" shouted Rohit, with his hands over his hips. He reached the boys, loafing alongside the road, and reprimanded Tillya. His eyes flashed, and mouth stiffened at the sight of Tillya.

Bapu cringed and his face dropped, but Tillya looked away puffed up. "If you don't pay my fees, they throw me out," he sneered, observing Rohit from the corner of his eyes. Rohit shook his head, and dropped his hands. The answer rebuked him.

"Damn the education!" fumed Rohit. His face contorted, and he found his anger melt.

Tillya grinned mischievously at the sight.

Rohit saw the gleam in Tillya's eyes, and his ego flared up. He wished to show Tillya his place in the hierarchy. "You go home and don't loaf around the village square," he snapped his fingers.

Tillya looked down, hitched his pants and nodded his head. He understood the message, his brother wished to convey.

Rohit appeared satisfied with the meek submission but wished to test Tillya's resolve. "I don't want to hear that you loafed around in the village square playing marbles," he thundered, with a gruff voice, and stared at Tillya.

Tillya nodded his head meekly.

"Huh!" snubbed Rohit; he shook his head, and stomped along. "Damn this education!"

Tillya watched Rohit from the corner of his eyes, and whirled around to see him go. Bapu's face paled, and his eyes turned moist. He regretted the encounter, which they could have avoided deftly, but it seemed too late. Rohit appeared to have thrown the spanner in their revelry.

"Don't tell me you're going home!" cried Bapu, turning around and looking at Tillya, with his face scrunched.

"Sssh," Tillya shooed; he stabbed his finger over Bapu's lips, and then raised his eyebrows, winked and edged closer to Bapu. "I said it to please him," he whispered in Bapu's ears. A mischievous smile crossed his face.

Bapu's eyes lit up and the gloom over his face vanished. He wiped his eyes and asked. "Why did you lie to Rohit? Do you fear your elder brother?"

Tillya fell silent and confusion scarred his face. "Hmm," he murmured to himself, as if thinking of an answer. He did not wish to loose the advantage he wielded over Bapu. "Not exactly," he said softly, shaking his head gently, as if conjuring a reason. He looked at Bapu, who appeared confused with Tillya's reply. "Nah!" clucked Tillya; he hitched his shorts and shook his head with vigour. He took his gaze off Bapu and wrinkled his nose. "It's because he's bigger than me, so I have to respect him," he spoke, with a tinge of carelessness in his voice, hitched his shorts, whirled around and hit the road.

Bapu pivoted on his heels and followed Tillya. He scratched his head and mused over the answer. He touched Tillya's hand, which remained occupied in saving his honour. "What?" questioned Tillya, heaving his shorts.

"Even Shoba's bigger than me, but I fight with her," bragged Bapu.

Tillya halted in his track, rolled his eyes skywards and faced Bapu. "She is a sister and sister's love. He is a brother and brother's bully. If you had a bigger brother, you wouldn't dare argue with him," reasoned Tillya, with a smirk on his face.

Bapu nodded his head and confessed. "O.K.—I understand," he confessed and kept quiet. It seemed the day did not belong to him. Tillya scuttled all attempts to get the better of him.

Tillya fixed his eyes on the empty seed bag that he carried. "This picture adorns the Sahukar's shop," he stated, smoothening the rumpled bag on the flat of his palm. "I wonder what's written below this picture?" he said, straining his eyes to read the letters, inscribed in the tiniest of fonts.

"Show it to me!" snapped Bapu; he snatched the bag from Tillya's hands.

"Damn it! What do you think of yourself?" questioned Tillya; his face scowled, and he seemed angry at the manner in which the bag left his hands. He hitched his shorts. "It's in English," giggled Tillya, a wry smile dangled from the corner of his lips. He seemed to revel in another opportunity to pin down Bapu. "I doubt you can read what's written here," he mocked, pointing at the letters inscribed on the rumpled packet. "Ha! Ha! Ha!" he pawed his stomach, hunched over and laughed with glee. He pointed at Bapu and mocked. "You've always failed in English," he uttered the words, with a lace of contempt, and hitched his shorts.

The snub agitated Bapu and his forehead puckered. His eyes flashed at the affront, and he took it as a challenge to prove Tillya wrong. He wished to make the most of this opportunity and win the duel. He glared at Tillya. "I am better than you for sure," he bragged, with his hands over his hips, and jerked his head. He inhaled a deep breath. "I'll read it out," declared Bapu, in an imperious tone

"Oh!" blurted Tillya; his eyes widened and lips pursed. He heaved his shorts and challenged Bapu to prove himself. "Let's hear you read."

Bapu flattened the rumpled bag on the flat of his palms, gouged the tiny particles of mud glued to the scrap and read aloud. "B . . . E . . . S . . . T," he hesitated, straining his eyes to read the alphabets of the first word aloud.

Tillya stared at Bapu and nodded his head in disapproval. "What's the word?" he asked, and then giggled.

Bapu wary of his reputation thought it best to conceal his ignorance. "I'll tell you later," quipped Bapu; the muscles on his face stiffened and he pursed his lips. Tillya hitched his shorts, chuckled and slapped his forehead. Bapu continued his ordeal and blinked owlishly. "G . . . R . . . O . . . W . . . N," he faltered.

Tillya observed him keenly and heaved his shorts. "You can't spell the words," he mocked, stabbing his finger into Bapu's chest. "I can bet on that," riduculed Tillya, with a cocky wink.

"Shut up!" shouted Bapu; he shoved the bag at Tillya's face.

"Damn you!" yelled Tillya, grabbing the bag, staring at Bapu and giggling.

"I know the words, but I'll not tell them to you," taunted Bapu, with a wry smile that dangled on the corner of his lips. He clenched his fists, brandished his thumbs and teased. "Dingo!" he blurted, turning his fists upside down. "I doubt you can read the alphabets. Why don't you prove yourself by reading the remaining words?"

Tillya's eyes flashed, he straightened the creases of the bag on the flat of his palm. "I.N I.R.R.I.G.A.T.E.D A.R.E.A.S," he rattled through the alphabets, without taking a breath, and flung the bag away. "See!" he gasped, inhaling a sharp breath. "I am faster than you. I've proved it!" he bragged, hitching his shorts. He stuck his tongue out, wrinkled his nose, and wielded his clenched fists, with the thumbs jutting out before Bapu. "Dingo!"

"Huh!" scoffed Bapu. "It's no big deal, you can't spell the words."

"I can spell the words and know the meaning, but I'll not tell them to you."

Bapu giggled and rocked back and forth on his heels. He stuck his tongue out and booed at Tillya. "Boo!" he wrinkled his nose, and raced down the road.

"Damn it!" howled Tillya, chasing him.

The boys' egos got the better of them, but the fact remained that neither could spell the words: BEST GROWN IN IRRIGATED AREAS, inscribed in the tiniest of fonts as a warning on the Bt25 cottonseed bag. Thanks to the Vidyamata School that ran like many other Government aided schools (shikshan sansthas) in Maharashtra. The citadels of tender learning, which nurtured the future of the State, lay in pitiable conditions. The State Government's policy of allotting schools to private institutions came across as another ploy to feed the party workers. Education remained one of the biggest rackets in Maharashtra, and most schools administered by political leaders and their cronies' embraced corruption. The Union Government boasted that, "sarva shikshan abhiyaan," or its policy of "education for all" remained a sincere attempt to educate all the youth of the nation. The Government of Maharashtra went a step further, and introduced English at the elementary levels, because it wanted the Maharashtrians to compete with the outsiders for global jobs created by foreign investments in the State. However, in reality it appeared, as if the schools symbolized a means of subtly channeling more funds to the institutions run by political thugs, who milked these for personal gains.

Many schools fudged registers to show that they possesed the required strength of students and teachers for grants. The salaries of the ghost teachers and subsidies of the ghost students went into the pockets of those who owned these institutions. Majority of the teachers employed in these institutions stayed forced to pay bribes for the jobs. Most teachers of Maharashtra, who epitomized Gurus that would mould the future generation of the State, appeared least competent and most corrupt. Moreover, these same teachers never admitted their children in these schools, because they lacked confidence in their teaching ability, so they preferred to send their children to private schools. This only reflected upon the political leaderships concerns for the poor and needy, as if the poor existed, as game for thuggery.

If this remained the awful condition of schools in Maharashtra, it came across as no surprise that Abba, who owned, "Vidyamata Vidyalaya," in Ramwadi, as most of his political class across the State, treated this school as a milch cow for corruption. Bapu and Tillya only symbolized the fate of lakhs of poor students across the State, who could barely read English alphabets, leave aside spell and understand the meaning of alphabets. If this remained the fate of English, one shudders to contemplate the fate of other subjects. These quarter baked products churned out of tax payers money, which the Government channeled into rogue institutions, pipped to reap the benefits of Globalization, also, happened to increase the literacy level of India. How beneficial will these remain to spur the economic growth of India, raises serious questions about the Governments intent?

The Government brags that the, "sarva shikshan abhiyaan," will benefit rural India, and equip the rural children with education that will help them take up jobs created by the market economy, so that they need not rely on agriculture for a living. The facts speak otherwise, despite the census (government sponsored), which shows high levels of literacy, and suggest that these quarter baked products will neither grab the jobs in the market nor be in a position to till their lands. In reality, they stay groomed to starve. It appears of no consequence whether Bapu and Tillya dropped out of school due to economic conditions? Because the condition of their school foretells that, the school would have eventually dropped them out of the global market. Bola Jai Jai Maharashtra Majha!

The two dropouts reached the Hanuman temple, which remained the cradle of dropouts in Ramwadi. They joined the other dropouts, as marbles dropped and rolled on the village square. A somber mood loomed over the village square. The rains played truant, most of the crops dried up, and the number of gamblers in the hall of the Hanuman temple increased. While Tillya played marbles, his father, Munna, tried his fifth hand at gambling. As usual, he lost, and stormed out off the temple. He noticed his son, squatting on his hams, and tossing marbles in the ring.

"Come here you waste!" howled Munna, from the ramparts of the Hanuman temple.

Tillya picked up the tone in the voice, and quivered. He looked up, and saw his father, descending the stairs of the temple. The anger in the tone suggested, his father lost a game, and Tillya appeared the whipping stone. Tillya got to his feet coated with dust; his face had streams of sweat flowing over, and his shirt appeared soiled. He could sense his heart miss a beat and legs heavy, as he heaved his shorts, and shambled towards his father.

"Come here quick you brat!" yelled Munna, hunkering down on the stairs of the temple.

Tillya wiped the sweat, gushing down his forehead, to the sleeves of his shirt. His palpitations increased at the sight of his father, and his legs seemed fastened to iron balls. He mustered all the courage he could, shut his eyes, and prayed to Hanuman. "Oh Hanuman, save me," he muttered, between his lips, and halted a few steps from his father.

Munna's eyes flashed at the sight of his son. He gritted his teeth, clenched his fist, and rammed it on the flat of his palm. "Why do you loaf around here, during school hours?" he grunted, hunching over, and dropping his hands over his knees.

Tillya's body quivered and his face paled. He dropped his head and stood silently.

Munna slapped his knees. "I pay through my nose for your education, and you squander away my money on marbles," fumed Munna; his cheeks puffed up.

Tillya felt a lump in his throat. "The school . . . won't take me . . . because . . . I haven't . . . paid my fees," his voice stuttered.

Munna's jaws dropped and his shoulders sagged. He propped his elbows on the stair behind him, and leaned on it. He whirled his neck, and his eyes rolled skywards. "Damn it!" he muttered to himself, while he stared at his son.

Tillya continued to look down at the earth. He shot a glance at his father from the corner of his eyes and pursed his lips.

Munna inhaled a deep breath and dropped his palms over his head. He shook his head in disgust and his heart melted. His eyes turned moist, he leaned forward and appealed to his son. "Come closer," he said, in a gentle tone.

Tillya sensed the change in mood, and slowly tilted his head upwards. His face remained confused, with a faint grin, lurking on the corner of his lips, ready to vanish if required. He tugged at his shorts, and hobbled towards his father, wary of mood swings. Munna slithered to the edge of the stairs, and hunched on his knees before Tillya. Munna gently lifted his hands, stashed them over Tillya's shoulders, and looked him in the eyes. "Doesn't matter," he said softly, dusting Tillya's shirt.

Tillya saw the tears in his father's eyes, and his heart melted. "Don't cry father," he pleaded, wiping the tears rolling down Munna's cheeks.

Munna broke down and hugged Tillya. "Tillu," he sobbed, kissing his son on his forehead. "Please forgive me," he apologized, burying Tillya's head in his palms.

Tillya wept, he understood his father's misery and sensed his somber mood. "Don't cry Papa," he entreated; his head gently wiggled out of his father's grasp. "I can work with you on the farm. School's boring," he said, gently wiping the tears off his father's eyes.

Munna shook his head vigourously. "I've failed you, because I'm a poor, unlucky father," he moaned, kissing Tillya on his forehead. "Remember one thing," he advised, squatting on the earth. "If you ever get a chance, leave this village. Go to the city and look for a living, but never remain a farmer. Do you promise me?" asked Munna, showing Tillya the flat of his palm.

Tillya looked away for a moment; his face scrunched and eyes moist. "Why do you want me to leave? I wish to stay with you," he protested, with a heavy heart.

Munna wiped the tears off Tillya's eyes. "No! No! You must always stay with winners. Loosers infect and if you stay with them, you run out of luck. Remember to always stay in the company of winners," insisted Munna, with a smile slowly appearing over his lips.

"Look Papa!" exclaimed Tillya. He shoved his hands in his pockets, and yanked out a handful of marbles. "I'm a winner. I've won these, this morning," he proclaimed, showing the bounty to his father.

Munna beamed. "Good" he complimented Tillya, with a gentle pat on his shoulder. "You have started well. I stayed bad at marbles and always lost, but you seem a winner. I have something to give you," said Munna, rummaging through his pockets, while Tillya stared with cow eyes.

"What?" inquired Tillya, smacking his lips.

Munna yanked out a ten-rupee note from his pocket, and dangled it before Tillya's eyes. Tillya's eyes glittered at the sight. "Now stop crying," admonished Munna; he crammed the note into Tillya's breast pocket.

The boy looked aghast; he could not believe his luck. "Ah!" he exclaimed, and then beamed. He pawed his pocket. "Do you mean it?" he questioned his father unable to come to terms with the generosity.

"Yeah!" smacked Munna, ruffling Tillya's hair. "For the winner; keep it. It's all yours."

"Papa will you give me a note each time I win?" asked Tillya, with a slight tilt of his head, pocketing the marbles, and heaving his shorts.

Munna fell silent and looked away. His eyes turned moist for a moment, and then he turned his gaze towards Tillya, and patted his shoulder. "Go and enjoy yourself," he said, with a feeling of remorse.

The boy looked into his father's eyes. He felt uneasy at the sight, and his heart stayed heavy, as he gradually withdrew. Tillya wished to stay, he sensed something wrong, as if he must stay and not leave. Munna smiled, but Tillya's face stayed glum as if dissatisfied. "Thank you Papa," he thanked his father and then managed to squeeze a grin. "You remain the greatest father in the world," he confessed, and then swirled around on his heels.

"Tillu," Munna called out to him, as if he wished Tillya must stay in his arms forever. "Come here!"

The boy whirled around, and hugged his father. Tillya sensed a strange beat; he felt uneasy. "What's wrong?" he questioned his father, as he withdrew.

Munna stared at Tillya like a mother looking at her newborn child and nodded his head. "Nothing! Just stay a winner!"

"Hmm," murmured Tillya, heaving his shorts, and racing away to celebrate his feat.

CHAPTER 15

▼

R amwadi never witnessed, what followed the next day, although, it happened all over Vidharbh. The village gathered around the corpse, laid it on a funeral pyre and lit it. Last night, Munna strung a rope around his neck, and hung himself to death on the neem tree in his farm. It appeared; his actions hinted that he staggered unsteadily to his deathbed and then keeled over. He left a note, "My debt burden has killed me." His family did not have the money for the last rites. Abba stepped in and paid for the expenses.

The media rained down on Ramwadi. The reporters from the media came with their camera crew, and gheraoed Munna's wife: Why did he kill himself? Did he borrow from the moneylenders? How much did he borrow? Did he tell you that he would kill himself? Did you witness his death? How did you react, when you first saw his dead body? Did you cry? How does it feel after his death?

Next, they hounded the children: When did Papa last talk to you? What words did he last utter? How does it feel to have lost a father? Have you married? When did you last drop out of school? How many times did you drop out of school? Did you like school?

They then focused their cameras on the man, who saw the hanging body and brought it down, and badgered him for answers: How did you react on seeing the dead body? Did you hear him scream? Did you hear him blabber? How did you bring him down from the tree? From which branch of the tree did he hang himself? Can you describe the tree? Can you describe the colour of the tree: black, white, blue, red or a rainbow shade? Do you confess that the tree had green leaves? Can you tell us the size of the rope? Can you tell us the type of rope Munna used to hang himself? How did you bring him down? Did anyone help you? How did you feel, when you shouldered the dead body? What did you do next? How did you communicate the death to his family: with your mouth, tongue, ears, legs, hands or stomach? How did the first person react when you relayed the news? These and many other questions kept spouting from the responsible fourth estate; the watchdog of democracy.

The entire day, the media broke this news on television—actually pounded it on screen. They braked all other stories, to break this news. In fact, this breaking news devoured all the time on the channels: prime time, breakfast time, lunch time, tea time, kitty time, play time, party time, launch time, baby time, children time, evening time, dinner time, late night time and adult time. Many companies jostled to sponsor it—deodorants, under garments, baby diapers, mobiles, beverages, biscuits, sugar free sugars, automobiles, finance, gels, tea, coffee, milk, ooof!—All kinds of products. The channels bustled with talk shows, debates, sawals, jawabs, pahelis, raaz, etc.etc.—on this subject. Celebrities, eminent panelists, intellectuals, spokespersons, fashion divas and many other types, who mostly wished to remain in the limelight-dressed in the latest garb with lipstick stuck on their lips, appeared to whet their views on this subject. Suddenly, it seemed as if, "on the blink of flashlight, India awoke to wisdom—Yes, Ramwadi, indeed, existed in India."

Next, the media put questions to the gullible viewers: Do you attribute this death to the Government? Does the common man (gender bias) exist in our democracy? Send us your views via sms; type space, yes/no, space, XYZ news and send it to XYZ. All media channels competed in the gladiatorial arena of the market economy and the competition stayed stiff. We broke (hammered, pounded, pulverized) the news first, boasted the news channels. They beamed the dead body from a thousand angles the whole day and after each shot; they requested the gullible intelligent viewers not to go anywhere, because they would return with a detailed angle after the commercial break. Most viewers obliged, but the channels returned to show the same angle in slow motion and then retired for another commercial break. Yellow journalism appeared its best and the commercial sponsors added to its irony. The younger journalists scouted the streets in search of celebrities, who happened to venture out and shoved the microphone up their noses, "what have you to say about the suicide?" they asserted. Then they beamed the views of the celebrity intermittently on the revolving band of their news channels.

Next, the political leaders visited the family in Ramwadi, as if, they suddenly realized they represented the sentiments of the people, and so they stormed into Ramwadi. First, the opposition alliance leaders raced into Ramwadi, in their saffron coloured SUV's. A fleet of twenty odd, luxurious vehicles choked the village square. The netas dressed in starch white kurta-pyjamas, with saffron coloured scarfs strung around their necks stomped into the family's home. They inquired about the death, shed a few crocodile tears, and promised them a twenty five thousand rupees compensation package. However, they conveniently forgot that similar deaths occurred under their regime. Then, the leaders gathered before the media, took a deep breath, pointed their fingers at the cameras, and ranted into the microphone, "this Government kills not just farmers." They paused and exhaled slowly. Then looked around, wrinkled their noses, flashed their eyes and hollered again, "but most important, we repeat; most important." They paused again for the words to sink in and went on, "it has conspired to kill the Hindus. If, the Government heeded our repeated appeals to declare the region draught hit, and declare a compensation package for the bereaved farmers, this suicide would not have happened," they shook their heads in disgust and prattled on. "However, this Government wants to kill the Hindus because it appears that no other communities have committed suicide. All the farmers killing themselves remain Hindus. The matter needs investigation, but we do not expect this anti-Hindu government to act. We have faith in the people, who will not vote for this Government. The opposition alliance vows to uproot this callous ruling alliance from power."

Although, this remained the common tune of the opposition alliance, each partner in the alliance wished to garnish the rhetoric to cater to its vote bank. The leaders representing, "Marathi Manoos," in this alliance chimed in. "We would like to add that the suicide represents not just a farmer or a Hindu but most important," they paused for an impact and then went on, "we repeat most important, it symbolizes the systemic killing of a Marathi Manoos. The matter needs further investigation: Why do immigrants and non-Marathis not committ suicide. Our party warns this anti-Marathi Government, that if it does not take measures to stop the suicides, our party will protest in our trademark style: destroy public property and set the State ablaze. Jai Hind! Jai Maharashtra!" they howled. After giving constructive opinions, the opposition alliance leaders vaulted into their expensive vehicles and hurtled out of Ramwadi.

A few days later, after the anger fizzled out, the leaders of the ruling alliance steered into Ramwadi. Dada accompanied the Chief Minister and a battery of Cabinet Ministers in a fleet of red-beaconed police escorted vehicles, which slipped into Ramwadi. It seemed as if the entire administration of Yavatmal had descended on this tiny village. The police encircled the house, while the leaders slithered through the door, shut it, met the family, jotted down the grievances, ordered an inquiry to confirm if Munna really died, made secret promises, and reluctantly ordered the District Magistrate to help the family. They then sneaked out and held a press conference. "The situation though tense, remains under control. We have ordered a thorough; we repeat a thorough investigation to probe the death of Shri Munnaji, because the suicide may have happened due to other reasons. We will wait for the report and when it arrives, we will immediately send it to the high command, which will decide whether Munna committed suicide or performed an act of insanity. Once the high command decides, we will comment on this unfortunate incident. Meanwhile, we appeal to the farmers to keep their hopes alive, because if the farmers believe in us, and vote us back to power, we will give free power to the farmers, and most important the beneficiaries will include Muslims, Dalits and Other Backward Classes. The ruling alliance remains committed to the secular tradition of our country, and till the report from the high command arrives, we view this death as a secular death."

The ultra-nationalist sub-regional party in the ruling alliance wished to garnish this alliance tenor with its own views, so the party leaders heaved a sigh of relief when the reporters wriggled the mike under their noses. They grabbed the opportunity and proclaimed. "Our party remains the real, actual, true and original farmers' party," they paused, and then stole a glance at their alliance partners, which squirmed in their seats. They went on, "We wrote to the PM, and requested him to give a special package to the farmers, and also bail out all the co-operative banks and sugar mills that have liquidated.

Our leader in Delhi has pursued the matter with the PM, and stays committed for a loan waiver scheme for the indebted farmers. As and when it comes, our nationalist party will ensure that the benefit percolates to not only the farmers, but also the poor farmers, and primarily the poorest of poor farmers and most importantly the poorest of the poorest farmers. We stay committed whole-heartedly to the farmers, but the compulsion of coalition politics has undermined our exclusive agenda for the poor, poorer and poorest of poor farmers. We do not relish staying in an alliance, because it appears difficult to pursue our party agenda, which entails eliminating suicides, but we have to respect the people's opinion. We appeal to the farmers to not loose hope and give us an exclusive majority in the coming elections." After which the red-beaconed entourage wobbled out of Ramwadi.

Abba waited patiently for all the political parties to finish their rhetoric. He wished to milk this opportunity. He appeared before the media, with the twin purpose of nailing his adversary and outling his course of action. "Ramwadi has witnessed a show of rhetoric and empty promises, from all the political parties. The truth remains that none of them wish to develop Vidharbh. I sacrificed my entire life for the ruling party and pleaded the cause of Vidharbh, but the party ignored me. If, Dada wants to prevent suicides, he could have done it long ago, but the suicides increase. The debt burden of the farmers cripples them, and drives them into the hands of unscrupulous input dealers and moneylenders, because the co-operative banks have turned bankrupt. Most of the political leaders, cutting across all party lines, have looted these banks. Vidharbh needs a change and I will change it. I kept silent all these years, hoping the high command would some day see reason but it appears otherwise. Munna's suicide has fuelled my resolve, and I will contest this election as an independent candidate for a separate Vidharbh. I propose to hold a rally to mark the death of Munna in which I propose to lay down my vision for a separate Vidharbh. I appeal to the media to attend my rally and hear me out."

It appeared; Ramwadi achieved a momentary cult status. Never before, in its history did so many dignitaries visit Ramwadi, and never before did so many political voices express themselves for their personal motives. It appeared an irony that the death of a poor indebted farmer made this tiny village famous (read infamous). The village square brimmed with grapevine. All conjured a story and rumours flew thick and thin. The suicide touched the life of each person in some way or the other. Munna's family continued to mourn. They lost a breadwinner and fell from the frying pan into boiling water.

CHAPTER 16

▼

Vladimir Molotov, the Russian ecologist, grasped the chopper's lever and gently jigged it. The motor blades tilted upwards, propelling the helicopter against the force of gravity. The metallic blades, belted the air to a raucous tumult, which blasted the snow-covered pines. The pilot fixed his eyes on the needle of the speed indicator, while the tension on the lever accelerated. He gradually stirred the speed of gradient to hundred kilometers per hour. The chopper climbed higher and higher, until it touched fifteen hundred metres above sea level. Buckled to the pilot's seat in the chopper's cabin, he looked down through the dome of the chopper. The view astounded him; a white sheet of snow covered land stretched for miles and miles.

"Welcome to Siberia's national tiger reserve. This natural habitat of the Siberian tiger in Russia, sits next to the Sea of Japan," said Vladimir, steadying the chopper over the habitat, and pointing to the tiger range on the screen of his video. "It measures four thousand and forty square kilometers and nurtures the wild boar, brown bear, lynx and wolf."

An endless stretch of white forests, with snow covered pines and thickets of junipers, lay below the chopper. The spectacle stunned the mind, aroused the heart and reminded the onlooker of Wordsworth's famous lines: bliss was it in that dawn to be alive, but to be young was very heaven. Linda Kohl and Michael Strosberg, watched wonder struck; strapped to their seats they sat in awe of nature's creation and savored the moment, which destiny offered. It personified beauty, transporting the sightseer to the highest level of consciousness—eternal bliss; the closest one could get to feel what John Keats meant when he wrote, "a thing of beauty is a joy forever: Its loveliness increases; it will never pass into nothingness." The crew moved their gaze through the plexiglass bubble of the chopper to survey the vastness of this panoramic view.

Linda squirmed in her seat, her eyes blinked and she wrung her gloved hands in dismay. Her face wrinkled, heart missed a beat and her eyes sought something, which remained an integral part of this forest. "I don't see a single tiger," she moaned, with tears in her eyes.

Vladimir's forehead creased, and his eyes filled with tears, philosophizing. "The Lord of this jungle staggers on the verge of extinction. The population of these majestic cats, which once ranged all over Asia, shrunk to three thousand. They survive in and around this frozen wasteland. The greedy civilization eats into the forests, and ravages ten million acres a year. A criminal nexus exists between the Russian government and mining barons that threatens the forests. The lure of timber and minerals destroys the forests, and brings the coy and solitary tiger closer to human habitats, making it vulnerable to poaching. The forests around Siberia need protection, and I fight a lonely battle to save this majestic beast from extinction. I started my tiger project ten years ago, with support from the Packer Research Institute in America to save the Siberian tiger."

Michael reclined in his seat, tilted his head, and surveyed the forest wide eyed. "Why this reckless poaching and what does one get killing tigers?" inquired Michael Strosberg.

Vladimir inhaled a deep breath and pursed his lips. "The lure of money appears the root cause of poaching," replied Vladimir; he exhaled his breath out slowly. His brows bumped together in a scowl and face grimaced. "Myths about the tiger's medicinal value in some societies like China give impetus to poaching . . ."

Michael's body stiffened at the remark and he interrupted. "Damn the myth! What medicinal value can a Tiger's body parts have?"

Vladimir's lips cocked a wry smile; he gripped the lever, stationed the chopper in the sky, twisted in his seat and spoke. "The myth suggests that the body parts can cure diseases like arthritis and impotency."

Linda's face scowled, she nodded her head and interrupted. "Huh!" she scorned, shifting her gaze towards Michael.

Vladimir laughed and went on. "The myth also suggests that the skin and claws work like some sort of a talisman which wards of evil spirits."

Michael sagged in his seat, shook his head and slapped his thighs. "Oof!" he exclaimed. He wrinkled his face, thrust his palms out, bent his fingers and lunged at Linda. "Evil spirits!" he snarled.

"Stop it!" snapped Linda.

Michael laughed and slumped in his seat. "How does a tiger claw ward of evil spirits? Can science prove it?" he mocked, looking at Vladimir, who gave a wry smile. "Anymore myths," asked Michael, shaking his head. "Jesus Christ!"

Vladimir lifted his shoulders in a shrug and shook his head. "The myth about curing impotency rests on the analogy that the tiger epitomizes sexual strength, because it copulates three to four times a day in mating bouts. Its skin fetches twenty thousand American dollars and so do other parts that fetch high prices in the international market. The money appears to tempt poachers, who run this racket," argued Vladimir, with raised eyebrows.

Michael arched a sly brow. "The biological analogy fastened to the myth surprises me. Copulation strength of a tiger transferred to humans on chewing a tiger's penis. Holy shit!" he nodded his head.

Linda's eyes swelled with tears, as she heard the conversation, "how cruel?" she thought.

Michael stared out of the glass bubble. The mythology seemed to have blown his brains, and he desired to spend the moments watching nature. He wrung his hands, shoved them in his coat and straightened his back. He reflected about Dad. "Dad must be racking the Senate to sabotage the Kyoto Protocol," he mused, with a slight smile, which hung from the corner of his mouth. "Wonder what dad would say, if he hovered over this paradise. I do not think this thought would have ever crossed his mind, its business and politics that clog his mind. He needs people around him all the time. Tiger love! Huh!" he tilted his head, biting his lips in cold contempt. His eyes continued to scan the topography below, while his mind pondered. Suddenly, he shouted into his headset, "I have a sighting, look!" he called out, pointing to his left. "A wild boar racing! There!"

Linda bounced in her seat on hearing Michael. Her heart galloped, and eyes widened with excitement. She twisted her body, and stretched it to get a view of the sighting. Her eyes glittered at the spectacle, and she beamed. "A Siberian tiger runs after a wild boar. There," she pointed below. "I can see it!" she shouted, with excitement.

Below, a three hundred pound giant cat sprinted on snowshoes, padded with retractable claws. It blasted through the snow, scooping out snowflakes, and chasing a boar, which scampered to save his life. The struggle for survival animated the crew in the chopper. The cockpit simmered with excitement.

"Quick! Mr Molotov that way! Follow them!" urged Michael; he lunged forward, pointing in the direction of the chase.

"Wow!" blurted Linda, with her eyes glued to the spectacle.

The pilot jigged the lever and set the chopper in motion. Linda picked up her camera to track the chase for survival. The chopper roared over the pine covered terrain, as Vladimir deftly stirred the lever for a descent. The closer he descended, the more the rotor blades hollered, as they blasted the snow covered pines, shattered the forest calm, and drowned the drill of the jungle chase. Below, a wild boar squeaked for life, while a hungry tiger plowed the snow for a kill. Above, an excited crew tracked the race for survival.

"Closer! Closer!" egged Linda, focusing her lens on the chase.

Vladimir stirred the lever; the chopper tilted and plunged through the icy air, as it ripped the silence of the terrain.

The brave Siberian plodded on, while the chopper hovered closer and closer over him. He accelerated to wrap up the hunt, with his mighty feet, which clawed the snow, and propelled him closer to his target, but the snow stayed deep, and the wild boar way ahead of him. The brave cat continued undaunted and covered ground to strike, with that one giant leap that would end the expedition. The chopper dropped further and further, to fifty meters over his head and split his concentration. He must take on one—either the boar or the chopper?

The brave Siberian skidded to an abrupt halt; his giant legs dug into the snow to control the kinetic velocity of his huge frame. He decided to take on civilization and granted the wild boar a reprieve. The Lord of Siberia appeared to have picked an unequal war. Three people ensconced in a chopper pitted against him stranded in the snow exhausted from a fruitless hunt. It appeared he possessed nothing, but his raw animal guts to defend him; yet, he remained defiant. It sprouted from his genes, the instinct to defend his territory, and he seemed prepared to fight to the finish. Any other beast would have scurried for cover at the slightest pretext of danger, but not this one, for he remained the undisputed Lord of this jungle, and the moment beckoned he prove it.

The chopper quivered at the sight, as it hovered overhead. The fierce Siberian clawed his way up a pine stump, and perched on the summit to face the chopper. His fearless persona resembled that of a sentry on a watchtower, overlooking his territory. He cocked his head, stretched his jaws, flashed his teeth, looked the crew in the eyes, with the flamboyance of a warrior, and roared with all his might. For a moment, it seemed, as if the growl had drowned the metallic din of the chopper. His body language seemed to suggest, "I will embrace death to defend my territory, but fight my enemy to the finish."

The scary spectacle sent a chill up the crew's spine. Their heart missed a beat, and the chopper made a hasty retreat, as the pilot jigged the lever to lift it. The brave Siberian stood atop his fiefdom undeterred and mocked at civilization's cowardice. "Come down and fight me you cowards, this Kingdom belongs to me, and I will defend it to my last breath," he seemed to say.

The chopper lifted higher and higher until Vladimir felt the chopper's lever go lifeless. His heart pounded faster, his forehead creased, face wrinkled, and eyes bulged at the sight. His fingers quivered, while he rattled the lever again, but the lever seemed dead.

"Damn it!" shouted Vladimir. He flung open the door of his cabin, slithered to the edge of his seat, twisted his body, popped his head out, narrowed his eyes, and peeked upwards.

The steel rod, connecting the rotor ball to the blades vacillated, and the chopper broke loose. He dropped his head and shook it in disgust. Below, he saw the Siberian tiger perched on the pine stump, as if waiting for the fall.

"What's the matter?" observed Michael, with his heart in his mouth. "Have you lost control?"

Linda blinked at the sight, sliding to the edge of her seat. Suddenly, her body jerked, tossing her off the seat.

"Huh!" she squeaked, grabbing the backrest of the pilot's seat, and slumping back in her chair. The chopper seemed to have ballasted on its own.

"Damn it! We have a serious problem," warned Vladimir, twisting in his seat, and facing Michael. "The lever lost control. We will rise to a maximum elevation of three thousand meters, and then crash down, when the fuel tank empties."

Linda and Michael's jaws dropped. They looked at each other bug-eyed, and squirmed in their seats. The tide seemed to have turned a full circle; the chopper fought for survival, while the tiger waited below. The chopper hoisted at fifty metres a minute, but the fuel could not sustain it for more than forty minutes.

Michael Strosberg lost his nerves; he grew impatient, and shouted into the headset. "What do we do, we appear to plunge down soon?" he stuttered, with a lump in his throat.

Vladimir seemed to have regained his poise. His face looked calm, as he leaned back, and pointed his thumb at Linda. "She needs to crawl up and fix the pitch or we will crash down," he reasoned.

The words hit Michael, almost, knocking him off his senses. His head reeled at the thought of Linda, risking her life. His heart pounded, and jumped into his mouth. He stared in disbelief and froze in his seat.

Vladimir reiterated. "Don't you get me?"

"Yeah," stuttered Michael; his face reddened. He took a deep breath to muster his strength and spouted. "I'll do it," he volunteered, fiddling with his belt. His hands fumbled, while he tried to unbuckle.

Vladimir shook his head. "Stay cool and listen," he said, with a slight tilt of his head. "You will not do it, because you cannot shuffle in this cabin. She stays closest to the door and will fix the damage."

"I'll do it!" volunteered Linda, slapping Michael in the hand. "Stay buckled!" she ordered, and then unfastened her seat belt.

Linda appeared bold and brave. The green peace activist from Germany carried engineering in her genes. Time, precision and discipline remained the forte of Germans and they stayed best at it. Back home, she had completed a flying course, and in Stuttgart, her grandfather owned the largest glider in the world. Avionics appeared her gifted legacy, and she stayed determined to prove it.

She unbuckled her seat belt, and swung the door open. The cold current of Siberia's frigid temperatures lashed her body. She yoked the seat belt around her wrist, and dropped her feet on the wire web of the freight bin beneath the aircraft. The holler of the engine almost split her eardrums to pieces.

Vladimir pointed to the pitch control arm that wavered. "Fix it to the rotor shaft," he instructed, and then turned his attention to Michael. "Salvage a borer from the tool gear under your seat and give it to Linda."

Michael rummaged through the toolbox, yanked out the tool, stretched out to reach Linda, and touched her gently, "here's the pin to thrust into the linkage," he said.

Linda removed her gloves to hold the pin. Her face wrinkled, and her fingers almost peeled off, when the cold wind stung her fingers. Her head reeled with pain, and for a moment, she felt dizzy.

"Come on Linda, you can do it," encouraged Michael, with his head popped out of the cabin.

The bolt and nut that fastened the arm and the rod appeared loose. Linda's job entailed to line up the holes of the assemblage, and then pierce through the pin. Linda posed subtly on the wire mesh, while her eyes narrowed to crinkled slits. She stretched out, aligned the arm with one hand, but her eyes ached, vision blurred and when she stabbed through the hole with her other hand, she missed and almost flew off her feet, when the strong current ripped her body. Her fingers went limp and head spun, when she looked down; stranded thousands of meters above the ground. Her heart pounded, when she felt her feet resting on the wafer thin mesh. A slight twist and she would fall down. She needed to erase the thoughts from her mind and pursue her effort.

"Keep up the effort. You will do it," yelled Michael.

The problem with the assemblage appeared the spinning ball that joined the rod. The ball spun, making it difficult for the naked eye to judge and distracted the stabbing. A cavity existed between the ball and the arm that needed fixing to stir the pilot's lever and regain control. Linda pursued her effort again, despite the biting cold.

Vladimir looked at the fuel gauge. His face cringed at the sight. He squirmed in his seat. "Hurry!" he beckoned, slamming his eyes shut. "We have only fifteen minutes before we tank out."

Michael's heart vaulted in his mouth, and he sensed a lump in his throat. He dare not look down, because the spectacle frightened him. He leaned out to see Linda. "Hurry we have very little time," he shouted.

Linda hung in the sub-zero temperatures, with her eyes fixed to the hole of the spinning ball. She watched and waited for the hole to align with the arm. The arm pivoted round, and round, and round, Linda held her breath. She saw the cavity and stabbed the pin.

Suddenly, Vladimir's hands appeared heavy, as if iron dumbles dropped on them. He shook his head, slithered to the edge of his seat and beamed. "Bravo! You've done it!" he blurted, as the tension in his hands stayed. He stirred the lever, and the chopper began to descend. "Keep up the pressure till we descend," yelled Vladimir.

Linda's face stiffened, her teeth gnashed, as she piled up the pressure. The cold and the stress drained her energy. She shut her eyes, "I can do it!" she said to herself, as the chopper descended gradually, and touched the ground.

The pilot shut the engine, inhaled a deep breath, slammed his eyes shut and collapsed in his seat. "Ooof!" he sighed, releasing his breath slowly. "Miracles do happen."

Linda crawled back into the cabin, and collapsed in Michael's arms. Michael hugged her hard, "we're proud of you," he said, and then grinned.

Vladimir patted her on her back, "you're a brave girl," he said, in an imperious tone.

Linda gathered herself, and hunkered down on her seat. She gathered her thoughts, and looked around worried. "Where's the tiger?" she asked.

The crew seemed to have forgotten the tiger. They stormed out of the chopper, and looked around, but the tiger remained out of sight. The brave Siberian appeared to have figured that the crew wanted to save him from extinction. Perhaps, this bond of love for the tiger conspired to save the chopper. Perched on the snow-covered pine stump, the kindhearted beast appeared to have prayed for the crew's safety. "God, please save them if you wish to save me."

Vladimir managed to fix a temporary repair, and the crew flew to the nearest village, Dacha. From there they took a hundred kilometers truck drive to Maltova, a fishing village next to the Sikhote Alin Biosphere reserve, where Vladimir stayed. The great chase ended.

CHAPTER 17

▼

Abba's rally at Phoolpur exhibited his political following. He managed to gather close to two lakh people, who applauded his rhetoric over Vidharbh, and booed and jeered, when he took potshots at Dada; the official nominee of the ruling alliance for the elections scheduled in October. Dada's ears stayed hooked to the rally, and when the media declared Abba's rally a huge success, Dada felt the jitters. The somber mood in the countryside along with Munna's suicide and incumbency worried Dada. The danger of defeat loomed over Dada, because the rally exposed his vulnerability. Abba remained an old warhorse capable of thrashing Dada's prospects. The night proved a nightmare, and Dada tossed and turned in his bed without sleep. He decided to appease Abba, and convince him to withdraw his candidature. He needed to act early to contain the damage.

He must also act against moneylenders, despite the truth that most funded his election expenses, because Abba's rancour at the rally against the moneylenders and input dealers: skin them alive, struck a chord with the farmers. Abba challenged Dada to act, and alleged that Dada worked hand in gloves with the moneylenders, so Dada needed to rebut these charges. The desperation forced Dada to pressure his Government to crack the whip, arrest a few moneylenders and input dealers, who sold duplicate seeds to the farmers. Swift action ensued, and the moneylenders and input dealers suffered September blues, and scurried for cover with the police stalking them.

The friction between these two political rivals generated heat that scorched Sahukar. The Marwari suffered nightmares, and squirmed at the prospects of an arrest. First, he suspended his activities until the dust settled, but the prospects of arrest and jail forced him to visit Abba for poltical asylum. He reached the peoples chamber and slithered through the door.

Abba's confidence appeared high after the rally, though, his mood waivered at the thought of voter vulnerability. He knew that numbers at a rally did not always convert to votes. Although he held a newspaper before his eyes, his mind stayed busy plotting his next move, when the Sahukar greeted him with folded hands.

"Namaskar huzoor," he said, softly.

Abba stayed glued to his newspaper.

"What brings you here?" asked Abba, in an imperious tone, flicking a page.

"It's the arrests happening around the countryside. The police visited me on two occasions, and threatened to detain me," he stuttered, looking around furtively.

"Hmm," murmured Abba.

The Marwari scratched his head, arched a sly brow and muttered. "I offered them money, but they refused to accept it. They say that the orders come from above and they need to act. I need your help," he paused.

Abba stayed silent. The Marwari's face dropped, and his heart pounded at the sight. He came with big hopes, but the situation so far hinted that Abba seemed unnerved. Abba coughed, and then turned over the page of the newspaper.

The Sahukar racked his mind for a way out of the impasse. He figured he must tickle the ego of the politician or say something that will wriggle him out of his arrogance. He gritted his teeth, staring angrily at Abba. "I stand here like a peasant cringing before him," he thought to himself, shaking his head. "Huh! Huh!" he cleared his throat, but Abba remained unfazed, and continued to read the newspaper. The Sahukar's face dropped and he felt insulted. He creased his forehead and muttered. "I gave your reference to the police, but they seemed unmoved. It appears they wish to arrest me—"

Abba dropped his hands, folded the paper, tossed it on the table and then grinned. "I'm not the one, who orders your arrest. You should question Dada," said Abba, looking away. He drummed his fingers on the armchair and flapped his knees.

The Sahukar heaved a sigh of relief and pursed his lips.He folded his hands and bowed slightly. "Why don't you settle your differences? We suffer because you squabble," moaned Sahukar, looking at Abba from the corner of his eyes.

Abba straightened his back, stiffened his face and stared at Sahukar. "He started the squabble," cribbed Abba, with a wrinkled face. "He suspended my ration shop, as if I'm dispensable," riled Abba; he pointed at himself, and took a deep breath. "If he thinks I'm dispensable," boasted Abba, exhaling slowly. "I'll teach him a lesson. I will rout him in the elections. You wait and see," fumed Abba; his face stiffened, and he gnashed his teeth.

"Abba please," implored the Sahukar; his face contorted as a beggars, and he hunched over in a low stoop. He bowed his head, clamped his palms together and squeezed them tight. "I beg you to compromise. Huzoor!" he pleaded, shaking his head. "Our business suffers. Dhanda hai, par Thanda hai."

"Compromise huh!" snapped Abba, taking his gaze off Sahukar's for a moment. He twisted his lips and straightened his shoulders. "Why should I compromise?" he sneered, with wide eyes, and then pointed a finger at Sahukar. "If he has the gall, let's wait till October. The results will show," he challenged, with an arrogant tone. "How dare he pick on me and expect me to cower and cringe before him?" shouted Abba; his face reddened and blood boiled. "I," he thundered, with his finger stabbing his chest. "Belong to a martial race. I will fight to the finish," he argued, clenching his fist.

The Sahukar cringed at the reaction. "What happens to us?" he asked softly, paused and shrugged his shoulders. "We suffer and loose business."

Abba stamped his foot on the floor, and slapped his arms against the arms of his chair. "Nothing happens to your kind," he yelled; his eyes flashed.

The Sahukar quivered at the sight, and hunched over shame-faced.

Abba pointed at him. "You people never spend on anything. You cheat and hoard. Have you ever heard of an input dealer committ suicide?" asked Abba; he uttered the question slowly and clearly. "It's the poor farmers that kill themselves," Abba's body shook violently, while he gasped for breath.

The Sahukar pursed his lips. "Abba that's not true. I have my problems. I need to take goods on credit," he stuttered.

Abba raised his hand and interjected with a huff. "Enough!" he shouted, staring at Sahukar. "You can fool the ignorant peasants with that crap. I'm not the kind, who will fall for the bait," he ranted, and then paused. He pointed at Sahukar, who stood with his eyes to the floor. "Your family came to Ramwadi with a lota. The famous line you uttered, 'jahi nahi jati bailgadi, waha pahujta marwari'. The truth remains that you alone have prospered in this village. It won't make a difference, if you spend some time in custody."

"Abba please," begged Sahukar. He looked at Abba and squeezed a tear from his eyes. "Izzat ka sawal hai! Dhanda hai, par thanda hai. You must not desert me in difficult times. I need your help," he insisted, with a wrinkled face.

Abba sat up in a regal poise and nodded his head. "Nothing comes free," he spoke, in an imperious tone.

The Sahukar grinned for the first time and added. "How much money will it take?"

Abba looked at him and nodded. "I don't want money."

The Sahukar's jaws dropped. His heart missed a beat and he kept quiet.

Abba scratched his head and looked away. "You have plenty of sale deeds in your name. What do you wish to do with so much land? A Marwari knows nothing about farming. You cannot go about swallowing all the land in and around Ramwadi with impunity. At this rate I gather you wish to challenge me."

The Sahukar sank on his knees and folded his hands before Abba. "Thoba, Thoba, Huzoor," he clucked, holding the tip of his earlobes and bowing his head. "Hamara dhanda hi dhanda hai. Bhala hi thanda hai," he muttered. He nodded his head and explained. "I can never think of such a sin. I am a small man with little needs. Politics is too big for me; it is for big people like you. I manage to eek out a living through money lending. The peasants insist for credit and if I lend, I have to recover, otherwise—"

Abba lifted his hands and interrupted. "Cut the crap. Get up and take your seat," he ordered Sahukar, who stood up and then plunked down next to Abba.

Abba slumped in his chair. "I heard you forced Vasu to convey his three acres of land in your name, I'm interested in the three acres, which borders my baandh. You transfer the land in my name," demanded Abba.

The Marwari stayed mute. He wriggled in his chair and crossed his hands over his chest. Abba looked at him, raised his eyebrows and jerked his head up, as if signaling a reaction.

Sahukar scratched the nape of his neck. "It's a prize catch, after Vasu struck water," he said, softly, but Abba stormed in, and cut him short.

"Damn it!" he fumed, slapping his knee. "Stop beating around the bush. I want that strip of land on the dry patta, or I'll have you burnt alive in that shop of yours," threatened Abba, staring angrily at Sahukar.

The Marwari squirmed. "Le lo huzur! Dhanda hai par thanda hai!" he surrendered softly, and then grinned. "I cannot deny Abba. I'll have it transferred in your name immediately, but what about the police?"

"As of now you court arrest."

Sahukar interrupted with a frowned face. "Abba it isn't fair . . . ," he stuttered, without completing his sentence, when Abba interposed. "You listen to me," Abba commanded, pointing at Sahukar. "Court arrest and then apply for bail. I will make sure the police treat you well. Remember Gandhiji went to jail."

A scowl appeared over the Sahukar's face. "I will transfer Vasu's land in your name," he squeaked, worried at the outcome. He folded his hands and begged. "I don't want to go to jail. Izzat ka sawal hai!" pleaded Sahukar. He feared the Police hospitality.

"Damn your honour! You blood sucking leech!" bawled Abba; he stamped his foot on the floor, and looked at Sahukar with wide eyes. "Jail remains the best protection you can have; otherwise the farmers will skin you alive in the square. Did you not hear of input dealers beaten balck and blue, because they sold duplicate seeds, and charged exorbitant interests?" Abba paused, and then grinned.

The Sahukar's face sulked like a dry twig. His shoulders slagged and he sat resigned to his fate.

Abba looked at him and spoke like a priest giving a sermon. "Presently, I will not tone down my rhetoric," he insisted, with a slight nod of his head. He took a deep breath and then explained.

"Because it'll harm my political prospects," he reasoned, shrugging his shoulders, and exhaled slowly. "You keep out of this and do as I say. I will ensure that the police do not touch you in custody. I will also talk to the Magistrate, and have you released on bail. The Court will not attach your properties so you must not worry. Didn't you just say that a marwari ka dhanda hi dhanda hai?"

The Sahukar's face stiffened and he crossed his hands over his chest. He cursed the deal, but he did not have a choice. The countryside reverberated with stories of moneylenders and input dealers brutally attacked and beaten. He feared for his life and knew that Abba could save him from pillory. He nodded his head meekly and questioned. "Abba will you guarantee that the Magistrate will grant me bail?"

Abba slapped his knees and rattled. "What do you think that the judges descend like angels from the heavens?" he asked, with a smile that dangled at the corner of his lips. "Huh!" he scoffed, with a slight tilt of his head. "They stay human beings and susceptible to all the temptations of life. In fact, the judiciary remains susceptible to corruption. Have you heard of any judge convicted for injustice or misappropriation of assets?" he queried, and then smacked his lips. "The dispensers of justice must stay liable for acts of omission and commission, but the law only seems to apply to them but in reality it doesn't. They have the most convenient weapon, 'the contempt of court act,' to shield them from corruption. No one can dare question a judgement, because it will affect the independence and fairness of the justice system. It remains the biggest joke, because it shows them infallible," he laughed and then continued. "The truth remains that many in the judiciary join hands with us. I have seen many black coats groveling before politicians for work. Most lawyers want big fat criminal clients or thieves, caught in scandals or neck deep in corruption, so that they can fleece them and make big money. They wish to work like legal advisors to co-operative banks, sugar mills, textile mills, trusts, educational institutes, local governing bodies, corporations and the like. What do you think they seek?" asked Abba, with aplomb.

Sahukar looked at Abba and stayed silent.

Abba laughed, nodded his head and went on. "Definitely not justice!" he blurted, with sarcasm. "It's the money to bail out corrupt practices that they want. To me it appears as if in most cases the most successful black coat have corrupted clients. First, they make filthy money in the bar and then they crave for power and lobby with the politicians for an elevation to the bench as judges. The law requires the Cabinet's consent for elevation to the higher judicial services. It seems that they lobby with us, but in reality, they strike a deal. How do you imagine the system works in this country?"

The Sahukar listened, with his eyes fixed on Abba, who babbled with an air of dignity.

"If you ever happen to visit the chambers of most of the senior counsels in the Higher Courts, you'll find a majority of the interns; sons and daughters of Judicial Magistrates, Session court judges, District Court judges, High Court and Supreme Court judges. Does this mean that they appear as the most competent lawyers?" Abba cocked a wry smile, and shook his head. "Nah!" he clucked. "On the contrary, they seem good managers," he winked. "They build their practice on the edifice of judicial management. They rope in the kith and kin of judges as interns to promote their corrupt practices. Most orders, decrees and judgements passed in the courts of law hinge on 'discretion;' a euphemism for 'whim and fancy'. In most cases, it implies corruption. The one who doles out a favour or pays will get the discretion. The gullible people falsely think that the erudite judges with loads of books stacked behind them interpret the law, but the truth remains that in most cases the discretion exhibits corruption. In most cases the, 'case laws,' do not influence the judgements of the Courts, the 'face laws,' do," explained Abba, drawing a circle around his face with his finger.

"In other words it implies the lawyer appearing before the bench. Does the lawyer belong to the judge's camp? Do the judge's kith and kin, train under him? Does the lawyer belong to a particular caste, gotra, language, religion, region or district? If any of these parameters stay satisfied, the discretion crystallizes into a ruling. This explains how bails happen, injunctions and restraining orders pass, adjournments stay granted and proceedings appear stalled. The lawyers call these, 'litigation tactics,' which actually imply corruption. Laws resemble a jugglery of useless words and maxims in Latin framed by the British to suit their interests. Presently, the politicians draft laws to suit their interests. My opinion based on solid experience suggests that justice goes to the biggest bidder, and lawyers represent the bidders, with the judges acting like an auctioneer. The grand judiciary takes years and years to decide cases. Petitions and plaints filed by petitioners and plaintiffs have concluded in the times of their grandchildren. Do you call this justice or some kind of rude joke?" mocked Abba, and then laughed. "The so called, 'independence of judiciary,' manifests a charade, which in reality means, 'insulation from corruption.'At least, we politicians have to face the electorate after five years or earlier. Presently, one cannot guarantee that people will take money and vote for you. It appears risky, because the people may take money and vote for someone else. However, the judges and bureaucrats have no such accountability to the people. They virtually stay unpunishable and untouchable. Can you imagine an entire Parliament impeaching a corrupt judge? It will never happen, because the judge undergoing impeachment proceedings would have some sort of political patronage. If the judge accepts a favour, he has to mortgage his discretion as collateral. Throughout his career on the bench, he must have ruled in favour of his political mentors on numerous occasions. Is it possible for these politicians or political parties to vote against a judge, in an impeachment motion, brought against the judge in the Parliament? It appears a rude joke to proclaim that this country runs by the rule of law. In fact, experience betrays this and shows many unequals, a few equals and an elite class that seems more than equal. A country runs on, 'faith and trust,' but when these appear the consort of sleaze, the entire system decomposes. Don't worry about your bail the system will ensure you get it," said Abba, and then beamed.

He spoke with such aplomb, like a seasoned politician that the Marwari's eyes twinkled and he grinned. It appeared that Abba had experienced a lot in his political career. He hobnobbed with the high and mighty, and knew the nuances of the system he controlled, which made him a formidable opponent. He also possessed the ability to mesmerize his listeners, with his encyclopaedic experiences, and he used this talent to the hilt. His experience in politics taught him how to control the levers of power. If one wishes to rule, one must learn to control the minds of people, with the display of strength—to the poor display wealth and to the rich exhibit influence. It will force them to wriggle before you. The Marwari looked convinced with the subtle message, which Abba delivered. "I remain bigger than you. You may have the money, but I have the power. You don't fit into my league."

The Marwari bowed his head and stood up with folded hands, "thik hai, Abba. I'll do as you say, kya kare dhanda hai par thanda hai," he accepted the verdict, and walked out of the mansion.

Ever since, the tubewell struck water, Vasu's family rejoiced. The cottonseeds sprouted and rippled in the wind, despite the rains having duped Ramwadi. Although, a bulk of the farmers lost their second sowing, the borewell saved Vasu's cotton crop. He now watered his crop regularly and hoped for the best. However, his other concern stayed—Shoba's proposal. Although, Vasu asked many in Ramwadi to look for a suitable match for Shoba, he still pursued the Borgaon proposal, which stayed close to his heart, while he channeled water for his cotton crop this afternoon.

"I wonder why Angad has not turned up," he pondered, while he stooped down, scooped out a lump of wet mud, and piled it in a heap to log the water in the channel.

"Papa, Papa," shouted Bapu.

Vasu straightened his back, and whirled around to see Bapu darting towards him.

"What's the matter?" inquired Vasu; he swiped the sweat trickling down his face against his forearms.

The boy reached Vasu. "Mamaji has arrived," he gasped.

"Hmm," murmured Vasu. His heart palpitated faster on hearing the news. He hunched over and rinsed his hands in the water channel. "Did he say anything?" asked Vasu, splashing the water on his face.

"Nah!" clucked Bapu, jumping into the water.

"Damn your pranks! Get out of the water," scolded Vasu.

Bapu's face shrank. "I'm washing my feet," he retorted, while he slyly looked at Vasu from the corner of his eyes.

"You'll break the channel if you jump around like that," warned Vasu, wiping his face against his shredded towel.

Bapu nodded his head. "No, I'm only washing my feet," he reiterated; he bent over, and scooped out water from the channel.

"Are you sure Mama didn't say a word," Vasu maintained, dabbing his face with the towel.

Bapu nodded his head, and then splashed water on his face.

"Get out and tell him I'm coming," ordered Vasu.

Bapu stepped out of the water, and ran away to relay the message.

"I hope he has some good news," thought Vasu, walking towards the neem tree to meet Angad. On Vasu's arrival, the two men exchanged greetings.

"What brings you here?" asked Vasu, with a heavy heart.

"Shoba's proposal," uttered Angad, and then grinned.

Vasu sat himself down next to Angad.

"The family agrees to accept Shoba, but demands more money," said Angad.

Vasu's face dropped and he nodded his head. "How much more?"

"One and a half lakh rupees; as dowry, which excludes wedding expenses."

Vasu slapped his head in disgust. "It's a heavy amount. The total expenses will touch nearly two and a half lakhs."

"I tried my best to haggle, but they persisted that the boy has a sarkari naukri."

"I think we must reject the offer!" Mangala interposed.

Vasu stared at her, "will you shut up, I haven't asked you far a suggestion," he snapped.

"It's pointless discussing the matter, when we don't have the money," retorted Mangala, with a scowl.

"Didi you keep quiet. Let jijaji decide," suggested Angad.

"I think we must accept the offer," said Vasu.

"Is it final?" asked Angad, wary of Vasu's mood.

"Yeah," muttered Vasu, with a slight nod of his head.

"How will you arrange for the money?" asked Mangala.

"That's my business. You need not bother," said Vasu, irritated with Mangala's unwanted intervention.

"I suggest, you first arrange for the money and then I'll convey your consent," cautioned Angad.

"I'll need to talk to Sahukar. He promised to give me the money. If he agrees, then we can go ahead with the proposal. Keep them hanging till then."

"Yeah," Angad replied.

CHAPTER 18

▼

The death of Munna compounded Lekha's difficulties, with three children to look after and no knowledge of the loans, which Munna piled up from unknown lenders in and around Ramwadi. The financial aid promised by the opposition never came. In fact, the day the leaders spoke to the media, denounced the government and warned it of dire consequences seemed the last day they stepped in Ramwadi. They disappeared, never to come back again. Lekha possesed a ration card, which in reality appeared ornamental, because food prices in the ration shop remained congruent with food prices in the private shops. In any case, assuming she carried a BPL card, it would still make no difference, because the ration shop in Ramwadi stayed suspended and forced her to buy goods on credit.

The State Government declared a compensation of rupees one lakh, subject to inquiry and forty pre-conditions. In reality, the compensation appeared a farce and another red tape affair. Despite making tall claims of an, "unlicensed raaj," the Government seemed loath to shed its habit of creating avenues for the bureaucracy to make money. The forty pre-conditions appeared so stringent that they would have driven a battered family to another bout of suicides. The ruling alliance claimed to represent farmers, but in reality, it made things more difficult for the farmers. While the five star hoteliers, corporates and Ministers deliberately failed to clear their electricity bills and then bargained for a discount, which the Government readily accepted, yet, it would not tolerate any such concessions to a family that lost a breadwinner, because of its faulty agrarian policies.

Munna's family failed to qualify for the compensation, because of no bank account, no bank loans and it appeared to have borrowed money from Sahukar, who remained a private unlicensed moneylender. The irony compounded because most of the co-operative banks in Vidharbh, which doled out rural credit, appeared robbed by the political class and a few banks that managed to survive the loot did not have money to lend the farmers. So much for the first two grand pre-conditions (sarkari nikash) laid down for compensation. The last seemed even more flimsy, because, according, to the tehsildar it constituted an offence to borrow from unlicensed moneylenders and commit suicide. This implied the Government punished the family of the deceased, for an offence commited by the deceased for which the deceased hanged himself to death. It appeared the Government did not wish to compensate the deceased.

There appear umpteen cases in which the Government attempts to bail out bankrupt co-operatives with public money, rather than punish political leaders, who mismanage the institutions. These political thugs, who belonged to all political parties, stay unfazed, because they remain unpunished. In fact, many hold Cabinet berths in the Government and enjoy political patronage for the money they swindle. The forty pre-conditions meant that Lekha would have to go back to a private moneylender and take another loan to bail out her woes. The Government pushed her into the vicious circle of debt, which would some day strangle her to death. The farmer's Government appeared to throw out the baby and the bath water. It systematically killed the farmers in Vidharbh. Who says democracies do not run concentration camps? The Nazis seem far more honest than the Government of Maharashtra. At least, they openly proclaimed and then butchered Jews, but here in Maharashtra, the Government claimed to belong to the farmers but in reality, its policies killed them.

Lekha soon learned that her husband borrowed money from other gamblers. He owed Mesba, Lakya, Ganpat and Banku money, besides piling up debt at the taanda. Hira visited Lekha and demanded his share of money. The borrowing matrix worsened by the day. The biggest shock came, when the tehsildar, while making the preliminary inquiry informed her that Munna transferred his land to Sahukar. The family's fortunes appeared like stilts on sinking sand. Lekha owed the creditors, over two lakh rupees and needed to provide for her three children. Her biggest concern remained her daughter Sushma's marriage. "Will she ever marry?" wondered Lekha. Sushil though educated to some extent found no work in the village to make money. He learnt from Pandu about the paper mills and mines in Gadchiroli and Andhra Pradesh, which constantly required new hands. He thought of going there to support his family. At first, Lekha protested, but the conditions did not favour her motherly affection, because debt has no room for family bonding. Once it enters the home, it starts breaking it and finally throws out the host. She finally relented and let him go.

Lekha possesed a few gold ornaments that could fetch her about twenty thousand rupees. She paid for Sushil's journey and cleared the debts of the gamblers and bootlegger. Sahukar's debts remained unraveled and his absence a temporary breather. She knew that once he returned from prison, he would summon her and make her pay. Tillya would never go to school again. The Government and the intelligentsia may talk about the grandeurs of, "sarva shikshan abhiyaan," but it would not feed the family. Debt does not follow the dictates of the Government. It has its own Constitution, which does not grant rights, but lays down duties and the fundamental duty of Tillya beckoned him to clear the family debt. The twelve-year boy, forced to mature into a responsible man overnight, took up the job of a sheep and goat herder.

Every year, thousands of sheep drove into Vidharbh from Gujarat for penning. Farmers penned their fields to improve fertility of the soil. Penning occurred between the months of January and April, but, if the rains played truant, it extended to almost the entire year. Manibhai and his family tended a herd of over thousand sheep and regularly visited Ramwadi. This year Manibhai's family fell short of hands, because of domestic compulsions and employed Tillya to help them, for a sum of twenty-five rupees per day. The shepherd would use a long wooden pole, with an iron hook wrapped around the tip, to rattle the branches of the acacia tree. The herd would gather under the tree and feed on the fallen leaves. At night, the herd gathered on the fields of the farmers that wanted penning. Manibhai charged fifteen hundred rupees for a night and this year he stayed back to pen Abba's fields. Tillya guided the sheep and supervised their grazing activity.

Lekha and Sushma slogged on Abba's farm. Abba decided to clean and rebuild his ten surface wells, which caved in, because the black soil around them loosened. To stall further damage, he planned to buttress them with iron rings and cement. Lekha and Sushma helped the masons, working on these wells. They earned fifty rupees each for a day's labour. The family struggled to make ends meet and barely made enough to survive.

CHAPTER 19

▼

Destiny blessed Tatya with a legacy, which envied many, but the only son of Abba and the scion of Ramwadi, like most aristocrats displayed debauchery. While most farmers in Ramwadi struggled to make ends meet, Tatya grappled to satiate his unending appetite for depravity. His extra-marital affair with Kanta, the nurse, at the Primary Health Centre (PHC) remained the talk of the village. It seemed as if no one dared question Tatya, because his filthy wealth and power gave him the license to defy customs and norms. It appeared like customs, norms and values loomed over the poor and powerless while the rich and powerful laid them down. Abba alone could dare question Tatya but not anymore.

Kanta stayed his mistress for two years, but like most mistresses, she wanted security. Like a typical mistress, she suffered from diffidence and feared desertion. Her caged relationship desired legitimacy and the question nagged her for the past few months. So she hinted to her lover on several occasions but the man in him deliberately ignored the clues. The cat and mouse game continued for long until Kanta's patience reached the tip and boiled over when Tatya came to meet her this afternoon.

Tatya drove into the compound as usual, with his bullet roaring. His starch white attire resembled that of a desi politician—gold rings fastened to his fingers, lockets dangling around his neck, his shirt half open baring his hairy chest and he wore tanned kolhapuri chappals that glittered in the sun. He wore glares and maintained a moustache with pointed tips. He parked his bike, hunched over the handle mirror,

149

twirled his moustache, yanked out a comb and forked it through his curly hair. He dusted his shirt, stretched his legs, jigged his crotches and ambled into the room, whistling and swirling the keys over his index finger.

Kanta waited nervously in the hall; her mind waivering over the issue. She sat glumly with a contorted face and fiddled with her fingers. Tatya sauntered into the hall as a matter of routine and flung himself on the couch opposite Kanta. He pawed his moustache, crossed his legs over and sat leaning on his arm against a pillow. He pulled down his glares to the tip of his nose and watched Kanta.

Kanta twitched in her chair and twisted her nose. "Huh!"

"Hey! What's wrong?" inquired Tatya, grinning mischievously.

Kanta looked away, and then took a deep breath.

Tatya raised his eyebrows, pursed his lips and continued to stare at her.

"How long will we continue like this?" asked Kanta, releasing her breath slowly.

Tatya laughed and slapped his thigh. He seemed least perturbed. "Till death," he replied, forking his fingers through his hair.

"Damn your jibes!" snapped Kanta. She stood up in a huff and her face turned red.

"What's the matter?" asked Tatya, sitting up, with a wry smile hanging on the corner of his lips. He rummaged through his breastpocket, and then yanked out a gold pendant. "I've bought this for you."

Kanta's eyes burnt with hatred at the sight of the pendant. She stamped her foot on the floor. "To hell with your gifts!" exclaimed Kanta, while she placed her fingers on the edges of her temple and shook her head. "I'm fed up!"

"Darling, why are you so agitated?" asked Tatya, with a soft voice. He stood up, removed his glares, walked towards her and grabbed her hand. "I'll get you something else. Anger doesn't look good on you," he whispered in her ears, attempting to cool the temper simmering in her.

She snatched her hand in irritation. "Do you dislike my anger or my face?"

Tatya grinned, tilted his head and gazed at Kanta. "You possess the most beautiful face in the world," he complimented, uttering the words slowly and loudly.

The words made Kanta tizzy and for a moment, she seemed to have forgotten her mission. She blushed, then looked at Tatya from the corner of her eyes and saw him grinning. She hated his carefree attitude and decided to talk tough. "Huh!" she scoffed, with her back at him. "The same old crap that you must have uttered to other women," she remarked and then curled her lips with contempt.

"I have only you to look at," Tatya blabbered smoothly, crossing over to face her. "You are my world," he hissed in her ears, and then kissed her.

Kanta's heart raced and she felt a current, which ignited her emotions. However, she wanted more so she stepped away and crossed her hands over her breasts. "That's what all men say, till they have their fill," snapped Kanta, stiffening her face.

Tatya tossed his hands over her shoulders and gently nudged his cheeks against the back of her head. "I'm not the kind you think. I can do anything for you," he declared, while he squeezed her shoulders.

"Really!" exclaimed Kanta; she stretched her eyebrows and widened her eyes.

"Don't you believe me?" Tatya whispered into her ears.

"Let's test your love for me," said Kanta, with a wry smile.

Tatya kissed her on her nape. "Go ahead. I'm willing to do anything for you."

"Marry me," said Kanta, and then smacked her lips.

The offer rammed Tatya like a bull, tossing a matador in the air. His hands dropped and he withdrew in a huff. "Huh!"

"What happened to your boast? The moment I ask for marriage, you withdraw," Kanta retorted, whirling around to face Tatya.

Tatya's face dropped and he looked away annoyed at the suggestion. "What's the big deal about marriage? It's just another ritual," stuttered Tatya, shrugging his shoulders. "We tie a knot and circle the fire seven times."

"Good!" blurted Kanta, as she bit her lips. She looked at Tatya with piercing eyes and laughed. "If it's a ritual, then why does it bother you? We can go through it like every other couple does."

Tatya's face stiffened, while he clenched his fists tightly and vented. "Damn the ritual! I don't approve of it."

"Does the ritual bother you or the commitment that follows?" badgered Kanta; she twisted her face.

Tatya gritted his teeth and shook his head. The rebuke offended him and he hated the nagging. "When I'm committed; it stands," he shouted, pounding his fist against the flat of his palm. He whirled around on his heels. "I don't need to go through a ritual to prove it, unless you don't trust me," he rambled, with a scowl on his face.

Kanta stayed unfazed, knowing she trapped him. She flung her hands on her hips and turned on the heat. "Men betray."

"Damn your suspicion!" thundered Tatya. He squirmed on his feet and his brows knitted in a frown. Suddenly, he changed the tone of his voice and sounded melodramatic. "Is this what I get for giving my heart to you?" he moaned, with a heavy heart, and slowly turned around to face her. He looked at her wearily like a lover, who just lost his love. "Even Radha doesn't live with me anymore. She wants me to leave you," he complained, with the intention of provoking empathy.

"I didn't tell your wife to leave your house," snapped Kanta, with contempt in her eyes. She bit her lips and pointed her fingers at him. "It's between you and her. I'm asking for my share of commitment."

"I'm always with you, what more do you want," Tatya shouted, as he slammed his foot on the ground.

"Why do you get so agitated, when I ask you to marry me?"

"Because, it's only a ritual. I'm married to Radha, but I love you more than her and that's what matters," fumed Tatya.

"Who knows, maybe tomorrow you will set your roving eyes on some other girl? Men betray," Kanta continued with her jibes.

"If that's the case, then why did you love me?"

"I didn't throw the bait, you cozied up to me."

"Come on Kanta! Do not sound so innocent. You wanted me and that's why you warmed up to me."

"Let's not fight over who came first—chicken or the egg. The time has come to entangle our love to a knot. We must marry."

Tatya scratched his forehead, as he slammed his eyes shut. "Marriage! Marriage! Marriage!" he drawled, while he opened his eyes. "What's this obsession with marriage?"

"Stop throwing tantrums. It means everything to me," shouted Kanta; her nostrils flared and eyes flashed with anger. She dug her finger into Tatya's chest. "You just said that you can do anything for me. I do not ask for the moon. I ask you to marry me."

"It isn't that simple. It means that I'll have to divorce Radha."

"I'm not asking for that. It's fine with me, as long as I get to be your second wife and have my children."

Tatya lost his cool and slapped his forehead. "Why don't you realize that it's not possible? You are a chamar!" he shouted, as his body shook violently

Kanta shut her eyes and clenched her fists. "Don't raise your voice!"

A momentary silence engulfed the argument.

Kanta opened her eyes, which had turned moist. "I didn't hide it from you. You knew it from the beginning," her voice choked, while she broke down. She gasped for breath and tried to talk but the words drowned in grief.

Tatya embraced her and patted her back. "You must know that I love you," he reiterated, trying to straighten the situation. He withdrew and pinched his throat. "I swear!"

Kanta nodded her head but continued to wail.

Tatya sensed the mood and felt it ripe to justify his protest. "Marriage is complicated. It entails political suicide. I have ambitions," he explained, with a soft voice, as he held the tip of her chin on his fingers and gently shook it. "All for you," he said, wiping the tears flowing down her cheeks. "They will fall apart, if I marry a chamar."

Kanta pushed him away. "Wah! Wah!" she mocked, clapping her hands. "It doesn't matter when you bang me in bed. You have touched me all over and squeezed the lust out of me. It's so damn hypocritical!"

Tatya straightened his shirt and stiffened his face. "Love and politics don't go hand in hand. You cannot mix the two. In politics caste matters because if my community gets to hear that I've married you, it will mean the end of my political career."

"Then, why don't you sacrifice your political career for me? You just bragged about doing anything for me," demanded Kanta.

The rebuttal stung Tatya to silence. It appeared as if the pressure showed no signs of abatting. He lay trapped under the pile of logical incongruities of the caste system in Hinduism, which fossilized mobilization for centuries. A strange social structure raised on the bedrock of a casteist order, which forced the Hindus to swear by caste rather than religion. It appeared a strange geometrical design in which the parts seemed bigger than the whole, making Hinduism a matrix of logical contradictions.

"I cannot sacrifice my political fortunes on the altar of love. I'm a Kshatriya and I cannot marry a chamar," stated Tatya, with an imperious tone.

"If you think, you can play around with my feelings, you better think twice. I will not let you off so easily. You'll have to marry me," threatened Kanta.

"Do you threaten me?" Tatya questioned, as he pointed his fingers at Kanta and twitched his lips.

"I do what I think right."

"Don't you ever talk to me like that? You bloody chamar! If somebody else would have said it, I'd have pulled out the tongue and burnt it," warned Tatya, fuming with rage.

"Do what you like? I am not afraid. I'll have my way," said Kanta, remaining steadfast in her demand.

Tatya walked towards the door in a huff. "I'll teach you a lesson," he said, and then vanished out of sight.

CHAPTER 20

▼

The ground lay tucked under the Siberian snowfall, while lumps of snow dangled over treetops. A thick air blew over the white terrain, as Vladimir and his team wrapped in thick winter coats, with mufflers strapped around their necks, tramped on snowshoes towards Vladimir's tiger enclosure. The snow crunched under their boots as they waded through the frozen landscape with a reindeer ranch in the background. The whistle of the wind mingled with the sweet rhyme of milk squirting into the pails as ranchers churned the udders of mother reindeers. At a distance, the clutter of locked horns and grunts of flared nostrils whoosing thick plumes of white breath rattled the icy air, as the boisterous males fought for domination.

"In the towns and villages around Siberia people have learnt to live with tigers," observed Vladimir Molotov, plodding through the snow along the fence of the ranch.

"I find it difficult to believe that tigers and humans can co-exist," proclaimed Linda Kohl, trudging through the snow.

"They can co-exist," maintained the Russian conservationist, halting in his track.

"Tigers like other carnivores will kill human beings to survive. I don't think they can co-exist with human beings," fretted Michael Strosberg, with a slight nod of his head. He stood between the other two and cast his eyes over the ranch.

Vladimir looked at Michael and smacked his lips. "This confusion arises because of insufficient scientific knowledge about the Big Cat's survival instincts. In the Sundarbans, tigers do attack human beings for food, but not in Siberia."

Linda stuffed her hands into the linings of her overcoat and interjected. "Do you imply that certain breed of tigers remain man-eaters?" she asked, with a curious look on her face.

"Hmm," murmured Michael, as if she spoke his mind.

Vladimir took a deep icy breath and gazed pensively at the sky as if conjuring a plausible answer. "I'll put it this way," he replied, exhaling a stream of white air that gushed out of his nostrils. "In order to understand any breed of tigers, we must study the eco-systems in which they live, including the watersheds where they drink water and the topography of their habitat, which together, determines their choice of prey. To illustrate my point, take the case of the Sundarban tiger that inhabits the mangrove forests of Bengal. The topography of the Sundarban delta makes it difficult for the tiger to kill his normal prey. The delta stays underwater, which makes it difficult for the tiger to catch prey. In fact, the tigers of Sundarban have acquired a talent to swim and stalk prey in water. They have mastered this technique as a means to survive. The dense forests stay submerged in water throughout the year and compel the tiger to attack from behind to maximize success. However, this does not happen at the Ranthambore and Kanha tiger reserves of India, which have plenty of game like Sambhar, Cheetal, Barasingha and Bison. Besides, these forests remain open and not submerged in water. Similarly, the Siberian tiger appears unconditioned for man-eating, because the forests of Siberia provide it with wild boar and elk. This explains why the bionetwork of the terrain determines the feeding habits of any breed of tigers."

"Do you suggest that tigers and human beings can co-exist, but the eco-system determines the degree of compatibility?" asked Michael, with a creased forehead.

Vladimir nodded his head in agreement and hypothesized. "Yes, my study has revealed that we need to protect the natural tiger habitats from shrinking in order to maintain an ecological balance in the environment and preserve the rich bio-diversity of the planet."

"How will we protect these habitats?" asked Linda, she angled her head and fixed her eyes on Vladimir, as if curious to know the solution to the impending crisis.

The scientist dug his hands into his overcoat, looked at the ground grimly, while he flirted with the question and formulated a few questions. "What do you think? Why restrict ourselves to Siberia? Why don't we think of a universal solution?"

Michael stifled a laugh, and then grinned. He spoke casually. 'I don't think we need to think much. We need to have stringent laws diligently enforced to deter poachers from killing tigers and other animals."

He looked at Linda, who joined him and added her suggestions. "Hang the poachers!" she spurted, with an angry glare. "Set up fast track courts to try poachers and deter others from such criminal activities."

Vladimir maintained a stoic silence.

Michael barged in with another solution. "Evict all human settlements from the jungles; especially, those that exist in developing countries of Latin America, Africa and Asia, where poverty and the lure of money spurs poaching and ruins natural eco-systems," he concluded in a huff.

A grim silence engulfed the intellectual tiger discourse, after three solutions appeared in rapid succession. The Russian ecologist shook his head and smiled cockishly while he mulled over the answers. It occurred to him that he needed to educate the world about the importance of preservation and conservation. He scrunched his forehead, "I'm afraid, I disgree with your answers. You belong to the conventional school of thought," he concluded, with a heavy heart.

Linda and Michael's faces contorted and they looked at each other wide eyed.

"Why do you say this?" inquired Linda.

Vladimir laughed and replied. "Your answers frighten me, because they reflect the opinion held by policy makers and common people the world over. Unless these views change, I see little hope for the tiger and ecology," lamented Vladimir.

"These opinions stand on evidence gathered and whetted by experts," asserted Michael.

"True, but the studies have outlived their times. I am thinking of newer ways to mitigate the menace. I feel we need to go to the root of the problem, which lies in the subconscious mind of the human populace and begin from there. We need to educate the masses and particularly the children of our planet, the future generations, about the importance of preserving the rich bio-diversity of our planet. We cannot restrict our solutions to stringent laws, fast track courts, severe punishments or eviction of human settlements anymore. These piecemeal measures adopted for decades have failed to curb the rapid deterioration of our eco-systems. Take law for example, we have the wildlife law and other laws to protect the environment, but what has happened? The population of the Siberian tigers has dropped alarmingly over the past decade. We need to follow the spirit of the law and not the form and this will happen through an aggressive eco-friendly education curriculum, which must begin at the primary school level, so as to nurture in the innocent minds of our children the importance of bio-diversity.

'Children appear the most innocent, imaginative, curious and affectionate species. I prefer to call them a species in themselves, because we must distinguish adult attributes, which remain the biggest threat to this planet. Adults forfeit childlike innocence and affection when they grow up and adopt greed, hate and other competitive and wicked survival traits, which tend to sprout from the mind and not the heart. These traits found in history books, which glorify bloody conquerors and inculcate parochial nationalism force children to think within the confines of boundaries. We forget to think of the world as ours rather we think of boundaries created by bloody wars and conquests as our homes. The heroes of these senseless conquests displayed in the national museums act as icons of children, who look up to these as role models. In the process, we convey a subtle and dangerous message to children. Kill one and the law will punish you for murder, but kill a million and the museum will honour you as a conqueror. What kind of history do we teach our children? A history, which glorifies violence and bloodshed against fellow beings, animals and nature so that they grow up thirsty for violence, if they cannot kill their fellow beings, they will vent their anger on animals.

'The truth remains that we have stopped evolving to higher forms as the theory of evolution will want us to believe. On the contrary, we have accelerated the process of extinction, by bequeathing violence and mayhem to future generations. We brag about rat race and competition to our kids, without mulling over the consequences this has for our environment. We need a tectonic shift in our education curriculum, from competition to co-operation. We need to inculcate in our children, the values of co-operation and co-existence and the philosophy of live and let live. Biology calls this, 'symbiosis.' We need to teach our children about the symbiotic relationship that we share with the environment and fellow beings . . ."

Suddenly, Michael interrupted the lengthy discourse, "I disgree on this point, because you contradict the law of nature, which doesn't believe in co-existence. Take the simple case of a tiger, if all the tigers abide by your theory, they would die of starvation. The tiger has to kill to live and risk death to survive," countered Michael Strosberg.

Vladimir heard him and smiled. "You've got me wrong Mr Strosberg. The tiger remains a dignified animal with integrity and character. It will not kill for sport and thrill nor misuse its power. On the contrary, the tiger kills when hungry and feeds on its kill for days. It will not waste, like a conservationist it displays wisdom and understands that it cannot outlive its resources. It abides by the rule of nature—kill for need not for greed. This explains why it never indulges in reckless killings to terrorize the jungle. Unlike us human beings, who live off terror?"

Linda interrupted with a doubt that nagged her mind. "What happens if the tiger population explodes and outlives its resources? They cannot co-exist peacefully."

Vladimir shook his head, and then smiled wryly. "When this happens we can safely conclude that we made it happen," declared the ecologist. He took a deep breath and continued. "Nature on its own will not let it happen. I propose to give you an interesting bit of information," he exhaled slowly. "Did you know the mortality rate of the Siberian cubs, in the wild?"

Linda and Michael watched and shook their heads.

Vladimir raised his three fingers, "thirty percent," he replied, paused and went on. "It means that only seventy percent of the cubs survive after birth? Moreover, the ones that survive remain vulnerable to attacks by strong male tigers and other animals in the wild. I know this sounds cruel, but it answers your doubt. These mechanisms adopted by nature control population explosion. Therefore, the conclusion remains that nature will not permit the tiger to outlive its resources. If it ever happens, it will happen due to human intervention. We remain the biggest threat to the tiger," confessed the ecologist.

"Why we?" questioned Michael, with a scowl on his face. He looked disturbed and irritated with the ecologist. "The tribal settlements in the jungles must be blamed for this threat. So I proposed the eviction of human habitations in the forests."

The ecologist looked at him and grinned. "The eviction of a few tribal dwellings from within the forests of the world will not settle the dispute between man and environment. The poachers kill tigers to cater to the rich and affluent class of society—those who pay heavy sums of money. I do not understand this obsession for evicting tribes from forests. In fact, most tribal societies co-exist peacefully with the environment. On the contrary, we need to educate the mainstream populace living off myths about the perils of environmental degradation. Once the demand for tiger parts seizes, the tiger count will rise. I followed the same in Siberia and succeeded in convincing the people about the importance of maintaining the ecological balance of the environment and saving the tiger. But, this solitary effort needs support and participation from the world and a humungous education curriculum so that we get bigger and faster results," he proposed, and then paused for a breather, with his eyes moist with passion and concern for his mission. He thought back upon his struggle and the risks he faced to come this far.

Vladimir Molotov appeared a passionate and eccentric environmentalist prepared to follow his weird imagination and make it happen. He stayed the pioneer of the first breeding enclosure for Siberian tigers in Russia, and seemed determined to study the behavioural traits of this animal. His mission appeared a bumpy ride from the start, but he braved it all to make his dream a reality. In fact, he and his wife Anna pooled all their savings to start this ambitious project. Despite the risk, the zealous couple willed to go to any extent to protect the Siberian cat. They roamed the vast endless patch of white land, educating the Siberian people and stalking poachers. They waited for days and weeks to win the confidence of the coy and ferocious cat and nurtured the frail and abandoned cubs orphaned by ruthless poachers. They also braved threats, escaped attempts on their person by vested poaching cartels, and pushed hard against the Russian bureaucracy to get them to work overtime to save the rare breed of tigers. The effort showed from the wealth of knowledge the ecologist exhibited in this excursion. Vladimir sacrificed over half his life to save the Siberian tigers from extinction, traveling the length and breadth of every tiger habitat on earth, before descending on his home turf in Siberia to protect the biggest cat on earth. It seemed that nothing could deter him, because his heart stayed convinced about this mission. The selfless Russian believed that if he could convince one of his audiences, he would have saved the life of at least one tiger on earth.

Linda observed and listened to Vladimir in rapt attention. She mused over all he said and continued to question him. The morning seemed to have opened to a vibrant discourse and she reveled in intellectual arguments. "I appreciate your effort and respect your knowledge, but I wish to know how you will save the depletion of forests in Siberia?" she asked.

Vladimir shook his head, and then put his hands to his chest. "We have to understand why forests face depletion?" he said, as he tapped the tip of each finger on the flat of his palm. "The trees provide firewood, timber, paper and the forests have mineral resources like coal and bauxite," he dropped his hands and continued. "We need to develop alternative sources of energy or non-conventional forms, like wind, tidal, solar and the like. It may seem impossible to beginners but it can happen with great political will of political and business leaders, especially those from the advanced nations, which have the technical expertise and research and development capacities. The present economic model pursued by the world remains highly energy driven. Every nation vies for high economic growth, which in turn means, higher energy consumption. However, the non-renewable oil and gas reserves, which presently drive economic growth have depleted and may not last beyond 2050. In fact, geologists have failed to locate new reserves of oil and gas, since the early sixties, which implies we will run out of conventional sources of energy that drive economic growth and warm the globe. In addition, we loose millions of hectares of forest cover, when we exploit mineral resources in the forests without substituting forests with trees. We need to start a heavy afforestation programme that will help restore the capacity of our earth to absorb carbondioxide gases emitted from fossil fuels, which deplete the ozone layer of the atmosphere. The forests remain the lungs of the world and you know what happens, when the lungs of the body get damaged," said Vladimir, wheezing heavily and gasping for breath. You . . .

know . . . how . . . the . . . earth . . . suffers . . . now," he demonstrated, uttering each word with difficulty.

Linda laughed at him and then shook her head. "You're impossible," she commented.

Michael seemed distraught and interjected the banter. "I repeat human habitations in the forests remain a bigger threat to the world and not the economic growth rates, which ensure a higher standard of living. We will have to evict the primitive tribes that burn firewood and slash and burn trees to preserve the forests. We cannot cut down on energy consumption and stall the march of civilization; at least the economists will not agree to that."

"Where will you rehabilitate these human settlements?" asked Vladimir.

"Anywhere, beyond the forests," replied Michael.

"Do you assume that the problem will end and it will make a difference?" inquired the eclogist.

"It will make some difference," replied Michael; he shrugged his shoulders and twisted his face.

"How big a difference will it make?" asked Vladimir; he raised his hands, squeezed the flat of his palms together and then separated his palms. "This big," he showed, and then expanded the distance.

Michael nodded his head.

"This big," Vladimir demonstrated again, increasing the distance.

Michael slammed his eyes shut.

"Or this big," Vladimir concluded, with his arms wide open and then jerked his head in anticipation of an answer.

"Come on," cribbed Michael, chopping the air with his hand. "It sounds silly."

"I find your hypothesis stupid," replied Vladimir.

"Why do you say that?" asked Michael, unable to comprehend the absurdity of the argument.

"Because you blame the tribes for the misdeeds of civilization," retorted Vladimir; he tossed his hands over his hips. "Rehabiltation happens because we wish to exploit the mineral resources that the tribes sit on. Therefore, we start this argument of convenience that tribes destroy the forests. How many tribes live in the forests? Much less than civilization, which inhabits most of this earth? If you wish to rehabilitate them, then I suggest that the Americans and Russians must be booted out of this planet first."

"A ridiculous suggestion!" exclaimed Michael, nodding his head vigourously. He cocked a wry smile, and then argued. "The tribes chop trees and live in the jungles. Why should the Americans or Russians rehabilitate?"

Vladimir pointed his finger at Michael, and then dug it in his chest. "Because both of us have piled up weapons of mass destruction in our backyard; I mean America and Russia. These weapons of mass destruction endanger the planet more then the firewood of primitive tribes," declared Vladimir. He thumped his chest, "we started the cold war on the pretext of ideological differences, and terrorized the world to assert our supremacy," he dropped his hand, and then shook his head in disgust. "Some stupid intellectuals that advised these Governments proposed the theory of mutually assured destruction (MAD) as a means to maintain peace on this planet. They snubbed the Einstein-Russell Manifesto, which condemned nuclear weapons. On the contrary, these war mongerers suggested that preparation for war would ensure peace—the most dim-witted theory ever proposed in the annals of international relations to maintain peace and security in the world. What followed appeared worse; Britain, France, China, Israel, India, Pakistan and North Korea joined the bandwagon and went nuclear. India, Pakistan and North Korea have millions of citizens living below the poverty line; yet, they have invested billions of dollars on building nuclear weapons. The lunatic leadership of these nations continues to spend more and more each year on upgrading their deterrence capabilities. If all these powers thrashed out their differences and invested a fraction of the same money in developing non-conventional sources of energy, our world will appear a safer and healthier place to live in. These nuclear blokes and their weapons of mass destruction must be kicked out of this planet," fumed Vladimir, his face turned red, and he twisted his face in disgust.

Linda and Michael stood dumb-founded and their jaws dropped. A feeling of guilt and remorse enveloped an otherwise objective tiger discourse, which none imagined would lead to nuclear warfare.

Vladimir shook his head and concluded. "It's high time the Americans and big powers sign the Kyoto Protocol and abide by the spirit of the treaty, because they remain the biggest polluters and biggest threat to the environment."

Linda's face lit up, her eyes twinkled and she clapped her hands. "Hurrah! Mr Molotov, I'm glad we think alike," she brimmed with excitement and stared at Michael, who nodded his head in agreement. Linda inhaled and spoke, "our green peace movement opposes all forms of weapons of mass destruction," she stated, with her hands on her heart and then exhaled. "I recall my journey to the Murara Atoll islands in the South Pacific, where the French conducted their hydro-nuclear tests, which ravaged the marine life and severely affected the livelihoods of the tribal people living around the Pacific islands. The fat powers must introspect and work towards disarmament and de-nuclearisation rather then coax the non-nuclear countries to sign a discriminatory nuclear non-proliferation treaty. It amounts to making the poor tribes of the South Pacific islands sign the treaty, while France opts out of it. In fact, I suggest that the Kyoto Protocol must include disarmament and de-nuclearisation so that nuclear powers first clean their backyards and then preach sermons to the world."

"Hmm," Michael nodded with a grim face.

An opinion appeared to have crystallized in the frigid temperatures of Siberia that co-existence would define the fate of a world mired in greed and competition. Ecological degradation remains a global problem, which concerns us, and unless nations move beyond, 'me,' and 'you,' this problem will aggravate. The Siberian tiger remains an indispensable part of this world and it has the natural right to a habitat. Human civilization cannot drive the tiger to extinction because they have not created it. The big nuclear powers who pose as larger than God must give up on their quest to dominate nature and phase out their weapons of mass destruction. They must learn to co-exist and not just exist.

"I wish to see your tiger enclosure and how you conduct your experiment, besides the education curriculum which you impart to the children of Siberia," said Linda, as the team started to walk towards the enclosure.

"I want to touch the Siberian tiger and do a few close-up photo shoots, so that I can boast a little," added Michael, while he winked at Linda.

Vladimir halted in his track and looked over the fence. He stuffed his hands in his sidepockets, lifted his shoulders, pursed his lips and gazed at the reindeers philosophically. "I marvel at nature's varied creation and fail to fathom the mind of the creator. It mesmerizes me and repells me, making me doubtful," he pondered, as he hit the road, with his mind steeped in thought.

"Anything wrong," asked Michael.

Vladimir shook his head and a smile appeared at the corner of his lips. He tilted his head, looked at Michael and Linda and remarked. "Someone rightly said, 'the trouble with this world is that the intellectuals are full of doubt and the stupid cocksure.'"

CHAPTER 21

▼

Vasu waited for a week, but Sahukar failed to turn up. The rumour mills in Ramwadi grinded all kinds of stories. "He'll never come back fom jail," concluded a few. Others sounded coarser, "the Government will hang him. These money lenders deserve more." Some expressed skepticism, "It's only a farce. He'll pay and come out." A few seemed anxious, "he's our only source of credit. If he doesn't return, we will never get loans."

Whatever, the conjectures, the fact remained that Vasu needed the money for Shoba's wedding. He instructed Angad to keep the proposal in limbo, until he arranged for the money, because he exuded confidence in Sahukar's promise. However, as the days passed he soon ran out of patience and decided to approach Abba. The headman basked in high spirits ever since he got wind of his son's discord with Kanta. He had plotted, prayed and hoped for the relationship to end, so when he heard the relationship tottered, he waited for the fall. He lolled in his chamber formulating a plan for his son's political future, when Vasu arrived.

"Namaskar Abba," Vasu greeted him, bowing humbly.

"Come in and sit down. What brings you here this morning?" asked Abba, with a loud and cheerful voice.

Vasu's heart bumped with joy. He gauged the mood and came to the point. "I need money," he said, with his head bowed and in a soft voice.

Abba stared at him, reclined in his chair and plopped his hands over his head. "Hmm," he murmured.

Vasu cast a glance from the corner of his eyes. He gathered that Abba would create a scene, and then relent, so he stayed unfazed.

"I don't have money to lend you and even if I have, I will not lend you," stated Abba, in a gruff voice.

Vasu's heart cringed on hearing the last few words. He knew they appeared when earlier loans stayed uncleared. He squeezed his palms tight. "Abba please," he implored, hunching over in a low stoop. He did not dare to look Abba in the eyes.

"You know what happened to Sahukar?" said Abba, shaking his knees.

Vasu nodded his head.

"That's what happens when you lend money," complained Abba, with a stiff face.

"I need money for Shoba's wedding," Vasu hesitated and paused. "She's my only daughter."

Abba looked away and thought to himself. "The same old crap they mutter." He then turned his sight on Vasu, dropped his hands on his knees, pointed his finger at Vasu and sat up. "If you don't have the money, then don't marry her off," he suggested, slumping in his chair. "Wait till you make money and then marry her off."

Vasu's face dropped, as he he slowly looked at Abba. "I swear," he entreated, squeezing the skin on his throat. "I'll pay you back on time. I've plenty of water."

Abba raised his eyebrows and stretched his face. "I see," he said, slowly and loudly. He then nodded his head, "I'm impressed. You seem a big man now," he declared, smiling sarcastically. He then laughed and crossed his legs. "I gather you owe others money."

A lump appeared in Vasu's throat and forced him to keep quiet. He gulped down the lump and his eyes bulged.

Abba leered at the sight. "Haven't you borrowed from Sahukar?" asked Abba, in a soft voice.

Vasu's face crumpled, as he nodded his head.

Abba drummed his fingers on the arms of his chair. "Haven't you taken rations on credit?" he toyed like a cat playing with a mouse under its paws.

"Hmm," Vasu stuttered.

Abba took a deep breath. "You have too many debts. How can you guarantee me my money?" he asked, exhaling slowly. Like a typical moneylender, he gradually strangled his prey.

Vasu said nothing.

Abba smiled wryly. "Your silence speaks for itself," he said and then giggled. "You clear your debts first. But I'm not lending you any more."

Vasu's eyes turned moist and he quivered at the thought of loosing the proposal for Shobha. "What happens to my daughter? It remains a matter of honour. I beg on her behalf. You alone can help me."

Abba shut his eyes for a moment, as if wary of the emotional outburst. "All the trouble starts here," he fumed, slapping his knees. "The entire village assumes that I have a magic wand. I crack it and money spills over. The people fail to realize that I too have to toil to make ends meet. You have a problem, but I have problems of an entire constituency to redress. Everyone expects me to solve his or her problems. If I say, 'no,' the people feel offended and complain, 'Abba doesn't care about our needs.' I give them money and they hang themselves to death, because they cannot pay back and I appear the villain—the bloodsucking vampire, who exploited them and drove them to the gallows. The police then come looking for me," Abba complained, as he shrugged his shoulders and paused for a breather. He put his fingers to his temple, stroked it and continued. "Thousands borrow from the banks and kill themselves. The bank remains a legalized money lending institution, but the Government will not arrest the bank. On the contrary, it questions the competency of the borrower. However, in Vidharbh everyone accuses the moneylender, as if, the moneylender forced the loan down the throats of the borrowers. The Government must address the question, 'why do the farmers borrow from the moneylenders?'" Abba questioned, with his arms spread wide. "Because the institutions that lend credit have collapsed, and the farmers have nowhere to borrow. In your case, you want to borrow, for your daughter's marriage. Why do you want to spend on a marriage? Huh!" exclaimed Abba in a huff. "Marriage comprises a dead investment. How can you guarantee me my money?"

"I have three acres of land, next to your patta. I'm willing to mortgage the land," said Vasu.

"How much do you wish to borrow?"

"I need two lakhs."

"Two lakhs!" exclaimed Abba; his eyes bulged and he crossed his hands over his chest. His face looked shocked. "It's a very big amount for a mortgage," he muttered each word slowly and loudly with his eyes wide open. "I suggest you register the land in my name so that I stay assured. I'll talk to Tatya, he'll give you the money and you complete the formalities."

Vasu nodded his head and then interjected. "I have one more request."

"What?" snapped Abba, with a scowl on his face.

"Bapu needs to join school. Your principal suspended him for non-payment of fees."

Abba sliced the air with his hand, as if the request sounded inconsequential. "I'll talk to the principal. You send him to school tomorrow."

"Thank-you," said Vasu; he bowed humbly and walked away.

"Tatya," Abba called out to his son.

Tatya walked into the hall, buttoning his shirt.

"Vasu needs money for his daughter's wedding. You get him to sign a sale deed in your name and give him two lakh rupees," ordered Abba.

"Yeah," nodded Tatya.

"I want the money to reach Vasu. If I get to hear, that you have splashed it on that wench," Abba gritted his teeth and shook violently.

Tatya's face dropped and he felt irritated. "Why don't you believe me? I am not interested in her anymore. It's over for me . . ."

"You may think so but that bitch will not give up so easily."

"I've done my bit. You stop bothering me.'

"I fear that she may keep pestering you. My hands stay tied due to the elections; otherwise, I would have transferred her to some unknown place. I warn you not to loiter around that hospital. You go to the farm and supervise activities there."

"Hmm," murmured Tatya.

The two-drop outs continued to share company. Tillya, who donned the mantle of a shepherd and worked for Manibhai stayed close to Bapu's farm. The penning in Abba's field had reached the fringes of the fifty-acre sugarcane plot, whose boundaries stayed lined with acacia trees. There lay a huge surface well in the middle of this plot and the masonaries had arrived here to build it. Sushma and Lekha worked on this well and after having lunch with them, Tillya would race down to Bapu's farm for a game of marbles. Sometimes, Bapu would come over and help Tillya with the herding. In short, though the boys dropped out of school, they remained in company.

This afternoon, they conjured a different plan. They decided to raid the jamun tree in Abba's orchard after lunch. The tree stood on the land next to the main road that led to the Hanuman temple. Abba's huge estate stretched from Vasu's land to the main road. It included a hundred acres swathe of fertile land, with a fruit orchard, standing next to the main road. The jamun tree that the two brats targeted stood in this orchard. After stuffing their tummies, they pocketed their plastic bags and sauntered down the track leading to the orchard, which included a ten to fifteen minutes walk. They sweated in the hot and humid afternoon of September, but it did not matter to the boys.

"I hope the orchard is empty," began Bapu, strutting down the dirt track behind Tillya.

"I've gathered that Kanha's on leave for the past two days, while Ganpat and Daya seem busy at the well. You've seen them haven't you?" asked Tillya, heaving his pants. He seemed well informed about the situation.

"I worry about our school boys. If they get there before us, they will take all the jamuns. We'll have to rummage through the scrap," complained Bapu.

"No!" exclaimed Tillya, shaking his head. "Today remains physical training day. The boys will tire out and not have the energy to climb the tree. We'll reach there first and take all the jamuns.'

"You still remember the schedule in school. I can barely recall the subjects and days," declared Bapu; his face scrunched and he looked dejected. "I may have to rejoin school. Papa says that he will ask Abba for permission."

"You appear lucky," beamed Tillya, halting in his track and whirling around to face Bapu. "I don't stand a chance."

Bapu motioned him to walk.

Tillya turned around and proceeded down the narrorw track that led through the plantation. "It appears I will work with Manibhai as long as he's here. Once he leaves, I will take charge of another flock, which Mother has fixed for me. She says that Mesba has arranged for twenty goats," said Tillya, with a heavy heart. His face dropped and it seemed he missed school.

"Damn the school! I hate it!" blurted Bapu. He hopped over a lump of cow dung spluttered on the road and swiped the sweat trickling down his forehead to his forearm. "It seems a waste going to school and studying subjects like English which make no sense when I know that one day I'll end up in the fields tilling my land. Look at what happened to your brother, Sushil. He studied for a long time and has ended up in the fields. However, Papa seems determined to see me through. He doesn't want me to end up farming."

Tillya hitched his shorts. "My father said the same to me. It seems everyone hates farming. Your father can still provide for you especially after you struck water on that dry patta. My father never appeared lucky, though he did his best. He should not have killed himself. I would have seen him through, but I regret staying small. I wish I could grow up quicker so I can make money," revealed Tillya, with a tinge of nostalgia in his voice. His eyes turned a little moist as he recalled his father's sermons. "My father promised me ten rupees if I win at marbles. I would have gathered nearly a hundred rupees had he lived. I need new pants, you see these with patches all over, my hands ache tugging at them all the time."

Bapu stifled a laugh and Tillya joined him as they entered the orchard. They reached the jamun tree, which stood in the centre of the orchard. The orchard comprised of many other trees like papaya, mango, custard apple, orange and a few coconut trees, which encircled a huge concrete well. The jamun tree stood at a distance of fifty metres from the main road, with a cattleshed hemmed in between the tree and a small farmhouse perched on the fringes of the main road.

"You climb up there and shake that branch," said Bapu, pointing at a huge branch that wilted under the weight of ripe jamuns.

Tillya shoved his hands in his pockets and yanked out two plastic bags. "Here keep these," he said, handing over the bags to Bapu. "Make sure you fill these with ripe jamuns."

"Hmm," murmured Bapu; he grabbed the bags and scoured the surroundings. "I don't see anyone around. Climb the tree. Quick!"

Tillya hitched his shorts and skimmed the tree. "I'll climb the tree, but you make sure you back me," warned Tillya, hugging the trunk of the tree and preparing to heave his body. "Keep guard and help me mount."

"Yeah," nodded Bapu, lifting Tillya and setting him in motion.

"Huh," Tillya gasped, scrambling up the tree.

"Easy," cautioned Bapu.

Tillya mounted the tree nimbly like a toddy tapper. His shorts slipped and revealed his buttocks. Bapu stuck his tongue out and giggled. "Your pants are falling off."

Tillya chuckled and winked at Bapu. He paused for a breather when he reached the middle of the trunk. "Stop giggling and go and check the main road. The school boys must be on their way," he ordered, and then leapt higher.

Bapu raced to patrol the main road. He reached the road and cast a glance on either sides of the road. It remained deserted. He cupped his ears and craned his neck to catch the sound of any boisterous cackle or cycles racing towards the orchard. He heard the faint whistle of the wind. He beamed then whirled wround and darted back to the jamun tree.

Meanwhile, Tillya reached a branch that jutted out of the trunk, mounted it, sat astride and gorged on the jamuns that dangled overhead. Bapu reached the jamun tree and skid to a halt. He hunched over panting for breath and waived his hand to Tillya. "No one around," he gasped.

Tillya grabbed the branch overhead, vaulted and stashed his feet on the branch below.

"Shake it hard," yelled Bapu, unfolding the plastic bag and preparing for the fall.

Tillya took a deep breath and bounced on the branch. The leaves rustled while the ripe bunches of jamuns tossed, lashed, bumped and plopped down on the ground.

"Harder!" shouted Bapu, crouching and gathering the jamuns.

Tillya used all the force his tiny body could muster and rattled the branch hard. The jamuns hurtled down and pelted the earth like raindrops falling from the sky. Bapu gathered them and tossed them in his plastic bag.

Tillya paused to regain his breath. Beads of sweat gushed down his body and trickled on the branch. He looked down on Bapu and gasped for breath.

"Don't forget to fill my bag," he reminded Bapu, who moved around on his hams picking the jamuns.

Bapu waived a bag crammed with jamuns. "I've stuffed it. I will fill the others. You continue to shake hard."

Tillya nodded his head.

Bapu brandished a dark purple coloured jamun. "You see this," he said, jumping to his feet. "We need more of this. It tastes delicious," he said, sinking his teeth into it. "Crunch!" the jamun spluttered, staining his lips. He munched on it and pointed to a bunch of jamuns on the tree. "You move further down the branch to the centre and shake harder."

Tillya twisted his face. "It's difficult to move further without a prop," replied Tillya; he cast his eyes overhead and shook his head at the sight. The branch curled upwards and stayed out of reach.

"Let it stay, when you come down. We'll pelt stones," suggested Bapu; his eyes scouted the tree for more jamuns. "I can see a few bunches of jamuns just above your head," he said, pointing to a cluster of ripe jamuns that dangled over Tillya's head. "Why don't you climb up there and stir that branch?"

Tillya shot a glance upwards and noticed a cluster concealed behind the leaves. He examined his chances, "I'll try," he accepted the suggestion, and then inched his way towards the trunk of the tree.

Suddenly, a raucous sound of an engine sliced the air. Bapu turned his attention to the main road and strained his ears. "Tillya do you hear that?"

Tillya remained stranded on the branch and swung like a hammock with his legs and hands fastened to the branch. "Huh!" he gasped, trying to grapple forward.

The sound grew shriller and then a motorcycle swirved round the bend and raced towards the orchard. Bapu froze in his tracks.

"Damn you thief!" yelled Tatya, hurtling on his bullet and screeching to a halt under the jamun tree.

Bapu quivered at the sight; his face cringed and heart sank. Tillya hammocked to the branch hung on to save his skin and feared jumping down because he had clamoured too high. Bapu's situation remained precarious, because Tatya had spotted him, while Tillya hung overhead. His mind failed to discern the right course of action. He stood as if resigned to his fate.

Tatya kicked the sidestand, alighted in a huff and charged towards Bapu; his face bursted with rage and eyes burned with anger. He had squabbled with his father, who drove him to the farm and now this spectacle offered him the perfect valve to vent his anger. He grabbed Bapu by the scruff of his collar.

"You bloody thief!" howled Tatya, shaking him hard. The puny boy's head shook like a weathercock struck by a Gayle and he froze.

"You steal fruits from my orchard in my absence," grunted Tatya.

The scrawny boy blinked owlishly. "Forgive me," he begged, with folded hands that trembled. "You can have the jamuns."

Tatya snatched the plastic bag from Bapu's hands. "Empty your pockets!" he demanded.

Bapu's fingers fumbled, as he groped his pockets stained with purple dots. He thrust his hands inside and emptied his pockets. The jamuns plopped down and the sight provoked Tatya. He gripped the tips of Bapu's earlobes and squeezed them.

"Ouch! Ouch!" squealed Bapu, like a chicken under the knife.

"How long have you robbed my orchard?" grunted Tatya, twisting the ears harder.

Bapu squeaked in pain, with his eyes turning blood red. "Ouch!"

"You thought you could get away with it. Now I have you. These trees belong to me. Do you get it?" hollered Tatya.

The boy howled and wept. "Sorry! Ouch! Ouch! Ouch!"

Tatya pushed him away. The boy drained off energy staggered and slumped on the ground. Tatya hauled him to his feet and slapped him under the ear.

"Ouch!" screamed Bapu. The blow stung his cheeks, which turned red and bore the imprint of Tatya's palm. He collapsed on the ground wailing in agony.

Tillya snooped down and cowered at the sight. He mulled over his fate and wet his pants. He slammed his eyes shut and prayed. "Oh Hanuman, please help me!" he murmured to himself.

Tatya grunted with anger, as he clenched his fists, slammed his foot on the ground. "Damn you rascal! All these months you robbed me. No wonder Abba forced me to come over. The village treats this orchard like a public property. They can come over to steal, shit and piss at will," he yelled, shaking his head, and then turning his eyes upwards. The sight made him mad. He saw Tillya hanging above with his eyes shut.

"Damn you!" Tatya shrieked with his eyes shut. The veins on his throat bulged and it looked as if they would burst. The sound tore through the sky like a knife ripping a canvas. He pointed at Tillya. "Come down," he ordered, with a stern voice, and then looked around for something to hurl.

Tillya's hands and feet wriggled and he struggled with the grip. Tatya hauled a stone that lay by the tree and brandished it before Tillya. Tillya's face contorted and his nerves stiffened. Tillya hung in a catch 22 situation. If he descended, he feared the pounding and if he hung on the stone would pelt him. He sobbed and begged for mercy, "please don't hit."

"You come down and face me or I'll break your head with this stone," warned Tatya, drawing his hand backwards to fling the stone.

Tillya stared horrified; he grappled with the branch and tried to mount it, while Tatya stood below with the stone in hand. Bapu lay on the ground and whimpered with his hands over his cheeks.

Meanwhile, the wind carried the squabble to the people working on the well. Ganpat and Daya knew Tatya had raked up a wrangle and Tillya's mother Lekha feared it must be the two boys who prompted him. Her motherly instincts forced her to run to rescue her son. She dropped her work and fled. Ganpat and Daya wary of their master's mood anticipated trouble and raced towards the orchard.

"What's the matter?" questioned Pandu, who had sauntered to the well after his lunch.

"Tatya's yelling at someone," replied Sushma, watching the people hurtling down the track. "Mother fears for Bapu and Tillya who visit the jamun tree."

"Damn that Bapu!" shouted Pandu, and then joined the chase.

Tillya appeared stuck in a precarious position. He grappled with the branch and shuffled around to wriggle free but failed. The panic had unnerved him and he cried.

"Come down quick," Tatya pestered; his hands twitched and he grew impatient. "Damn you thief!"

Lekha reached the spot and saw Bapu whimper. The sight made her uneasy.

"Where's my son?" she worried, running towards the tree.

"There hangs the thief," mocked Tatya, pointing at Tillya squirming to break free.

"Aai," whined Tillya, when he saw his mother. The effort had drained him and it seemed he ran out of vigour to hold on to the branch.

"Someone help him come down," cried Lekha; she twitched her face at the sight and asked for help. "Daya, Ganpat, do something."

Bapu's ears bled and the sting on his cheek ached. The pain had sapped his energy and dampened his shrieks to a wail. He lay on the ground confronting his fate. Pandu rushed to him and embraced him. "Don't cry," he said, stroking Bapu's head.

Lekha crumpled on the ground like a sack of potatoes and grabbed Tatya's feet, "I beg you to forgive him," she pleaded, while she cried. "Hit me, if you want, please spare my son."

"Damn your son! He's a thief!" shouted Tatya, pulling his feet away. He swirled on his feet to face his men. "What do I pay you for?" he hollered; his nostrils flared and he pointed at them. "I don't pay you to let thieves into my orchard. Look!" he showed the plastic bag, gnashed his teeth and trampled a jamun.

Ganpat cringed at the sight. "We labour on the well whole day. We don't know what happens here," he stuttered in a soft voice and looked at Daya from the corner of his eyes.

"Yeah," nodded Daya.

Tatya interjected with a frown on his face. "Damn the well!" he lambasted, spreading his hands wide open. "You have also to protect my orchard from thieves. I hate to hear excuses!"

"Aai, aai," cried Tillya.

Lekha gathered herself, lunged to her feet and raced to the trunk of the tree. "I'm coming," she said; she flung her hands around the trunk, and tried to ascend, but slithered down. "Someone please help him."

Pandu dashed to the tree, cuddled the trunk and clamoured up like a panda. "Hang on, I'm coming," he assured Tillya, who found his hands slither.

The sweat on Tillya's palms and feet slackened his grip. "Huh! Huh!" he wrestled to hang on.

"Damn the thief!" blurted Tatya; he swooped on Pandu and hurled him down. "You keep off and let him hang!"

Lekha grabbed Tatya's feet. "Please save him. He will fall," she cried.

Tatya kicked her in the ribs.

"Ouch!" screamed Lekha, hunching over and writhing in pain.

Pandu grabbed Tatya's collars and pushed him away. "What's wrong with you? Do you want that kid to fall down," he fumed.

"Damn you peasant! How dare you touch me?" howled Tatya; his body shook at the affront and he charged towards Pandu brandishing the stone.

Ganpat and Daya stepped in and seized him. "Tatya please don't loose your cool."

"Damn this peasant! How dare he touch me?" Tatya ranted and then pressed forward, but the two men held on to him. "Let me go," he yelled, as he jostled the two men.

"Please understand that the boys wanted some fun so they came over, but look what happened to Bapu. He bleeds and why kick Lekha?" said Pandu.

Tatya squirmed in the human barricade. "Shut up!" he howled. "This orchard belongs to me and I will decide the fate of these thieves," he wrestled the two men and tried to break through. "Why do you defend them? I gather you incited them to rob my orchard."

Pandu slammed his eyes shut. "I wish you settle this matter amicably. Why should I defend them?"

Daya interrupted, "Pandu please stay quiet."

Pandu shrugged his head, raised his hands and dropped them in disbelief. "What do I say? I prevented Tatya from getting sore and flinging his wrath at Lekha."

"Huh!" scoffed Tatya. "Leave me alone.'

"Aai, aai," Tillya cried out again.

The mother looked up and saw him slithering.

She squealed, "Tillya my son."

Tillya lost traction and dropped down.

"My son," yelled Lekha, charging towards him.

Pandu twisted his face and plugged his ears at the sight. He hobbled towards the boy, lying on the ground.

Lekha tapped his cheeks, shook his hands and lifted his head. He lay still. She hugged him. "My son, wake up," she shouted, beaingt her chest.

Pandu kneeled and shook Tillya. "Tillya, get up," he said. Tillya did not respond. Pandu's face dropped and he quivered at the sight. "Water, get some water please."

"Take him to the hospital. Daya go fetch a tum tum," ordered Tatya, straightening the creases on his shirt.

Ganpat raced to the cattleshed and shouldered a pitcher of water. Pandu sprinkled water on Tillya and shook him again. Lekha continued to weep.

In a short time, a tum-tum arrived and drove the boys to the hospital at Ashti.

CHAPTER 22

▼

The Siberian Tiger School of Vladimir stood half a kilometer from the tiger enclosure. The classroom reverberated with the cackle of kids, and shuffle of chairs and feet, as the children settled down for the early morning lecture. The hall contained a projector, screen, board and table; posters of the Siberian tiger hung on the walls of the hall and a dog lounged on the floor in a corner fastened to a leash. Vladimir and his team stood around the table, which contained tiger parts of a model tiger, while the kids giggled, gossiped and waited for the session to commence.

"Why study tigers in captivity?" asked Linda Kohl, holding a hind leg of the model tiger in her hands.

Vladimir dipped his brush in the bucket of black paint and striped the body of the tiger. "The Siberian tiger appears a solitary and shy animal, which makes it difficult to study tigers in the wild. Moreover, we wish to make the study interesting to children and show them how the tiger looks and behaves," replied Vladimir, as he marked the body of the model tiger, while his wife Anna held the bucket.

The children watched the team working on the model and chatted.

"I don't like to see tigers with black stripes," said Victor, who stood with his hands on his hips at the back of the classroom.

"It must be painted red," added Emily, who stood next to Victor and observed Vladimir paint the model tiger.

"Why not use some other colour? Maybe yellow or blue," opined Victor.

Emily nodded her head. "No! No!" she replied, as she inched closer to Victor. "I think red will look better."

"Colour him red and he'll look like Victor," jeered Katrina, popping her head from behind and giggling.

Victor swirled on his heels and faced her, "even you look red so the tiger will look like you," retorted Victor, staring at her red faced.

"See, he'll look like this. Boo!" Katrina pointed at Victor's face, and then stuck her tongue out.

Victor giggled at her.

"You look stupid laughing on your own. Turn around and look ahead," interjected Sarah, from behind.

Katrina put her hands to her mouth and laughed.

The arrogant Victor felt slighted and dug his heels. He hurled his hands over his waist and turned his gaze on Sarah. "I want to look at you. I will not look ahead."

"Stop fighting and look ahead," pleaded Emily, while she tossed her hands over Victor's shoulders and tried to twist him around.

"Huh," snapped Victor; he shrugged his shoulders, stiffened his body and resisted. "I don't wish to turn around."

"Grrrrr," Sarah roared at him, twisting her nose.

Victor smiled wryly. "I don't fear tigers," he boasted, manipulating his fingers in the shape of a gun and pointing them at Sarah. "Bang!"

"Grrrrr," roared Katrina, joining the fray. It appeared as if, the two tigresses wanted to take on the hunter.

Victor swiftly flashed his other hand out and pointed it at Katrina. "I'll shoot you too!"

The two girls appeared undeterred and continued roaring at him. Victor retreated and accidentally bumped into Little John standing between Sarah and Katrina.

"Damn you," shouted Little John, shoving Victor aside.

Victor lost balance and crashed on the ground.

"Ha! Ha! Ha!" the two girls laughed at the sight.

"He cannot even stand," joked Sarah, as she looked at Katrina, and then shook her head.

Emily's ribs tickled, but she put her hands to her mouth to suppress the giggle.

Little John joined them and roared with laughter.

The sight maddened Victor; his blood boiled and eyes flashed with anger, while his brows bumped together, as if his mind seemed confused, because he suffered humiliation and wished to vent his anger, but did not know whom to target. It appeared he made too many enemies in his first tiny hunting expedition: two tigresses, who roared at him, an angry bystander whom he trampled and a pacifier whom he snubbed. The dilemma added to his powerlessness and aroused his chauvinist instincts. He jumped to his feet, seething with anger and pounced on Little John. It appeared, he wished to take him on and warn the pretty girls, who taunted him. It seemed, as if the bugle sounded and declared war—Victor versus Little John.

The puny warriors looked fierce, with their reputations at stake and pretty spectators watching them. It resembled a knight duel with chivalry to prove. Little John crashed on his back, while Victor mounted over his chest, sat astride and pinned his shoulders to the floor. Little John gasped for breath, groveled on his back, kicked his feet, gnashed his teeth and resisted with all his might. He wished to thwart the tackle in this kinder garten category of free-style wrestling. The girls appeared uninterested in this duel and rushed to extricate the puny warriors.

"Stop it!" shouted Katrina, tugging Victor.

"Get off his chest!" yelled Sarah; she seized Victor's hands, while Emily tried to push him over.

Victor snatched his hand and stayed put. He clenched Little John's collars and resisted. The tackle shifted gear and helped Little John free his shoulders. Little John reacted; he clenched his fists and pounded Victor, who bucked. The blow knocked the hat off Victor's head and Victor now gripped Little John's neck and stifled it. Little John's eyes reddened, as he gasped for breath. His fists dropped, and he kicked the air, wriggling for breath. "Huh, huh," he panted, squirming as a fish scooped out of water.

The girls continued to shuffle Victor by tugging in three directions. Emily happened to drift and come across Little John's feet that kicked around, and took the boot. She screamed, "Ouch!" and then tumbled on the floor. The other two girls rushed to rescue her. The pandemonium in the hall attracted attention.

"What is happening there?" yelled Anna, while Linda and Michael raced to the venue. Anna put down the bucket and charged to Emily, who sat up weeping.

The wrestlers continued their bout. It appeared as if Little John's boot worked to his disadvantage. Victor regained the upper hand, having brushed the three girls aside. He took full advantage of the situation and choked Little John harder, who gasped for breath. "Huh! Huh!"

Victor brandished his right hand, clenched his fist to punch Little John. Just then Michael appeared. "Stop it," he yelled, seized Victor's puny fist, and hauled him to his feet.

Little John sat up and devoured the air. He blinked like an owl and straightened his collar.

Anna hastened to the scene with the girls in tow.

"Victor pushed him down," deposed Sarah.

"Shut up. You started the fight," alleged Victor, as he tidied his hat. He glared at Sarah and pointed his finger at Little John. "He pushed me to the ground and she laughed," he argued, as he plopped the hat over his head.

"You pushed me first," added Little John, as he emerged from behind Michael and faced Victor.

"Yeah, it's true," corroborated Katrina.

"You joked and laughed at me," accused Victor.

It appeared as if allegations flitted thick and fast in the hall. Anna plugged her ears, slammed her eyes shut and intervened. "Quiet," she ordered, dropped her hands and glared at the children. "You have come here to watch an experiment and not fight."

"Mam we stood behind and watched you stripe the tiger black but Victor complained and says he hates the colour black and the fight started," said Emily, wiping the tears streaming down her puffed cheeks.

"I hate the colour black. Why stripe the tiger black?" interrupted Victor, with a frown on his face. He lifted his shoulders and questioned. "Why not yellow or blue?"

"Tigers have black stripes. Haven't you seen Bruno and Maria?" replied Anna.

"They look real and beautiful not like this paper tiger," complained Victor, twisting his nose in disgust. "This paper tiger looks bad."

"I understand what you mean," said Vladimir, as he approached the kids. "This tiger cannot look as good as Bruno and Maria. But this remains an experimental model."

The last two words seemed heavy for Victor and his brows popped up. "What ex . . . peri?" he hesitated to pronounce the lengthy word and blinked.

Anna dropped down on her knees and placed her hands over his shoulders. "Repeat what I say," she said.

Victor nodded in agreement.

Anna stretched her lips wide, "Ex," she demonstrated and paused. "Now say it."

"X," repeated Victor.

"Good," Anna complimented. "Now say pe," she bleated like a goat.

"Pe," Victor followed.

Anna nodded her head and smiled. "Peri."

"Peri," repeated Victor.

"Say experi," suggested Anna.

"Experi," Victor repeated the words.

Anna smacked her lips and muttered, "ment."

Victor pressed his lips and uttered. "Ment."

"Very Good," Anna patted him on his back. "Now we will utter the complete word."

"Hmm," nodded Victor.

"Experiment," Anna repeated the word in a loud and emphatic tone.

Victor cast a glance at his colleagues, who observed him keenly. He gulped the saliva down his throat, widened his eyes, and took a deep breath. "Experiment," he breathed the word out, and then paused for the reaction.

Anna beamed and clapped her hands, "very good," she said.

The hall exploded as the children clapped and applauded Victor. He blushed and lifted the rim of his hat to acknowledge the appreciation.

Vladimir raised his hands to signal silence. "I will explain what it means," he said; he swirled around to face the table and pointed at the tiger parts. "These parts as you can see look like the parts of our real tigers—Maria and Bruno," he explained, pointing to a picture stuck on the wall. He veered back to face the children. "We will create a tiger like that and place it in our tiger enclosure to study how Bruno and Maria will receive it? If they like it, they will accept this tiger but if they hate it, they will fight it and even kill it. Tigers defend their territories or homes fiercely and will not like other animals to enter. Since the entry of a new tiger may lead to a bloody fight, we will not place a real tiger in the enclosure, because we have to save tigers. We have few tigers in the jungles of Siberia and we have to protect them so we decided to use this copy or model, which means experiment," Vladimir elucidated his simple version to the tiny dots, who nodded their heads.

"But why don't you colour him differently?" inquired Victor.

Vladimir tilted his head, looked at him and smiled. "This tiger must look real and a real tiger has black stripes. Remember this is our secret, which Bruno and Maria don't know," replied the conservationist.

"It means we cheat Bruno and Maria," said Victor, with a creased forehead. It appeared he disliked the idea.

"Bruno will find out. He's smart," Sarah interjected, with a toothy smile.

"Even Maria will find out," gushed Emily.

"What will happen, if they find that we have cheated them?" asked Little John, with his hands across his chest.

Vladimir stretched his jaws, popped his brows and nodded his head as if amused by their curiosity. He took a deep breath. "That's what the experiment will answer. We will have to wait and watch."

"Why do we wait? We must go and see," declared an impatient Victor.

"Our model tiger remains incomplete unless we fix the tail and we can fix it if you stop fighting," revealed Vladimir; he spun on his heels and walked to the table. He picked the tail and plastered it to the back of the model. "Now we can begin our experiment," he addressed the audience. "I request Linda and Michael to help me prop up the model for all to see."

Linda and Michael helped haul the model to its feet.

"Wooooo," snarled the dog tethered to the leash in the corner. It stood up, glared at the model and whirled about as if examining the beast. "Bowwow," the dog barked and lunged at the beast. The leash tugged it and the dog veered around barking. The kids guffawed at the sight and made the dog the butt of banter.

"Sssh," they shooed him, with their fingers stubbed to their lips and beckoned him to keep quiet.

"He thinks the model is real," snapped Victor. "Ha! Ha! Ha!"

"Bowwow," the dog continued to bark.

Anna rushed to him and patted him on his head, "Banjo, keep quiet," she said, seizing his collar.

"Woooo," whined the dog, wagging its tail as if it hated the model tiger's intrusion.

"Our model must be a good copy of the real tiger, because Banjo seems convinced," joked Vladimir.

"How will this tiger walk inside Bruno's home? This tiger needs help," muttered Little John.

"We'll carry him inside the enclosure and nail him to the ground," replied Linda.

"Let's bring down the model," said Vladimir.

The three pair of hands lifted it and parked it on the floor.

Banjo's ears stood up and his face stiffened at the sight. He rose to his feet and growled at the tiger, while Anna gripped his collar and appeased him. "No, Banjo, no."

"Dumb dog," commented Sarah, as she slapped her forehead and waggled her head.

"Look, he can't walk," said Katrina; she ran upto Banjo and stroked his coat. The dog whined and plunked down on the ground. Banjo continued to stare at the model tiger; his face scarred with confusion.

Linda switched on the recorder. A raucous recorded roar electrified the atmosphere and scared the tiny dots, who seemed taken aback. "It's working," she said.

"Bow wow," the dog barked gain.

"No!" screamed Victor, cringing at the sudden outburst, which ripped the air. He slammed his eyes shut, hunched over and plugged his ears.

Linda twisted the knob to lower the volume. The roar subsided, as abruptly as it started. Victor continued to shiver with his eyes shut.

Little John shook him hard, "It's over," he said.

Victor opened his eyes, and saw the girls laugh at his timidity. He lost his temper again. "Why do we need the recording?"

"To scare you," taunted Sarah and then laughed.

"Grr . . . Grr," roared Emily, spurring a peal of laughter.

Little John took the cue and grabbed the opportunity to avenge his pounding. "He looks scared," he sneered, and then laughed with his fingers pointing at Victor.

The intentional slight aggravated the situation and provoked the temperamental Victor. A bitter Victor, who found himself subjected to humiliation, pounced on him. But this time Little John resisted and Linda spotted the scuffle and raced to the scene. She grabbed Victor's collars and looked him in the eyes.

"What's wrong with you?" she asked.

"He says that I'm scared," gasped Victor, shaking with anger.

"How does it matter what he or others say? You cannot keep beating up people like this. What you think of yourself matters," reprimanded Linda.

"I'm as brave as Bruno," boasted the hotheaded Victor, in an imperious tone.

"Why did you have to pounce on Little John for the second time?"

"He says that I'm scared and says it before the girls," replied Victor.

Little John intervened, "earlier he pointed a gun at Sarah and Katrina, when they roared at him. But, the moment you switched on the recorder, he screamed and shut his eyes," said Little John.

"I only taunted her," argued Victor, with a scowl on his face.

"If you pointed a gun at the tiger and intended to shoot it down. You had better watch your ways. We have gathered here to save the tiger and not shoot it," chided Linda, with an angry stare.

The tone forced Victor to mellow down and he stuttered. "Both of them roared at me and the gun looked like this," he displayed his palm, curled the lower two fingers inwards, and pointed them at Linda. "Look."

Linda nodded her head in disgust. "Victor, you should know that tigers love and don't harm. You have to grow up to protect them and I hate this act of pointing a gun at a tiger. Any gun—be it a real gun or a toy gun. Don't play games with weapons," she lambasted, as she shook his shoulders. "Do you understand?"

"Hmm," nodded Victor, with his eyes to the floor.

Linda faced the children. "Have you all understood? No pointing guns and weapons at tigers," she repeated, and then turned her attention to Victor. "Do you think you're braver than Little John?"

Victor flung his hands over his waist, and stomped his foot on the floor. "Of course," he declared, with his jaws jutting out. "I pinned him to the floor."

"Huh," Little John twisted his nose, and faced Victor. "I'm braver. I would have thrown him down and beat him up if no one stopped us."

The atmosphere appeared tense and it seemed the puny warriors wished to settle things. Both looked each other in the eye and itched for a showdown.

"Let's test your bravery," Linda said, with a wry smile.

The challenge motivated the two. They pulled up their sleeves to take on each other. Linda stood between the two warriors, and made a declaration. "The one who will put out his hand," she paused, and then looked at the two fighters. Both swiftly raised their hands and clenched their fists, ready for the bout.

"The one who will put his hand out first, offer a handshake and apologise will stay the bravest kid in the world," said Linda, stepping aside.

The two warriors bumped into each other. "Sorry," they apologized to each other, and offered a handshake.

Linda walked towards them, as a boxing referee, held their hands, and raised them high. "Victor and Little John are the bravest kids," she declared, with a smile on her face.

"Like Bruno," added Victor.

"And Maria," insisted Little John.

They blushed at the girls applauding them.

"And all the tigers in Siberia," said Victor, with his arms spread wide open. He spun on his heels and did a jig. Little John joined the pirouette. Round and round they swirled, like a merry go round and invited the girls to join them, while the others looked on. The girls took the cue and joined the bandwagon and the hall exploded with revelry.

The dog looked surprised at the turn of events. He wagged his tail, stood up, angled his head and tugged at his leash. It seemed he too wished to join the celebration. Finally, he squatted, with his chin on the floor, dropped his ears and watched the children dance.

CHAPTER 23

▼

The police report stated that Tillya trespassed into Abba's property, with the intention of committing theft. However, on Tatya's arrival, he panicked and clamoured up the jamun tree, when he slithered, dropped down and died.

The boy appeared too insignificant in this world for the Maharashtra police department. He remained the son of an indebted farmer, who had committed suicide and his mother lacked the strength to defend him, because she stayed indebted to Abba. The witnesses wielded little influence and stayed indebted to Abba. Ganpat and Daya remained bonded to Abba for life; they dare not state the truth. Pandu protested and argued with the investigating officer, when they recorded his statement. However, the police as a matter of convenience dropped Bapu and Pandu as witnesses from the scene of offence. Even, if they included Pandu as one of the star witnesses the investigation would remain biased, because the other three witnesses would have contradicted his version of the story. In short, even if Pandu wished to help, he could not do much about it. "If the mother appears least interested in telling the truth, why should I bother?" Pandu said to himself.

Abba summoned Lekha and showed her the book of accounts. He also reminded her of the gratitude that she owed him and assured her of financial aid. In short, justice lay buried under the pile of gratitude and debt like most other cases in Maharashtra, which remain at the mercy of the police department and their political masters.

The only ones to gain from this tragedy appeared Tatya, who wielded influence and the police department, which remained on Abba's payroll. It appeared an irony that the so-called custodians of society in cases, which involved political leaders, remained at the disposal of the political leaders. This system implied that there appeared certain conventions and customs, which the police followed when they ignored the written laws and traded their conscience for money and favours. This invisible (visible in practice) police manual, operated with a preamble.

"WE, THE POLICE, SOLEMNLY RESOLVE TO PROMOTE THE VESTED INTERESTS OF THE POLITICAL PARTY THAT CONTROLS THE HOME DEPARTMENT."

This police manual appeared more concise, swift, efficient and user-friendly than the authorized manual. It operated the parallel system, scissored the red tape that entangled speedy justice, conducted investigations at will, diminished political rivals and disciplined rebellion in the party. There existed a few rules on how to conduct investigations.

Rule 1—Verify the accused against whom the complainant wants to register a First Information Report (FIR). If the accused belongs to the political party that controls the Home department, do not enter the complaint in the station diary. Note it down on any scrap of paper and wait for the corroboration process to conclude.

Rule 2—A corroboration process stays established, when the station-in-charge receives a call from any Cabinet Minister that informs him/her on how to conduct the investigation. If the call advises the officer to drop the case, the officer must burn the scrap of paper on which he/she scribbled the complaint. The I.P.C., Cr.P.C or any other penal legislation will not apply in this case.

Rule 3—If the verification process fails then the station-in-charge will register the complaint in the station diary and strictly follow the letter and spirit of all the laws enacted to deal with the offence. The Home department will tolerate no lapses in this regular investigation procedure, because the matter remains non-political.

Rule 4—If a police officer wishes to indulge in corrupt practices in non-political cases, the officer must indulge at his/her own risk and guard against sting operations, provided, the officer pays the regular kick-back to the police department. If a new recruit lacks experience, the recruit must keep off, until the recruit develops a good hand and succeedes in undermining his/her conscience.

Golden tip—Please contact the seniormost corrupt officer of the department for guidance.

Rule 5—If any police officer runs out of luck and gets caught in the act of corruption, the police department must conduct an inquiry, headed by the most corrupt officer in the department. The accused officer stays suspended or transferred, until the investigation finishes for the satisfaction of the media. The investigation must acquit the corrupt police officer after the media publicity fizzles out.

"Satya me jai the-Jai Hind-Jai Maharashtra"

In Tillya's case it appeared, as if the police diligently followed the rules laid down in the invisible police manual. Tillya remained the son of an ordinary indebted mother and suffered at the hands of an influential political leader, who managed the police. He seemed destined to die, because the parallel system created for political patronage worked against him. Even if he survived, he would have suffered under the law. It appeared safer to die, because at least it guaranteed a fair trial, somewhere beyond this world, if the scriptures speak the truth. Bapu on the other hand suffered more damage, because the pounding injured his eardrums and impaired hearing for the rest of his life. Vasu's financial condition stayed bad and he could not shell out twenty thousand rupees for the surgery. Bapu paid heavily for the jamuns and Vasu warned him not to venture near the orchard again. The boy seemed too small to understand the responsibilities and risks of running a cotton farmer's family in Vidharbh. The golden rule stipulated, never annoy the moneylenders, because the one thing certain, besides death remained; a farmer would need him for credit throughout his life.

Vasu registered his three acres of land in Tatya's name and received one and a half lakh rupees for Shoba's marriage. Mangala stayed unhappy with the events that transpired and especially with the manner in which her son suffered. The motherly instinct in her aroused and she threw her tantrums.

"I see no point groveling before money lenders. They charge exorbitant interest rates, swallow our lands and now they kill our children. Why did Tatya damage my boy's ear?" she asked in a huff, her heart simmering with anger.

Bapu quietly swallowed the rice and dal served to him, with a bandage wrapped around his left ear and face swollen. His jaws dare not chew on anything because his ears hurt.

"Eat slowly my dear," clucked Mangala, as she stroked his head gently.

Pandu sat and observed Bapu eat his meal. His cheeks puffed at the sight and he still carried the bitter memories of the orchard tragedy. The rebel in him itched for a showdown and his hands twitched. He picked up a stone and flung it in anger. "If this happened around Gadchiroli, Tatya would have a bullet through his head by now. These moneylenders need a pounding."

Mangala put her hands over her heart. "This incident shocks me. It appears as if Bapu and Tillya stole diamonds from the orchard. They only picked a few jamuns and look what has happened to the boys," she pointed her finger at Bapu.

"They should not have stolen the jamuns. They knew that the orchard belongs to Tatya. Why go in there? You cannot compare diamonds and jamuns. The fact remains that they stole something," reasoned Vasu.

Mangala's temper flared and her eyes flashed. "He should have reported the matter to me. I would have paid for his jamuns," she argued, twisting her face. "He killed Tillya and damaged Bapu's ear. Does the law permit what he did? Don't defend Tatya."

Pandu nodded his head and thumped his chest. "I requested him to settle the matter and clamoured up to help Tillya, but he pulled me down and warned me not to interfere. We lost time over the argument and Tillya fell," said Pandu; his eyes turned moist and his heart swelled with guilt. "Damn it!"

"Pandu stop digging around. You did what you could. I do not defend Tatya. We must not mull over the past," said Vasu.

Mangala hunched over with a stiff face. "He hit my son and a mother knows what it takes to deliver a child. If he does it again, I'll teach him a lesson," warned Mangala, as she trembled and gnashed her teeth.

Vasu shook his head. "He's my child too and I feel for him. But we also owe Abba money for the rations and Shoba's wedding," explained Vasu.

Shoba the listener-barged in. "You need not worry about me," she interrupted, with a frown on her face. She seldom spoke but now that the buck plopped in her hands, she decided to straighten things out. She pointed at Bapu, "If this is what it takes to have me married, then I'm not interested in marrying. I cannot sacrifice my brother on the altar of my wedding. I wish to have a wedding and not a funeral."

Vasu shook his head. "Such things are easier said than done. You cannot stay home all your life. I have a responsibility towards you and I'm doing my best," suggested Vasu, wary of social obligations.

"You also have a responsibility towards Bapu. What have you to offer him? You have given away all your land to those wicked moneylenders, who bay for Bapu's blood. He has nothing on him. Huh!" ridiculed Mangala, with tears in her eyes. She pulled the ends of her saree and wiped her eyes.

Vasu wriggled in his seat. It appeared as if all hell broke loose. He slapped his forehead and buried his head in his hands. "Damn if you do and damn if you don't," he thought to himself. When in debt, even your near and dear ones do not spare an opurtunity to kick ass.

"Damn the barbs!" he exclaimed, raising his head. "I don't control the rains and you can't blame me for the debt. Is this what I have to live with all my life?" he questioned, with a long face. He stabbed his finger around. "Each one of you, sitting here remains a farmer and you all know what it takes to stay a farmer? Munna's debt strangled him. What do you want me to do?" he questioned, pointing at the tree. "Hang myself like Munna!"

Pandu interjected angrily. "Munna's a fool, if he hung himself to death because of the debt," he fumed, and then waived his hand. "Did it resolve the issue? Look how his family suffers. What is this big thing called debt? Everyone has some form of debt. Does it imply that all the people should kill themselves?"

"I agree. What about the money you borrow? You have to return it and with the rains playing truant the debt fattens. You cannot get away with that. I dare you to name any one farmer in and around Ramwadi, who paid his debts and lives a life of comfort. It has not happened. We're lucky to have that tube well pump water," said Vasu, pointing to the well. "Otherwise, things would spin out of control."

Pandu gnashed his teeth, and smashed his fist on the flat of his palm. "If the debtors unite, the moneylenders can't do a thing. They dare not levy such exorbitant interest rates; the rates kill us. If you borrow money, you sure have an obligation to pay, but not at sixty plus percent per year. It is criminal! Even the money lending laws do not permit it. They take advantage, because nobody questions them and the system protects them. What happened to Sahukar? He is out on bail and the story will go on and on, because the system works for him. Unless the people organize and revolt, this system will not mend its ways. I protested against Tatya to the police, but Lekha seemed uninterested. She is a mother, isn't she? How will things change?"

Vasu smiled wryly. "Why don't you calm down?" he snapped, scratching his stubble. "You have a long way to go in life. When you marry, you will speak more responsibly. Lekha did not have a choice. The least that could have happened to Tatya—arrested and released on bail," mocked Vasu; he lifted his shoulders in a shrug. "The courts take years to decide cases and she may not live to testify. Why fight with crocodiles in water? We stay poor and have to endure."

Pandu shook his head in disagreement. "You may brag about marriage, responsibility and fate, but I believe these remain excuses to justify this system. If Tatya ever crosses my path, I'll skin him alive, because I'm not the kind, who takes things lying down."

"Neither will I, if he dares touch Bapu again, he'll meet his match," added Mangala, flashing her eyes.

"Do as you wish. Shoba and Bapu remain my responsibilities. I'll do my best for them," said Vasu, patting Bapu on his shoulder.

The boy smiled. He did not understand what the adults talked about, but he appeared lucky to have his parents by his side. He cozied up to his father. "Papa, will you buy me new clothes for Shoba's wedding?" he asked in a soft voice.

"Of course I will! The bride's brother runs the show," said Vasu.

"I want long pants. I hate running around in these shorts."

"Ha! Ha! Ha!" cackled the gathering.

"I'll take you with me to the bazaar and you choose your clothes," said Vasu.

The boy smiled back and looked ahead at the tube well. He remembered the days, when Tillya and he splashed around in the pool, next to the tube well. They played together and dropped out of school together. They even planned to play pranks in Shoba's wedding.

However, as destiny would have it, Tillya disappeared. Bapu's fond memories crystallized into tears and rolled down his cheeks.

"What's the matter Bapu? Why do you cry?" asked Mangala, inching closer to him.

"Everyone wants to leave me. Even Shoba will leave me soon," he cried.

Mangala hugged him gently. "Nothing stays forever," she said, with a voice lost in a flood of tears.

CHAPTER 24

▼

The elections approached and each day Dada worried. He knew Abba's substantial chunk of voters could deny him victory. So far, he had tried every trick in the hat, but Abba remaind insolent. The party's top brass from Delhi to Mumbai talked to Abba and persuaded him to withdraw, but their pleas fell upon deaf ears. Abba shared a cordial relationship with the Chief Minister and many felt that he rebelled on his behest. Dada succeeded in getting the high command to pressurize the Chief Minister, who then spoke to Abba, but to no avail. The party remained wary of disciplining him, because it feared incumbency and infighting might damage the party's prospects of retaining power in the coming elections.

The situation forced Dada to try his luck for the last time. He decided to meet Abba and negogiate a settlement; he sent word to Abba that he stayed keen on a dialogue and open to compromise. Abba the wily politician laughed, because his efforts paid, but accepted the offer after much delay to show he did not care. Finally, the two men met and sat down in the people's chamber, to iron out their differences.

"Why challenge the party's dictat to further your political agenda?" questioned Dada, with a creased forehead. He appeared stout with a big belly, dark complexion, prominent forehead and a beard.

Abba kept quiet and looked him in the eyes.

Dada took a deep breath. "The Centre will take a call on Vidharbh's statehood," he exhaled slowly, cracking his knuckles.

Abba cocked a wry smile and watched Dada with a slight tilt of his head. "The high command cannot play ball with the sentiments of the people of Vidharbh anymore," he snapped, and then looked away. "It must not expect the regional people to toe the Delhi line. The issue has reached the tipping point after the creation of Jharkhand, Uttarakhand and Chattisgarh."

Dada waived his hand, as if dismissing the demand. "Come to the point. The agenda of Vidharbh's statehood appears a prop to further your personal interests. It does not bother the big political parties fighting this election," he stated, with an imperious tone, and uttered the last sentence with an air of arrogance. "The marginal parties and a few independents like you clamour for a seperate Vidharbh to rake up regional sentiments."

Abba remained calm and steadfast. He smiled, "if you call me marginal, then why waste your time, talking to me," he mocked and then laughed.

Dada's face dropped, as he looked away.

Abba went on, "a big political party," he said, with his arms spread wide. "Must ignore me and fight the elections with ease, unless the candidate nominated by the high command finds himself on slippery turf," he paused, with a smile dangling on the corner of his lips, and dropped his arms.

Dada slammed his eyes shut.

Abba hunched over and watched him. "I can sense the fear in your eyes and you know that a few votes flitting out of your kitty can seal your fate. It appears terrible when you cannot hold on to your seat. I gather," Abba derided, and then slumped in his chair.

Dada squirmed in his seat, but regained his poise. "Assume I loose," he conceded and then paused. "What will you gain? Bravado!" he exclaimed, glaring at Abba. "You remain a pariah and if the party comes to power, you will face the music. Our businesses need the law to run them or they cannot survive."

Abba twisted his nose and waived off the threat. "I can join the opposition and seek their protection. You know how the system works. At the end of the day, all the political parties need each other. The ruling alliance has offered me nothing substantial, except empty promises."

"What do you mean by substantial?" grunted Dada; his brows puckered.

Abba laughed, drumming his fingers on the arms of his chair. He pressed his lips, straightened his face and nodded. "I wanted the party ticket which you snatched."

Dada raised his hands and showed Abba his palms, as if he conceded. "Fine, forget what happened," he surrendered, dropping his hands. "It's a fair deal. The party offered you the MLC ticket and guaranteed your election. You remain equal to me. What more can you ask for?"

Abba frowned and snapped his finger. "A member of the Council does not carry the same weight as a member of an assembly."

Dada smiled, crossed his legs and shook his head in disagreement. "Both wield proportionate powers, which matters most in politics."

"The party made similar offers umpteen times in the past, but dishonoured its words. Unless the party looses, it will not honour its word."

"You made your point. This time the party will keep its word. The high command spoke to you and not many get a chance to talk to the high command. I do not see sense in damaging the party's prospects in Vidharbh. I repeat that we need the party to run the show. Power matters in politics. Why don't you look ahead?"

"Precisely," thundered Abba, slapping his knees. "You speak to me, because I wield the power to scuttle your prospects. I am not the only dissident in the state. Thousands of dissidents will work to wreck vengeance against the party, but only a few will succeed. You know my chances of spoling the party."

Dada slumped in his chair and took a deep breath. The negogiation seemed to lead nowhere. But he wished to persist. "I agree," he snorted and went on. "Listen, I'm alluring to the bigger power—government. We burnt our fingers, when we lost power to the opposition alliance for four and a half years. They hounded us and forced us out of business. Do you wish to re-live that nightmare again? We have our businesses and other issues that depend on the government and we need power to protect them. Take the case of Tatya, the police could have arrested him, put him behind bars and he would rot in jail. However, I talked to the police department on your behalf and settled the matter. These petty matters also require power. If you fail to oblige you earn the wrath of the party," hinted Dada, using tact to convey the consequences.

Abba laughed. "The same party suspended my ration shop, planted anti-dalit stories against me in the newspapers and conspired to end my political career. The party should understand that times have changed and we live in an era of coalition politics. The days of the monolith party have dawned. Presently, party workers have a variety of parties to join. If the party continues its vindictive politics, it will drown," retorted Abba.

"Damn the party!" Dada interrupted. He seemed ruffled and wished to reach a conclusion. "The party offers you the MLC ticket, guarantees your election and offers you a position in the cotton federation. I suggest you withdraw."

"Damn the cotton federation!" shouted Abba, slapping the arms of his chair. "It's in losses. What remains in that federation to swindle?"

Dada raised his hand and signalled Abba to cool down. "Relax, you shouldn't get wild, because a few years ago you roosted on that federation, and made your kill. In other words, you made your fair share of money while other party workers complained. If you reject the offer, someone else will grab it. We must not allow someone outside our league to fatten and challenge our supremacy in this district, while we squabble over the spoils. You know that money matters in politics and if someone else lays hands on it; someone may challenge us."

"The cotton federation doesn't excite me, especially, after the government banned the monopoly cotton procurement scheme. I have other demands, which appear more promising. I want the party to offer the Zilla Parishad ticket to Tatya and make him chairman of the body," demanded Abba.

Dada's jaws dropped and he hesitated. "I don't think the party will accept your offer," he muttered, scratching his beard.

"Why?" asked Abba, looking in his eyes.

Dada's eyes blinked, as he looked away. "You know the party hates dynastic politics."

"What?" Abba's eyes squinted, as he cocked a wry smile.

Dada shifted course. "I'm repeating what the high command said in Delhi. Take my case, I lobbied hard for my wife to become the chairman of the Zilla Parishad but the party refused."

"Hmm," murmured Abba, tilting his head. "I got what you imply. You seem the best replica of the Delhi dynasty, which runs as a family fiefdom—hates dynastic politics. Ooops," Abba mocked. He pursed his lips, rolled his eyes upwards and jigged his head. "You remain a MLA, chairman of the District Co-operative bank, chairman of the sugar mill, director of many more institutions and lobby hard for a berth in the Cabinet. The reason I rebelled against you. Does this sound democratic or dynastic?" Abba asked, jerked his head and continued. "How did you react? First, you suspended my ration shop; next, you blocked my files at the DCC and now you have the gall to remind me that you intervened and saved Tatya from the clutches of the police— typical political vendetta, which will end with the CBI hounding me," ranted Abba; he looked disappointed and hurt.

"Abba, relax," suggested Dada, motioning him to cool his nerves. He folded his hands before Abba. "I apologize. Forgive and forget, I request you. What occurred, happened because I wished to persuade you to withdraw your candidature? Please do not make a mountain of a mole. I'll have your license restored and clear all your files."

Abba nodded his head and his face bore a grim look. "What about my son's political future?" he asked, squinting his eyes. "The party claims that it rewards dog like loyalty. Correct me if I'm wrong."

Dada scratched his beard and ruminated for a moment. He inhaled a deep breath and stabbed his chest. "I can assure you of the ticket," he boasted, as he dropped his hands and exhaled slowly. "But the positions you hanker for," he paused, gripped the arms of his chair, stiffened his back and nodded. "The party will decide. I don't have the powers to take a call on that."

Abba laughed. "Well, well, then I suggest you offer me a stint as chairman of the DCC," he paused, and then gazed at Dada, who wriggled in his seat. Abba smiled wryly. "Damn the party! You give me what you can, make room for me. The party will not mind because you have headed the bank for a decade."

Dada gripped the arms of his chair and frowned. "He's asking for too much," he wondered to himself. He appeared unhappy with this proposal, because the politician in him would not permit the surrender of power. He knew the importance of holding on to the levers of the District Co-operatve bank, which controlled the nerves of the farmers. He crossed his hands over his chest. "I have another proposal for you," he spoke softly. "If you wish Tatya head the Zilla Parishad after the next elections then I agree to move a resolution in his favour for half the term."

"Why half the term?" interjected Abba.

"I wish my wife serves the other half. It's a win-win deal," stuttered Dada.

Abba's lips pouted. He creased his forehead and mulled over the offer. "Why don't you adopt the same pattern for the DCC?" asked Abba.

Dada interrupted in a huff. "You demand too much!"

Abba grinned and retorted slowly and clearly. "I ask for too little too late," he imputed, with a scowl on his face. He stabbed a finger in his chest. "I should have contested the elections ten years ago!"

Dada dug his heels. "The DCC has bursted," he declared, shrugging his shoulders. "Bankrupt! Nothing to loot!"

Abba stormed in. "Yeah," he tilted his head, and then smirked. "Then, why do you cling on to it? You know that the RBI will pump money into it. It has happened for decades, because the high command knows that the DCC feeds party workers. The party workers will not work for nothing. They stay in politics because it pays."

Dada tapped his finger on his lips. He feared loosing his seat and dampening his chances of a Cabinet berth. "I propose you let me complete my term and then take over for the next term. I will keep my word." "Done," answered Abba, sealing the deal.

"You withdraw from the election fray and get those cane harvesters to break their strike," demanded Dada.

"Hmm," murmured Abba, nodding his head in agreement.

"I'll restore your license and clear your files."

"What about Vidharbh?" quizzed Abba.

The two men looked at each other and cackled.

"Ha! Ha! Ha!"

"The high command will decide," said Dada.

CHAPTER 25

▼

In the first week of October Vasu stayed busy with Shoba's marriage proposal, which hinged on dowry. Vasu wished to deliver the money he received from Abba to the Jadhavs of Borgaon, because he feared that the money might invite unnecessary expenses. Angad, his brother-in-law, fell sick, which forced Vasu to hold back his plans. He thought of visiting Borgaon, but the cotton crop, which needed watering deferred his plans. The erratic load-shedding schedule shifted to morning hours, and forced Vasu to channel water in the nights. Vasu ate his dinner, left for the cotton field at eight o'clock and waited for the load shedding to end. The abrupt load shedding appeared a menace and increased in duration, because the electric cables snapped.

Vasu lay under the neem tree with his palms tucked under his head and marveled at the skyline. The full moon light flitted, as white puffs of clouds glided across the moon, and a gentle breeze wafted over the terrain. Vasu gazed at the moon in the midst of millions of stars that dotted the sky and dwarfed his presence. He looked with awe and imagined. "I wish I hung like a star that looked down on earth. I would stay happy, throwing light on earth. I wonder if the stars know me, though, they can see me, lying on this land. The cloud veiling the moon looks like a ball of cotton drifting in the sky. How I wish, I could ride on it and reach the stars? I would also reach out to those black clouds and wrench them dry so that the water trickles over my field and soaks the soil. Imagine if it happened, shooting a cloud. It would wipe the miseries of the farmers," he fancied, as he flirted with his thoughts.

"Ouch!" he shrieked, and then sat up. It appeared something stung him and broke his fancy. He dusted his back and found a black ant crawling on his arm. He jerked it off and looked ahead. The loadshedding continued; he failed to see any bulb burning over the terrain. "Damn the loadshedding! I need to grab some sleep!" he stifled a yawn and then stretched down. "I hope I wake up. No I must stay awake and wait for the lights," he reconsidered his decision, rubbed his eyes and arose.

"Chum, Chum" he heard the sound of anklet bells jingling in the air.

Vasu's attention diverted and his ears straightened to catch the sound. He clamped his arms around his knees and craned his neck. His eyes widened to catch a glimpse of the person, but the mound of rubble screened the view.

"Chum, chum, chum," the footsteps accelerated towards him.

"A woman at this hour of the night?" it occurred to him; he looked around for a weapon and grabbed a stone lying on the ground. He knew robber bands disguised as woman roamed around the terrain.

"Chum, chum . . ." the feet staggered and fell.

Vasu stood up and heard the sound of a body groping in the dark. Vasu's face tightened and his mind deduced mischief. "It maybe a thief drunk to the brim and disguised as a woman," he concluded, as he raced sideways and gathered his wooden pole.

"Chum, chum, chum," the feet cluttered again.

"Who is it?" yelled Vasu, as he brandished the stone to hurl it at the intruder.

"It's me," a woman answered, and then showed up on the mound.

Vasu dropped the stone, nodded his head and hunched over the pole. "What brings you here at this hour of the night?" he asked.

"Have you seen Pandu?" inquired the woman, as she hobbled towards Vasu, gasping for breath. She unwound the black tattered shawl wrapped around her face and looked around furtively.

"Damn that Pandu!" exclaimed Vasu, with a grim face. He flung the pole and squatted on the ground. "What's wrong with my family? Women roaming around the dry patta at this hour . . ."

"Did Pandu come over to water the crops?" Mangala inquired, as she hunkered down opposite Vasu.

Vasu shook his head. "No. What's the problem?" inquired Vasu, shaking his knees.

Mangala slapped her forehead and started to weep. "You shouldn't have trusted him. It's all because of you," alleged Mangala, burying her face in her palms.

Vasu blinked as confusion scarred his face. "Damn the drama!" chided Vasu, slamming his fist on the mud. "What brings you here?"

Mangala raised her head and pointed at Vasu, with tears streaming down her cheeks. "It's because of you . . . ," her voice choked and drowned the words.

Vasu's mind cluttered like a traffic snarl. He did not understand a thing. He shrugged his shoulders and wondered. "What could have happened?"

Mangala continued to sob, cursing her fate, "It's all happening to us!" she blurted, tossing the shawl over her shoulder. She bit her lips, scrunched her face and vented her woe. "Whenever, something good happens . . . ," she moaned and then jigged her head. "An evil eye casts its spell on us."

Vasu's confusion simmered into irritation. He tried to figure out what happened. "She says Pandu, but what has happened to him. He watered the crop last week," he mulled over for a lead. "Did he pick up a fight in the village?" asked Vasu, rocking back and forth on his seat.

"I cannot help it. He may fight," Mangala bawled, wiping the tears to the ends of her shawl. "Huh! My dreams . . . ," her voice stuck in her throat.

Vasu's head wobbled with confusion. He shook his head, blinked and anxiety pervaded him. He cocked his head and stared at Mangala. "Who squabbled with him?"

Mangala continued to cry.

Vasu's blood boiled and his patience exploded. "Will you tell me, what has happened?" he thundered.

"Go and ask Shoba. She knows," Mangala turned hysterical.

Vasu stood up in a huff, slammed his foot on the ground, and hurled his hands over his hips. "Do you expect me to run all the way back to the village to find out what happened?" he questioned in disbelief, as he spun his eyes upwards. He dropped his hands, hunched on his knees and looked Mangala in the eyes. "Look, I don't understand a word. You say Pandu and mention a fight and now you tell me to ask Shoba."

"She's not home, you will find her at Pandu's place," interjected Mangala. Her voice trembled, as she she stuttered. "Don't blame me . . ."

"Stop this cat and mouse game and come to the point," yelled Vasu, rising to his feet. His heart pounded heavily and his instincts fluttered.

"I'm not the one playing cat and mouse . . . ," Mangala quivered, with a lump in her throat. She dabbed the ends of her shawl on her eyes and wailed. "Shoba and Pandu played cat and mouse." She stabbed her finger in the ground, "right here, under our noses and we remained ignorant."

Vasu's instincts groped around and got a faint sense of the problem. Then his heart froze, mind numbed and he staggered. He blinked and tried to come to terms with the situation. "Hmm," he murmured to himself. Sudddenly, his heart melted and whipped up frenzy. His adrenalin pumped up his heartbeat and blood boiled. He clenched his fists and gnashed his teeth. "I ran from pillar to post. I begged, groveled and prostrated before moneylenders for money," he paused, slammed his eyes shut and shook his head when the memories came to mind. His heart congealed and sight blurred with tears in his eyes. His body shuddered; he sank down on his knees, buried his head in the mud and wept. "Is this what I get in return?" he sobbed and sobbed until his heart wrenched dry.

Mangala crawled upto him and shook his shoulders.

Vasu cocked his head; his face appeared smeared with mud that stuck to his wet cheeks. He wiped his cheeks and twisted his face. "Huh," he snubbed, and then stood up.

"What do we do?" Mangala's lips quivered, as she staggered to her feet.

Vasu's heart simmered with contempt. He trembled, "I'll kill her!" he shouted, tightening his face and clenching his fists.

Mangala caught Vasu's hand. "You're not doing anything of that sort," she pleaded.

He snatched his hand. "Then what do you expect me to do? Just sit back and enjoy the spectacle!" he ranted, jigging his head. "What does Shoba say?"

"Shoba says that she wants to marry Pandu . . . ," stuttered Mangala.

"Hmm," murmured Vasu; his lips curled with contempt.

"She may say anything, but what about the people? Will the village approve of it? What happens to the Borgaon proposal?" Vasu rattled question after question, slapping his forehead. He dug his finger in his chest. "I sent word with Angad and collected the money from Abba. What happens to my reputation? Such news will spread like a forest fire."

"I don't know how to react? I went to Pandu's home and Kamla revealed it to me. Shoba stays holed up there and refuses to come home," disclosed Mangala, tossing her shawl over her shoulders.

"Does the matter appear too serious?" Vasu stuttered. He feared the inevitable and the village grapevine.

"I don't know a thing. I heard the affair and came running here. We need to ask Shoba," retorted Mangala, with her hands on her heart.

"Damn the blot!" blurted Vasu. He remained tensed, confused and apprehensive of the consequences. "What happens to our honour? I gave word to Angad and this news will dent my image. No one will accept our proposal anymore. Oh! Vitthal! What have you done?" moaned Vasu, looking upto the sky. "I hope you haven't spilled the beans?" whispered Vasu, wary of the gossip.

"No!" replied Mangala, as she sneaked around, inched closer to Vasu and whispered in his ears "I left the house and came over to tell you."

"Did you bump into anyone?"

Mangala nodded her head. "Luckily no!"

"Why does it happen with us?" questioned Vasu.

Mangala lifted her shoulders and twisted her lips with a slight nod.

Vasu turned it over in his mind and recalled. "Pandu must have lured her. He talks big and sounds rebellious. He spoke against marital expenses, festivities and ceremonies. I challenged him to marry the way he wants and he replied, 'we'll see.' Is this the way he accepted my challenge?" Vasu's eyes flashed, as he clenched his teeth and spluttered. "Damn that swine!"

"What happened?" queried Mangala.

Vasu nodded his head and his heart stirred at the thought of Pandu's betrayal. He slammed his fist against the flat of his palm and took a deep breath. "If Pandu thinks that he can get away with this," he murmured to himself and stiffened the muscles in his face. "I'll kill that bastard!"

Mangala, who regained her poise after relaying the news, had sobered down. She looked at Vasu and reasoned. "What's the point? This anger will do us no good."

"Then, what do we do?" howled Vasu, hysterically.

"Sssh," Mangala stabbed her finger on her lips, looked around slyly, dragged her feet towards Vasu and whispered. "We'll have to think of a way out of this."

Vasu pinned his fingers to the edges of his temple and racked his head for an answer, but failed to figure out what to do. "For a girl like Shoba, with a marriage proposal in the pipeline things seem complicated. I fear how the village will react to all this. We may suffer a boycott," thought Vasu, worried of the implications in a patriarchial feudal society.

Mangala waived off the fear. "Huh," she snapped, twisting her lips. "What's there to worry? Pandu belongs to our caste."

Vasu's face reddened and he interrupted. "What do you imply?" he grunted, as he glared at Mangala.

Mangala's face dropped and she stood silent.

Vasu nodded his head in disagreement. He pointed his finger at Mangala. "Don't even think of it?" he warned, as he dropped his hand. "What does Pandu think of himself? He's just an ordinary tiller of this land," said Vasu, kicking the mud beneath his feet and spitting on the ground, "thu!" He wiped the tiny drops of spit perched on the tip of his lips against his forearm. "A farmer with an uncertain future condemned to live and die in debt. He keeps bragging about revolutionary stuff that he picked up from the LOFA in some unknown jungles. Even his parents do not trust his ability to shoulder responsibilities. And you expect me to give my Shoba to him."

Mangala frowned and looked at Vasu as if he did not understand her. "I don't suggest that you accept Pandu, but will Shoba agree with you? She went off her own will. We must not overlook that."

Vasu interjected angrily. "What makes you think so? That swine lured her. He betrayed the trust, we reposed in him," alleged Vasu. He walked upto Mangala, pointing his finger at her. "Whatever occurred between them? You should not have looked away!"

The insinuation stirred Mangala. Her eyes glowered, as she stashed her hands on her hips. "I didn't tell her to go along with Pandu," she grunted in a gruff voice, with a tinge of sarcasm. "Huh!" she sneered, raising her eyebrows and lifting her shoulders in a shrug. "Why blame me? You contracted Pandu and as a father you bear the larger responsibility to discipline a daughter when she comes off age."

Vasu's jaws dropped as the rebuke maddened him. "Stop arguing with me!" exclaimed Vasu. He whirled around, put his palms over his head and shut his eyes. He knew Mangala sounded right, but the truth remained that his mind stayed occupied with other problems.

"What do you suggest?" asked Mangala, having smothered Vasu's domination.

Vasu steeped in confusion now faced an ego hassle with his wife. He had turned down her suggestion, forced the decision on himself and now suffered a rebuke.

"What happened?" Mangala pestered.

Vasu spun on his heels to face her. "Stop the nagging," howled Vasu; it appeared his helplessness overwhelmed him.

"Huh," snapped Mangala, as she looked away.

"Enough of coddling Shoba! I'll visit Angad tomorrow and get her married," Vasu announced his decision.

"I don't think she will follow, what you suggest. She stays committed to Pandu."

"Do you defend her?"

"I defend the family, because if she disapproves of what you suggest; it will complicate matters. Imagine the village grapevine, rife with rumours. It won't take time for the rumours to reach Borgaon."

Vasu kept quiet. The reasoning forced him to reconsider his decision, because of the possibility of a backlash. However, his ruffled ego got the better of him and held him back. He had proposed in a fit of rage that he would not permit Pandu to get away, but he seemed helpless against reality and found it difficult to swallow his words.

Mangala on the other hand knew the ways of her husband and decided to concede. "I don't think you must feel ashamed of anything. All fathers will react the way you did," she said softly and then paused.

The words restored Vasu's honour and assuaged his ego. His heart lightened and washed down the clutter in his mind. He breathed with ease and his eyes twinkled. Mangala witnessed the change and decided to pursue her proposal.

"I think we must let them marry and bury the matter. We know Pandu and his family for years and its useless picking a fight with our neighbours. We must accept that they have remained good and always helped us. This marriage will further strengthen our bonds," said Mangala, with a soft voice, while she observed Vasu from the corner of her eyes.

Vasu sat with his head facing the ground in a state of submission.

Mangala continued her persuasion. "We remain in debt and to make things worse, we have borrowed heavily at an exorbitant rate of interest from Abba. This marriage will help us save on money. You can return the money to Abba and take back our land, because Pandu's folks refuse to accept dowry. It seems they wish to see Pandu married and settled."

"Hmm," murmured Vasu, grappling with his ego again. "Damn the money! The swine will not get a match like my Shoba. She's one in a million," bragged Vasu, venting his frustration on Pandu.

"Sssh," Mangala shooed and smiled. "Be careful with your words. He may be your son-in-law. If you wish to take my suggestion," Mangala cautioned, adding the last sentence emphatically to reassure Vasu that he remains the boss. She stretched down on the ground, confident of the outcome, pulled the shawl over her face and shut her eyes.

Vasu sat up for a while and then sprawled on his back. He saw the moon looking down on him and wondered. "What a strange twist of events?"

CHAPTER 26

▼

Vladimir looked through the wire mesh that stood fifteen feet tall and enclosed six acres of snow covered land. He looked for Bruno the tiger and Maria the tigress.

"They remain out of bounds," said Anna, with a bucket of tiger urine in her hands.

Linda and Michael stood behind her, holding the model tiger to watch the controlled experiment.

"We'll brush this tiger with urine and then move him inside the enclosure," informed Vladimir, as he dipped the brush into the bucket and smeared it over the model tiger.

Michael's nose wrinkled in distaste. "Yuk! It stinks!" he complained, pinching his nostrils to ward off the stench.

"Its tiger cologne," explained Vladimir, as he looked up and smiled.

"Why do we need to polish the model tiger with 'tiger cologne,'?" asked Linda, grinning, as she uttered the last two words and raised her eyebrows.

"Bruno and Maria will get scent of it and approach this model tiger. Tigers spray urine on the trunks of trees and earth to mark their territories. It resembles a marker that distinguishes territories and warns the intruder to keep off or face the consequences," replied Vladimir, looking at Anna and nodding. "Done."

Anna proceeded to park the bucket at a distance.

"I'll nail this model in the enclosure," said Vladimir, while he tilted his head and studied the model. "It's fine."

"I hope the kids stayed back to watch this experiment," said Linda.

Michael nodded his head. "A bunch of brats especially that Victor," he added, with a grin.

"I liked the way he uttered the word experiment," recalled Linda. "But he kind of gets worked up easily."

"Yeah, short headed," said Michael, stretching his face and lifting his eyebrows. "It's not easy to control kids that small, with an attention span which digresses easily."

"Yeah," nodded Vladimir. "They dictate terms and we need to make things interesting. I will bring them here someday."

"I miss them," hankered Linda.

"They will come here again someday. The last time they came here, they appeared scared. I wish to conduct this experiment for you, so that you observe it carefully without bother," explained Vladimir, lifting the model tiger. "With the kids around, you need to watch over them."

"I understand," said Linda.

"Did you test it?" Vladimir asked Anna, who arrived with a speaker in hand.

"Yeah," she replied.

"Let's move," said Vladimir.

Linda unbolted the door of the enclosure. Vladimir and his wife sneaked in and scoured the surroundings for Bruno and Maria as they tiptoed.

"Its fine keep walking," whispered Anna, who followed Vladimir.

The conservationists tiptoed to a distance of fifty metres and halted.

"Yeah, we'll nail it here," stated Vladimir, and then hunched down. He nailed the four legs of the tiger to the ground, while Anna kept guard. "Done," he concluded, standing up and fastening a leash to the collar of the model tiger, which carried a camera.

"Where do we fix this?" asked Anna, showing him the speaker. Vladimir pored over the surroundings; his eyes caught sight of a pine tree.

"There," he pointed, dropping the leash and proceeding with Anna in tow.

The couple hurried to the tree and fixed the speaker to the trunk. They then scurried to the model tiger, picked the leash and dragged it to the door. They stepped out and Linda bolted the iron gates.

"Hold on to this," requested Vladimir, handing over the leash to Anna.

Anna tugged the leash, which jigged the head of the model tiger. She nodded in satisfaction. "Good it moves," she said to herself, whirling around and following the team, which alighted into the van.

"Turn on the recorder," instructed Vladimir.

Linda switched on the recorder, which roared. The team members gazed through the lens of their binoculars, anticipating a response.

"I can see a tiger totter in our direction," descried Michael, with excitement.

"That's Bruno," replied Anna.

Vladimir twisted around to face Linda. "Switch off the voice," he ordered, and then turned around to observe the reaction. Linda followed the instructions and continued to peer through the lens.

"Where's Maria?" asked Linda.

"She must have buried herself in a dug out. She'll emerge when she gets wind of this situation," replied Anna.

Suddenly, Bruno halted in his track. He popped his ears, harkened, cast his eyes about, angled his head, stuck his nose in the air, and sniffed. The aroma tickled his nostrils, which flared. He wrinkled his nose, bared his teeth, stuck his tongue out and lowered himself on the snow.

"He's got scent of the intruder," quipped Vladimir.

The clock ticked on but Bruno continued to crouch and sniff the air. Michael's fingers twitched and he shook his knees tired of the wait. Bruno stayed seated. Michael lowered his binoculars. "It's almost fifteen minutes, since, he saw the trespasser, but he remains squatted," complained Michael.

"He will study his enemy and size him up. A tiger stays cautious because it remains a solitary animal. It will not want to injure itself recklessly, because it will affect his hunting ability and he may starve to death," explained Vladimir. He signalled Linda, who twisted the knob of the recorder. The speaker howled.

Bruno's tail curled upwards and he crawled a few steps forward. Michael beamed at the sight. "He's moving stealthily!"

Vladimir snapped his fingers; Linda switched off the recorder.

Linda scanned the enclosure with the binoculars. "I don't see Maria. Why hasn't she turned up?" she asked, with a frown on her face.

"I gather, she hasn't got wind of anything," replied Michael.

"Even if she does, Bruno will fight this model tiger because it remains his territory," explained Anna, tugging at the leash.

"Why? If I have gathered correctly, they live together," Michael questioned.

Anna took a deep breath and answered. "We have studied them for months. You see that tree, where we fixed the speaker. Bruno has clawed the trunk to mark his dominion; he urinates around there, which implies that he rules this territory."

"Do tigers share territory?" inquired Michael.

"The tiger is a solitary animal, unlike, the lions that move around in a pride. A tiger does not share his territory, except, during a brief mating bout with a female," retorted Vladimir.

"The other day, when we hung in the chopper, the tiger clamoured up a stump and roared at us," Michael recalled.

"It defended its territory. This experiment will show, how Bruno will react to any intruder," said Vladimir.

"It's almost thirty minutes and Bruno hasn't inched forward," maintained Michael, irritated with the delay. He checked his watch and shook his head. "What's he waiting for?"

"The tiger remains a tolerant and cool animal like a cat. It remains patient and studies the enemy. I remember my expedition in the Ranthambore tiger reserve of India, where I first witnessed the unending patience of this animal. On a hot summer season, early in the morning, I tracked a tiger around a lake surrounded by tall grass. An ambush occurred in the lake and the tiger killed a Sambhar that weighed roughly two hundred and fifty pounds. The task that followed appeared more difficult, because the tiger needed to drag the carcass across the lake to reach the shore and gorge on it quietly. The lake remained infested with crocodiles, which attacked the tiger in the middle of the lake and snatched the prey from the tiger. The tiger withdrew from the battle, outnumbered, and waded through the waters to reach the banks, where it settled down and watched the proceedings. The four crocodiles tried to tear the tough hide of the sambhar, but failed, despite their efforts. The crocodile's teeth designed to spin and cut failed to tear the hide apart. The tiger sat unstirred and waited for an opportunity. The wait tired me, because it stretched for nine hours, but the tiger sat unfazed. The crocodiles, finally, gave up the effort. The tiger swam to the middle of the lake, retrieved its kill, dragged it to the banks of the lake and and devoured it. Patience remains the strongest attribute of a tiger. It will never give up," narrated Vladimir.

"What's the history of these tigers?" asked Linda.

"Their mother Sarah, the first collared tiger, gave birth to a litter of four cubs. I radio tracked her for months, but one day the signals from her collar showed her movement had stalled. I traced her signals and found her lying dead; killed by poachers. Her litter lay scattered on the road, about half a kilometer from her, awaiting her to feed them. When I gave chase, they disappeared in the forest, so I drove back home, agonizing over their fate. I knew that the cubs would die in the forests without their mother. I tried to sleep, believing nature will decide their fate, but in the morning my mind beckoned that, I intervene and save them. I took a crew of twelve helpers with me and rescued the cubs. Unfortunately, within a few days, two of the cubs died from genetic abnormalities. Bruno and Maria survived," narrated Vladimir, with a smile.

"How long do you propose to keep them?" inquired Michael.

Vladimir smacked his lips and replied. "This remains the first captive breeding experiment of its kind in Russia, similar to the type pioneered by the Packer Research Institute in Alaska. I do not want these two tigers to breed, because they carry the same genes. We propose to send Bruno to Alaska and import another Siberian male to copulate with Maria. If Maria succeeds in giving birth to a litter of cubs, then we will release her back into the jungles. Captive breeding appears the last hope for this endangered species. It sounds ironic that the natural habitat of the Siberian tiger appears the biggest threat to its survival," explained Anna.

"Let's prayer we succeed," said Vladimir, marking a cross on his chest.

"When everything else fails, prayers do work," affirmed Linda, with a smile.

Anna tugged the leash and switched on the recorder. The roar electrified the atmosphere.

"He's crawling towards the model," proclaimed Michael, who observed Bruno creep towards the model.

Anna continued to jig the leash. Bruno sprang to his feet, snapped his jaws and roared back.

"It's the last warning," quipped Vladimir, peering through the binoculars.

Bruno tramped through the snow and faced the model tiger, which roared and defied him. Bruno lunged on the model and ripped it apart.

"Holy, Christ!" exclaimed Linda, with her hands on her heart.

"It happened brutally," stuttered Michael, stung by the assault.

"It resembles a blitzkrieg," replied Vladimir, unlocking the door of his van and stepping out. "Come out," he waved to the inmates.

They dropped out and followed him to the door of the enclosure.

"Bruno," Anna called out.

Bruno continued to maul the plaster.

"Let him vent his anger," said Vladimir.

Linda and Michael quivered at the sight.

Vladimir pointed at Bruno. "A typical tiger attack; sudden and lethal. It unleashes all the energy it conserves in waiting. Many opine that the tiger remains the most unpredictable and dangerous hunter. It stays unnoticed and waits endlessly untill the enemy looses guard and then attacks," explained Vladimir. He whirled around to face Linda and Michael. "Remember this when you fly to India to study tigers there. Never loose guard in a tiger expedition."

CHAPTER 27

▼

It took a month's time for Vasu to get over the shock. Shoba married Pandu, shifted to Pandu's house and the couple stayed happy. Pandu worked harder and took care of Vasu's cotton field. This gesture eased the burden on Vasu's shoulders and by November, he appreciated his decision. The marital alliance strengthened the bond, between Vasu and Gangaram. In fact, Gangaram looked happier because Pandu settled down. Mangala seemed happy to have her daughter, by her side, while Bapu appeared content because Shoba did not leave him. In short, everything fell in place, except the load shedding.

In the elections of October, the people of Maharashtra voted the ruling alliance back to power. However, this alliance immediately reneged on its promise of providing free electricity to the farmers. To make matters worse, when the media questioned it about this volte-face, it gave the most flimsy excuse in the annals of political history—a printing error in the election manifesto.

The irony continued because such backtracking appeared customary in Indian Democracy. Most political parties promise the sky in the elections; most people believe in these promises and vote these parties back to power and these parties then renege on their promises. Maharashtra's ruling alliance remained a part of this pattern and though the people voted it back to, 'power,' the ruling alliance out of gratitude rendered the electorate powerless. Many contended that it seemed unfair to blame the government, because in reality the government kept its word—it indulged in power expansion.

The ruling alliance filled every Cabinet berth in the government. Despite this, many contenders within the ruling alliance wanted power (ministries). The high command ordered the Chief Minister to accomadate (generate more power), the disgruntled power contenders. It decreed. "Expand the Cabinet (generate more power) and fulfill the promise made to the electorate, by distributing more power. Make the government more powerful, so that it completes its five years term. Don't bother of the cost (taxpayer) ensure power expansion in Maharashtra."

The Chief Minister obliged and created more Ministries (power expansion) and distributed the surplus to the dissidents. He proclaimed; "we will not betray the people. If we promised them power; we will give them more power, because our secular and socialist alliance believes in the equitable distribution of power and in keeping with this idelogy, every poltical member of the alliance will receive power." So, in this way the ruling alliance kept its promise and if the people complained about powerlessness in Maharashtra they must know that the ruling alliance generated and distributed more power when it came to power.

The government also demonstrated that it stayed committed to the United Nations repeated demands for a higher Human Development Index (HDI), particularly one parameter that included health or longevity. The load shedding would ensure that, by the end of the coming summer season, the people of Maharashtra looked leaner and meaner, because the afternoon heat coupled with the load shedding, would force the people to shed their fat. The more they sweated under the grueling heat without fans, air conditioners and coolers, the more they would sweat and shed their fat. This government sponsored, "free fitness regime," would result in reduced risks of high blood pressure, hypertension and cholesterol. The health index of the state would surely soar, thanks to the load shedding, which showed that this government succeeded because it ensured both, "power expansion" and "load (fat) shedding". The United Nations must declare this phenomenon a, "UN Heritage site," and preserve it for the delight of future generations.

The erratic load-shedding schedule made Pandu more prompt, because he could not afford to waste a minute. The moment the electricity came, he would switch on the motor that pumped water from the tube well and water his crop. This morning at about eleven o'clock, Pandu ambled to the switchboard and stabbed the switch. "Thuk!" but the motor faltered.

Pandu pursed his lips and wobbled his head in disgust. "Damn the light," he blurted, and then stabbed the button again. "Thuk!" the motor hesitated again.

Pandu's face frowned; he shot a glance upwards at the bulb hanging over the pole. "The lights are on," he murmured to himself.

He thumbed the switch repeatedly. "Thuk! Thuk! Thuk! Thuk! Thuk!" the switch snapped, but failed to start the motor.

"Damn it! What's wrong?" Pandu ranted in frustration, as he thumped the switchboard, wiggled the wires and stabbed the switch. "Thuk!" it wavered.

Pandu shook his head and slammed his eyes shut. "Damn the motor," he slapped the switchboard, and then whirled around in a huff. "What happened?" he thought back, as he scratched his stubble.

"Maybe the fuse," he swirved around and set his eyes on the fuse fixed above the switchbox. His face dropped at the sight. Someone had tampered with the switchboard and stolen the fuse.

His eyes glowered as he wondered. "Who could have taken it?" He turned it over in his mind and creased his forehead. "If it happened, it must have happened in the evening, when no one hangs around," he reasoned.

Whatever, the cause, he must first water the crop to save it from wilting and arrange for a fuse from Ganpat who worked on Abba's land. He got along well with Ganpat though he hated Tatya and Abba. "Why take a chance if Tatya gets to know?" his mind hesitated, but the circumstances compelled him, because he did not wish to waste a day traveling to Ashti and back.

"I can borrow for the day and return it," he weighed it in his mind and then decided to meet Ganpat.

He raced to the edge of his field, reached the baandh, which overlooked Abba's sugarcane plantation and halted. Ganpat usually watered the sugarcane when the lights came and then proceeded to work on the well. The sugarcane leaves rustled against the strong wind, which lashed Pandu and almost knocked him down. He staggered as he yelled, "Ganpat, Ganpat," at the top of his voice.

He waited for a response, as he wobbled against the wind. "Damn the wind!" he exclaimed, shaking his head.

He gathered himself, cupped his hands, stuck them to the edges of his mouth and shouted. "Ganpat, Ganpat."

There appeared no response.

"This wind will not carry my voice," he deduced, ramming his fist against the flat of his palm. "I'll have to walk down and find him," he said to himself, and then forced his way into Abba's land.

The sugar cane stalks stood tall and dense and the leaves rustled against the wind. "I hope I find him quick," thought Pandu, trekking along the dirt track that led through the plantation. He elbowed his way through the dense sharp leaves, which lashed and ripped his skin. "Ouch!" he cringed and shoved aside the leaves, which invaded his path. "No wonder Ganpat can't hear me," he inferred, as he jostled his way through the plantation.

"Huh! Huh!" a stifled voice squeaked from the undergrowth and caught Pandu's attention.

Pandu froze in his track and strained his ears to listen. Now, he heard the tinkle of glass and grapple that mingled in the rustle of leaves.

"Huh! Huh!" the voice choked, as if crying for help.

Pandu's face stiffened and his brows bumped together in a scowl. He hunched over and spotted a stone in the undergrowth. He picked it up and trailed the voice.

"Huh! Huh! Huh!" the voice grew shriller against the sputter of leaves.

"Must be an animal trapped in the undergrowth," he thought, as he peeked through the leaves. He could not see a thing, because of the tall stalks and leaves, rustling against the wind.

Pandu hurled the stone in the direction of the disturbance.

"Hurr . . . Hurr . . . ," he shouted in an attempt to scare the disturbance.

"Help! Help!" a violent cry ranted the air, and then dissipated to a grapple.

"Shut your mouth! You bitch!" a voice snapped.

"Help! Help!" the voice recurred.

Pandu took the cue and raced towards the scuffle. He had covered twenty metres, when his eyes caught Sushma groveling in the mud, with Tatya sitting over her and gagging her mouth. She bit Tatya.

"Ouch! Bitch!" howled Tatya, slapping her.

"Help, help," shrieked Sushma.

"No one will help you," Tatya snapped, throttling her neck.

"Huh!" Sushma gasped for breath. Her eyes reddened and feet kicked the air.

Pandu's blood boiled at the sight. His face turned red and he clenched his fists. He charged towards Tatya and grabbed his collars from behind. "Get up you swine!" howled Pandu, as he dragged Tatya away.

Tatya taken aback wrestled to extricate himself. "Leave me!" he squirmed.

Sushma sat up gasping for breath and weeping. Her clothes appeared torn and ruffled, hair disheveled, face shocked and wrists cut by pointed pieces of smashed bangles.

"Pandu . . . help . . . me . . . ," her voice quivered; she pointed at Tatya. "He . . . raped . . . me . . ."

"You lured me," retorted Tatya, whirling about and trying to break free. "You keep out of this!"

"Shut your mouth! You filthy swine!" snapped Pandu; he released his grip and kicked Tatya in the back.

"Ouch!" yelled Tatya, tumbling on the ground.

Pandu lunged at him, mounted his chest, slapped him across his face and strangled his neck.

"Huh!" Tatya gasped for breath.

Pandu looked at Sushma. "Don't worry," he said, squeezing Tatya's neck. "I'm here to deal with him."

"Ouch!" Tatya squeaked and resisted. He struggled for breath. "I'm not to blame."

"You forced me," shrieked Sushma.

Pandu's anger soared; he clenched his fist and rammed it against Tatya's jaws. Blood sputtered from Tatya's mouth and he went dizzy in the head. "She lured me here," his voice choked, trying to defend himself.

"He's lying," cried Sushma, with her voice stuck in her throat.

"I'm not a stranger to your ways. You can't get away with this," yelled Pandu, whacking Tatya across his face, and then releasing his grip.

"How dare you touch me? You debtor!" ranted Tatya, pushing Pandu.

Pandu grabbed Tatya's hands and pinned them to the ground. "Watch your tongue! You swine! I'm a debtor, not a rapist like you," howled Pandu, strangling Tatya's wrists.

"She owes me money and hasn't paid a penny," gasped Tatya.

"She owes you money, not her honour," replied Pandu, slapping Tatya again.

"Don't hit me!You'll pay for it!"

"It's the end of you and your tyranny!" thundered Pandu, grabbing Tatya's neck and squeezing it.

"Huh! Huh!" Tatya choked and wriggled.

"That's how it feels, when someone chokes your neck," sneered Pandu.

"Please leave me," Tatya begged for his life.

"Pandu please control your anger. You'll kill him," pleaded Ganpat, who arrived on the spot, seized Pandu's shoulders and pulled him over.

Tatya sat up panting and blinked. "Take him away . . . ," he gasped.

"Leave me!" shouted Pandu, trying to wrest free. "I'll kill the swine!"

Tatya breathed heavily and his face bled. His clothes looked rumpled, hair tousled and eyes smarted from the pounding. He quivered and pointed to his right. "If it's the fuse you want. It's there . . . ," he disclosed.

Pandu hustled Ganpat and tried to break free. "Damn you thief! You tampered with my switchboard!"

Tatya wriggled in his seat at the sight of Pandu. He tried to stand up, but staggered and crashed down in the undergrowth.

"Let me go! I will kill him!" shrieked Pandu, grappling with Ganpat, who held him with great effort.

"Pandu don't," panted Ganpat, pulling him away.

Tatya crawled away scared of the wrath.

"Why do you wish to save this rapist?" inquired Pandu; he bulldozed Ganpat, who lost his balance and collapsed on the ground. Pandu bolted towards Tatya, but Ganpat trapped Pandu's foot in his hands and dragged him back.

"Pandu please don't fight," begged Ganpat.

Pandu twisted his foot to extricate it. "Why did you remove my fuse?" he asked Tatya, wriggling about.

"Your tube well sucks all the water beneath the ground. Did you know that since you drilled that hole in the ground my tube well pumps less water? If you do not believe what I say, then ask Ganpat," grumbled Tatya; he gestured towards Ganpat, who held on to Pandu's foot. "He reported the matter to me."

Pandu's nostrils flared; he stared down at Ganpat.

Ganpat cringed. "I've repeated a general assumption," he responded, with a crumpled face.

Pandu fixed his gaze on Tatya and shook his head. "Damn you coward! Don't make him a scapegoat!" he fumed, fisted the air and hauled his foot.

Ganpat lost his grip, while Pandu lunged at Tatya and seized him by his collar. "It's my tube well and I have a right to water. You may assume anything you wish, but don't you ever tamper with my fuse," he grunted, looking him in the eyes.

"I returned your fuse . . . ," quivered Tatya.

"You have to," maintained Pandu, dropping his hands.

Ganpat gathered himself, scurried towards Pandu, and embraced him from behind. "Please stop the fight," he pleaded.

Pandu twisted around and kicked Tatya in the ribs.

"Ouch!" groaned Tatya; he hunched over and stumbled.

"You dare touch Sushma again and I'll burn you alive! I'm reporting this matter to the Police!" riled Pandu, squirming in Ganpat's grasp. "Let me free!"

Tatya stumbled holding his ribs and smiled wryly. "You can go to the Police if you wish," he grunted, as he staggered, gasping for breath. "Remember, I'm a Deshmukh by blood and descent and we run this state," he bragged, pointing to himself.

"Shut up! Thu!" Pandu spat, with a scorn on his face and pressed forward.

"Hold him tight," Tatya squeaked and retreated. He squinted in a furtive manner and blabbered. "The land your father-in-law tills belongs to me. You have forfeited your right over that land and of course that tube well lies beneath that land. You tell Vasu to evict the land immediately. I don't wish to see you there anymore."

"Don't you dare try to rob that land? Vasu approached Abba and returned the money he borrowed but Abba refused the money because he wants the land. True to your blood, Deshmukhs remain thieves in Ramwadi," yelled Pandu, twisting in Ganpat's grasp.

"Hold him," quivered Tatya, and then receded.

Pandu stared at him. "Don't take me for granted. I will not give in so easily. If you do not return Vasu's land, I'll not let you live in peace," threatened Pandu.

The intensity of the threat sent a chill down Tatya's spine and a lump appeared in his throat. He blinked and gulped down the lump quivering. His mind seemed rattled and ego pulverized to the core. His body language exhibited that he suffered insult beyond reproach, because he never imagined that he would encounter such a situation. He lay exposed committing a wrong. He felt guilty, angry, humiliated and helpless at the same time. So far, he appeared accustomed to beating and abusing people with impunity. The victims never resisted and swallowed all the abuse humbly, but this seemed a different scenario. He never thought he would meet his match. This unexpected retaliation shocked and unnerved him from head to toe. His mind froze and failed to discern how to react to this situation. His lips quivered when he reacted.

"When you need money; you come to us and once you take it, you never turn up," grumbled Tatya, in an attempt to sound like the good Samaritin.

Pandu interrupted. "Shut up! Do not change the subject. You raped Sushma!" he reminded Tatya, wriggling in Ganpat's grasp. "Let me go! I'll kill him!"

Tatya's face dropped and he looked away.

"Tatya, why don't you leave?" suggested Ganpat, struggling to hold on to Pandu. "Go! Go!"

"Why do you protect him?" fumed Pandu, dragging Ganpat along.

"Tatya, why don't you run? I fear he'll kill you!" Ganpat reiterated, trying to pull back Pandu.

Tatya spun on his heels and fled.

"Leave me you idiot!" yelled Pandu, twisting about in Ganpat's grasp.

"Pandu, try to understand that you may have killed him," shouted Ganpat. He glimpsed ahead and saw Tatya disappear.

"I will not do anything silly. Leave me," promised Pandu.

Ganpat released Pandu. "You would have killed him, if I was not here."

"He deserves to die," snapped Pandu, straightening his rumpled clothes and flicking the dust off his shirt.

"It will add to your woes. Remember you are married and have responsibilities," cautioned Ganpat, stretching his arms. "Look what has happened?" he showed Pandu his arms, which bore red patches.

Pandu looked around. "Where is Sushma?" inquired Pandu. It suddenly occurred to him that the girl had disappeared.

Ganpat continued to fold and unfold his arms for the blood to circulate freely. "She must have gone home," he answered casually.

"Sushma! Sushma!" Pandu shouted.

The wind whistled with the rustle of leaves, but no one responded. Pandu's heart throbbed. He called out again. "Sushma! Sushma!" but no one replied.

The two men looked at each other worried.

"Sushma! Sushma!" Ganpat yelled.

"I hope she hasn't fainted in here," said Pandu, tramping around and rummaging through the undergrowth. "Damn it! Where is she?"

Pandu motioned Ganpat, who joined the search. The two men hustled the sugarcane stalks, surveyed the surroundings and took to the track, which led to the orchard. They called out to her, but she did not respond.

"Where is she?" wondered Pandu.

"I'm sure she must have gone home," replied Ganpat.

They reached the orchard and Pandu called out again, "Sushma!Sushma!" but no one responded.

"I'm sure, she must have gone home," Ganpat reiterated.

"You go and search that cattle shed," ordered Pandu, pointing in the opposite direction. "I'll search the orchard."

Ganpat raced to the cattle shed perched on the edge of the main road, while Pandu stomped around the orchard calling out to her. "Sushma! Sushma!"

Ganpat burst inside the cattle shed, which reeked of animal dung and looked around frenzied. He halted for a breather, slammed his eyes shut and shook his head. "There she lies," he sighed, walking up to her and tapping her shoulders.

"Sushma get up," he appealed to the girl, who lay twisted on one side, with her head facing the wall in the corner of the shed.

Sushma lay still.

"Do you hear me?" said Ganpat, tugging at her shoulder.

Sushma rolled over on her back.

Ganpat's face crumpled at the sight; his eyes widened and a lump appeared in his throat.

"Damn it! What has she done?" thought Ganpat. He slapped his forehead, sank on his knees and stared in disbelief.

Sushma lay sprawled on the floor, with her eyes wide-open and white froth perched on the corner of her lips. An open can of endosulphan lay scattered on the floor.

Ganpat jumped to his feet and hobbled out. "Pandu . . . Pandu . . . ," his voice quivered and heart throbbed.

Pandu ran towards Ganpat, who narrated the discovery.

"Damn that Tatya!" fumed Pandu; his eyes turned moist.

"Should we call Lekha?" asked Ganpat.

"Damn the mother! First rush her to the hospital!" said Pandu, as he pursed his lips and shook his head. "Ganpat go on the road and stop a tum-tum. We need to carry her to the hospital."

Ganpat charged to the main road, while Pandu scurried to the shed.

CHAPTER 28

▼

The police constable at the chowki in Vithalwadi, a stout, pot-bellied man consumed his lunch and hunkered down on his wooden chair. He burped, while he rummaged through his breast pocket, yanked out a tobacco pouch, scooped out a pinch of tobacco, stashed it on the flat of his palm and smeared it with a tinge of wet lime. He yawned, slumped down on his chair and pinched the tobacco. It appeared he would fall asleep any moment.

Tatya sneaked inside the police station in his hammered avatar. His shirt appeared soiled, mangled and bloodied; his face looked swollen and slashed with a black patch under his left eye, while blood oozed from the corner of his lips. He hobbled to the desk.

"Namaskar Kendre Sahib," Tatya greeted the police officer.

Kendre snorted with his eyes shut and head tilted against the backrest.

Tatya nodded his head, hunched over and knuckled the table. "Sahib," he called out again.

"Hmm," the cop's head dropped; he blinked and tossed it back.

Tatya took a deep breath. "Sahib," he breathed out, with a loud tone.

The cop wriggled in his seat and then opened his eyes. The sight shocked him. He stared bug-eyed. "Who the hell are you?" he questioned, while he straightened his back, rubbed his eyes and discerned. "Is it Tatya?"

Tatya nodded his head, and then looked away.

"Damn it!" the cop exclaimed; he pored over the spectacle, pursed his lips and jigged his head. "What has happened to you?" he questioned, uttering the words slowly and tossing the tobacco in his mouth.

Tatya hurled his hands on his hips. "I want to register a FIR," he demanded, with a gruff voice.

The cop jumped to his feet, dusted his palms on his buttocks, shoved his chair aside, scurried to the corner of the hall, grabbed a chair and dragged it to his desk. "Please sit down," he bowed, and then motioned Tatya to take his seat.

Tatya squatted down. "Ouch!" he groaned, with a wrinkled nose.

"Easy," cautioned the cop, holding the chair for Tatya. "I'm sorry about the chair, the chowki's on a shoe-string budget," he apologized, and then stomped back to his seat and slumped down on his chair. "Will you have water, chai or nimbu pani?"

Tatya waived his hand, and then elbowed the desk. "I need to talk to you."

The cop leaned over the desk, and then fixed his eyes on Tatya. "You look troubled."

Tatya nodded his head. "Yeah," he murmured, taking a deep breath. "I need police protection" he asserted, exhaling slowly. He then gestured and drew a circle around his face. "Look how he beat me black and blue," he showed his avatar, reclining in his chair.

The cop observed the spectacle, and then smacked his lips. "I can see that."

"I am lucky to escape or I would have died."

"I understand. You should have visited the Doctor, before coming to me or do you want me to send for him?"

Tatya wagged his palm and brushed aside the offer. "We don't have the time," he complained, rolling his eyes upwards. "I want you to arrest him or I fear he will kill me."

"Damn the rascal!" snapped the cop, slamming his fist on the table. "Who did it?" he inquired, with a gruff voice.

"Do you remember that Pandu?" Tatya retorted.

The cop blinked, while he creased his forehead. He crossed his hands over his chest, and then reclined in his chair. He ruminated for a moment. "Pandu," he turned it over in his mind, and then nodded in disagreement.

Tatya hunched over the desk. "Recall the incident of that boy who stole jamuns from my orchard."

"Yeah," recalled the cop; his eyes twinkled. "I got it," he snapped his fingers. "The arrogant guy, who argued over the matter."

Tatya shook his head. "Yeah, he beat me up."

"Tring, Tring," the telephone rang.

Kendre stretched his hand out, grabbed the receiver and stuck it to his ear. "Vithalwadi police station," he announced, as he drummed his fingers on the desk and twitched his face. "I'm busy, call up, some time later," he yawned, as if a programmed bureaucrat trained to avoid work.

Suddenly, he jumped to his feet and hunched over the line. "Sorry Sir, Yes Sir, Good afternoon Sir," his voice quivered, while his jaws dropped. His palm fumbled and fingers groped around the desk. He pulled the drawer, rummaged through the papers and yanked out a pen.

"Yes Sir . . . , I'm writing," he stuttered, flicking over a page in the diary. "Three men infiltrators, hmm," he nodded his head. "I'm listening, please go ahead, hmm, hmm, hmm, red alert, hmm, comb and patrol the villages, hmm, hmm, hmm, yeah, I'm listening, they are on field visit, hmm, yeah, Jai hind," he concluded and then hung up. He leaned over the table with a stern face and his eyes flashed with rage. "Damn the headquarters!" he blurted, pounding the table with his fist.

"Shaikh, Bhosale, Kulkarni come over. Quick," he shouted, snapping his fingers. He paused, and then slapped his forehead. "What's wrong with me?" he muttered, shaking his head. "They are on field duty. Why do I forget? I'm tired," he confessed, slumping in his chair.

Tatya, who had snooped on the conversation and mulled over, arched a sly brow. "What's the matter Sahib?" he inquired, with a soft voice.

Kendre sat quietly; his eyes glued to the table as if pondering over the confabulation. He wobbled his head in anger. "Damn the job!" he shouted, smacking the table with his hands. He plonked his elbows on the table. "The District headquarters called up, because the intelligence informed them that some LOFA guerillas have infiltrated this area. They ordered us to patrol the area and arrest them," he yawned, while he reclined in his chair and rubbed his eyes. "I haven't slept for the past two days due to overtime. The government will not pay us for overtime. It only issues order after order," he complained, and then inhaled a sharp breath. "Comb the area, arrest the terrorist, record a dying

227

declaration, stop investigating this matter, investigate that matter, barricade the road, conduct a search operation, provide security to this V.I.P., Ganpati bandobast, Id bandobast, Ambedkar jayanti bandobast, oooof," he heaved a sigh, while he twisted in his chair. He clenched his fist, and then pounded the table. "This country celebrates festivals and jayantis half the year! I don't have time to breathe! I'm sick of it!"

Tatya's eyes lit up. "I understand you handle a real tough job," he emphatized, with a gleam of deviltry in his eyes.

The cop nodded his head in agreement. "It gets tougher, when we have to track revolutionaries because they mingle with civilians and appear better equipped and trained than our police force. It looks stupid running behind them, because we risk loosing our lives," lamented Kendre, shrugging his shoulders. "They remain ruthless against policemen. I remember, when I worked in Gadchiroli, I lost ten of my colleagues in an ambush and managed to survive by God's will," Kendre looked up, raising his hands. "If I ever get to lay my hands on them; I'll shoot them dead," he raged, clenching his fists and stiffening his face.

Tatya cocked a wry smile, and then pointed at him. "I must admit you remain one of the toughest cops and most efficient," he stated to flatter the disgruntled cop.

Kendre beamed at the suggestion, and then straightened up. "Yeah, I straighten people who mess with the law."

"Hmm," Tatya nodded his head in agreement.

Kendre stabbed the bell on his table. "You must have tea," he insisted.

"Yeah, if you insist I cannot refuse," replied Tatya.

A minor boy dressed in a soiled vest and shorts, burst into the police chowki and halted at the desk. He bowed before Kendre. "Sahib. Your order please," he asked, with folded hands.

Kendre assumed a regal poise, and then stared down at him. He motioned him to come closer. The boy complied. "Get two cups of tea," Kendre demanded, in a gruff voice.

The boy nodded his head, and then whirled around.

"Listen carefully you brat! I haven't finished!" yelled Kendre.

The boy cowered, as he slowly turned around.

"Make special kadak chai!" demanded Kendre.

"Yes Sahib," the boy quivered.

Kendre snapped his fingers. "Get going," he commanded the boy, who meekly veered around, and hobbled out of the chowki.

Tatya sized up the situation, grinned and winked. "He almost pissed in his pants," he commented, and then stuck his tongue out.

Kendre laughed, and then waived his hand. "This is nothing. Hardened criminals shit when I interrogate," he bragged.

Tatya looked around furtively, and then slithered to the edge of his chair. "Sahib, do you think it fair, when the revolutionaries kill and loot at will and then surrender before the government? I mean, the license to kill and get away," he whispered, and then smacked his lips.

"Nah," clucked Kendre.

"Precisely," added Tatya; he snapped his fingers and slithered back. His forehead creased and he wore a grim look. "I hate it when the police loose their lives. They work hard and brave the odds to protect society, but what does the Government give them in return?"

Kendre's eyes turned moist. He brandished his fist, popped his thumb out and turned it upside down. "Nothing credible," he answered, dropping his fist. He took a deep breath. "The government offers little compensation. A pittance," he sighed; his shoulders sagged and lips pouted. "A rusted medal or plaque of honour and family thrown to the winds at the mercy of fate," mocked Kendre, with a sarcastic smile. "In some States, I hear, the revolutionaries receive a rehabilitation package on surrender and our Government considers replicating the same. I suggest; hang them."

"Yeah, your right. Hmm," agreed Tatya. He tilted his head, gave it a thought and continued. "These swines contaminate society. They have lived in jungles. They behave like animals. This character Pandu, who beat me, worked as a revolutionary," alleged Tatya.

Kendre's eyes flashed. He gripped the arms of his chair. "What did you say?" he inquired.

Tatya cocked a wry smile. "Yeah," he nodded, pinching his throat. "I swear. The village says so. I hear it everyday. The village cannot go wrong on this assumption unless it appears true."

Kendre stared at Tatya, and then wobbled his head in agreement. "I see," he stated, tapping the table. "What happened to you? I need to hear your story."

Tatya jigged his head, and then commenced. "This Pandu, the revolutionary, trespassed into my sugarcane field and raped one of my labourers. Ganpat my employee informed me about it and both of us raced to the scene of offence, where I saw Pandu forcing himself on this girl. I warned Pandu to stop, but he threatened me not to interfere. The poor girl agonized and cried for help. I could not bear to see her in pain, so I pounced on Pandu to save the girl. The brute overpowered and beat me up. You know these revolutionaries behave like animals. Ganpat joined the melee and caught hold of Pandu, while I escaped to save my life. I do not know what has happened to Ganpat and the poor girl. I fear for my life and want police protection," Tatya concluded his twisted story.

Kendre slapped the table. "Don't worry. I'll arrest him; he can't run away from the law."

Tatya interjected, "he's a tough nut to crack and I doubt the police can get him," he taunted.

Kendre's blood boiled, while his nostrils flared. "Damn the swine!" he slammed his fist on the table. "I've handled criminals worse than him. He can't take on me."

Tatya's eyes squinted; he bent over the table and whispered. "Are you sure? This monster appears too strong. You see this," he pointed at his face.

Kendre's ego flared and he barged in. "Damn the monster! He'll wet his pants when he meets me!" he shook with rage.

Tatya raised his hand. "Please listen. I do not want you to harm yourself. I warned him about police action, but he laughed at me and bragged that he gives a damn to the police. 'I shot them in the jungles,' he claimed."

Kendre stood up in a huff. His face stiffened and his hands twitched. "Damn the jungles! How dare he challenge the police? I'll shove the baton up his ass and he'll never say that again!" hollered Kendre; he crashed on his chair, grabbed the pen perched on the table and scribbled the complaint. "That's it; I've done my job," he stated, dropping the pen.

Tatya grinned. "What about the terrorists?" he reminded Kendre.

"Let that stay. First, we will arrest this terrorist. The Headquarter has ordered to comb the area, so we will pick him up first, get him to talk and extract the lead to pursue the others."

The boy arrived with the cups of tea.

"Have your tea and don't worry. We will track him down," said Kendre.

CHAPTER 29

▼

Kendre and Tatya drove into Ramwadi to arrest Pandu. The sight of the police jeep created a flutter in the village square. The gamblers scurried for cover, but the jeep rattled on and halted at Pandu's doorstep. Gangaram, who had finished his lunch, staggered to his charpoy in the portal, plopped down and almost stretched out, when he felt his bed wobble.

Kendre kicked the charpoy. "Get up you swine!" he yelled.

A stunned Gangaram twisted about and noticed Kendre staring down on him, while Tatya cowered behind Kendre.

"What's the matter?" Gangaram hesitated.

"Where's the terrorist?" Kendre questioned, stashing his boot on the charpoy

"What?" inquired Gangaram; his face looked perplexed, while he cupped his ear to catch the words.

Kendre rolled his eyes upwards, propped his elbow on his knee, huched over and shouted into Gangaram's ear. "Where is the terrorist?"

Gangaram stared dumbfounded and looked bewildered. He shook his head, puzzled by the events and shrugged his shoulders.

Kendre slammed his eyes shut, annoyed with the response. He caught him by the scruff of his collars and looked him in the eye. "Don't pretend, you know that I ask for Pandu," he howled, and then hauled Gangaram to his feet.

The women working in the kitchen scampered out on hearing the commotion.

"What happened?" inquired Jija; she stood slack-jawed at the sight. Kamla followed her and stood by her side.

Shoba ran towards Gangaram and stood behind him, while Tatya snooped on her from behind Kendre. A group of villagers assembled outside to see the tamasha. They had followed the jeep to know what compelled the police to come over.

"Why have you grabbed him?" quizzed Shoba.

Kendre cocked a wry smile, let loose Gangaram, stepped aside, and then tossed his hand over Tatya's shoulder. "Look at what Pandu has done to Tatya," he showed Tatya to the audience.

Shoba gawked at the sight. Her face scowled and mind tried to figure out what happened.

Tatya bore a pale look and rolled his eyes around slyly. He observed the people gaped and goggled at him. His heart bounded with glee, but he maintained a sullen look.

Kendre stepped forward and pointed at Tatya's attire. "Pandu pounded him black and blue, tore his clothes and threatened to kill him," he declared before the crowd.

The people stared in disbelief and looked at each other. Many felt their hearts thumping with joy, but they suppressed their emotions and hung on to learn more.

Shoba recovered from the shock and stepped forward. "I don't believe what you say," she protested at the allegations, hurling her hands over her hips.

Gangaram held her arm, drew her back and motioned her to silence.

Kendre pouted his lips and frowned. He looked up at the crowd and pointed at them. "I wish to know if anyone of you witnessed what happened?" he questioned.

The gathering remained silent.

Kendre curled his lips with contempt, and then glared at Shoba. "There appear no witnesses so you must believe what you see and hear," he claimed, motioning Tatya to speak.

Shoba interrupted, "why should we believe him?" reasoned Shoba.

Kendre stiffened his face and gnashed his teeth. "Because I say so and I am a policeman," he dawdled, and then stabbed his finger to his lips. "Shut up! Hear him out!" he ordered, and then gestured Tatya to talk.

Tatya nodded his head and shot a sly look at the audience. "He beat me all over. See," he showed his face and pointed to his nose, eyes, lips and cheeks. He twisted and showed his shoulder and flicked his rumpled shirt.

Shoba rolled her eyes upwards and took a deep breath. "I can see it, but there must be some provocation, if you are right, because, of late, you complain about the tube well. Besides, I need to hear Pandu's version of the story," she snorted.

The crowd nodded in consent.

Tatya's face dropped, as he squirmed on his heels. He hesitated and looked at Kendre, who slammed his foot on the ground.

"Damn the story! Pandu raped Sushma and Tatya tried to save her so Pandu beat him up," snapped Kendre, staring at the crowd.

The gathering stood stunned.

Gangaram's heart vaulted to his mouth and choked his voice. He felt his head reel under a hammer; he staggered and dropped on his charpoy bewildered. Shoba's face scrunched and her heart sank, while Jija and Kamla looked at each other, unable to comprehend the situation.

Shoba sifted her sight on Tatya and observed him cock a wry smile. His face displayed guile and his eyes betrayed what he said. She smelled mischief and shook her head in disbelief.

Tatya observed the reaction of the people and his confidence soared. He straightened up and cocked a snoop at the gathering. "Why does everyone here keep quiet?" he questioned; his words laced with arrogance and his heart brimming with joy.

The silence hinted that Pandu remained at large.

He flung his hands over his hips, glaring at Shoba. "Tube well. Huh," he scoffed at Shoba, pointing at the gathering. "The village knows that if I loose a little water, it will not make me poorer," he bragged, as he dropped his hand. He gloated at Shoba. "The truth stays. I fought hard to save Sushma's honour," he boasted; his eyes squinted and a wry smile dangled on the corner of his lips as he harangued. "The village knows that he played around with you before he married you. Now he seems to have forsaken you," he jeered, casting about his sight. He pointed at Kamla and Jija and looked at the crowd. "This family encouraged him, because they knew that no girl would ever marry a revolutionary like Pandu," he alleged, arching a sly brow.

"Rubbish! Stop these accusations!" Shoba objected; her eyes burned with rage and body trembled. "My husband will never do a thing like that," she defended, shaking her head. The thought bolted across her mind like lightning and struck her heart, which melted and streamed down her eyes in tears. She clenched her fists, stiffened her face and glared at Tatya. "Vile men like you sniff around for helpless women!" she ranted, and then pointed to the crowd. "The village knows that your wife dumped you, because you visit Kanta."

The crowd giggled.

Tatya wriggled at the sight and intervened. "Shut up," he stuttered, with a crumpled face and blinked.

"Keep your bloody mouth shut!" Kendre yelled at Shoba.

"Why don't you stop Tatya, from making allegations?" retorted Kamla; she stepped forward and faced Kendre.

"How dare you tell me what to do?" questioned Kendre, with a gruff voice. He cast a glance at the crowd and watched a few faces giggle. The sight unnerved him and hinted that he must assert his authority. He set his eyes on Gangaram, who sat hunched over with his hands over his head. The old man appeared traumatized. Kendre clenched his collars, pulled him to his feet, looked him in the eyes and imputed. "Your son can't run away from the law!"

The three women rushed over, grabbed Kendre's hands and pulled to extricate the old man, who quivered. "Leave him!" they screamed.

Kendre released his grip and pushed Gangaram, who dropped on the charpoy gasping for breath. "Where is Pandu?" inquired Kendre.

"He's not come home," wheezed Gangaram.

Kendre sifted his sight through the crowd. "Has anyone seen Pandu?"

The villagers looked at each other hoping someone will come forward, but it seemed as if no one sighted him.

Tatya pried the crowd, sighed and snooped in. "Why don't you search the house?" he suggested to Kendre, with a gleam of guile in his eyes.

Kendre jerked his head and gestured to Tatya. "Go in and search the home," he ordered.

Tatya launched across, but Shoba stepped in and barricaded the door. "You will not step inside my home!" she warned, with her hands spread across the doorframe. "I don't want you to pollute my house."

Tatya cocked a wry smile, spun on his heels and addressed the gathering. "Did you see that?" he queried the crowd, and then laughed. "They hide him inside and this wench," he pointed at Shoba and continued, "prevents me from going in."

"Mind your tongue," warned Kamla; she stepped in front of Shoba and fortified the barricade. "You don't have the right to enter our home and humiliate us."

Kendre lost his temper, lunged at Kamla and slapped her across the face.

"Ouch!" Kamla shrieked, staggered and rammed against the wall. Shoba and Jija darted to rescue her.

"I'm the law and you cannot obstruct me from searching your place," thundered Kendre, with his hands on his hips. It appeared his khaki ego got the better of him and he failed to discern that the law did not permit him to assault woman. He snapped his fingers. "Tatya go inside and take a good look!" he commanded, and then signalled a man in the crowd. "Come here!" he ordered the man, who blinked and quivered at the prospect of facing Kendre.

The man looked sideways and hesitated.

"Don't you get what I say? Come here!" repeated Kendre, gnashing his teeth.

"Yeah," the villager gulped the lump in his throat and lumbered up to Kendre. He grabbed the skin on his throat. "I swear I haven't seen a thing," he swore, wiggling it.

Kendre flashed his hand. "Go inside and help Tatya search the place."

The man heaved a sigh of relief, and then staggered inside the house.

The women whined and failed to discern how to react to the situation, while the villagers looked curious and wondered what will happen next. In short, it appeared like an audience in a theatre on the threshold of climax.

Kendre looked down on the crowd, pointed his finger at them and shuffled it across. "I warn everyone, standing here not to hide Pandu. If you sight him, bring him to me. Inform the village," he proclaimed.

The crowd nodded in agreement.

Kendre proceeded with a stern face. "If I get to hear that anyone in this village sheltered Pandu from me. I will break his back," threatened Kendre.

"Sahib, Sahib," the searchers bursted out of the house with worried faces and reached Kendre.

"What's the matter?" asked Kendre.

"He's not inside," replied Tatya.

Kendre looked at the other man and jerked his head.

"No," he replied.

Kendre signalled him to leave and tapped Tatya's shoulder. "Don't worry, I will nab him. He can't go far," he assured Tatya, and then pointed to the crowd. "I've instructed the people to catch him and bring him to the chowki. Meanwhile, we'll go the farm and conduct a thorough search. Come along," said Kendre, as he stomped towards the jeep.

Tatya followed him and they hopped inside. The jeep wobbled down the road, reached the village square and took the main road leading out of Ramwadi.

Raghu, the Sahukar's servant boy, sat at the counter and watched the jeep whiz past the square. He got to his feet, dashed to Sahukar's home and broke inside panting. The Sahukar remained wary of the police ever since the police cracked down on moneylenders and arrested him. He instructed Raghu to keep a close watch on the police and inform him about their movements in Ramwadi.

The Sahukar lolled on his diwan and chatted with Vasu, who squatted on the carpet.

"Sahukar the police van zoomed out of Ramwadi," Raghu informed Sahukar, gasping for breath.

"Damn you idiot!" snapped Sahukar, glaring at Raghu with contempt. "I wish to know why they came to Ramwadi."

Raghu nodded his head. "I don't know," he admitted, with a blank face.

The Sahukar's face twisted and he felt irritated. He slammed his eyes shut and took a deep breath. "Go and find out," he dawdled, gloating at Raghu.

Raghu pivoted on his heels to haul off, when Sahukar called out. "Listen."

Raghu turned around.

The Sahukar added. "Stay at the counter and inquire from the customers or people loafing around the square. I don't want to hear that you left the shop to gather information."

"Yeah," replied Raghu, and then sprinted back.

Sahukar turned his attention to Vasu. He jigged his head. "What did I last say?" he questioned, trying to gather the threads of the broken conversation.

"The sale deed," Vasu reminded Sahukar.

Sahukar nodded, "yeah." He looked at Vasu and continued. "I don't want to cheat you. I wish to come straight to the point. I have transferred your land in Abba's name."

Vasu's face dropped. "What?" he blurted in surprise, and then blinked. "How could you do that without my consent?"

Sahukar raised his hand, beckoning him to listen. "I will explain what happened," he said.

Vasu shook his head in disbelief. "I transferred my land in your name and now you tell me that you gave it to Abba," he fretted, shrugging his shoulders. "How can you do such a thing? I just gave you one and a half lakh rupees, which I borrowed from Abba."

Sahukar interjected. "Will you listen?" he fumed.

Vasu remained peeved and his heart melted.

Sahukar proceeded. "I needed money for my legal expenses, because whatever little remained I gave on credit," he explained in a soft voice, pointing at Vasu. "You know that this draught has ruined all the farmers so none of my creditors, including you paid back my money. You should have given this money, when I needed it most," said Sahukar, pointing at himself. "I go out of my way to help farmers, but not one farmer stood up for me, when the police dragged me out of my house," he grumbled, as he shifted the blame to arouse guilt in Vasu.

Vasu's heart congealed; he pinched his throat. "I swear I didn't know, when the police came and took you," he defended his absence, and then dropped his eyes.

Sahukar watched him and his voice assumed a sarcastic tone. "Huh!" he scoffed, dropping his shoulders. "Everyone says the same thing," he moaned, twisting his lips. "They come to me, when they need money, but when I needed help, no one turned up," he complained, in a melancholic voice, and then looked away and watched Vasu from the corner of his eyes.

Vasu's gullible heart churned in guilt. He felt he owed an explanation and his eyes turned moist. He happened to cry, because he lost his land, but it now appeared his heart whirled in a pool of guilt.

He gawked at Sahukar, who gauged his dilemma and continued his guilt arousing babble.

He pointed at Vasu with a somber face. "Would you have paid for my bail?" he questioned, dropping his hand.

Vasu squirmed in his seat and blinked.

The Sahukar wrinkled his face. "You know what the lawyers charge?" he questioned, jigging his head.

Vasu nodded.

Sahukar went on in a sullen voice. "Justice has a price," he said Sahukar, flicking his fingers. "That's the reason I approached Abba. I do not carry all the money in the world on me, as the village thinks. Money lending stays tough. I too have my problems and Abba refused to bail me out without a guarantee, so he forced me to transfer your land in his name," revealed the Sahukar; he paused, lifted his shoulders and pursed his lips. "Do you blame me?"

Vasu's mind wobbled and his heart whirled and entangled his emotions. He remained bewildered and dropped his hands over his head. "I don't know what to say?" he conceded, slapping his forehead and weeping.

The Sahukar's heart leapt with joy at the sight, but he concealed his delight with a despondent look. Vasu stayed stuck in an emotional whirlpool, churning in guilt, despite the truth that he could not have done a thing, even if he saw the police arrest Sahukar. He stayed helpless.

Sahukar arched a sly brow, and then hunched over. "Approach Abba and request him to release your land," he said softly.

Vasu slapped his forehead and his voice squeaked under the deluge of tears that gushed down his cheeks. "I'm in a fix," he stuttered; his lips quivered, while he shook his head. "I borrowed money from Abba for Shoba's wedding and registered a sale deed in his name. Then, it so happened that I did not need the money, so I went back to Abba to return the money and reclaim my land. He refused to accept the money and insisted that I return it later. Then I came to you to pay back my debt and reclaim my land and now I hear that you have transferred my land in Abba's name. It means that Abba has all my land in his name. What do I do?" wailed Vasu.

Sahukar bore a cunning look and he relished the mood he designed with the intention to provoke Vasu. He sensed the time ripe and cleared his throat. "Huh," he coughed, spilling his intentions. "Why don't you go and file a complaint against Abba in the police station?" he suggested, in a wry voice.

Vasu shook his head. "How can I fight Abba?" he hesitated, with a crumpled face.

Sahukar scowled at the meekness. "The village will not spare me because I'm good. I spent a forthnight in jail and no one bothered to visit me. They take advantage of my goodness and complain, but with Abba, things look different. Abba lends money, but no one has the guts to point a finger at him. Look! What he has done to you?" riled Sahukar, pointing at Vasu. "He made you a landless peasnt. I too lend money, but I will never do such a thing, because I stay honest and clean in my dealings. Assume that I did the same to you. Would you hesitate to complain against me?" questioned Sahukar, with scorn. He stared wide-eyed at Vasu. "You would have dragged me to Court and shoved me behind bars," he deduced, and then smacked his lips. "But, when it comes to Abba, you put up an excuse and declare that you cannot fight him," sneered Sahukar; his eyes burned with hatred. "He stole all your land, yet, you fear to take on him. Don't you have dignity and self respect? I remember you once told me that you desired freedom, dignity and self-respect. What happened to your tall claims?" mocked Sahukar, curling his lips in contempt. He thumped his chest. "If he did this to me, I would not have wavered," he boasted, and then shook his head. "Nah! I believe that if a man is down and out, he must fight to the finish. Why fear Abba? Take him head-on. I will back you as I always do. You never turned up to save me from the police. Forget it and move on. I have a big heart and I forgive you, but it pains me to see what he made of you. He trampled your honour and reduced you to beggary."

Raghu raced in and then halted before Sahukar. "Sahukar," he gasped for breath.

Sahukar glared at him. "Damn you idiot! Can't you see me talking to Vasu?" he chided, jerking his head. "Is this the way to barge in and disturb an important conversation? Don't you respect Vasu?"

Raghu's eyes blinked and he looked puzzled. He failed to gather his master's sudden fondness for Vasu. He panted as he apologized. "Sorry Sahukar. You asked me to find out why the police came," he hesitated, wary of his master's foul mood.

"Go ahead," Sahukar nodded.

Raghu cast a glance at Vasu and looked ahead. "The police came to arrest Pandu," he hesitated, and then paused for breath.

Vasu wriggled in his seat, as if an earthquake occurred and staggered to his feet. "What!" he blurted bewildered and faced Raghu.

Raghu stuttered. "I heard that Pandu beat Tatya and Kendre Sahib came to arrest him."

The news hit Vasu like a bolt from the blue; his heart congealed and then melted into horror.

Sahukar's eyes twinkled and heart galloped; he slapped his knees and stood up in a huff. "Damn you unlucky brat!" he chided, storming towards Raghu and grabbing his arm. "You barge in with bad news. What happened between Pandu and Tatya?" he asked, with a gleam of guile in his eyes.

Raghu narrated the story.

Vasu shuddered, flaundered, sank on his knees and dropped his hands over his head. Sahukar's mood soared and his face lit up, but he creased his forehead to show concern, hunkered down next to Vasu, and gripped his shoulder. "Calm down," he entreated.

Vasu nodded his head.

"I know, I know. This village loves stories," he alleged, standing up in a huff. He seized Raghu's arm and glared at him. "Tell me the truth," he shouted, slapping him across his head.

Raghu cringed; his nose wrinkled. "Ouch!" he groaned and trembled. "I swear I heard what I told you," he swore, with folded hands. He rolled his eyeballs around and gulped the chunk in his throat. "If you wish you may ask anyone in the square."

Sahukar cocked a wry smile, and then released Raghu's hand. He pointed at him. "If it turns out a lie, I'll pull your tongue out of your mouth," warned Sahukar.

Raghu nodded his head in agreement.

Sahukar flipped his fingers. "Get going you curse," he ordered.

Raghu bolted out of the door.

Sahukar saw him leave and beamed. His face bore a crafty look, while his mind plotted a script. It appeared his stars favoured him and this news would strengthen his argument and convince Vasu to seek vengeance. He spun around, and then dropped on his hams. "I don't believe a word of what Raghu narrated. I smell a ploy to frame Pandu and grab your land. The village knows Tatya's character and maybe Tatya raped Sushma. I suggest you lodge a cross complaint against Tatya at the police station, but first find Pandu," he rambled in excitement, patting Vasu's shoulder.

Vasu appeared comatised. He stared with a blank face and his mind hung like a computer with many windows open. He appeared shocked, full of scorn, dejected, angry, disgusted, and alarmed all at once. His mind failed to figure out what to do and he suffocated.

Sahukar shook him hard. "Vasu you will have to react. How much more will you endure?"

Vasu shook his head. "What do I do?" he questioned, slapping his forehead. "I must visit Abba and find out."

Sahukar slammed his eyes shut. "Stop behaving like an idiot," he fumed, glaring at Vasu. He straightened Vasu, and then gripped his shoulders hard. "First protect Pandu. Damn it!" shouted Sahukar; he shook Vasu, who still appeared dazed. "You just heard Raghu say that the police wished to arrest Pandu. They will track him down, because Tatya and Abba must have poisoned their ears. They will hound him."

Vasu's eyes widened and he trembled in Sahukar's hands. "No, no. It cannot happen," he hesitated; his voice quivered and he shuddered. "Please help me."

Sahukar held him tight, and then whispered in his ears. Vasu nodded, "Hmm, hmm, hmm," he murmured, with a stunned face.

Sahukar pulled back, and then jerked his head. "You get what I say, otherwise the police will cook a case and throw him behind bars," explained Sahukar. He cast a wry look at Vasu, who appeared to have gained his poise. "If you need money, then I'll lend you some, but I want you to act against Abba. First; he stole your land and now he framed your son-in-law. It's a plot to destroy you," he urged, rising to his feet.

"Yeah," Vasu agreed; he staggered to his feet and shambled out of the hall.

CHAPTER 30

▼

Pandu and Ganpat appeared frustrated as they waited for thirty minutes for a tum-tum. They lost patience and almost gave up, when they sighted a bullock-cart swerve round the bend of the main road. It appeared that Hira, who had visited the village, now rode back to the Taanda. Pandu and Ganpat explained the urgency and Hira agreed to help. The trio drove Sushma to the Government hospital at Ashti, which like every other Government hospital ran at will and refused to attend to Sushma, until the doctor returned from his field visit. The three men unhitched the bullock-cart under a banyan tree next to the hospital, sat down in a circle and waited for the doctor to return.

"I'll go ahead to Vithalwadi and file a complaint," proposed Pandu. He appeared anxious.

"I feel you must wait for the Doctors report and then proceed," urged Ganpat.

Pandu curled his hands over his knees. "The doctor may arrive late, but I need to move on and inform the police to save time," reasoned Pandu.

Hira adjusted his eye patch and yawned. "I suggest that you first inform Abba and then proceed to the police station. The matter appears too delicate," advised Hira.

Ganpat nodded his head. "I think he's right."

Pandu's mind waivered and he looked confused. He sat with his chin resting on his knees and speculated, "I wonder where Tatya must have fled." His mind thought back upon the incident and he simmered with regret. "I should have killed him," he proclaimed.

Hira nodded his head. "You have a family to look after. Leave the matter to the police," he suggested.

"I said the same to him. He appears to hold a grudge against me," added Ganpat, with a frown on his face.

"Hey Pandu," someone called out from a distance.

"Lakya," said Pandu, who saw him coming with his daughter in his arms. "I wonder what he has to say."

Hira and Ganpat twisted around and saw Lakya hurry towards them.

"What do you want?" inquired Pandu.

Lakya cuddled his daughter in his arms and patted her back. "Stop crying, my little doll," he crooned to appease his daughter who cried.

"She looks ill," said Pandu. "Come sit down."

"Chicki's suffering from loose motions so I visited the private hospital but the doctor's away. So I came here," he replied, standing before the trio.

"You'll have to wait, because the doctor's on a field visit," said Hira.

Lakya's face contorted. "Seems a hard day for this girl," he said, dropping on his hams. He stared at Pandu. "I hope things have sorted out," he asked, stroking his daughter's back. "Stop crying, little doll."

Pandu looked at Ganpat and Hira and raised his eyebrows. "What are you talking about?"

"Kendre and Tatya came over to Ramwadi and created a scene at your house. Kendre wants to arrest you," said Lakya.

Pandu's face grimaced. "When did it happen?"

"I heard it in the village square, about half an hour ago, when I waited for a tum-tum to drive chicki down here," replied Lakya, fondling chicki and trying to appease her. "Just a little while and the doctor will arrive; my little doll."

Hira hunched over and whispered. "What more did you hear?"

Lakya narrated all he heard.

Pandu raged. "Damn the liar!" he fumed, clenching his fists. "I'll kill him for twisting the story!"

The little girl jolted in Lakya's arms and shrieked. Lakya interrupted. "Easy or you'll frighten her," he cautioned, stroking the girl. "My brave little doll," he chanted, caressing her back. The girl's shrieks tapered down to whimpers.

Hira grabbed Pandu's hand. "Stay cool and control your temper," he pleaded in a low voice.

Pandu snatched his hand away. "I'll pull that tongue out of his mouth!" he shouted.

"Ssssh," Ganpat put his finger to his lips and motioned Pandu to keep quiet. "You're under watch. Don't give yourself away."

"The village may not believe Tatya, but the police appear convinced. I think that we must approach Abba and tell him the truth," reasoned Hira.

"I don't think Abba will help Pandu. It's a question of his son's reputation," Lakya added; he patted his daughter, who appeared to stupor.

Pandu stood up. "That's the reason I want to go to Vithalwadi and report the matter to the police," he said.

Hira looked up and pulled Vasu's hand. "If Kendre's looking for you, it doesn't make sense going to the police chowki. He'll put you behind bars."

Pandu snatched his hand away. "I can't sit and wait, after hearing Lakya," he replied, and then pointed at Ganpat. "You should not have let him go!"

Ganpat's face scowled and he jumped up to his feet. "You still can't get over it can you," he snapped, facing Pandu. He stuck his finger in his chest. "If I didn't turn up, you would have killed Tatya and complicated matters for yourself."

Hira stood up and interjected. "Stop arguing over what has happened" he appealed, trying to douse the squabble, and then looked at Lakya. "What's the mood like in the village?"

Lakya rose to his feet slowly, with the little girl fast asleep, and then whispered. "I told you that the village does not believe Tatya. But you must remember that Kendre warned the village to report the whereabouts of Pandu, I fear someone will inform him; gamblers and drunkards, who wish to please the police," cautioned Lakya, walking away. "I need to lay her somewhere. Take care."

"I feel that Pandu must not go to the police station," said Hira.

"What does he do?" questioned Ganpat.

Hira pointed at Pandu. "You keep away from the village, till Ganpat and I meet Abba. We'll see what he has to say and then get back to you," suggested Hira.

Pandu crumpled his face, and then shook his head. "No, I will not meet him."

"I feel that Tatya must have informed Abba and then gone to the police station and the police have acted on Abba's advice," conjured Ganpat.

"Hmm," murmured Pandu.

"We don't know, but Pandu will have to hide from the police. Assume Abba acted on Tatya's behest; he may change his mind after he hears our version of the story. We can then inform Pandu and take him to Abba, but if you go to the police, they will not hesitate to throw you behind bars," explained Hira.

Pandu bit his lips, and then jigged his head. He hated both the options. He flung his hands on his hips. "I will not meet Abba and I will not go to jail," he submitted.

Ganpat stepped forward, and then stashed his hands over Pandu's shoulders. "I think, what he says makes sense. You disappear first and decide. We will keep you informed."

Pandu rolled his eyes upwards, and then slammed his eyes shut. "Damn the complication! Where do I hide?" he questioned.

Hira motioned Pandu to close in. Pandu lent an ear to Hira, who whispered into it.

"Hmm, hmm, hmm, don't expect me to meet Abba, hmm, hmm, fine," Pandu nodded, and then pulled away.

"I'm going but don't forget to tell my folks the real story," urged Pandu, waving his hand and disappearing in the fields behind the hospital.

In the meanwhile, Kendre and Tatya searched the fields around Abba's estate and failed to trace Pandu, Ganpat and Sushma. Tatya suggested that they visit the Government hospital at Ashti; he reasoned that Pandu and Ganpat must have rushed Sushma to the hospital at Ashti. Kendre consented and contacted the police station to confirm if Pandu had reached there. Then the men drove to Ashti, which lay ten kilometres from Ramwadi in the opposite direction of Vithalwadi. The doctor had arrived at the hospital and summoned Sushma.

Hira rushed to the bullock-cart. "I've talked to the nurse, she wants us to carry Sushma inside," he said to Ganpat.

Ganpat hopped inside the bullock-cart. "I'll haul her shoulders and station her on your back. You carry her on your back," he suggested, clenching Sushma's shoulders to lift them, when the raucous sound of a jeep rattled the air.

"It's the police jeep," said Hira.

Ganpat looked up to see the police jeep screech to a halt under the banyan tree.

Tatya hopped out, waved out to the men and raced towards the bullock-cart. He looked nervous and confused. "What's the matter? Did you visit the doctor? Did you reveal anything to him?" he gasped, snooping down on Hira and Ganpat. His eyes sneaked around and face dropped at the sight of Sushma. "Where is Pandu?" he stuttered, with his lips quivering and glazed at Hira. "What are you doing here?"

Hira and Ganpat noticed his behaviour and looked at each other.

Hira stepped forward. "The doctor will examine Sushma shortly," he replied, scratching his stubble. "Hmm . . . he has just arrived . . . ," stuttered Hira.

Tatya twisted his head and then shot a glance backwards. He observed Kendre closing in; he turned about to face Hira. "Leave the body here. Let Kendre examine it," he gasped, shooting a sly look at Ganpat. "Where is Pandu?" he whispered.

Kendre arrived at the scene, examined Sushma's body and glared at Hira. He shifted his sight on Ganpat, stared at him and inquired. "Who amongst you witnessed what happened?"

Ganpat and Hira looked at each other.

Tatya interposed in haste, "none of them saw what happened," he spoke slowly, leering at Ganpat.

"Let them explain," Kendre asserted in a gruff voice, and then jerked his head to signal them to talk.

"Huh," Tatya swallowed the lump in his throat and sputtered. "I told you that Ganpat came over to save me, when Pandu pinned me to the ground and threatened to kill me."

"Do you agree with what Tatya says?" Kendre questioned, with his eyes fixed on Ganpat.

Ganpat squirmed, and then looked at Tatya, who jerked his head and glared at him. Ganpat gawked and his voice choked with fear.

"Can't you hear me?" Kendre yelled in anger.

Ganpat cringed and stayed dumbfounded.

Tatya walked up to Ganpat. "Don't fear Pandu, come on speak out and tell Sahib that Pandu pinned me down and threatened to kill me. You saw it didn't you?" he suggested, winking at Ganpat.

The servant in him showed up; Ganpat wilted under pressure and nodded his head. "Yeah," he stuttered.

Tatya swirved around, and then faced Kendre. "He seems terrorized by Pandu. I told you that Pandu's a tough junglee," he added the last sentence to provoke Kendre.

"Damn the swine! I'll teach him a lesson for life!" howled Kendre. His sight caught Hira; his brows bumped together in a scowl. He looked at him with suspicion. "What about Hira?" he questioned, and then recalled with squinted eyes. "If I gather correctly, he finds no mention in the FIR."

Hira quivered and dropped his eyes.

Tatya interrupted, "he was not present when all this happened," his voice hesitated, while his mind tried to fix the puzzle in the slot.

"Why does he not speak?" Kendre questioned, grabbing Hira's shoulder and staring down on him. "I reckon you know all."

Tatya's face wrinkled; he looked at Ganpat in fear, pointing at Hira to ascertain if Hira knew what happened. Ganpat stayed dumdfounded. Tatya's heart pounded with fear; he intervened to contain the damage.

"He . . . ," Tatya barged in, when Hira opened his mouth simultaneously. "I . . . ," he paused, on hearing Tatya.

Kendre straightened the confusion. "He's talking. I want to hear him speak," he demanded, shaking Hira's shoulder.

Tatya shuddered, shut his eyes and nodded his head in despair.

"What are you waiting for? Talk," pursued Kendre.

Hira gulped the saliva down his dry throat. "I rode on my bullock-cart down the road, when I saw the two of them wave out to me. I stopped and they insisted that I take Sushma to the hospital."

Kendre interjected, "you said two of them, who two?" he asked, with a gleam of suspicion in his eyes.

Tatya twitched around and interrupted. "I told you that he doesn't know anything, because he came later," he stuttered, and then looked at Ganpat. "You must know because you held him. Where is Pandu? He threatened the police."

Hira and Ganpat appeared confused under immense pressure. They failed to gather their thoughts and speak freely.

"Where is that swine?" grunted Kendre.

Ganpat's mind seemed cloistered and burst out. "We don't know," he stammered, and then blinked.

"Damn the coward! He ran away after bragging about thrashing the police. He must have threatened Ganpat as well," riled Tatya.

Kendre's eyes squinted; he fixed his eyes on Ganpat. "You dare hide anything from me and I'll hang you upside down in the chowki," he howled, slamming his foot. "I suspect you are hiding something from me."

Tatya wriggled on his feet; he pursed his lips.

"The doctor's waiting for you. Come quickly. He will leave soon," said the nurse, who arrived on the scene.

Tatya heaved a sigh of relief. "Yeah, we will come soon," he replied.

The nurse walked away.

Tatya pointed to the body. "Carry it inside, quick," he ordered. Ganpat and Hira positioned themselves. Tatya arched a sly brow and took a deep breath. "Sahib will talk to the doctor and inform him about what happened," he declared, casting a glance at Kendre. "Is it fine, Sahib?"

"Yeah," nodded Kendre.

Ganpat hunched over to haul Sushma. "Sushma drank endosulphan and I found her lying in the cattleshed," he spilled the beans, and then stuck out his tongue.

Tatya's face lit up; his eyes twinkled. He assumed a regal pose.

"When did it happen?" inquired Kendre.

Tatya jumped in to add. "It must have happened when Ganpat held Pandu. She must have fled in fear and consumed the pesticide in disgrace," he looked at Kendre from the corner of his eyes, and then grinned. "Don't waste time. Carry her inside. Quick."

The two men carried the body inside the hospital, while Tatya and Kendre met the doctor and explained their version of the story to him. The doctor examined the pulse beat of Sushma and declared her dead.

"I'll prepare the medical report and give it to you. You can then carry the body back to the village," said the doctor.

"Yes Sir," said Kendre; he saluted the doctor and ordered Hira and Ganpat to load the corpse in the bullock cart and carry it back to Ramwadi. He then addressed Tatya, "accompany me to the police station to complete the paper work and gather the force. We'll then hunt down the criminal."

Tatya and Kendre clamoured into the jeep and drove to Vithalwadi.

CHAPTER 31

▼

Hira's taanda resembled a jumbo circus and comprised of a cluster of tattered canvas tents nailed to the ground. The canvas appeared a collage of ragged clothes and blankets sewed to cover the yawning holes, which dotted the tents, propped against bamboo poles fixed to the ground. The encampment perched on the dry patta, fluttered against the wind, which carried the clutter that emanated from the tents.

Vasu roamed around the fields in Ramwadi in search of Pandu, but failed to track him. His last hope remained the taanda where he hoped to pick up some information from Hira. He wore a gloomy look as he trudged through the rugged landscape late evening. The cold began to set in and bite, but Vasu's mind mulled over the events that transpired. His heart melted when he thought of Shoba's future. "What will happen to her?" he wondered, looking up to the skies. "Oh Vitthal, please help me. Spare my daughter," he begged the heavens, plodding through the dry land. He recalled the night he argued with Mangala and protested against Pandu's proposal. "Why did I relent?" he regretted.

"Ouch!" he howled, when his toe stubbed a stone in the middle of the path. He felt a current run through his spine. He shook his head and blinked. "I'm tired of running around this patta," he sighed, and then hobbled ahead. "How much more to suffer?" he pondered on reaching the fringes of the taanda and heard the cacophony that resonated from the tents. "Ouch!" he stumbled over a body sprawled on the ground and almost collapsed. "Damn these drunkards!" he exclaimed, gathering himself. "They'll lie here all night, till the police pick them up and throw them in jail," he muttered to himself, lurching towards the charpoy stacked in the centre of the camp.

"Hira," he gasped, approaching the centre of the taanda.

Hira, who reclined on the charpoy smoking a hookah waved out to him. "Come over."

Vasu shambled towards Hira, looking around furtively. "Have you seen Pandu?" he inquired, standing before Hira.

Hira sat up and rolled his eyes sideways. "Sssh," he shooed, with his fingers on his lips, motioning Vasu to take his seat.

Vasu wrinkled his forehead and his face paled. "What's the matter?" he inquired, plonking down next to Hira.

Hira inched closer to Vasu and spoke in a low voice. "I'll tell you everything," he said, twisting about and casting a glance over his shoulders. "I don't want the word to spread."

"Yeah," nodded Vasu, with his heart pounding fast. His face wrinkled as he lent an ear to Hira, who narrated the story.

Meanwhile, Kendre and Tatya reached the police station and found Sheikh, Bhosale and Kulkarni had arrived from their field visit. Kendre relayed the details to them.

Bhosale's face grimaced. "Damn this job!" he fumed, slamming the table with his fist. "We just arrived from a field visit and you want us to join you in tracking Pandu and the revolutionaries. I'm sick of this job!"

"I can't help it," retorted Kendre; he shrugged his shoulders.

Kulkarni, who sat reclined in his chair with his legs spread out rose to his feet. "Stop arguing and let's leave. We must not delay," he declared, tapping Sheikh's shoulder.

The group ambled out of the chowki, clamoured into the jeep and headed for Ramwadi. They first visited Pandu's home and inquired in the village, but failed to get a lead. Tatya suggested that they search the dry patta and adjoining areas so they decided to visit the taanda.

"Any short cut to the taanda?" inquired Sheikh, who steered the wheel of the jeep.

Tatya pointed to the road ahead. "If we drive down the dry river bed then swirve right and course along the dirt track we will reach the taanda from behind the village," replied Tatya, who sat behind Sheikh.

Sheikh narrowed his eyes, hunched over the wheel and peered. "I hope the road's big enough to accomadate the jeep," he asked, wary of the roads in the countryside.

Kulkarni nodded his head with contempt and yawned. "Damn the adventure! I suggest we take the pacca road that leads through the village square and get over with this ordeal," he argued.

Bhosale nodded his head. "He's right," he affirmed, twisting his head to face Sheikh.

Kendre, who sat next to Kulkarni and opposite Tatya squirmed in his seat. "It's pointless taking the main road. We will have to come back to survey this road so drive on quick," suggested Kendre; he tapped Sheikh's shoulder from behind. "Go ahead don't waste time."

Sheikh stamped the clutch, swapped gear and floored the accelerator. The jeep wobbled and clattered along the dusty road, with a trail of dense black fumes, which choked the air. Potholes and yawning ditches scarred the surface of the road.

"Damn these roads!" riled Sheikh, working the wheel around. "It's difficult to drive on them," he complained, and then decelerated and changed gear.

The convoy shuddered and almost died down on the edge of a pothole that criss-crossed the road, which lead down the dry riverbed.

"Drive carefully," warned Kendre, who sat with his hands clenched to the edges of his seat.

The jeep descended the riverbed at snail pace and rocked the crew like a cradle.

"It'll take years to cover distance on these roads," jeered Kendre.

The crew swung like a pendulum, when the jeep rolled down the descent. Dust seeped through the holes in the faded canvas, which covered the jeep and tickled the noses of the crew. "Huh, huh, huh," the crew coughed, fanning the air to ward off the dust.

The jeep bumped into a huge stone perched in the middle of the road and vaulted into the air.

"Ouch!" howled the passengers seated behind, bouncing up and smashing their heads against the iron grill, which supported the canvas.

The jeep crashed down in a crater in the middle of the riverbed and the tyres squealed.

"Ouch!" shrieked the inmates, bumping into each other and ramming against their seats.

Sheikh felt his spine rattle and his nose crumpled. "Boody hell! This road will chew my tyres to shreds!" groaned Sheikh, miffed with the spiked road. He gripped the wheel, decelerated, gently released the brake, pounded the clutch, swapped gear and floored the accelerator. The engine croaked and almost exploded under stress as it wobbled out of the monstrous crater and took to the far end of the tract. Sheikh blinked his eyes, and then shook his head. "I'm sick of driving this tinbox!"

Bhosale clenched the gripband, which dangled overhead and shuffled inside. His belly wobbled, like jelly as he reclined in his seat. "It's impossible to ply these roads!" he protested.

Kulkarni sat with a frown on his face. He looked fatigued and irritated. "Why doesn't the Government build these roads?" he complained.

Sheikh laughed. "The netas promise to build them when the elections come but do nothing later," he said, with a scorn on his face.

Kendre stared at Tatya. "You can surely bring political pressure on them," he proposed, rocking on his seat.

Tatya rolled his eyes about, and then looked away. "It will happen this summer," he stuttered, and then cleared his throat. "Huh! Huh!"

"Why wait for the summer? It can happen now," asked Kulkarni.

Kendre bounced and slithered to the edge of his seat. "Damn this ride," he ranted, slipping back. "They start laying and repairing roads in summer so that the rains devour the roads and they float tenders again and make money each year."

Suddenly, Sheikh slammed the brake to avoid crashing into a pit. The tyres screeched and the body almost broke loose and flew over the axles of the jeep. The crew jolted, tossed about and rammed against their seats.

"You'll kill us all!" howled Kulkarni, holding his back.

Sheikh landed back in his seat and grabbed the gear. "Can't help it," he admitted, and then changed gear. He wheeled around the pit, slithered to the edge of his seat and shot a glance downwards. "It's a pothole big enough to break our backs," he mocked, slipping back.

"Thank God, they have no speed breakers on this track," jeered Kendre, bouncing up and down on his seat.

Sheikh swirled the jeep around a bend, and then jigged the beamer for a closer beam. "Why do you need speed breakers, when you have so many natural back breakers?" lampooned Sheikh.

"Ha! Ha! Ha!" cackled the men.

"Beep! Beep!" the wireless beeped.

"Answer it," ordered Bhosale.

Kulkarni picked up the receiver. "Sir, we're in Ramwadi combing the outskirts for the suspects. Hmm, hmm, hmm, hmm. Yes, yes we have a lead. Hmm, hmm, hmm. Over and out," he concluded, and then hung up.

"What's the command?" inquired Bhosale.

"The same old crap they ask: what's taking so long? The home department wants results! Arrest the revolutionaries immediately!" blabbered Kulkarni.

Kendre slapped his knees. "It's easy to pass orders, sitting in the head office. Let them come on a field visit and drive on this road. They'll understand our difficulties," snapped Kendre, with a scrunched face. "Just look at this rust we're driving in and the road we're plying and the Government wants results in a jiffy."

Kulkarni stifled a yawn. "I'll break that Pandu's back the moment I get to lay my hands on him. He's the cause of this trouble," he alleged.

"Don't get worked up. It is a routine call. We're doing our best," said Sheikh, trying to pacify his angry colleagues.

"We're almost there," said Tatya, pointing to the cluster of canvas tents, fluttering against the wind.

"Thank God," said Sheikh, swapping roads. He bent over the wheel to get a better view of the road and floored the accelerator. The vintage roared and raced along the dry terrain. He tickled the dimmer for a high beam. "It isn't working!"

"Nothing's working! I wonder how we reached this far?" lampooned Kulkarni.

The jeep headed for the taanda.

Hira finished narrating the story to Vasu. "I went over to Abba's place but failed to meet him. I'll speak to him in the morning," said Hira.

Vasu regained poise after he heard Hira, but the fear of the law haunted his mind. "If we delay the police will reach him. I wish to go to the talav and meet him," Vasu insisted, jumping to his feet.

Hira grabbed his arm. "Don't go there. I'll go," said Hira. He stood up, preened himself and twirled his moustache. "He must be hungry."

Vasu nodded his head and volunteered. "I'll go home and bring some food for him."

Hira straightened his eyepatch. "You need not go all the way to the village, because it'll consume time and create suspicion. You know how news travels around here. I'll take some food from my home and inform him that you met me," suggested Hira.

Vasu motioned him to wait, and then whispered in his ears. "I have some money," he said, shoving his hands in his pockets. "Pandu may need it," he assumed, yanking out a few notes. He held Hira's palm and crammed the notes on it. "Give these to Pandu."

"Yeah," nodded Hira; he closed his fist and stuffed the notes in the pocket of his vest.

Vasu's eyes turned moist. "Tell him not to worry," he broke down.

Hira patted Vasu on his back. "This is not the time to cry. I will meet him and we will work out something," consoled Hira.

Vasu wiped the tears. "You come to the village in the morning and we'll meet Abba," he said.

"Hmm," murmured Hira, whirling around to leave.

"Police! Police!" someone shouted, bumping into Hira.

Hira lost his balance and crashed on the ground, while the man scrambled on, flashing his hand and alerting the camp.

"Damn it!" yelled Hira, while Vasu shuddered as he hunched over and helped Hira to his feet.

The jeep trailed the man and halted in the centre of the taanda with its headlights on.

"Damn the cops! What do they want?" snapped Hira; he raised his arms to screen the light shining on his face.

Vasu froze in terror.

The lights died down when the engine shut. The cops alighted from the jeep and charged towards the charpoy.

"Have you seen Pandu?" inquired Kendre; he stood before Hira and glared at him. The other cops encircled the two men, and then looked around to survey the taanda.

"I haven't seen him. I delivered the dead body at the village and came over," stuttered Hira.

Tatya caught up from behind, and then pointed at Vasu. "This is Pandu's father-in-law," he stated, with a wry smile.

Bhosale raised his eyebrows. "I smell a conspiracy. What's he doing in your company?" asked Bhosale, pouring his eyes over Vasu. "Have you conspired to hide Pandu from the law?"

Hira's face dropped, but he managed to control his nerves. He nodded his head. "No Sahib," he replied, bowing before the cops. He pointed at Vasu and declared. "Vasu happened to pass by so he stopped over."

Kendre wrinkled his face. "Thu," he spat on the ground, and then hurled his hands over his hips. "Don't give us that shit! We can smell a lie!"

"Where did you hide that terrorist?" quizzed Bhosale; he grabbed Vasu by the scruff of his collars.

Vasu's face dropped and he wriggled with fear. "I don't know a thing," he hesitated, with a lump in his throat.

Kulkarni, who stood behind Vasu raised his leg and kicked Vasu in the butt.

"Ouch!" screamed Vasu.

"He needs more of this to talk," shouted Kulkarni; he pursed his lips and frowned. "He's spoilt the night and forced us down in that rust. I'm sick of these goons," he complained, kicking Vasu again.

"Ouch!" shrieked Vasu; he squirmed and grabbed his buttocks. Bhosale shoved him away; Vasu staggered, and collapsed. The cops booted him indiscriminately.

"Ouch! Ouch! Ouch!" Vasu screamed for mercy. He curled his legs, hunched over and screened his face to ward off the blows.

The cops stopped for a breather.

Vasu continued to beg for mercy. "Spare me Sahib. I swear I don't know a thing," he wept.

Tatya beamed and his heart jumped with joy. He enjoyed the spectacle and interjected. "Pandu brags about killing policemen. He dare challenge the cops."

Kendre's anger reignited and he clenched his fists. "His son-in-law says that he gives us a damn," gasped Kendre. His face reddened; he lost control and booted Vasu in the back. "He can't hide from us!"

"Ouch!" Vasu squeaked, going dizzy in the head. He groveled with pain and gasped for breath.

"Stop the tamasha and tell us where is Pandu?" screamed Kendre; he raised his leg to kick again, but Bhosale intervened and pushed him aside. "Leave him or he'll die," cautioned Bhosale.

Kendre fumbled, and then gathered himself. "Swine," he screamed, dashing towards Vasu.

Bhosale and Sheikh barricaded him. "Control your self," urged Shiekh, but Kendre continued to forge ahead.

"He challenged us and declared that he has killed khakiwallahs in the jungles. I'll teach him a lesson!" howled Kendre, trying to wrestle his colleagues to break free.

Bhosale grabbed Kendre's shoulders. "He is not Pandu. You have lost your head. Stay calm. I'll handle this," he explained, twisting his head to face Sheikh. "Take him away and offer him a drink to cool his nerves. The overtime's killing him."

"Yeah," murmured Sheikh, and then dragged Kendre away. "Let's go."

Kendre dropped his hands over his head and racked his head. "I will go mad," he said, walking away with Sheikh.

Bhosale pointed at Hira. "Go and get some water," he ordered.

Hira stood bewildered and failed to catch the message. He strained his ears and asked. "What?"

Bhosale rolled his eyes upwards, and then slammed his eyes shut. "Get the hell out of here and bring water," snapped Bhosale.

Hira quivered and staggered off.

"Get a jug full of cold water," reiterated Bhosale, dropping on his hams before Vasu. He waved out to Kulkarni. "Kulkarni hold the torch to his face," he ordered.

Kulkarni lit the torch and directed the beam against Vasu's face. Vasu's face bled; his lips looked sliced and his forehead swollen.

Kulkarni stiffened his face. "He needs more of that. He will not talk easily," he griped, holding the torch overhead.

Vasu gasped for breath and appeared weak.

Tatya beamed at the sight like a sadist. "I'm sure he knows where Pandu is?" he alleged, with a wry smile. He arched a sly brow, and then pointed to his attire. "Look, what your son-in-law did to me," he showed, with the intention to provoke the cops.

Vasu tried to haul himself but he collapsed. He looked at Tatya. "You're lying," he stuttered.

"Damn you swine! How dare you call me a liar?" fumed Tatya, and then looked at Bhosale with intention to incite.

Bhosale motioned him to silence. "We'll take care of that, you keep quiet," he replied, standing up. He waved to Kulkarni, who shut the torchlight.

Tatya's face dropped and he nodded his head in agreement.

Bhosale turned around and cast about his eyes. "Where is Hira? What's taking him so long?"

Kulkarni squatted on the ground and sprawled his legs. "I'm tired of this job. I need to sleep," he complained.

Meanwhile, Hira ran helter and skelter to clear the mess in his fiefdom. He yelled from the top of his voice, "Stop the gambling! Leave the place! The police have arrived," he flashed his hand, storming into each camp.

"What's the matter? I'm not leaving," argued a gambler; he appeared adamant and drunk to the brim.

Hira stooped down and pulled the rug from under the cards. "Leave the place you bloody thickhead!" shouted Hira.

The man cringed but protested. "I don't see them around," he persisted.

Another gambler, who went out to relieve him-self burst into the tent. "It's the police!" he gasped, zipping his chain.

The gamblers snatched the money in the ring and fought over it. The coins rolled around and they groped about to trap them. Hira fumed at the mess, "get out you idiots!" he ordered, and then grabbed a man, who crawled around searching for money. "Don't you understand the urgency?"

The gambler dug his heels. "My money," he insisted, forging ahead on his fours to find the coins buried in the stampede.

Hira hauled him to his feet, and then pushed him away. "Get out!" he shouted.

The drunkard staggered, tumbled out and kicked the bamboo pole that hoisted the tent. The tent collapsed over the heads of the gamblers, entangling them.

"Damn the swine!" exclaimed Hira, wriggling under the canvas.

The other men trapped under the canvas groped about to break free. They squeaked and squirmed around for breath. "Huh! Huh!"

they snorted, kicking about and flashing their hands around to extricate themselves.

Kendre and Sheikh reached the scene of turmoil.

"Damn these gamblers!" blurted Sheikh; he hunched over and surveyed the muddle.

"Kick them hard," suggested Kendre; he drew his leg back and rammed it into the canvas.

"Ouch! Ouch!" groaned the gamblers.

Hira begged for mercy, "Sahib it's me, don't hit," he pleaded.

"Get out you blind son of a gun!" shouted Sheikh, pulling the canvas from over Hira's head.

Hira breathed a sigh of relief and straightened the eye patch over his eye. He folded his hands and apologized. "Sorry Sahib, the tent collapsed over our heads."

Kendre's face frowned. "What are you doing in here?" he inquired.

"Bhosale Sahib sent me to get water," stuttered Hira.

"Damn the water! Go and get us something to drink!" ordered Kendre.

"Yeah," nodded Hira, standing up and dusting his back.

Kendre stared at him, and then flicked his fingers. "Get going!" he snapped.

Hira shambled away.

Suddenly, a gambler rolled out of the canvas onto Kendre's boots. "Get up you bloody dog!" yelled Kendre.

The man reeked of liquor and failed to discern the cop. He blinked, pointed at Kendre and his words faltered. "Who the hell are you?" he swaggered.

Kendre's blood boiled; he kicked him in his ribs.

"Ouch! Ouch!" squeaked the drunkard; he sprawled on the ground and groveled in pain.

Kendre bent over and grabbed his collars. "Do you need more introductions?" he scorned, hauling the emaciated man to his feet. The man hung in the air and fluttered, as if a laundered cloth pinned to dry. Kendre released him, and he slumped on the ground, like a sack of potatoes.

Sheikh sat on his hams, dug his hands inside the man's pockets and yanked out a wad of notes.

"Ha! Ha! Ha!" he cackled, tucking the notes in his pocket. "Wow ! What a prized catch!"

Kendre's eyes glimmered. "Let's frisk these gamblers for money," he suggested.

"Hmm," murmured Sheikh.

The two cops rummaged through the gamblers pockets for money.

Meanwhile, Bhosale tired of the wait sent Kulkarni to fetch water. Kulkarni brought a jug of cold water and handed it to Bhosale, who poured some water over Vasu's head.

"Do you wish to drink some water?" asked Bhosale.

Vasu nodded his head, cupped his hands and gulped the water that Bhosale poured out. Vasu felt a relief from the dehydration that sucked him dry.

"How do you feel?" asked Bhosale.

Kulkarni overlooked the spectacle with disdain. He twitched about and interrupted. "He's bound to feel good. Just drag him to the police station and make him talk. I'm tired," he fretted, and then twisted his lips. "Huh!"

Bhosale stared down at Vasu. "Now tell us, where is Pandu?"

Vasu pinched his throat and swore, "I swear, I have no idea," he spoke with difficulty.

Bhosale got irritated and slammed his eyes shut. "Don't waste our time or you'll wet your pants!" he warned, gripping Vasu's throat.

"Huh! Huh!" Vasu struggled for breath; his legs and hands fluttered and his eyes went red.

"Drag him to the police station and shove a baton up his ass. He'll start talking," raged Kulkarni.

Bhosale released the throttle, hauled Vasu to his feet, handcuffed him and pushed him towards the jeep.

Kendre and Sheikh arrived on the scene.

"Has he given any information?" inquired Kendre.

"Not yet," replied Kulkarni.

"You shouldn't have stopped me. I would have thrashed the truth out of him," bragged Kendre.

"Where the hell were you?" shouted Bhosale, when he spotted Hira, crouching behind Sheikh.

"He was with us," replied Sheikh.

"I asked him to fetch water," complained Bhosale.

"Forget it. We have something better to offer you," said Sheikh; he pointed at his breastpocket and winked.

Hira emerged from behind and folded his hands. "Sahib, I pay you your regular hafta. If you turn up like this my business will suffer," he muttered, unhappy with the raid. He rolled his eyes sideways, and then wrinkled his face. "I swear, Vasu is innocent," he entreated, when he saw Vasu handcuffed, and dragged to the jeep.

Bhosale's face stiffened. "Damn your hafta!" he ranted, slamming his foot. He gnashed his teeth and grunted. "We can come and go at will. Who the hell are you to question us?" shouted Bhosale. He stomped towards Hira, and then stuck his finger on Hira's chest. "Don't abett terrorists and offer shelter to fugitives or I'll throw you behind bars. You get what I say!"

Hira looked down, and then nodded his head.

Bhosale whirled around and followed his colleagues who shoved Vasu in the jeep. They hopped inside and drove away.

CHAPTER 32

▼

ordering Gadchiroli, and next to the river Indravati that divides Maharashtra and Chattisgarh, stands a dense forest in which the rays of the sun barely kiss the ground. The floor of the forest resembles a carpet of withered sal, mahua, teak and bamboo leaves that rustle, when lizards slither underneath. Red ants dig out mud and pile it on earth mounds, lying scattered on the ground. A fragrance of mud, wood, leaves, flowers and fruits drifts across the jungle, tossing the white clouds, which hover over lush green mountains, dotted with white streams of water spouting downhill. The mountains appear, as if patches of terraced paddy fields cut by Gond farmers, along the hillsides dotted with colourful scarecrows perched on them. The air resonates with the twitter of unseen birds, cries of animals, whistle of tall trees and clatter of drums, which the farmers pound to shoo away wild boars, elephants and bears that trespass on their fields. Monkeys hoot and jump around trees, while giant squirrels slither over trunks, sniffing and nibbling at the mahua flowers that hang from the trees. Butterflies of different shades flit around bamboo thickets, creating a riot of colours, and bees hover around the honeycombs dangling from treetops, while a freak bark of a sambhar deer and pecks of a woodpecker echo from the forest. This landscape, home to the Madia Gond tribes that inhabit the Bhamragarh tehsil of Gadchiroli, seems a virtual paradise.

In the middle of this dense jungle, sits a square patch of cleared land, with four machans, overlooking the forest and perched on trees along the fringes of the patch. In the machans, young boys and girls dressed in olive green uniforms, with guns slung around their shoulders, peers through a pair of binoculars and watches over the forest. Below these machans, a group of child soldiers sits on a tarpaulin spread on the ground and cleans their guns or mends their rucksacks, or learns ABCD from adult instructors, with a radio playing Gondi songs in the background. At a distance, along the rim of this square patch, five tarpaulin tents stand nailed to the ground, next to which, a few fighters tend to a pot of rice, cooking over the firewood, while a few women fighters ferry firewood from the forest to fuel the fire. Inside the tents, fighters not engaged in cooking and guarding, take instructions from teachers or stay glued to books. Whatever their vocation, all these fighters either wield a gun or stay close to a gun of varied types: •303 rifle, double barrel gun, shot gun, self-loading gun or AK47. In the middle of this square patch, a platoon of thirty revolutionaries stands in six files of five each, facing a commander dressed in a black outfit, with a gun slung around his shoulder.

"Comrade Number thirty!" shouted the Commander, with a gruff voice, standing upright with his hands perched on his hips.

Pandu stepped out in his olive green uniform, slammed his foot on the ground and saluted the commander. "Lal Salaam."

The Commander grabbed the stopwatch that dangled around his neck, and then adjusted the reading. "Ready, steady, go" he yelled, and then pressed the knob of the stopwatch.

Pandu bolted towards a ramp, ran over it and lunged into a ditch below. He seized a rope, which hung overhead, swung over the ditch and landed on the other side. He released the rope, charged towards a rope ladder that hung from a wall, gripped it and clambered up to a height of six feet above the ground. He paused to regain his breath.

The commander glimpsed at his stopwatch. "Hurry!" he beckoned.

Pandu leaped into a sand pitch below, staggered, gathered himself, dashed towards the second wall, climbed the rope ladder to ten feet above the ground and halted for a breather. He panted and wiped the sweat off his brow with his forearms, trudged nimbly along the wall, snatched a rope, which dangled overhead, swung over the third wall and dropped into a pit of soft mud below. He scuttled ahead, hopped onto a line of wooden logs laid on the ground, trampled across five logs, scurried to the drums stacked ahead, leaped over them and zig zagged through five plastic inverted cones stationed on the ground.

The commander flashed his hand. "Faster!" he goaded.

Pandu wrinkled his face and panted. He mustered all his strength, forged ahead, ascended an elevated stand and shouted back. "Number thirty," he gasped for breath, descended, sprinted another fifty metres to reach the commander and then crossed the finishing line.

The commander stabbed the knob of the stopwatch. "You clocked eight minutes and forty five seconds," he declared.

The company applauded Pandu, who hunched over gasping for breath.

The commander beamed. "Excellent. You have recorded the fastest timing," he complimented and then thrust his hand out to compliment Pandu, who reciprocated the gesture. "Congragulations," said the commander, shaking Pandu's hand.

"Thank-you," replied Pandu; he slammed his foot, saluted the commander and raced back to join the platoon.

"Attention," thundered the commander. "Take your positions."

The revolutionaries dropped on their tummies, and then tucked their guns under their chests.

The commander walked a few steps forward. "We must study the habits of the police and para-military forces and then plan our line of attack. They have the numbers and loads of ammunition, which we do not. In most cases, the police take routine routes or common ways, but we must always avoid these routes and especially roads built by the state. One of the golden rules of guerilla warfare states that you must create your own routes in the jungles and make the most of the dense foliage. When the forest cover appears scanty; lie down and move cautiously. Avoid firing in upright positions, unless, you have a tree or a wall or anything substantial to protect you. If you wish to advance in the middle of a skirmish; crawl on your elbows and if you intend to move sideways; roll on your sides. Do not run in the open without cover from your colleagues. These and many other rules appear in your manual, 'jungle warfare.' Read them daily, before and after your training," instructed the commander, overlooking the boys, who continued to lie still with their guns under their bellies. The commander pivoted around, and then pointed to the forest. "I want you to lie still for two minutes and focus your guns on the trees over there."

A faint breeze rustled the leaves of the trees, which lined the clearing and carried the rhythmic sound of water that gushed downhill, and plonked on the river, which meandered through the valley below. The lukewarm rays of the early morning sun nudged the forest, as the ball of fire appeared over the distant hills. A group of young boys and girls sat and watched the proceedings of the training camp.

The commander took a deep breath and then continued his lecture on guierella tactics. "A small force can maul a big enemy by employing guierella tactics. The core of guerilla warfare lies in ambush and subterfuge," he exhaled slowly, and then went on. "You must provoke, leading the enemies into the forest, and then encircle and ambush. The success of an ambush depends on how you position on strategic locations. This, in turn, demands the thorough study of the topography of the region of operation. You must study the maps and memorize the routes. Remember stealth warfare demands that you avoid a head on collision, and if it becomes inevitable, then try retreating inside the jungle. The jungle remains the guerilla's most loyal friend, because the guerilla knows it better than the paramilitary tropper. Most paramilitary troppers change duty frequently, so they will not know the terrain. You must draw them deeper and deeper into the jungle, because your chances of victory will increase. Similarly, your chances of victory will diminish, if you choose to fight your enemies in open fields, because you lack the numbers and ammunition. However, if it becomes inevitable then you must never run across open fields. Drop down quickly and crawl on your elbows to advance and roll over if you wish to move sideways. Remember you cannot run without a guaranteed and competent cover so crawl and roll. Dalam number one! Get ready to move!"

Six guierellas crawled out of the platoon.

"Position," yelled the commander.

The guierellas lay still, with their fingers on the triggers.

"Fire," ordered the commander.

The guierellas pressed their triggers.

"Move, position and fire," the commander repeated the instructions, until the dalam advanced fifty metres.

"Roll right," instructed the commander.

The guierellas turned over.

"Good," said the commander; he then turned his attention to the platoon. "Dalam number two," he shouted, and then repeated the same instructions, until the entire platoon advanced fifty metres.

The commander then clapped his hands. "Stand up," he instructed. The guierellas stood up.

"Single file," ordered the commander.

The fighters formed a single file, facing the commander.

"Comrades and most esteemed members of the Liberation of Forests Army, who have gathered at the Kolamarkha forests. I take this opportunity to commemorate the martyrdom of our first revolutionary, Comrade Konda Ramesh, who on this day, 25 November 1980, laid down his life for the LOFA. He and his dalam of ten revolutionaries entered Gadchiroli from Karimnagar in Andhra Pradesh with the slogans: land to the tiller; land, water and forests for the adivasis; democracy for the poor and downtrodden.

'Within a few months of their arrival, another contagion of five dalams entered the Bastar region of erstwhile Madhya Pradesh to spread the same slogans. In this manner, our movement first started in the Dandakaranya region of India, with Bastar zone at the core. Presently, the zone comprises of the districts of Bastar, Kanker, Dantewada, Bijapur, Narayanpur, Rajnandgaon in Chattisgarh, and Gadchiroli, and its adjoining areas in Maharashtra.

'Presently; despite, the formation of the Chattisgarh State, our movement continues to spread, and we have declared this area, 'a liberated zone'. The Indian bourgeoise State does not exist in our liberated zone, except the para-military forces that patrol this area. This remains our greatest achievement, and the LOFA salutes Comrade Konda Ramesh, who risked his life and dared to sow the seeds of our revolution in Dandakaranya. As a mark of respect for this martyr we must all observe two minutes silence," said the commander.

The platoon bowed its head and stood still for two minutes.

The commander lectured on. "As a member of the Bastar zonal committee of the LOFA, my responsibility entailed supervising this combined intensive divisional training camp in Kolamarkha. Our Supreme Council; the highest decision making body of the LOFA, has decided to start a Company to operate in Gadchiroli and the areas around Indravati, which will resemble the Company, which commenced operations on 4 June 2004, in the Koraput region of Orissa. As you, all know, our organization comprises of dalams or squads at the lowest level, which operate in twenty odd villages. Presently, you represent these squads, which clubbed together, make a platoon, which operates over a larger area. The newly formed Kolamarkha Company will include the Gadchiroli and Indravati platoons. This new Company will conduct revolutionary activities in Gondia, Chandrapur, Gadchiroli and the three neighbouring districts of Chattisgarh, and will comprise of thirty cadres, which must increase to hundred cadres by the end of 2005.

'The Company's objectives include the following: educating tribes living in these areas about our class struggle, and the fundamental tenets of Maoism; seeking new recruits for our war against the bourgeoise state; engaging the police and other para-military forces in warfare, and guarding our shipment of arms and ammunitions, transiting through Gadchiroli. The intelligence wing of this Company will also have to investigate the reasons behind, 'Tendukheda desertions,' in which, many of our cadres surrendered to the police. Such desertions will have to stop, if we want our movement to spread. The Company will have to assemble here every two months, on a given day and report its activities. If the Supreme Council has any instructions for you, I will convey them to you. The Bastar zonal committee also decided to appoint Comrade Sameer, as the Company commander. Comrade Sameer remains a dedicated cadre of the LOFA, who served this organization for a decade and hails from Madhya Pradesh. He remains an engineer by profession and holds a doctorate in aeronautics, besides, having post graduated in political science and sociology. He also appears a well-read master tactician. I order Comrade Sameer to step out and take the oath of honour."

A tall, slim and dusky guierella, who appeared in his mid-thirties stepped out of the platoon. He slammed his foot on the ground, and then marched towards the commander.

"Raise your hand, and repeat the oath of honour," said the commander.

Comrade Sameer followed the instructions and took the oath of honour. "I, Comrade Sameer, solemnly swear in the name of the Liberation of Forests Army that I will diligently work for the cause of the LOFA, leading the Company justly, without fear or favour, and faithfully obeying the commands of my superiors, knowing fully well that any dereliction of duty will lead to punishment," he concluded, slamming his foot on the ground; he saluted the commander, and then shouted at the top of his voice. "Long live the forests! Long live the LOFA!"

The commander pinned a badge on his breastpocket, which bore the inscription: Kolamarkha Company Commander.

"Congragulations and good luck," remarked the commander, shaking Sameer's hand.

"Thank-you Comrade," replied Sameer; he saluted the commander, and then turned around to face his Company.

"Everyone raise your right hands and repeat the oath of honour," ordered the commander.

The guerillas obeyed and took the oath of honour. "We, Comrades of the LOFA, owe our allegiance to the Kolamarkha Company Commander, Comrade Sameer. We, solemnly swear to obey the orders of our Company Commander, knowing fully well that any disobedience will invite punishment. Long live the Forests! Long live the LOFA!"

"Dismiss," ordered the Commander.

The guerillas relaxed and waited for Comrade Sameer, who walked to them and shook hands with each of them. He reached Pandu.

"Congragulations Comrade," said Pandu, thrusting his hand into Sameer's hand.

"Thank-you," replied Sameer, looking at Pandu in the eyes. "I need to talk to you about the Tendukheda desertions. Come along," he said, pointing to a tent. "We will walk there and discuss the matter."

'Yeah," nodded Pandu.

"What happened at Tendukheda?" asked Comrade Sameer.

"Comrade Dinesh, our dalam leader, informed us that the police would visit Tendukheda. We thought, the police would engage us in another ambush, so we followed him to Tendukheda. When we reached the village, we waited on the outskirts for our informers to inform us about their arrival. At this point, Comrade Dinesh revealed that we would not fight the police. This shocked us and one of us asked him, 'why?' To which he replied that the police force wished to make peace with the LOFA, and that they would help us negotiate a settlement. We remained bewildered, but could do little, because he remained our leader. He then ordered us to empty our guns, because the condition stated that we meet the police unarmed and face-to-face. We smelled a rat, but did as he commanded," explained Pandu.

"Hmm," murmured Sameer. He creased his forehead, mulled over the narration and wrinkled his nose, as if not convinced with the happenings. He continued his interrogartion. "Did he ever provoke you to quit the LOFA?" he inquired, with a slight tilt of his head and lifted his shoulders in a shrug. "I mean, express any grievance against the organization. Show signs of frustration."

"He did complain about the injustices meted to him. He appeared sour about the fact that promotion eluded him, because he remained a non-Telugu. He hated the Andhra domination in the LOFA. Comrade Sitaramiah appeared the source of his frustration, and he constantly argued against LOFA's policy, which objected to the construction of roads in the interiors. I gathered that the road contractor, Waman Tikre wielded considerable influence over Comrade Dinesh, although, Comrade Dinesh once ordered his execution, but retracted after Waman agreed to pay more than the regular commission to Comrade Dinesh. It baffled us to know that Comrade Dinesh charged more money from Waman than the rates stipulated by our area committee. When quizzed, he replied that the area committee revised the rates and instructed him to collect money as per the new rates. He even permitted Waman to construct five new roads, into LOFA's territory."

Comrade Sameer interrupted. "What happened to Sajjid Khan?" he asked.

Pandu nodded his head and then raised his hand. "I'm coming to that," he assured, dropping his hand. "All the contracts went to Tikre's firm. Then one day Comrade Dinesh instructed us to kill contractor Sajjid Khan, because he alleged that Sajjid stopped paying ransom to the LOFA. Waman betrayed Sajjid and handed him over to us. Before his execution, Sajjid admitted that he paid his hafta to LOFA through Waman, who agreed to deliver the money. He also declared that he paid three commissions of the LOFA to Waman, but Waman denied Sajjid's claims."

Comrade Sameer nodded his head and intervened. "About this Sajjid guy, I want to know if you believed what he said."

Pandu nodded his head. "If you ask me, then honestly, I found Sajjid's defence genuine. Comrade Dinesh beat him black and blue, but Sajjid did not retract. In fact, he revealed how Waman violated the partnership deed between them, and failed to pay Sajjid the initial capital, which Sajjid put into the venture. Comrade Dinesh shot him dead and the matter stayed buried. Besides this, there appeared numerous such instances when Comrade Dinesh went all out to help Waman. He even helped Waman with arms and uniforms."

Sameer's brows bumped together and he interjected. "What's this new thing, I'm hearing?" he questioned, with surprise.

Pandu laughed, and then took a deep breath and exhaled. "We opposed him and refused to part with our uniforms and weapons, but Comrade Dinesh forced us to follow his dictat," replied Pandu.

"How many members in the dalam supported him?" asked Comrade Sameer.

"There were ten of us, but six were particularly close to him and readily consented to his demands. They lent their unloaded guns and uniforms to Tikre's hired goons. I was shocked, because it appeared a ridiculous demand. Later, I learnt that Waman used these to threaten a social activist, named Chandan, who had filed a complaint against Waman's brother, Sunder, who happened to run an Employment Guarantee Scheme. Waman hired the goons that dressed themselves like us and threatened Sunder and his family against pursuing the matter. The ploy seemed to imply that the LOFA backed Waman. Comrade Dinesh also increased the work-a-day tax to two days. Earlier, the LOFA charged a days labour from the tribals as compensation for higher wages for tendu collection. However, Comrade Dinesh increased the tax to two days. Many of the tribes protested, but Comrade Dinesh blamed it on the higher ups in the LOFA. In short, he worked to defame the LOFA and it culminated in that surrender at Tendukheda," said Pandu.

Comrade Sameer listened with rapt attention and continued to dig for information. "Did you surrender or were you tricked into surrendering to the police?" he asked.

"I had applied for leave to visit my village. Comrade Dinesh refused to sanction my leave, because he needed a replacement, but the squad area committee refused to send one, because as he always claimed, the Andhra dominated command hated him. I persisted for six months, but he refused to let me go. I also contracted malaria and dysentery and suffered physically, finally, I decided to run away within a week. However, the Tendukheda incident took place and the police came in full force. Comrade Dinesh took away all our weapons, and declared that we had surrendered to the police. He made us face the squad and declare the same. Four of us remained shocked, because we remained uninformed about this line of action. The police gave us an option, surrender or die. We agreed to leave LOFA, but not surrender, because that would invite trouble from the LOFA and give us unnecessary publicity. We feared that it would affect our family reputation and marriage prospects. We appeared lucky, because the police agreed to let us go, because they had achieved their purpose. The other six members and Comrade Dinesh surrendered, because they got good compensation. Waman Tikre brokered the deal, because he accompanied the police to Tendukheda," said Pandu.

"Interesting, information" said Comrade Sameer; he sneaked around, and then motioned Pandu to come closer.

Pandu closed in.

Sameer whispered in his ear. "Do you have any information about his whereabouts?"

Pandu pursed his lips, shrugged his shoulders and nodded his head. "I don't know a thing. Once we parted, I went to Ramwadi and never heard of him or any of our colleagues," confessed Pandu.

Comrade Sameer turned around and hauled his hands over Pandu's shoulders. "Can I trust you?" he asked.

"Yeah," nodded Pandu.

Comrade Sameer inhaled a sharp breath and exhaled slowly. "We received information from our intelligence wing that he works as a security officer for a coal mining company called, Coal India Private Limited, in the Tadoba-Andhari corridor of Chandrapur, but we don't bank on it. Because some say that, he runs an illegal coalmine next to the Tiger reserve, and operates from Nagpur. I think, in both cases, we will have to visit the Tiger reserve and Tendukheda to find him. I will supervise the operations personally so I want you to accompany me. You will join my dalam," said Comrade Sameer, patting Pandu's shoulders. "I need fit and swift fighters like you," he smiled and then dropped his hands.

Pandu mulled over what his leader said. "What do you want to do with Comrade Dinesh?" he asked in a soft voice.

"I haven't decided," replied Comrade Sameer, with a smile across his face.

"Do you hate him?" asked Pandu.

"I don't even know him. I want him, because I wish to restore our confidence amongst the tribes. If I want to recruit more people for my mission then I will have to prove that the LOFA did not sanction any of his extortionist activities. He systematically ruined the name of the

LOFA, and it appears a ploy planned by the Police. They could have made him surrender six months in advance, but they wanted him to defame the name of the LOFA and then surrender. It took the LOFA twenty years to build good will in Gadchiroli and the adjoining areas in order to win over the poor tribes. The bourgeoise state remained callous to the needs of the tribal people. The moment we stepped in we stopped the exploitation of the tribes at the hands of timber and tendu contractors, paper mills, forest officers, police and bureaucrats, and compelled the callous administration to react positively to the needs of the tribal people. Presently, the state accuses us of inhibiting progress and development of the tribes. This explains why the State provokes desertions from our ranks and lures our comrades with compensation. However, it will not happen now. We will get Dinesh and send a strong message to the police. 'We are back'," said Comrade Sameer.

"Comrade," Pandu hesitated. "I want to ask you a question?"

Comrade Sameer smiled. "Yeah, go ahead."

"Do you really believe in the revolution? I mean, will it ever happen," asked Pandu.

"You have to truly believe in something for it to happen. Keep working at it, because it gives you joy. It may not happen in your lifetime, but it will happen someday. When Comrade Kondu came to Gadchiroli and started this revolution. People laughed at him and called him a dreamer, but he stayed steadfast. He continued his struggle and died with the satisfaction that he fought for something that he believed in. Twenty-four years, since his death, the revolution continues to grow. Today, the state has deployed paramilitary forces in Gadchiroli to fight the LOFA. This proves the culmination of Comrade Kondu's dream. Earlier, the State never bothered about the plight of these tribals. Now, we have forced the state to listen and ameliorate their conditions. That is how dreams come true. The important thing is to believe in your dreams. A revolutionary must be a great dreamer," said Comrade Sameer.

A whistle blew outside the tent; Pandu saluted his chief. "Lal Salaam," he said, and then walked towards the cooking pots to grab his meal.

CHAPTER 33

▼

"Heaven has no rage like love to hatred turned, nor hell a fury like a woman scorned," wrote William Congreave. These words aptly described what a jilted Kanta reflected upon. Tatya may have thought that he dumped her, but she remained vengeful. The buzz in the village that Tatya raped Sushma and framed Pandu reached her ears and made her more restless. First, the woman in her put on a pretence. "It can't be. He loves me," she thought to herself. Like a typical woman, she possessed tremendous self-belief in her ability to lure any man she liked, but this self-belief bore doubts about the intentions of her lover.

She had waited for more than a month, but Tatya failed to turn up; his absence further fuelled her mistrust. She felt that the village hated Tatya, and always spoke ill about him, because he remained rich and powerful. However, the fact that Pandu disappeared reinforced her doubts about Tatya's intentions. In short, she resembled a classic case of a woman in quandary, because her mind and heart stayed at loggerheads and this confusion detterred her from acting decisively. She hoped that Tatya would turn up and give her the importance that every woman hankers after.

This delusion—if you may call it, forced her to stay optimistic, hoping for a miracle, without trying to influence the course of events. However, the news of her transfer rattled her and shook her out of stupor. Abba finally acted and succeeded in wielding his political influence to transfer her out of Ramwadi, because the politician in him knew that Kanta's presence in Ramwadi hung like a Damocles sword over Tatya's political career. The transfer crashed like a bolt from the blue and prompted her to act. The snub jilted her, but the transfer humiliated her. This disgrace further strengthened her womanly tenacity to cling until the end. She resolved not to leave and force Tatya to submit. Finally, the anger and vengeance, which simmered in her veins bursted; she exploded into Abba's chamber and boldly declared her intentions.

"Why have you done this?" she questioned, breaking protocol.

Abba, who sat in the chamber, chatting with his political workers, appeared shocked with this brazenness. He jumped to his feet; his face grimaced and mind baffled at the sight. "How dare you barge in the middle of an important meeting?" he fumed, quivering with anger.

Kanta's resolve seemed in no mood to follow decorum; she stashed her hands over her hips. "I've come here to demand justice," she bubbled, with anger and glared at Abba.

The party workers gaped at the spectacle. Abba cast his eyes about and sized up the situation. He realized that he could not afford a showdown before his party workers. He snapped his fingers, and then jerked his head. The party workers took the cue and shuffled out of the chamber.

Kanta twisted her lips. "Let them hear me out. Why fear the truth? Let the world hear it," she fretted.

A few of the men halted, whirled around and looked at Abba from the corner of their eyes.

Abba's eyes flashed and face flushed at the sight. He waived his hand. "Get out!" he shouted.

The men spun around and raced out of the chamber.

Abba looked daggers at Kanta. "What kind of justice do you seek," he queried, with a curt voice.

Kanta's eyes turned moist, her lips quivered and she turned hysterical. "Tatya has betrayed me," she nagged, curling her lips in contempt.

Abba cast a wry smile. "You lured him, with the intention of making money, knowing that he has wealth and power," he sneered, with a tinge of arrogance. He squinted in a sly manner and proclaimed. "I know woman like you, who always sniff around for quick money," he mocked in a haughty tone, and then dropped down in his chair. He took a deep breath. "But it will not work with me," he breathed out.

Kanta observed his attitude and raged. "Your son is no saint. He shares the guilt," she snapped. "Huh."

The wily politician laughed. "What happened is the past," he stated, squaring his ankle over his knees.

Kanta's eyes flashed and she interposed. "It may not matter to you; for me it remains a matter of honour. I will not cave in so easily," she warned.

Abba stiffened his back, flicked his fingers and looked away. "If it's the money you want, then quote the amount. I'll give it to you on condition that you leave Ramwadi," he proposed, in a haughty manner.

Kanta curled her lips in contempt. "Huh," she scoffed, glaring at Abba. "You cannot bribe me. Damn the money! He will have to accept me and I will not leave Ramwadi."

Abba squirmed in his seat at the affront. "Damn you wench!" exclaimed Abba; he hunched over and slammed his foot on the floor. "No one talks back at me in this village. You'll have to leave," he thundered with rage.

Kanta gauged the mood and sensed the irritation. "The village knows the truth of what he did to Sushma. You cannot shield his bad ways," Kanta snarled.

Abba's face contracted and his eyes blinked. He knew the truth and the fact that he had exerted influence to hush up the matter, but it simmered under the lid and Kanta made full use of it. The politician appeared foxed, but his ego persisted. "Damn the village!" he blurted, slamming his fist against the flat of his palm. "You worry for yourself. How much will you take to leave Ramwadi?"

Kanta smiled wryly. "It's no more a question of worrying for me," she retorted, pointing to her belly. "I'm carrying his child. Your grandchild!"

The news swept across Abba like a Tsunami and drowned his arrogance. He wriggled in his chair and quivered. So far, he assumed like most politicians that his power could control things and change the course of events, but this matter appeared complicated. He creased his forehead and reflected. "Tatya never said such a thing," he recalled, arching a sly brow. Yet, he knew his son and feared he must have concealed the truth. The sight bewildered him: a chamar girl carrying the genes of the most prestigious family in Ramwadi in her womb. For a moment, he went blank, but the politician in him trained to face any situation quickly recovered his poise and resisted. "You can't blackmail me into submission. I'm not the kind that you can fool," he pretended like an ostrich, burying its head to avert danger.

Kanta smiled wryly. "Whether you like it or not, you cannot hide the truth for long. The village knows that Tatya slept with me," she divulged, with aplomb and then fixed her eyes on Abba. "All it takes is a simple DNA test."

The confidence in her tone almost knocked Abba off his chair. He sensed the lid cracking over the Pandora's Box. He mellowed his tone and tried to assuage Kanta. "Why fight over this? I will give you whatever amount you quote to forget what happened. Why do you fail to understand that this bickering will lead us nowhere?" he reasoned.

Kanta knew her strength and persisted. "I don't want your money. Tatya will have to marry me. I'm not a piece of tissue paper that you use and throw away," she replied, remaining steadfast. "You can't use your power and money to intimidate me. I'm not the one to cower and cringe."

The rebuke threw Abba in a predicament. He weathered many a storm in his political odyssey, but this appeared a tornado, which threatened to uproot him and his family from the political arena. He understood the power of the Dalit community, which always united under these conditions. He also knew that the village hated Tatya and the people knew the ways of his son. The woman before him remained humiliated and looked vengeful. He stayed unsure of the claims she made, but the tone and tenor of her voice backed her allegations. Abba remained in a dilemma, but decided to talk tough and upped the ante.

"If you think you can threaten me with these insinuations; think twice. I am not the kind who will permit anyone to abuse me. All this while, I listened to you and tried to reason with you, but if you want a showdown then you have picked the wrong opponent. I have the entire system under my thumb. If you care for your safety then follow what I say. Forget the past, take the money and leave this village," he warned.

"What about this child?"

"Damn the child! Drop it! Get the hell out of here!"

"I will leave, but not before I get justice. I will take this matter to the police and the court. Tatya can't get away so easily," replied Kanta, storming out of the hall.

Abba slumped in his chair. He found it hard to take the humiliation heaped on him. "Damn the bitch! How dare she talk to me like that?" he thought back; his blood pressure rose and heart raced. He clenched his fists and gnashed his teeth in anger. He shut his eyes and nodded his head in disgust. For a moment, he felt like smashing his head against the wall. His sheer helplessness seemed the cause of his son. "Damn this idiot!" he uttered between his lips. The anger in him needed a valve, and he wanted to vent the frustration that choked his heart.

"Namaskar Abba," Vasu greeted him with folded hands and stood at the door.

"Damn this Vasu! I wonder what he has to say," thought Abba; he signaled him to come in. "What's the matter?" he asked, with a wrinkled face.

Vasu sensed the mood and seemed reluctant to say anything. He realized that he walked in at the wrong time, but he must talk so he shook his head and faltered. "Yeah," he murmured.

Abba twisted in his seat. "What do you want?" he grunted, flipping his fingers.

Vasu gulped the saliva down his throat. "I wanted to talk to you about my land," his lips quivered.

"What land?"

Vasu took a deep breath to summon courage. "The sale deed," he exhaled slowly.

"Damn your sale deed!" shouted Abba. He stared down at Vasu. "You pay back the principle and interest on the amount you borrowed and take back your land."

Vasu rolled his eyes sideways. "I am talking of the sale deed that Sahukar delivered to you. He says that you have my land registered in your name."

Abba raised his eyebrows and smacked his lips. "I see," he said loudly and slowly. He rammed his fist on the arm of his chair. "Damn the money lender!" he yelled, drew his leg up and stashed the heel on the edge of his chair. He placed his arm over his knee. "He owed me money and so he gave me the land. You have taken rations on credit and borrowed for your daughter's wedding. You need to clear all your debts. That's the deal isn't it?" reminded Abba.

"Abba please," begged Vasu; he fell on his knees and cried. "I have suffered for long. I do not know what transpired between Sahukar and you, so why drag me into it. What wrong have I done?"

Abba dropped his leg, sat up and placed his palms on his knees. "I'll give you a better deal, provided, you stop crying and listen," said Abba. He paused and then motioned Vasu to sit down.

Vasu squatted on the floor.

Abba smiled. "Good. Now listen to my offer," he demanded, slumping in his chair and pointing at Vasu. "You settle for a bataidari or thekedari with me. In either case, I will lease your land to you. You have loads of water running below your land so make good use of it and take a Rabi crop after you harvest the cotton crop standing on your land."

The offer shocked Vasu; his fears came alive. It happened all over Vidharbh; moneylenders swallowed the mortgaged land of indebted farmers. This offer conveyed a subtle message to Vasu; he had forfeited his land. He remained a lessee on his own land bonded for life. His face crumpled, he wept and pleaded. "It's my land," he cried, slapping his forehead in disbelief. "How can you do this to me?"

Abba sported a wry smile and his eyes glittered. "Of course it's your land," taunted Abba. He lifted his shoulders in a shrug. "Who says it's mine? You work hard, pay back the money you owe me, and I'll return your land," declared Abba, in a casual manner, as if nothing happened. He pointed to Vasu. "I've always cared for you. Have you forgotten the day the police picked you up and locked you behind bars? I spoke to them and set you free. I did not take a penny from you; also, I gave you rations on credit and the money for Shoba's wedding. When you wanted Bapu readmitted to school, I obliged. In fact, it appears as if only I oblige all your demands despite suffering heavy losses. I should cry; not you," Abba lamented, in a soft voice. He observed Vasu, who remained shocked and hurt.

Vasu nodded his head. "No, no," he gasped, weeping.

"Yes, yes," replied Abba, jigging his head up and down. "If you settle for bataidari, then both of us will bear the cultivation costs and share the yield equally. In case you cannot bear the initial expenses, I will pay your cost, charge interest, which you repay later. If you wish to settle for a thekedari, then you pay me a fixed amount per acre per annum. I will settle for two thousand rupees per acre, which for six acres of land adds upto twelve thousand rupees per year, so pay me twelve thousand rupees and do what you want with the land. You have plenty of water and can profit from it. Give it a serious thought, because I have other work to attend to."

Vasu cried like a child. His heart melted like butter over fire; it appeared he would go insane. He remained a helpless victim of a system which, entrenched itself in Ramwadi. For all the effort and hope to live a simple life of dignity, he seemed worse off then when he started. It seemed the freedom he yearned for resembled a mirage in the desert and his life looked doomed to endure. The grim reality of an Indian farmer stared him in the face. He remained a glorified bonded labourer, worse than the black slaves that toiled on the plantations in America. A farmer in India appeared nothing more than a living-dead: born in debt, lived in debt, died in debt and bequeathed debt to his progeny. Yet, it remained a cruel irony that the same farmer fed and clothed civilization.

Vasu dropped his hands over his head and racked it in disgust. He dare not annoy Abba, because he wanted Pandu back in the village. He must accept the offer, but after a hard bargain.

"What about Pandu?" Vasu asked.

Abba looked at him carelessly and replied. "What about him? What do you want me to do for him?" he inquired, in an arrogant tone.

"I want him back in Ramwadi. The police must not harass him."

"Hmm," murmured Abba. He glared at Vasu. "I don't want him to mess with my son. I will consider your offer, after you consider my offer," replied Abba, standing up in a huff. "I need to go," he excused himself, and then walked out of the hall.

CHAPTER 34

―――――――― ▼ ――――――――

Tucked deep inside the forests of Tadoba, Tendukheda looks beautiful, although, surrounded by coalfields and fifty kilometers from a thermal power plant, which feeds on coal supplied by "Coal Asia Private Limited," a multinational mining conglomerate that has secured many coal blocks in the region. Over the years, the Government made repeated attempts to evict the village, but the people refuse to vacate. The Madia Gond tribes, who lived here for centuries, depend on the forests for their living and call it their natural habitat. The coalfields have damaged the environment, threatened the existence of tigers, which live in this part of India and brought them in direct conflict with the villagers. The wildlife activists continue to press the Government to vacate all the villages near the Tadoba-Andhari tiger reserve to prevent a tiger-human conflict. Yet, the villagers protest and argue that the coalfields have caused this conflict. However, the coal blocks increase by the day and threaten to swallow Tendukheda, but the village remains defiant and refuses to evict. Whatever, the dispute, the village appears beautiful and the people continue to live in the midst of tigers.

On the fringes of Tendukheda, stands an old decrepit concrete structure called, "Vidya Niketan." The villagers call it a primary school set up by the Government to impart education to the tribal children of Tendukheda and a few neighbouring villages. However, the appearance of this school defies their claim. The name inscribed in bold black letters hangs illegible with some letters peeled off, and others blotched across the faint concrete plaster. The tin sheets on the fringes of this building look corroded and dotted with big holes, while the ceiling in the centre either caved in or seems never laid by a corrupt government contractor. The wodden skeletal frame that supports the ceiling looks moth-eaten, and ravaged by hungry termites. The walls of the school appear wrecked, with huge cracks opened in some areas that make it impossible for the building to stand, without the support of a divine hand.

The appearance of this dilapidated structure, makes it difficult to believe that it remains a school, because it resembles the ruins of modern civilization and not ancient civilization, because ancient monuments weathered the test of centuries, but this remains the vestige of a corrupt Indian civilization. Historians cannot name it an archaeological site because it symbolizes a, "corrupthaelogical site," and represents a modern marvel of engineering degradation built with slimy kickbacks and commissions paid to political rulers of the, "Great Indian Democracy."

If history must include something, it will record the valour and grit of the students, who risked their precious lives and dared to sit inside to take a lesson or two from the Indian education system. However, the official records of the State Government enlist this dangerous monument as a school so we will abide by the official records.

Early morning, the students gathered in the clearing opposite the school, waiting for the arrival of their schoolteacher, "Bapuji." A cool breeze gently tossed the leaves littered on the earth, while the faint rays of the morning sun kissed the ground beneath the childrens tender feet. A pack of monkeys jumped around the trees, which surrounded the school, while a mother in the pack picked lice from her infants' hairy body as he suckled her. Another little monkey stepped on her back and swung from one branch to another of a tree, which overlooked the roof of the school. Suddenly, he tripped, fumbled, lost his grip and crashed on the roof of the building.

The metallic din of the fall rattled the ambience, and attracted the attention of the children, who played below. They gathered down under and made merry of the spectacle; laughing and jeering at the young acrobat, who tumbled down the roof and almost fell down, when his hand managed to grab the ledge of the wodden frame that supported the ceiling. He now dangled in the air with one hand and feasted on the termites, which infested the ravaged wood. He appeared to enjoy his early morning breakfast, but the termites would not give in so easily. They swarmed his puny body with their numbers and stung him, forcing him to squirm and shriek in pain. He thought of jumping down, but the children below jeered him and he feared their presence. He tried to haul up, but the moth eaten ledge deluded him and the termites stung his arm and forced him to withdraw.

Caught in a catch 22 situation, he squeaked for relief from the termite agony and drew the attention of his mother, who wrapped her baby under her belly and hooted for help. The pack assembled and jumped into the war zone to rescue the suspended brat, but the children below threatened them so they spread out, gnashed their teeth and grunted at the children, who reveled in delight and mocked them.

The brat ached and screamed for help; his mother appeared anxious and wished to extricate her tiny brat, but the children below stalled her attempts. She jumped around nervously; her nostrils flared and she bared her teeth to scare the children, but they laughed and jeered at her and refused to budge. The mother surveyed the most dangerous monument in the world, and searched for a prop strong enough to hold her and her baby to cross over and extricate her brat, but her instincts seemed to hold her back. She watched helplessly, as the termites continued to swarm the brat and agonize him. It looked like a war of attrition to rescue a brat, who hung on the fringes of the most dangerous monument in the world.

Bandu the ringleader of the boisterous children picked up a stone and pointed it at the suspended brat. The gesture flared the tension, and angered the mother, who anticipated the assault and climbed down the tree; she shrieked and gnashed her teeth. The battalion took the cue and followed her. They closed down on the threat and it appeared that the count down would commence. A few of the children feared the monkeys, who snorted and shrieked in anger and took to their heels. Bandu and his gang dug their heels and challenged the monkey battalion. Bandu got a boost from his band, which egged him on; he drew his hand back to fling the stone at the brat.

Suddenly, a hand from behind seized Bandu's hand and snatched the stone. "Stop it," scolded Bapuji, who arrived at the scene, and then rushed to rescue the hanging brat.

Bandu's cronies receded into the background, while Bandu remained to face the music. Meanwhile, the brat seized the opportunity, jumped down and rolled on his sides to ward off the termites. The battalion dropped down, encircled the brat and feasted on the termites, which scurried for cover. They dusted the brat off termite agony, and then escorted him to the treetop.

The children assembled on the ground, and faced Bapuji and Bandu, who stood next to Bapuji, with a frown on his face.

"Why did you pick the stone?" inquired Bapuji.

Bandu stood silent, with his eyes to the ground. The teacher brandished his arm; Bandu baulked, shut his eyes and screened his face to ward off the blow. "Please don't hit," he pleaded for mercy.

Bapuji stiffened his face. "Look how you cringe and cower," he said and then dropped his hand. "Did you care to think what the monkey must have felt, when you threatened to hit him with this stone?"

"I swear, I aimed at the termites and not the monkey," replied Bandu; he pinched his throat and feigned innocence.

Bapuji cocked a wry smile and raised his eyebrows. "I see. Do you think this stone would have relieved the monkey of termite agony?"

Bandu kept quiet; his mind, trying to conjure a fancy answer. He looked around for a prompt from one of his cronies and hesitated.

"Come on. We want to hear you," the teacher persisted.

Bapu's face dropped. "Yes Sir, no Sir," he stuttered, racking his head. "Actually, I aimed at the wooden beam," he gasped.

"How would that save the monkey?" the teacher continued to interrogate.

"Hmm," murmured Bandu; he fancied a way out of the labyrinth. "The termites would fear me and leave the monkey," he gulped the lump in his throat.

The teacher insisted. "Why?"

"Sir, the beam would fall and drop the monkey," stuttered Bandu, and then blinked. It appeared that in an attempt to end the ceaseless interrogation, he decided to bring the monkey to the ground.

The teacher laughed, pointing to himself. "I just saved the building. Otherwise your stone would have reduced this mighty building to rubble."

The answer provoked a giggle, and forced most of the children to gag their mouths to suppress the tickle, which lingered on the verge of exploding. Others failed to suppress the tickle, which burst into a cackle. The guffaw appeared contagious and culminated into a boisterous roar of laughter.

Bapuji joined the banter.

Bandu heaved a sigh of relief and giggled.

Bapuji put his hand over Bandu's shoulder. "Don't be cruel to animals, because they too have a right to live like you and me. They cannot talk like us, but they communicate in their own ways and have feelings and emotions like us. They too have a heart and can feel the pain, so you must learn to live and let live on this planet. Today, I wish to tell a story called, 'The Bushman and the termites,' which will enlighten you and convince you about the importance of living in harmony," said the teacher; he sat down and motioned Bandu and the children to sit down. The children hunkered down with a twinkle in their eyes and Bapuji started narrating the story.

"Once upon a time there lived a Bushman, who headed a village in a jungle. The jungle appeared dense and full of trees, animals, birds, reptiles and insects, which lived off the jungle. It comprised of caves and a river, which flowed through the middle of the jungle. The law of the jungle prohibited the cutting of trees so the trees grew taller and taller, until two of them grew the tallest and towered over the jungle. These twins, which stood in the centre of the jungle and village, symbolized prosperity and overlooked the jungle around them.

'The villagers remained proud of their twin towers, because they symbolized might so the Bushman and the villagers declared the trees their totem. Every year in the month of September, the villagers gathered around these trees and worshipped them. They performed religious rites, paid their obeisance, and prayed to God to bless the trees and protect them. They then danced around the trees in circles and feasted. The roots of these trees went deep down into the earth to thousand feet and sucked out water and nutrients that nourished the trees. The trees grew taller and taller, while the roots went deeper and deeper into the ground and spread beyond the jungle. They sucked on the soil and water and fattened like pigs. Soon, they grew so big that they started to kill the undergrowth. The roots grew so strong that they mangled the other roots, overpowered them and crushed them to shreds. It appeared as if the trees hated other vegetation so the jungle gradually reduced to a thicket.

'The animals, insects, birds and reptiles struggled against the onslaught of the twin towers and lost their homes. The villagers got easy game and appeared delighted. They thanked the trees for the largesse. 'Thank-you for the food,' they said, bowing before the trees. However, the animals, birds, reptiles and insects complained. 'Let us live. We too have a right to live,' they pleaded before the trees. The towers mocked them, 'haven't you heard the jungle law-survival of the fittest?' bragged the arrogant trees, dismissing their pleas. The creatures then pleaded before the villagers, who appeared least interested in their fate, they continued their twin tower worship and pampered the towers.

'The roots grew bolder and attacked the caves in the jungle. It appeared they wished to display their strength. 'We'll cut through the caves,' boasted the towers. The caves made of hard rock seemed difficult to break, but the roots stayed defiant. They wanted to tear through the rocks. The rocks resisted and refused to let them in. 'Go away,' they cried, putting up a stiff fight. 'Leave us alone! Live and let live!' they entreated the roots. But the roots remained adamant and continued to bulldoze the caves. 'How dare you challenge us?' they shot back, and then continued their ruthless plunder. 'Just one more push and we'll break the caves,' they bragged amongst themselves and succeeded in breaking them down.

'The caves collapsed and released millions of termites locked inside them. The termites hated the arrogance of the towers. 'How dare you bulldoze our home?' they questioned. 'Shut up,' replied the towers. The angry homeless termites swarmed the roots and bit them. The roots felt the sting and howled in agony. The termites continued their assault and reduced the roots to rubble. They then attacked the barks and branches of the trees. The massive trees cried in pain and despite their strength, they appeared helpless against the termites.

'The villagers watched in shock and dismay as the towers slowly lost their leaves, branches, barks and roots. Finally, on September 11 they crashed over the thicket and killed half the jungle. The catastrophe unparalleled in the history of the jungle traumatized the people, who looked up to to their towers and believed in their invincibility. They gathered before the Bushman and demanded action. The Bushman's head reeled at the sight. 'How to react to this termite strike?' he wondered, but stayed under pressure of his peoples demands.

'His blood boiled and he reacted without reason. 'We will avenge the death of our people and destruction of our twin towers. I will retaliate and kill every terrormite. Small insects that live in caves have challenged us,' he mocked, with a wry smile and pointed to himself. 'I will smoke the terrormites out of the holes,' he thundered.

'Hurrah! Hurrah!' the villagers egged him.

'Bushy we love you!' they exclaimed with joy.

'The Bushman felt jubilant with his people behind him and declared his war on termites. He called a special session of the jungle parliament and addressed the jungle. 'I declare war on the terrormites and expect all to join this war on terrormites. I will not rest until all the terrormites die. I propose to burn the caves and smoke the terrormites out of the caves,' he bellowed.

'The leader of the panguins stood up and interjected. 'Why burn the caves and threaten the jungle? We feed on termites and know their hideouts. We can help if you want,' he reasoned before the Bushman.

'The Bushman cocked a wry smile. 'Huh,' he scoffed, slamming his fist on the podium. 'How dare you oppose my war on terrormites and assume it will threaten the jungle?' he shouted, glaring at the panguin. He pointed at the assembly and warned. 'If you are not with me then you are against me. There can be only two possibilities and no neutrals,' he fisted the desk again, and then pointed at the panguins. 'I will not permit reason to prevail over my war, so don't give me your suggestions. I don't need your help, because I possess the best firepower in the world,' he boasted.

'The panguin insisted. 'Please don't waste it. It may cause collateral damage. We will kill the termites."

'The Bushman's face reddened and his eyes flashed. 'Damn you panguins!' he riled, shaking his head in disgust. 'I possess the strength to destroy the world. I do not need your help. Get the hell out of here,' he snapped his fingers, curling his lips in conmtempt.

'The panguins bowed their heads and disappeared inside the jungle.

'Hurrah!Hurrah!' yelled the mob.

'Follow me,' ordered the Bushman; he whirled around and led the mob to the caves.

'He rummaged through his pockets, yanked out a matchbox, struck a match and brandished the flame before the mob.

'Death to the terrormites,' he shouted, setting the caves ablaze.

'Death to the terrormites,' repeated the mob, with their fists pumping the air.

'The flames spread out and devoured the caves. The villagers looked on, as the fire spread out further into the thicket. They failed to ponder and question the Bushman, whether he saw the termites in the caves, before he set the caves on fire. Their zeal prevailed over reason and they looked excited. The cave fires scorched the thicket for days and burnt most of the life forms that inhabited the jungle. The villagers cheered the inferno in the delusion that it devoured the termites, but the termites scampered out of the cave and spread out beyond the forest. The war on termites lasted for months and the jungle burned, like a red ball of fire. Thick fumes engulfed the forest and gassed the villagers.

'The villagers gasped for breath. 'Huh, huh,' they choked for breath.

'A few of them complained for the first time. 'What has he done? He has choked us to death. We must douse the fire,' they stated.

'However, the fanatic supporters of the Bushman gagged the dissent. 'Shut up! How dare you question our leader? Bushy has done a great job. Let the fire burn the terrormites,' they retorted in a haughty manner.

'The dissenters reasoned. 'It's impossible to kill all the termites that have spread out beyond the jungle. The fire is burning the jungle. Can't you see it?" they questioned.

'The fanatics scoffed. 'Yeah, we can see it kill the terrormites. The war on terrormites will end, only, when all the terrormites have died. You cannot oppose the war or you will stand trial for treason. Remember what Bushy said, 'either you are with us or against us,'" they reminded the dissenters, who left the village.

'The village continued to reel under thick smoke. The smoke hovered in the air and clouded the vision, while the fumes throttled the lungs. The fanatics, finally, cracked under pressure. 'We've had enough!' they protested and searched around for the Bushman. 'Where are you? Stop the war on termites.'

'The Bushman worried, because he appeared to loose support for his war on terrormites. He thought hard for something to win back his support. An idea flashed in his mind; he dropped on his knees, crammed his hand in a hole in the ground and rummaged through it.

'Stop the war. Where are you?' the people demanded, continuing to track him.

'I've got him,' the Bushman shouted; his fingers groped about in the hole. 'Quick. Come out and save my neck. I need to douse this dissent,' he talked to himself.

'The fanatics turned euphoric. 'Hurrah! Hurrah! Bushy's great,' they cheered and applauded the Bushman, but failed to read between the lines. He said to them. 'I've got him.' When he should have stated, 'I've got them.'

'The stupid mob remained jubilant and restless. 'Where is he?' they asked, desperate to see the criminal.

'The Bushman jumped to his feet. 'I've dragged him out of a spider hole,' he declared, brandishing a spider in the air.

'Hurrah,' applauded the mob, looking around. 'Show him to us. We can't see him,' complained the mob, unable to see a thing in the smog.

'The Bushman winked and cocked a wry smile. 'Even I can't see him, but I have him in my hand,' he said, arching a sly brow.

'Hold on to him. Do not let him go,' warned the mob.

'We'll put him on trial. He has gassed the jungle.'

'He's slipping out of my hand. Come quick!' complained the Bushman."

'Hurrah! We cannot see you. Where are you?' screamed the mob. 'Bushy you're great.'

'I can't hold on anymore. Come quick! What do I do?' repeated the Bushman.

'The mob howled. 'Hang him! Hang him!'

'The spider paid with his life for the acts of the termites. Heavy rains followed and doused the violent fires, which reduced most of the jungle to ashes. The survivors crept out of their hideouts and thanked the rains. The smoke gradually dissipated and exposed the damage. The villagers faces dropped and they wept at the sight. 'What a disaster? Nothing remains,'they moaned.

'A few fanatics persisted. 'It's collateral damage. At least, we killed the terrormites,' they uttered.

'Ouch!' cried a young girl, when she felt a sting on her arm. 'Mummy, something has bitten me,' she complained to her mother.

'It's a termite,' replied the mother; she brushed it off the girl's arm.

'The little girl gawked. 'I just heard that the fire burnt all the termites,' she taunted.

'The villagers finally realized their folly. 'Where is the Bushman? He's cheated us all,' they lamented, and then searched around to track him.

'They searched and searched and searched in vain; till it dawned on them that the Bushman had vanished, after destroying their fate," concluded the teacher.

The bell tolled and the students stood up.

"Think over the story. We will continue tomorrow," the teacher announced, and then dismissed the class.

CHAPTER 35

▼

Bandu's two friends munched on their snacks, while Bandu reflected upon the story narrated in class. Bandu entertained a different notion and bared it before his friends. "The twin towers Bapuji talked about," reminded Bandu.

The two boys nodded their head. "Hmm," they murmured.

"I have seen them," revealed Bandu.

The two boys looked at each other and giggled.

"I swear, I'm telling you the truth," insisted Bandu.

"Nah!" clucked the boys in disbelief.

"It's only a story," said the boy in a blue shirt.

Bandu pointed at the other boy, "Kunju, you must believe me. Let Boria think what he wants to, but you come with me and I swear, I'll show you the trees," entreated Bandu.

Kunju's eyes twinkled and he felt an urge to see the trees. He looked at Boria. "If he says he can show us the trees, then let's go and see them," he suggested.

Boria nodded his head, and then twisted his lips. "Both of you go and have a look. I'm going home," he replied.

"Damn your home! Do not cook excuses. You don't have the guts to walk into the forest," taunted Bandu, with a wry smile. He wished to provoke Boria.

The challenge threw Boria in a difficult situation. His ego got the better of him. "I've visited the jungle on a number of occasions, all by myself. Look who talks! Huh!" he scoffed at Bandu.

Bandu smacked his lips, grinned and waved his hand. "I'm not talking of the jungle behind the school. Do you see that hillock?" asked Bandu; he pointed to the hills which towered over the forest. "That's where the trees stand."

"I haven't hiked that far," admitted Boria; he raised his eyebrows. "If my mother gets to hear that I went that far she'll spank the day lights out of me."

"Huh," scoffed Bandu; he smirked in contempt. "You still sound like a mother's boy. When will you grow up?" teased Bandu.

Bordia's face flashed and he hurled his hands over his hips. "I'm not afraid of going there, if that's what you mean," he clarified to defend his valour, and then looked away. "I find it difficult to believe you," he doubted, as if challenging Bandu's credibility.

Bandu laughed and sallied forth. "Come on then. Follow me," he gestured to the boys. "I'll prove my point."

The two boys appeared foxed. They looked at each other, jerked their heads and followed Bandu. The gang crossed the paddy fields behind the school and headed for the hillock. The track wound up the green hills, which basked in the afternoon sun. The canopy on the hills resembled a green carpet spread on the mountains, with streams of water running down and falling on the river below that flowed through the valley. The sound of running water mingled with the wind that rustled the littered foliage and echoed in the hills. The boys clamoured up the steep road, which slithered up the hills.

"How big are the trees?" gasped Kunju; he wiped the sweat on his forehead against his forearm.

Bandu halted in his track, poured over the trees that lined the track and pointed at a tall sal tree. "They are bigger than this," he asserted.

The two boys looked up.

"When did you see them?" asked Boria.

"In summer, when I went up there to collect tendu leaves with my mother," replied Bandu, motioning the boys to walk.

"It's too far and deep," said Boria; he stooped on a stone on the track and picked it up.

"We never ventured that far until the coalfields arrived, ate into our forests and forced us to move higher and deeper to collect tendu leaves," complained Bandu.

"Kunju knows more about those coal pits. He worked in them," said Boria; he nudged Kunju's shoulder and flung the stone.

Kunju wrinkled his nose. "It's filthy in there with dust hovering in the air. Your lungs get heavy and you gasp for breath," explained Kunju, with his hands over his lungs. He took a deep breath and breathed out. "The air around here smells fresh and light."

"Bapuji talked about termites and fire that destroyed the forest in the story, but here the coalfields have ruined the hills," alleged Bandu. He bent down, picked a stone and flung it at an orange tree, which stood on the fringes of the track. The stone hit an orange, which fell down. He picked it up and started to peel off the rind. "How much did they pay for that filthy work?" Bandu asked, and then sucked on an orange slice.

"The contractors pay a pittance for the menial work. They paid me twenty rupees for an entire day's work," replied Kunju; he took a slice of the orange offered by Bandu.

"How much for ferrying?" asked, Bordia.

"If you ferry coal on a bicycle and sell it to the traders. They will pay you thirty rupees. But, you have to trek twenty kilometers from the dumps and it tires," said Kunju. He sucked the orange slice dry. "This orange tastes delicious. Let's eat some more."

The three boys pelted the orange tree with stones. Oranges rained down on all sides and the boys hopped around on their hams and gathered them. They then squatted down in the middle of the track and sucked on them.

"These are gifts from our forests, which always feed us. But, I fear those coal dumps will soon destroy these trees," worried Bordia.

"These taste better than those, by the coal dumps, where the trees stay covered with dust and the oranges appear crumpled and dry," remarked Kunju.

"There stood many orange trees where the coal dumps sit. The coal dumps have devoured all the orange trees," observed Bordia, peeling off the rind.

Suddenly, the bark of a sambhar echoed from within the forests and birds fluttered. The boys twisted about and cast a glance.

"Don't worry. I have this," said Bandu; he jumped to his feet and pulled his shirt over. A dagger stayed tucked in the waist of his trouser.

"This tiger has scared the village," divulged Kunju.

Bordia waved off the threat. "The elders in the village say that the tiger does not move around here," he revealed, and then pointed towards the hillock. "He hangs around there."

Bandu laughed. "It will do us no harm. I'll stab it in the stomach," boasted Bandu; he yanked out the dagger and brandished it before the boys.

The two boys gaped at the pointed weapon.

"Why do you carry it around?" asked Bordia.

"I keep it ever since the tiger story erupted," replied Bandu; he dropped his hand and tucked the dagger back in his waist. "If you show it to the tiger, it will run away. Let's go."

The boys stood up and set off on their excursion. They lumbered up a bend of the steep road that wound up the hill and overlooked the valley. They halted on the edge and gazed at the valley. Below, the river meandered through the valley against the backdrop of lush green hills, which resonated with the whistle of the wind that swept across the valley.

"Those are the coal dumps where I worked," said Kunju; he pointed to a bald patch of excavated earth, next to the river in the valley.

Tiny dots of varied colours dug and loaded the coal into heavy dumpers parked in the quarries. Heavy earthmovers pummeled the earth, hauled up coal chunks and piled them on the mounds of excavated earth. Black dust hovered over the quarries and smothered the gasoline fumes emitted by machines. The ugly spectacle resembled a dagger that pierced the bosom of the pristine valley. Suddenly, the wind carried the sound of faint voices from somewhere.

Kunju strained his ears and stabbed his finger on his lips. "Ssh," I hear voices," he cautioned, twisting about. The other two craned their necks to catch the sound.

"It must be farmers coming down from the fields in the mountains," said Bordia; he straightened up and tapped Bandu on his shoulder. "Let's walk."

The three boys swirved around the bend, and watched four men in olive green uniforms, with guns slung around their shoulders stomp towards them.

Bandu looked from the corner of his eyes. "They appear Mauvadis," whispered Bandu, with his hand cupped around his lip.

"What do we do?" asked Kunju in a low voice.

"Keep your heads down and walk past them," suggested Bandu "They will not harm us."

The two groups met in the middle of the road.

"How far is Tendukheda?" asked Comrade Sameer; he halted in his track and looked at the boys.

The boys looked away without responding and shuffled past the revolutionaries. Pandu raced behind the boys and grabbed Bordia's collar from behind. Bordia cringed and stopped in his track.

"Don't you hear what the Comrade asks?" said Pandu, in a gruff voice.

Bordia's eyes blinked; he looked sideways at his colleagues who froze in their tracks. "It's half an hour from here," he hesitated, and then slowly turned around.

Comrade Sameer pointed to the boys, and then moved his finger back and forth. "Come here," he demanded.

The three boys scrunched their faces and hobbled towards him.

"Where do you come from?" questioned Comrade Sameer.

"Tendukheda," stuttered Bandu.

"Where do you go?"

The boys looked at each other as if wondering who will talk.

Bandu stepped forward. "We're going to the fields up there," replied Bandu; he twisted around and pointed to the hillock.

"When did the police last visit your village?"

Bandu creased his forehead and pursed his lips. "Hmm," he murmured, while he mulled over. "They came yesterday in the afternoon. I saw their jeep stationed opposite the ration shop," he recalled.

"Does Comrade Dinesh live in Tendukheda?"

Bandu's eyes squinted. "Do you mean Dinesh Dada?" he asked.

"Yeah. Where is he?"

Bandu nodded his head. "Not anymore," he stated, rolling his eyes about. "He's no more a Mauvadi. Whenever, he comes to the village, he comes with the police and leaves immediately," said Bandu.

"Hmm," murmured Comrade Sameer; he cast a glance at his colleagues and walked towards Bandu.

Bandu wriggled on his feet.

Comrade Sameer stuffed his hand in his trouser pocket and yanked out toffees. The boys eyes twinkled and they goggled at the chocolates.

Comrade Sameer observed the faces of the boys. He squatted on his hams before Bandu and offered him the chocolates. "Do you know where he is?" he asked.

Kunju stepped forward and grabbed the chocolates. "He used to run a transport line that ferried coal from the coalfields in the valley," he answered. Bandu seized Kunju's hand and tried to wrench the chocolates. "Damn it, stop it," shouted Kunju; he clenched his fist and snatched it away.

"He offered them to me," grunted Bandu; with a frown on his face.

Comrade Sameer smiled at the sight and seized Bandu's hand. "I'll give you more. Let him talk," he promised.

Bordia stepped forward. "What about my chocolates?" he asked.

Comrade Sameer slammed his eyes shut and nodded his head in irritation. "I'll give you your share. Let him talk, because I wish to hear him," he offered, and then patted Kunju's shoulder. "Speak."

Kunju took a deep breath. "Six months ago. I saw him at the coal dumps where I worked, but I don't work there anymore," he breathed out with aplomb.

Sameer looked him in the eyes and hurled his hands over his shoulders. "Does he run the business alone? I mean, who works with him?" he asked, with a slight jerk of his head.

Kunju mulled over for a moment, pressing his fingers on his lips. "I don't know all the people," he frowned.

"Anyone," insisted Sameer.

Kunju recalled, and then snapped his fingers. "A man called, 'Tikre Seth,' supervises the mining operations. I remember Tikre Seth employed me on Dada's recommendation," remembered Kunju.

Sameer raised his eyebrows. "I see," he muttered slowly and loudly. He dropped his hands, and then pointed to the road. "Is there a road that leads to the coal fields, from this hill?"

Bandu barged in. "You'll have to walk down to Tendukheda and take the main road," he rattled, and then flashed his palm. "My chocolates!"

The revolutionaries laughed at the sight. Comrade Sameer stood up, rummaged through his pockets, yanked out a handful of tofees and offered a few to Bandu and Bordia. The boys beamed and took their share.

Sameer then whirled around, and then gestured to his men. "Let's go," he said, walking ahead. The four men followed him; while the boys watched, the men disappear around the bend.

"Why do they ask for Dinesh Dada?" asked Bordia; he unwrapped the kismi tofee and plopped it in his mouth.

"Dada is a Mauvadi. Maybe, they know him," answered Bandu, sucking on the toffee. "Why bother?" he shrugged his shoulders and spun on his heels. "Let's go."

The boys turned around and continued their trek, along the track that wound up the forested hill. They sucked on their toffees as they climbed the hill and gasped for breath. The air seemed humid and the trees popped and whistled, with the call of birds. White clouds floated across the hill, while thick strands of foamy water coursed down the hillsides, with a deafening roar. The sharp bark like calls of the mousedeer resonated from the forests, while giant squirrels leaped nimbly on the thick canopy of sag, salai and tendu trees, which sheltered Forest Hawks, Pittas, Brahminy Mynahs, Malabar pied Hornbills and Paradise Flycatchers. Dozens of red ants scurried across the dirt road, with lumps of mud, which they dumped on the anthills that ringed the path. The littered foliage rustled, as Golden Geckos slithered beneath them and popped their tongues to sense prey. The boys treaded cautiously to avoid the dung heaps and animal scat littered on the ground. Sweat poured out of their skins, as they clambered higher up.

The vegetation under went changes; tall bamboo clumps gave way to fruit trees, like the mahua and mango. Finally, the trail led to a plateau, where the tree cover thinned out and made way for tall grass. The wind shrieked as it rippled the grassy meadows dotted with Gaur, Sambhar and Wild Buffaloes that grazed on them. The Plateau contained plenty of water pools, with patches of trees and bamboo clumps scattered across the grassland. The boys followed Bandu along the vanishing track and appeared nervous.

"Are you sure you're heading in the right direction?" asked Kunju, hacking his way through the thick grass.

Bandu pointed to a cluster of trees visible from where he stood. "That's where the two trees are."

"They seem very tall from here," acknowledged Bordia, jumping over a fallen branch on the path.

The boys progressed slowly through the thick grass that dwarfed their tiny bodies.

"Bandu, you're walking too fast," complained Kunju; he halted in his track and waited for Bordia to join him.

The wind shrieked so Bandu failed to catch the words. He appeared excited and eager to show the trees to his friends so he hurried across the meadow. The grass grew taller as the boys groped their way into the grassland. Suddenly, Bandu realized that he walked far ahead of his companions, so he stopped, turned around and waited for Kunju and Bordia.

"Kunju! Bordia!" he shouted, at the top of his voice.

A thunderous roar drowned the sound of the whistling meadow as the the man-eater of Tendukheda pounced on Bandu. The tiny boy taken by surprise stood motionless as the big cat swung its paw across his face. The puny figure collapsed on the ground, while the man-eater dug his jaws into Bandu's shoulder and lugged it.

"Help! Help!" Bandu screamed.

The two boys arrived on the scene of attack. Their faces trembled at the sight and they looked horrified. They spun around on their heels and vanished out of sight.

"Help! Help!" they cried out, scurrying through the grass.

The tiger stayed undeterred. He dug his canines into Bandu's neck and cracked the windpipe. Bandu lost his life. Kunju and Bordia continued to race in frenzy and reached the track, which lead down the hill.

"Help! Help!" they continued to yell, while they raced downhill towards Tendukheda.

CHAPTER 36

▼

Vasu's family suffered its leanest phase. Mangala turned more aggressive and complained. "It's your fault. You shouldn't have borrowed money from Abba," she nagged Vasu. On the other hand, Pandu's disappearance hurt Shoba, who knew that her husband remained innocent, but the fact that she could not do anything about it frustrated her. The anger a person endures, when unjustly treated needs an outlet, otherwise it moves around hurting the wrong people. Shoba by nature occured quiet and reserved, but unlike her mother, she sympathized for Vasu. Hardship prepones matuarity and forced Shoba to matuare beyond her age. Bapu, though, too small to comprehend the complications of life sensed the problems that his family faced. His helplessness lay in the fact that he remained powerless to confront them. He indicated to his parents that he would like to work and contribute to the family income, but his parents insisted that he continue his education.

Pandu's family seemed upset, with all that transpired. Gangaram remained old and counted his last days, while Jija and Kamla struggled to console Shoba. The family, though, derived solace from a steady income, which managed to feed them. They had experienced Pandu's vanishing act before and stayed confident that he would return, but their concern remained the police. If Pandu must return safely to Ramwadi, the police must co-operate, which meant that the family would have to make peace with Abba and forgive him for all that happened. However, the difficulty lay in convincing Shoba, who remained in a precarious situation. To forgive meant that they encouraged wrongs, which may occur again and again. It, also, meant that they lacked the strength to challenge Abba, and he could abuse them at will. Besides this, Shoba's larger concern appeared her marital life. To live without a husband in the village bore a stigma and made Shoba insecure. In Pandu's absence, she remained at the mercy of her in-laws. So far, they appeared good, but for how long. She knew that things could change any moment and put her in a difficult situation.

In theory, she could always go back to her maternal home, but it remained a taboo. Besides, she knew that Vasu and Mangala struggled to feed themselves and she did not want to increase their woes. Vasu and Mangala looked equally concerned about Shoba. In fact, Vasu remained in the worst situation, because he could not dare to take on Abba, otherwise, his son-in-law would never step in Ramwadi. On the other hand, Abba had swallowed his six acres of land and Vasu must do something about it, but the delicate situation forced Vasu to prayer and hope that Abba would return the land someday, although, it appeared a hopeless situation because it seemed never to happen. It also meant that Bapu inherited nothing but debt and looked bonded for life.

In one stroke, Vasu's dreams seemed shattered. He now lived a life of drudgery from whom Abba alone profited. Vasu often looked at Gangaram and thought, "he's lucky that he's old and will not live long. I have so many years to live and have no purpose in life." An unwelcome thought to occur for a person of Vasu's age, although, he sometimes prayed to God and hopelessly waited for a miracle to happen. The questions that stared Vasu in the face stayed: Would it ever happen? When will it happen? Vasu's attempts to plead with Abba failed and he stayed resigned to think over the offer. The more he thought over it, the more his heart burnt with anger. The sense that he remained exploited because of his vulnerability made it worse. He could not eat and sleep peacefully, except for the last ray of hope, his cotton crop.

It appeared the last crop that Vasu could call his own, because Abba had ignored it and allowed him to own it. He fancied that if he managed a good yield, he could settle for a bataidari or a thekedari with Abba and he need not borrow from Abba to get started. Otherwise, it meant another round of loans and interests, which would continue to pile up exponentially, so his immediate thought gravitated towards survival first and then living. Who knows, there may appear a miracle that would give him a chance to live his desired life with dignity. This fancy inspired him to labour on his cotton field. So far, his cotton had thrived, because of the tube well. In fact, it survived three months of draught and there appeared a fraction of a chance for it to fail.

The winter set in long ago and the mornings stayed shrouded in early morning dew. Vasu woke up early, this December, to water his cotton crop, because the load shedding had shifted to the evening hours. He usually slept in his home in Ramwadi and set out early morning to water his crop. He wrapped a torn blanket over his frail body to beat the cold and set off to his farm. The village rose for the morning chores, as he sauntered through the village. People hurried with their lotas in hand to visit the open-air toilets. The women cleaned their homes and lighted the chullahs, while the people hurried to the village well to fetch water. The teashops lifted their shutters and Raghu dusted the Sahukar's shop as Vasu walked past the village square, which smelled of gasoline smoke that emitted from the early morning bus that shrieked as the driver floored the accelerator. Passengers raced to hop in, while a few hovered close to the door greedily inhaling the last puffs of their cigarette butts before the bus moved. Devotees of Hanuman in naked torsos shouldered pitchers of water to the temple to perform their morning poojas. A few bullock-carts rattled along the bumpy road with pales of fresh milk and drowsy riders.

Vasu nodded his head and acknowledged the early morning greetings from those that he encountered on his way. He now dawdled along the main road that slithered out of Ramwadi. Vendors wheeled past him, carrying bakery products in aluminium trunks fastened to the rear of their bicycles. A crisp aroma of baked dough wafted in the air, luring farm dogs, who wagged their tails and raced alongside the bicycles. The vendors crooned filmi songs and peddled faster to dodge the dogs. Vasu reached, "Vidyaniketan," and watched a group of schoolchildren cycle to school. He remembered his promise to Bapu. "I will buy him his cycle, after I harvest the cotton crop," he thought to himself, gazing at the cyclists, who whizzed past him. "Damn the expenses! They just keep mounting," he raged at himself; he shoved the blanket back, which slipped over his shoulder and forged ahead. His mind brooded over the fate of his daughter. "My Shoba, how much more will she suffer?" he reflected, and then nodded his head. His eyes turned moist and his heart melted at her fate. "The village will keep talking till Pandu returns," he concluded, trudging along the road. The morning chill bit his hands and toes and seeped though the holes in his blanket. He wrung his hands to keep warm, and held the edges of his blanket, which covered his head, between his lips.

He accelerated his strides to warm his blood, reached Abba's estate and descended into the orchard. "I hate walking through this orchard. It reminds me of the death of Tillya," he thought back, dropped his head and crossed the jamun tree. He heard the sound of water dropping into the well and the putter of the motor pump. "The lights have come. I must be late," he realized; he reached the well, halted and peeked inside. He twisted about, and then scoured the surroundings. "I wonder where Ganpat is," he figured in his mind, scuttling to the fringes of the orchard. He swapped tracks and strutted towards the sugarcane plantation.

The narrow trail appeared moist from the dew, which fell off the grass that lined the path. Vasu's toes soaked as they grazed against the dew on the grass along the track. He looked down at his moth eaten chappals and chafed toes dampened with the dew. "I need a pair of tough chappals made from worn tyres. I must visit the cobbler and give my measurement," he inferred, and then shook his head. "It comes back to money repeatedly. I'll wait for the cotton harvest," he reviewed his decision, looked up and hastened ahead. The sugarcane stood tall and still under the morning mist that hovered over it. A sweet moist fragrance of grass, earth and sugar tickled his nostrils and lifted his mood. He took a deep breath and exhaled slowly as he stepped inside the plantation. The sugarcane leaves with razor sharp edges gashed his blanket and scooped up the wool. "Damn this blanket! Nothing remains of it," riled Vasu, hacking his way through the plantation. Suddenly, he stepped back, when a rabbit hopped on his path and scampered across at lightning speed. "Damn the bunny!" he fretted, slamming his foot on the ground. "I wonder where Pandu is?" it occurred to him, while he plodded down the path to the hedge and crossed into his field.

A thick misty haze engulfed the dry patta. It remained a little dark, when Vasu reached his field. The cotton field resembled a park lit on a late foggy evening with small white bulbs that distinguished the dark background. Vasu beamed at the sight of cotton that bursted out of the

301

green buds perched on the stalks. The cotton looked good and healthy from the hedge where Vasu surveyed his crop. Vasu's heart leaped with joy and his spirit soared. He felt a surge of energy gush through his blood. "At least, I have something, to feel proud of," he acknowledged his effort; he walked through the cotton field towards the tube well and switched on the motor.

The engine clattered beneath the land and propelled the water that dropped down in the pool. "I'll reap a windfall this season," Vasu conjured in his mind, trekking down the funnel to the fringes of his cotton field. The water from the pool logged the main shaft. Vasu dug his hands into the earth, and then scooped out a lump of mud to divert the water into the last channel that ran along the baandh.

The sun slowly lifted over the horizon and the faint rays gently sliced through the mist that hovered over the field. The view brightened as the sun rose higher up, transforming the dry rugged patch of land into a stunning landscape. Vasu's feet warmed up, while he plodded through the lukewarm ground water, racing ahead to log the channel. Vasu marveled at the sun lifting over the horizon and kissing his cotton buds. A feeling of earthy pride overwhelmed him. A man of the soil derives tremendous satisfaction, when his labour receives appreciation. This moment commemorated his toil, as if the sun saluted Vasu and complimented his effort by blessing his cotton crop.

The confidence gave him the liberty to brood over his effort and condemn fate. "If Abba played straight and nature supported my efforts. I will write off my debts by the end of the next season and make my family proud. Imagine how proud Mangala will feel, she will stop the nagging. I will get Bapu admitted to a good private school and make a few ornaments of gold for Shoba. Life will change for the better. I must figure a way out to get back my land. Maybe talk to a lawyer. A good lawyer to win back my land," he fancied; his face lit up as he reached the end of the funnel on the hedge.

The rays of the sun grew brighter and flashed over the corner of his field. He almost bent over to clear the clog, when he noticed the cotton stalks in the last row had wilted. He straightened up, and then his face frowned at the sight. "Damn the shepherds!" he fretted, shaking his head. "Why can't they keep their flock out of here?" he said to himself, plodding through the muck to inspect the extent of damage. The animals that grazed on the dry patta often strayed into the farms and gorged on the crops that stood along the fringes of the fields. When he reached the corner, he raged at the spectacle. An entire row of his crop had wilted. He rolled his eyes upwards, and then slammed his eyes shut. "You can't expect to stay away for a moment," he deliberated, pursing his lips. He recalled that he remained absent for two days, because he suffered from a headache and fever. Mangala refused to check in, because she appeared disinterested ever since Pandu disappeared. He fumed at the sight.

"Who could have done it?" he wondered in disgust, squatting on his hams to scrutunise the damage. His fingers trembled as they held a bud; his eyes narrowed as he drew the bud closer and examined the wilted leaves. The sight shattered him; his face crumpled and he stared in horror. He snatched a leaf and turned it over on the flat of his palm. The light from the morning rays had intensified and he examined the spectacle closely against the rays of the sun. He turned hysterical, dropped on his knees and slammed his hands over his head. Tears streamed down his eyes, as he shook his head violently. His voice appeared stuck in his throat, as if, he wished to talk and cry at the same time. He looked at the sky, and then wept.

"Lalya! Oh God!" he cried, slapping his forehead. The leaf he examined had turned to a rusty red colour infected with white flies. Vasu slumped on the ground weeping bitterly. His troubles seemed to mount and showed no signs of dissipating. His fears came alive, the cotton crop had succumbed to the dreaded sucker pest disease called, "lalya," in Vidharbh. Vasu's heart sank, when he crawled from stalk to stalk. It appeared that all the cotton stalks in the last row had suffered the same fate. His blood boiled; he gnashed his teeth. "Damn the Sahukar!" he fumed, recalling Sahukar's false claims. "He lied to me, when he said that this Santano variety of Bt Cotton stayed pest resistant," mourned Vasu, slumping on the ground. He dropped his hands over his head, and then shook it in disbelief. "Not again. I am tired of life. How many more problems to face?" he complained, weeping. He slouched; fixed his eyes on the ground; his mind blanked out and he looked traumatized.

The disease implied an invitation to spend. Vasu would need to borrow more to spray pesticide on his crop. It meant another one thousand and more rupees per acre per pesticide spray, but it never ended there, sometimes the crop required more pesticides. Moreover, with no money on him, the expenses loomed beyond his reach. It meant another round of borrowing, interest and humiliation. The cycle of debt seemed to whirl round and round his neck as if determined to strangle him.

The GM seed companies appeared to mislead farmers and took undue advantage of their gullibility. They trained their salespersons to puff the product to sell it. So the salespersons diverted attention from the terms and conditions typed in the tiniest of fonts and never explained these to the farmers. To worsen matters government agricultural officers on the pay roll of these multinational seed companies also promoted their products. This sophisticated blue chip thuggery bragged about the yield per acre, but the Santano Bt25 Cotton variety never increased the yield per acre. It possessed an inbuilt genetic pest resistant mechanism that saved the cost of pesticides, which reduced the total input cost of production and this increased the margin of profits. Again, this happened if the crop grew under ideal conditions, which rarely happened. The Bt 25 cotton variety consumed lots of water and like sugarcane it remained unsuited to Vidharbh and Maharashtra; a water scarce region. Why did the Government promote these water-sucking varieties in Vidharbh? Perhaps it exhibited another faulty agrarian policy drafted by intellectuals in South Block touted as the Messiahs of the Green Revolution in India.

The biggest draw back of the green revolution, the world over, remains the excess consumption of water, chemical fertilizers and pesticides, which sap the fertility of the soil and threaten the environment. The babus and scientists in South Block never foresaw the ill effects that seemed unsustainable and dangerous in the future. The reasons emphasized the need to feed India's teeming millions and achieve self-sufficiency in foodgrain production. Today, India boasts of an excess of foodgrain production, called buffer stock, but lacks go-downs or stocking yards to store these grains. The media rightly telecast how the buffer stock rots in the most unhygienic conditions. We destroyed the fertility of our soil, damaged the environment to create a buffer stock, which fattens rats and stray pigs, while millions continue to starve and suffer from malnutrition. The larger question about quality execution needs redressal first, before any grandiose scheme reaches the desired targets.

To make matters worse, the latest economic development model adopted from the World Bank and IMF remains powered by non-renewable energy resources, which will not last beyond the next twenty-five years. Presently, all nations seek a higher economic growth rate, which symbolizes development and progress, but also harms the environment. Higher economic growth means higher levels of fossil fuel consumption, more ecological degradation; adverse climate change that affects monsoon patterns and threatens farmers, who depend on agriculture for a living. Add to this the higher input costs of production in agriculture, with a tight regulation of market prices of agricultural goods to control inflation, and you have a sure recipe for suicides. The present cost of food production in Industrial Societies remains expensive and unsustainable in the future. Every calorie of food consumed, costs ten calories of energy to produce. It does not need rocket science to predict the fate of the world.

The most viable solution appears: in reviving organic farming; spending on research and development of renewable energy resources; promoting permaculture; investing in rainwater harvesting techniques, which require little investment; regulating cropping patterns that suit local conditions, with emphasis on crops, which nourish soil content; prohibiting indiscriminate growth of cash crops and facilitating a direct farmer to consumer business model, which eliminates middlemen, who exploit the farmers and the consumers.

Inorganic farming fostered by the Green revolution, has failed to alleviate the plight of marginal and small farmers, because of an unsustainable input cost. Besides, it remains capital intensive and centric to the rich farmers, who can afford to invest big money, but demands a shift to cash crops to recover the heavy investment. This explains the plight of farmers in western Maharashtra, who mainly cultivate sugarcane for cash. The monoculture practiced there has damaged the soil, polluted the rivers and underwater table, and encouraged the indiscriminate use of water, which if saved and diverted to Marathwada and Vidharbh can help address the water scarcity in these regions.

However, the stakes of political leaders has severely hampered this development and resulted in the misfortunes of small and marginal farmers. Farmer suicides remains largely a political phenomenon, and farmers remain pawns in vote bank politics of political leaders, who pose like farmers and encourage cash crop cultivation, which demands huge capital investment and big irrigation projects that gives an opportunity to political leaders to indulge in corruption.

Presently, in Maharashtra, setting up a sugar industry and becoming a MLA, with the backing of the sugar lobby, appears the norm. As long as this nexus stays, the plight of the small and marginal farmers will worsen over the years. Monoculture defies the basic law of nature, which remains diversity. Farmers in Vidharbh must adhere to the conventional local crops and not fall in the monoculture trap, which threatens the environment.

Vasu gathered himself slowly, and then staggered back home. The initial euphoria had vanished. His mind faced another challenge and he wondered. "How will I pay for the pesticides?"

When he reached home, Mangala sat by the chullah, cooking food. "When will you eat?" she asked, dabbing the bhakri, heating over the tawa with a rag.

Vasu wore a glum face. "I'm not in a mood to eat," he replied, squatting on the floor.

Mangala looked at him; her hands smeared with flour. "What's wrong? Are you feeling unwell?" she inquired; she pulled out a piece of half-burnt firewood from the chullah, tapped it on the floor to make a charcoal heap, and thrust the firewood back inside the chullah.

Vasu curled his hands over his knees. "Our cotton is infested with lalya," he said, in a low voice.

Mangala gawked, and then slapped her forehead with the back of her palm. "Not again!" she exclaimed, shaking her head. Suddenly, her face flashed with rage. "Sahukar said it was pest resistant."

Vasu curled his lips in contempt. "They will say anything to sell the seeds," he quipped; his eyes turned moist. "We have to endure the crap, because farmers remain free game for everyone."

Mangala knuckled the dough. "Damn the Sahukar," she fumed, staring at Vasu. "We must demand our money back," suggested Mangala; she flipped the bhakri over the tawa, sprinkled some water and spread it over the bhakri.

Vasu nodded his head. "He won't listen," he stated.

"It's his responsibility to inform us. Why does he run the shop? I reckon to kill us!"

"It's pointless, arguing with big people. We have to endure. I don't know what to do and where to get the money for pesticides?"

"Damn the money! Damn the pesticides! We will not go around begging for money anymore," retorted Mangala. She picked up a rag to cover her fingers, gently heaved the bhakri and tossed it on the pile of charcoals. The crust inflated like a ballon. She turned it over on its side. A delicious crisp aroma of charcoal and dough wafted through the air.

A measly stray brown dog got wind of it, and then wobbled to the door. He goggled at the bhakri; his tongue dripping with water. His stomach had caved in and he stood with his tail tucked under his legs. He looked hungry and wished to eat.

"Ssh!" Mangala shooed at him, but the dog did not budge.

"Give him something to eat," suggested Vasu.

Mangala picked up a dry piece of firewood and flung it at the dog. "Get out!" she shouted.

The dog took a hit, flattened on the ground and wailed in pain. It seemed he willed to take the blows, because his hunger overwhelmed him.

"Don't hit him. He's hungry," entreated Vasu.

Mangala flashed her eyes. "Everyone's hungry in here," she quipped, kneading the dough. "We're living on borrowed rations."

The dog continued to wail in agony. "Wow! Wow! Wow!" he whined. The fur on his coat had peeled off, one ear hung loose with holes in it and fleas swarmed his body.

Vasu raged. "Throw him, something to eat. The poor animal's starving," he yelled.

Mangal broke a quarter of the bhakri, and then tossed it over the skinny dog's head. He turned around, tracked it and gorged on it.

Vasu mellowed down. "I'll have to meet Abba," he admitted.

Mangala snapped in rage. "I just warned you against begging for money. Damn that Bt Cotton! We should have grown jowar it would have fed us and your dog."

Vasu scowled at the comment. "It's not for the money. I have to discuss the proposal he offered," explained Vasu.

Mangala punched the dough. "How dare he give us an offer? It's our land and he lays down conditions," she sneered, curling her lips in contempt. She could never digest what had happened. It lingered at the back of her mind. "Damn the offer! We will not give in!

"I don't mind what you say, but what about Pandu. I want him back home safe. Abba knows it so he's toying with us," lamented Vasu.

The hard reality forced Mangala to swallow her words. "Hmm," she murmured; she hunched over the chullah and blew at the tiny yellow flame below the tawa. The flame shot up; she pulled back and wondered. "I wonder where Pandu is?" she asked poignantly.

"We haven't received any word from him. I hope he comes back soon. I worry for Shoba," added Vasu.

Mangala folded her hands, and then looked up at the sky. "Oh Vitthal please protect him. Send him home," she prayed.

"He can only come back, if Abba permits. Otherwise, the police will arrest him."

"Damn the system! It shields the corrupt and tortures the innocent."

"We have to live it and work out something. What do you suggest? Should we settle for bataidari or thekedari?"

Mangala wiped her wet eyes against the tattered sleeves of her blouse. "It's up to you to decide, but I suggest thekedari. We will pay him his annual rent and grow jowar and soyabean," she replied, turning the bahakri over the tawa.

"I thought the same, but all depended upon the cotton crop. Since the crop is infested, we will not manage a good yield, unless, we spray pesticides to control the damage."

Mangala interjected angrily. "We will not borrow a penny for the pesticides. Let the cotton rot! I'm fed up of the input expenses for cotton," she riled, tossing the bhakri over the mound of coal.

"How will we manage the rent for thekedari? We will have to pay Abba in advance or take an advance loan on interest. Just imagine, what will happen?" reasoned Vasu. He cast a glance at Mangala. "We must save the cotton crop," he insisted, in a low tone.

Mangala rammed the dough, with her knuckles, and then interrupted in a huff. "Buy the pesticide and give it to me. I will swallow it and die. Then you do what you want with the cotton crop," scoffed Mangala. She appeared to loose her head at the slightest mention of cotton. "Damn the Bt Cotton! It's a murderer!"

Vasu got the message. He raised his hands and motioned Mangala to relax. "Don't get worked up. I'm only suggesting," he reminded.

Mangala plucked a chunk of the dough, and then flattened it on her palm. "Whatever you do, make sure you get Pandu back. I can't see my girl, live in misery all her life," cautioned Mangala.

Vasu nodded his head, and then stood up. "Abba assured me that he will think over it. I am sure he will agree, if we accept one of his proposals. He knows the truth, but will not admit it openly," he reckoned, walking to the door.

"Where are you going?" asked Mangala.

"I'm going to talk to Abba. The earlier the better," replied Vasu.

"Have your lunch and go," insisted Mangala.

"I'm not in a mood. I'll talk to him and come home for lunch," said Vasu, he walking out.

CHAPTER 37

───────── ▼ ─────────

Comrade Sameer and his revolutionaries had camped on the outskirts of Tendukheda. The news of the killing reached them through the courier, who carried dinner for them. He also informed them that the village would assemble the next day and the sarpanch would address the gathering. Comrade Sameer cancelled his trip to the coalfields and decided to attend the meeting. The village gathered in the square, at around half past ten in the morning. Bandu's death appeared the fifteenth death, at the hands of the man-eater of Tendukheda. This time the village looked determined to do something about the killings. Bapuji the sarpanch and teacher of the village sat on the charpoy and faced the crowd that squatted on the ground, while the revolutionaries stood behind Bapuji, overlooking the gathering.

"We made umpteen requests to the wildlife warden, but all our pleas fell on deaf hears. They do not seem interested in taking any action. Everytime, I made a request they insisted that we must evict the village. They say that the wild life act prohibits the killing of tigers and that we pose a threat to the forests. They want us to evict at the earliest," Bapuji broached the debate.

The audience scowled at the suggestion. The people nodded their heads in disagreement. A man stood up in a huff and interposed. "No one will leave the village. The forests belong to us. The coalfields out there," he said, pointing to the hills and continued, "have forced the tigers on us. The killings never happened before; they started when the mining began. Why should we leave our homes? Tell those mining companies to stop mining the forests," he stated.

The audience applauded.

Bapuji raised his hands, motioning the crowd to listen. The applause died down. "We must first stop the tiger menace. The forest officials refuse to kill the tiger and have warned us against it," Bapuji cautioned, but an angry man intervened.

"If they don't wish to kill the tiger, then why don't they capture it and cage it in the zoo. We live in constant fear of this beast. It kills our cattle, goats, sheeps, pigs and people. We have to do something," argued the man.

"Yeah," the gathering backed him.

Bapuji noticed the unrest and divulged his line of action. "I plan to hold a protest outside the District Collectorate. We'll go there, sit on an indefinite fast unto death and force the Government to act," he stated, and then paused for the audience consent.

"Damn the protest!" a voice protested from the gathering. The crowd applauded. The man stood up to face Bapuji. "If we choose to fast unto death; they'll let us die. I know the ways of this Government, which doesn't care for the people," he mocked, casting his sight about as if anticipating a response.

Another man took the cue and vaulted to his feet. "We have petitioned the Government so many times. What happened? Why should we sit on a fast unto death? I suggest we kill the man-eater."

"Yeah," nodded the audience, clapping their hands. "Kill the man-eater!" they shouted back.

Bapuji waved his hand and gestured silence. "If we do what you suggest. The police will arrest us for violating the law," he reasoned, in a bid to pacify the temper of the people.

A scrawny man with a naked torso stood up. "If they come to arrest us, we'll retaliate with our bows and arrows. They must not underestimate the might of the Gonds. We remain descendants of the Great Gond race that once ruled Gondwana. We will need to remind the Government," he bragged, pumping his fist in the air.

The gathering erupted to a thunderous applause.

Bapuji continued to assuage his people. "Fine, but how long will we defend ourselves, against their guns and bulldozers? We cannot win against them. It's pointless provoking violence," he persuaded.

The scrawny man's face flashed with rage. "They have compelled us to provoke violence, because they wish the man-eater to live. It does not matter to them that the tiger feasts on our tribe. It appears a conspiracy to terrorize us, so that we leave the forests and the mining companies take over. The coal dumps have trapped and killed many tigers, but nothing happens to the mining companies," the man fumed.

"Yeah," cheered the crowd.

Comrade Sameer heard the debate with rapt attention and gauged the mood of the assembly. He sensed the simmering tension waiting to burst. It appeared that the Government's callous attitude had pushed the villagers to the brink. Like a typical revolutionary and propagandist, he seized the opportunity to stoke the discontent and propogate the LOFA ideology. He whispered to his colleagues, "keep guard from the police," he said, signalling them to take positions in three different directions.

Pandu whirled around, while the other two rushed ahead and turned their backs to the audience.

Sameer then walked to the charpoy in his olive green uniform, with a Kalashnikov strung around his shoulder and signaled the angry villagers to silence.

A hush fell over the restless audience.

"The LOFA has heard your grievance and I promise to act. We have maintained that the bourgeoise state remains the handmaiden of capitalists, who want to ravage the forest wealth for profit," he announced, and then twisted around pointing at Bapuji. "Bapuji appears naïve, although, he commands respect. I bow before him," he said, and then turned back to face the crowd. "But I don't agree with his penchant for non-violent protests. Everyday thousands of social activists sit on similar fasts unto death all over the country, with one hope," he paused, and then smacked his lips. "that the Government will redress their problems, but what happens at the end of the day," he questioned, with a wry smile. "A few corrupt babus turn up, shove a glass of nimbu-pani down the throats of these non-violent protestors, gather their applications and give them another false assurance that the Government will look into the matter. Then they appoint a committee, which takes months and even years to prepare a flimsy report," he submitted, wrinkling his nose. "The report takes months and years to reach the Cabinet, which clears files that promise kickbacks with haste, but prefers to sit over the reports of common people like you and me, because we cannot pay them money," mocked Comrade

Sameer, and then flicked his fingers." If the report manages clearance then it must go to the committees of the legislature and finally to the assembly or any other time consuming forum, which will tire and kill the issue. These babus, committees, commissions, investigating teams, legislatures remain a hoax to delay and finally deny the social activists their demands. Bapuji's non-violent and peaceful protests will meet the same fate, although, he appears an honourable man," he revealed, casting a glance at Bapuji. He hurled his hands over his hips. "Democracy is a nautanki, which allows impotent peaceful protests a valve to vent frustration against Government inaction so that they will not fight the system. It will not let the have-nots direct their anger against the corrupt system, which favours the bourgeoise," he explained, pointing to the audience. "As someone rightly pointed that we belong to a Great martial race called Gonds," he asserted, thumping his chest. "Sixty lakh Gonds lack a nationality, because the bourgeoise state has conspired to divide and rule us," he shouted, and then pointed to the ground. "Today our people stand divided between five states, because the bourgeoise state fears our united might and wishes to subjugate us. The bourgeoise state has conspired to eliminate this great race. All other nationalties stand divided on linguistic lines, and have achieved Statehood, but not us, why?" he questioned the mesmerized audience, and paused for them to gather his message. He cocked a wry smile and answered. "Because we sit on mineral and forest wealth, required to spur the economic growth rates of other mainstream ethnic groups. History remains testimony to this reason. First, the British undertook mining explorations, set up plantations and constructed railroads to connect their Raaj by plundering our forest wealth. They took away iron-ore, manganese, gold, bauxite, dolomite, quartz and many other mineral resources. They also destroyed the forests for teak, bamboo, sandalwood and other forest produce and deliberately made laws, which prevented adivasis from enjoying their traditional rights of collecting forest produce. The laws punished and fined our people for flimsy things like collecting firewood to cook a meal and build a home," he alleged, took a deep breath and exhaled. He observed the audience, sitting spellbound and continued. "Then the bourgeoise State of post-independent India evicted adivasis from their natural habitats in the name of Industrial development. Millions of adivasis lost their homes and identities, when displaced by hydroelectric irrigation projects, steel plants, bauxite plants, thermal plants and other mining projects. The temples of modern India stand on our graves. Their so-called, 'development projects,' have destroyed the environment, contaminated rivers and polluted the air. They pose the biggest threat to the forests and wild life, not we," he asserted; his eyes turned moist and his heart melted. He regained his poise and proceeded. "The exploitation also appears cultural. They look down upon our way of life and call us primates. They say we must civilize by joining the organized religions like Christianity and Hinduism. The Christian missionaries, fanatic khakichadis and other right wing Hindu organizations force us to convert to the Christian and Hindu faith. The khakhichadis want to sanskritize us, by introducing us to Hindu Gods, forms of worship, rites and rituals. They wish us to join their notion of Hindu India. The mainstream communities dislike our Gondi language and force us to adopt Hindi, Telugu and Marathi languages. The banias have created a cartel, which buys our forest produce for a pittance and sells it at exorbitant rates," he thundered; his eyes flashed and he pointed to the audience. "Our people don't know greed, because we share a symbiotic relationship with the forests. Our adivasi culture considers land a non-commodity and treats it as collective property. We live by trust and believe in the spoken word. This explains why we do not carry documents to prove land titles. However, the greedy non-adivasi immigrants who came from outside snatched away our lands, because they see property as a commodity. They have ravaged and exploited our forest wealth to satiate their never-ending base desires," he fumed, and then waited for a breather.

The audience applauded him.

He waived his hand to gesture silence. They obeyed and he proceeded. "They create national parks, wildlife sanctuaries and reserves to protect the forests and animals, which they have threatened to extinction, but we receive nothing but eviction notices," he pointed out.

The scrawny man stood up and intervened. "We will not evict the forests!" he shouted.

"Yeah," joined the audience.

Comrade Sameer's heart bounded with glee at the reaction. He motioned the man to sit down, who bowed and promptly hunkered down. Sameer took a deep breath, exhaled and went on. "They call us uncivilized, savage and barbaric tribes, who stalk the jungles to ravage civilization's pristine natuaral resources. They have destroyed our identities; yet, call themselves the largest democracy in the world, a democracy that believes in Equality, Justice and Liberty," mocked Comrade Sameer; he stiffened his face and gnashed his teeth. He paused and smiled wryly. "Has their democracy embraced us? Does their democracy acknowledge our existence as human beings or considers us animals or something below these?" he questioned, curling his lips in contempt. "Let us assume they consider us animals, then the wildlife protection act, must apply to us, because we appear wild and barbaric, and if we seem endangered then we must find mention in the schedules of the wild life act as endangered species like the tiger. So what do we identify with?" he questioned, raising his hands. He smiled wryly and continued. "The only other category of animals remains the domestic variety of dogs, cats, horses and other such animals. Maybe they consider the adivasis domestic animals; plain, harmless and pliant, like the dogs. Let us assume they think of us as dogs; domestic and not wild, otherwise we will come under the wildlife protection act and compel the state to protect us," he spoke with scorn, prompting a giggle from the crowd. He paused for the chuckle to subside. "What kind of domestic dogs do we resemble? There appear many species of domestic dogs: Alsation, German shepherd, Bulldog, Hound, Great Dane, Doberman, Labrador, Pomerian, Cocker Spaniel and many more. These privileged hybrid species live in mansions, drive around in cars, sleep in bedrooms and receive palatial treatment," he sneered; he raised his eyebrows and widened his eyes in awe.

The audience laughed.

"Yet," he spoke, motioning the people to hear him. He wrinkled his face. "There appear many dogs, unfortunate, unpalatable and called derogatory names like; stray dogs, street dogs, rabies dogs, garbage dogs or filthy dogs. The civilized people dislike these; poor, ugly, weak, uncouth, unintelligent, mannerless, naked, illiterate, homeless and diseased dogs that swamp the streets and garbage dumps. Does the civilized race consider us street dogs?" he paused for the question to sink in and glared at the assembly.

The people frowned.

He nodded his head. "No," he snapped, and then stabbed his finger on his chest. "We appear worse off than street dogs, because our Great Gond race stays damned to that of rag pickers, garbage raiders and bhangar collectors in the name of rehabilitation, displacement and compensation. We have to fight garbage dogs, stray cows, pigs and crows for food from the garbage dumps of civilization. Eviction has forced us out of our forests into the garbage dumps of civilization to compete with stray animals for survival," he yelled; his eyes flashed and body trembled with rage.

A man stood up and interjected. "Damn the civilization!" he shrieked, slamming his foot on the ground.

The audience joined in and yelled. "Damn the civilization!"

Comrade Sameer took a deep breath and exhaled. His eyes turned moist and he sounded sympathetic. "Our dignity as human beings lies trampled, when our kith and kin beg on the streets of cities, railway stations and traffic signals. Eviction has forced us to risk our lives, working on towering construction sites, break our backs in stone quarries and mining pits, and pushed our women into the flesh trade. We walk around like the living-dead, live on pavements, under flyovers and in conditions of squalor under the constant fear of the police and civic authorities. The scrap merchants, mining barons, industrialists and builders profit from our labour," he paused, wiping the tears in his eyes and shouted. "Civilization treats our race worse than domestic and wild animals, as if, the living-dead and calls us eco-terrorists that threaten their natural resources. Their environmental laws appear a subtle conspiracy to eliminate the Great Gond race in order to plunder the natural resources we sit on," he fumed, pointing to the hills, and then clenched his fist and pumped the air. "Yeh jal, zameen, jungle hamara hai, koi pujipati ki jagir nahi," he sloganeered.

The audience fisted the air and chanted. "Yeh jal, zameen, jungle hamara hai, koi pujipati ki jagir nahi."

The orator motioned them to silence, and then spewed his vitriolic. "Democracy remains a discredited ideology, which seeks to legitimize the rule of an oligarchy of thugs, robber barons, timber mafias, oil mafias, ration mafias, sand mafias, tusker mafias and political mafias. The democratic state remains the biggest terrorist and source of violence designed to protect the bougeoise so it will never pay heed to peaceful and non-violent forms of protest. Democracy resembles a nautanki and the electoral process a farce in which you choose between thugs. If you wish to change the system, you will have to fight to overhaul it. Change will never happen from the ballot box; it will come from the barrel of a gun," he hollered, removed his gun, pointed it to the sky and pumped it with bullets.

The gathering cheered and applauded.

Sameer lowered his gun and stated. "I have joined the LOFA to fight this unjust state and liberate my forests from the clutches of civilized thieves. My conscience reckons it worth a million times to die to save my forests than stay condemned to eat from the garbage dumps of civilization. I have grabbed my fate in my hands; you too will have to make a choice. If not now then later, but choose you must—either the road, which leads to a filthy garbage dump or the path that leads to an honourable martyr's den. It appears possible that they may smash us today, but tomorrow will remain ours. Many will mock my belief and call it a myth, but I live by it," he clenched his fist and pumped the air. "Long live the revolution! Long live the LOFA!" he chanted, pointed his Kalishnikov to the sky and pumping it with bullets.

The spell of the oratory engulfed the audience, smothered the despair and gloom that appeared and rekindled hope and fervour. Like a forest fire, it spread out devoured the assembly and ignited their emotions, to a deafening roar. "Long live the revolution! Long live the LOFA!" shouted the gathering, with their fists pumping the air.

The garbage dump appeared the spark that fuelled their conscience and ignited their self-respect. It displayed romantic idealism at its best. Comrade Sameer raised his hands to signal silence and continued, "I'm glad to see that you possess the belief, but your belief will need direction, if it has to succeed, which the LOFA will provide. You will have to surrender yourselves to the LOFA and work selflessly to realize your dream. The State will not give in so easily. It will resist and try its optimum best to sabotage our dream. Equipped with violence and disposed to terror it will ruthlessly suppress our voices. To resist this bourgeoise State we will need arms, ammunition and to train in the methods of guerilla warfare. So, let us repose our faith in the LOFA and promise to stand and die for it, because the forests belong to us, since, generations and we will defend it to our last breath. Yeh jal, jungle, zameen hamara hai, koi pujipati ki jagir nahin," ranted the orator, and then fired his gun in the air. "Long live the revolution! Long live LOFA!" he shouted at the top of his voice.

The gathering exploded and joined the sloganeering, "Long live the revolution! Long live LOFA!"

CHAPTER 38

▼

Kanta's threat stayed real, because she meant what she said. The police station refused to register her complaint, because the police diligently followed their manual that stated complaints against party members of the Government must stay unregistered. However, this failed to deter Kanta, who immediately approached the Dalit Human Rights Organization and protested. The issue appeared serious and on the verge of grabbing headlines. The organization directed her to Dada, the local MLA, who seemed delighted and more than pleased to receive her, when she visited him in the afternoon. It seemed an opportunity that came with little effort and Dada wished to make the most of it. Dada appeared unhappy with Abba, ever since Abba piled up demands to withdraw from the election fray so after winning the elections Dada remained obliged to keep his word. This seemed Dada's opportunity to get even with Abba and haggle with him to whittle down his demands. After hearing Kanta, Dada requested her to wait outside and dialled Abba's number. "What to do?" he questioned, with delight.

Abba stuck in a fix knew the matter appeared too sensitive for the party to oblige, because if the Dalit Human Rights Organization acted then the opposition would raise the issue in the legislative assembly. Abba also knew that, if the matter snowballed into a political storm, the party would force him to resign. Abba's political fortunes hung on a cliff.

"Give me some more time. I'll work out something," replied Abba, with a scowl on his face. He hated to face such an awkward situation.

Dada beamed and upped the ante. "You should have done it long ago. We can't wait for the matter to make headlines," he asserted.

Abba took a deep breath and exhaled.

"Come on speak up," taunted Dada.

Abba raged and shouted. "Do you suggest, handcuffing Tatya and parading him through the village?"

Dada beamed and pressed on. "No of course not, he's like my son," pretended Dada. He cocked a wry smile. "I suggest he surrender to the police in the police station. The matter appears serious and will invite punishment under the Atrocities Act," he suggested, with scorn.

Abba squirmed in his seat and felt the heat. "I'll talk to her and try to convince her," he replied, knowing that he ran out of options.

Dada held his turf, with intention to show his importance. "She spoke to me at length," he revealed, slowly and loudly.

"What?" interjected Abba; he appeared agitated.

"Hey, cool down. Don't get worked up," advised Dada. He winked and rattled on. "She will not accept the money, although, I cancelled her transfer order to appease her, but she insists that she wants justice," teased Dada.

"Damn your suggestion!" Abba shouted into the receiver. "We're a prestigious family and will not accept a chamar girl."

Dada smirked and his heart vaulted with glee. "Tatya should have mulled over it before he lured her. You know that your political career hangs precariously. You must accept her and douse the matter," Dada persisted, pinching Abba where it hurt most.

Abba understood his intentions and decided to stay calm. He needed some time to settle the matter and found it futile to argue over the telephone. "Just give me two days and I'll work out something," insisted Abba.

Dada loved the sight of Abba pleading before him. "Make it quick, because I feel sorry for you and would love to help you, but the high command will not tolerate this. The least, I can tell the police to treat Tatya well in case he has to go behind bars. It is up to you to try to convince Kanta. I have made her wait outside my chamber. What do I say to her?" asked Dada.

"Tell her to hold on. I'll work out something," said Abba; he slammed the phone.

Dada kissed the receiver, and then put it down. He sent for Kanta. "Send her in," he ordered his sipahi.

Kanta hurried inside and stood before Dada.

"Please sit down," said Dada, softly. "I talked to Abba and he wishes to have a word with you."

Kanat twisted her lips in contempt. "Damn him and his words!" she fumed, sitting down on the chair. "He threatened me saying, he has the system under his thumb. I will not cave in so easily. Your party will have to act, against him or I'm going to the press," threatened Kanta.

Dada enjoyed the heat. He put on a pretense and pleaded half-heartedly on Abba's behalf. "Madam, please try to understand, I've cancelled your transfer order. Why don't you have another word with Abba and settle your differences?" he entreated, arching a sly brow.

Kanta nodded her head in disagreement. "What if he refuses to oblige? What do I do then?" she questioned, with a gruff voice.

Dada pursed his lips and jigged his head as if agreeing with her. "I'll make sure you get justice and promise you protection. I give you my word and I'll keep it," he pleaded, elbowed the table, looked around furtively and spoke in a low voice. "Stick to your demands and don't give up. If Abba refuses to listen, come and protest outside my house. We will call the media and report the matter. He'll be forced to accept you," advised Dada, with intention to incite her.

"What about the police complaint?" asked Kanta, overwhelmed with the support she managed to muster.

Dada slumped back in his chair. "Wait for two more days and then go to the police station. I'll make sure that the police register your complaint," promised Dada.

Kanta stood up. "Thank-you and I'll do as you say," she said, and then left the office.

Two hours passed, since, Dada talked to Abba, but the words kept buzzing in Abba's ears and made him restless. The system that he boasted lay under his thumb now sat on his head. He appeared helpless and angry at the same time. He stared down on his son, who stood before him and the sight of his own blood made him boil. He stiffened his face and rammed his fist on the arm of the chair. "Damn it! Look at what you did. My enemies have cornered me. They will make full use of this opportunity granted by you," Abba pointed at Tatya, "to vanquish me. I had warned you a hundred times not to play with fire," shouted Abba; he dropped his hand, slammed his foot on the ground and nodded his head in disdain.

Tatya looked nervous and quivered. "I'm sorry Abba. I never expected her to go to Dada," he stuttered and apologized, with sweat trickling down his forehead.

Abba's eyes flashed and his face reddened. "Damn your apologies! Your actions have ruined my political career. It took me years to build a reputation and you've wasted it," thundered Abba, breathing heavily.

"What do I do?" Tatya questioned, overwhelmed with fear and confusion. He bit his lips and moved his eyes around. "I'll run away and hide, till the matter settles."

Abba shook his head in disgust and pressed his lips. "Damn you thickhead! Your running away, will further aggravate the situation. The law will catch up with you. It's best that you surrender to the police," advised Abba; he slammed his eyes shut and racked his head.

"No! I don't wish to go behind bars!" Tatya cried. The very thought of jail frightened him. "You have the system under your thumb. You must protect me."

Abba slapped his knees. "Damn the system! You cannot play ball with the system, as and when you like. There remain certain rules in politics that you have to respect and one of these implies that you cannot annoy the Dalit vote bank; otherwise, the system will turn against you. And you have violated this rule," explained Abba.

Tatya's arrogance wilted at the sight of his helpless father. So far, he piggybacked on the belief that he could do anything and his father would protect him. This kind of an upbringing typical of spoilt children nurtures them to believe that life remains a bed of roses. However, they cower at the sight of adversity, because they stay used to getting what they want and the moment they do not get it, they appear clueless. Tatya whirled about in a similar situation. He fell at his father's feet and cried bitterly like a child.

"Abba, please help me," he begged, prostrating and groveling at his father's feet.

The father needed to do something, because he had induced the habit of saving his spoilt brat, whenever, he invited trouble. This habit seemed difficult to break. Moreover, the larger question of Abba's ability to defend his son remained at stake. The village would watch and rumour, so Abba needed to defend his reputation. He sat on his hams, and and then grabbed Tatya's shoulders. He looked him in the eye and consoled him. "Don't worry. I'll work out something," he confided to his son. He pulled him closer and whispered into his ears.

"Hmm," Tatya murmured, nodding his head in agreement.

"Go," said Abba; he patted Tatya on his back.

Tatya staggered to his feet, and then hobbled out of the house.

"Abba," a voice called out from the door.

Abba looked up. Vasu stood at the door.

"Come in," ordered Abba.

"I came to discuss the offer," said Vasu; he entered the hall.

"Hmm," murmured Abba.

The two men sat down to discuss the offer.

Tatya regained poise after Abba whispered into his ears. There appeared urgency in his gait, as he accelerated to salvage his diminishing fortunes. He reached the village square and saw Kanha the cowherd ambling towards him. Tatya cast a glance at his wristwatch. "Five o'clock," he murmured between his lips, hurrying towards Kanha.

"I'm looking for you. Idiot!" fumed Tatya; he took a deep breath and exhaled. "Where were you?" he questioned, looking around furtively.

Kanha baulked and wondered why his master wanted to meet him at this time in the evening. He seemed taken by surprise and it showed on his face. "I am heading to the waada. I just arrived from the farm," he stuttered, and then looked away.

Tatya seemed in a hurry; he waved his hand. "Damn the waada!" he blurted, staring down on him. "You first go to the taanda and look for Hira. Abba wants to talk to him," ordered Tatya.

Kanha's face contorted; it seemed he did not approve the idea of walking back all the way. He nodded his head, "yeah," he muttered, but hung on hoping his master will change his mind.

Tatya watched him and lost his cool. "What; yeah? Run, you dumbhead," snapped Tatya.

Kanha took to his heels and hit the main road.

Tatya tidied his hair, twirled his moustache and smoothed the creases on his shirt. He gathered his thoughts and scampered towards the Primary Health Centre. He saw the doors open; it appeared Kanta had arrived after having a word with Dada; she sat in the hall of her home, pondering over what happened. Tatya crossed the gate, paused, looked around, ascended the stairs and gently knuckled the door.

No one responded.

Tatya struck the door a little harder.

"Coming," answered Kanta; she walked to the door.

Tatya heard her footsteps advance to the door. He twirled his moustache and waited. The curtain opened and Kanta gawked at the sight. Tatya seemed confused not sure whether to smile or look grim. He moved his eyes sidewards and wondered how to begin. Kanta recovered from the shock; she creased her forehead, stiffened her jaws and cleared her throat. "Huh," she scoffed, twisting her lips, and then spun on her heels.

Tatya hesitated. "Kanta I love you," he entreated.

Kanta stood with her back to him and remained mute. Her mind still confused, fancied, how best to react, because she never expected her efforts to yield so quickly. Deep down in her heart, she appeared exuberant, because she felt she won the battle. Her prodigal lover stood at her doorstep begging for pardon. A sight envied by most women, who crave for such attention. This remained her finest hour of glory; she fancied this moment stay forever; although, her heart craved to whirl around and hug him hard, because she missed him, and yearned to have him by her side. So far, she spent days thinking about him and waited on him, hoping he would return and embrace her, but the wait grew longer everyday. Finally, the moment had arrived; a pleasant surprise and it beckoned her. She decided to toy around with him, and bask in his helplessness.

"What are you doing, at my door steps?" she asked in a haughty manner, tapping her foot. "You said, you'll never come here," Kanta sneered at her helpless lover, who sought asylum from political vendetta.

Tatya's heart raged at her tantrums, but reality demanded he face the situation. He crooned, the take me back tune. "I never meant it. I said it in a fit of rage. I love you and cannot live without you," he pleaded to woo his lost love and salvage his political fortune.

Kanta stayed silent.

Tatya pried about and persisted. "Won't you ask me, to come inside?" he sounded melodramatic.

The words worked as a balm on sprain. Kanta felt warm; her heart melted and churned. The endless wait had hardened her heart, as frozen butter, but the words acted like a flame, melting her heart. "I never stopped you from coming," she replied, in a soft voice; her eyes turned moist. "You decided to leave me and vanished," she added, with a tinge of sadness, wiping her tears.

"I'm sorry," Tatya apologized.

Kanta's heart jumped with joy. She stood at the peak of her conquest, basking in the triumph of her charm. She dabbed her hair to ensure it stayed in order and pressed her lips to keep the lipstick intact. She preened her sari and jigged her head as if facing a mirror. "He came back. He loves me," she exhilarated, in the thought of her magnetic charm.

"Please allow me to come in," pleaded Tatya; he feared standing at the doorstep and inviting attention from the village.

She realized, she forgot to call him in. She walked ahead without saying a word. Tatya tiptoed inside behind her like a thief wary of prying eyes. He cast his glance about and recalled how he walked out in a huff months ago. He challenged her and bragged, but here he appeared like a sheep meekly following the shepherd. Kanta reached the end of the hall and halted next to the window. She stood with her back to Tatya. The crimson rays of the setting sun filtered through the curtains drawn over the windows.

Tatya arched a sly brow and spoke in a soft voice. "Won't you turn around and show me your beautiful face. Oh! How I long to kiss your cheeks?" he crooned, going overboard to convince Kanta. It seemed difficult for his chauvinistic feudal ego, conditioned over years to demand and bully others to submit, but he hung on like an actor, waiting for the cameras to die down.

Kanta on the other hand revelled in high spirits. The attention she received appeared too intoxicating to resist. She continued with her tantrums. "Go on and on! Oh! How I love you talking so sweetly," she murmured, between her lips.

The feeling gradually dissipated; whatever, despise she had developed for Tatya. The mistressical love if one may categorize it, buried deep in the bottom of her heart lifted to the surface, and floated in her heart. Like every mistress, Kanta too wished to hear that her paramour loved her more than he loved his wife. In the darker world of romance, a mistress, who robbed a married woman's man delighted in the conquest. She got a high in the belief that she possessed the magnetic charm to lure a responsible man into her trap. The one attribute, which the champions of feminism failed to defend—a woman betraying another woman. Most feminist declared that it remained out of syllabus, so why study it.

"Say it to your wife or some other woman," Kanta taunted, with a heavy heart, but she did not mean it. It appeared a more diplomatic substitute to the curt word, pardon me or come again. It meant; repeat what you said, because I love what you said.

Tatya, a seasoned womanizer, bit the bait. He grabbed the skin under his throat. "I swear,' he crooned, wiggling his skin. "You're the only woman I love; the most beautiful divine apsara," he rattled off, cocking a wry smile, because this appeared a rare bait worth biting as it trapped the baiter, like a small fly tagged to a hook to trap a fish, leading a hungry shark to the fisherman for food.

Kanta whirled around and faced Tatya; her eyes moist and heart throbbed to embrace her lost love. The love that had buried itself at the bottom of her heart now surfed on nostalgic waves. She remembered the good old days; a memoric euphoria overwhelmed her.

Tatya appeared more than pleased with his effort, but wished to win with a huge margin or better net run rate. He crashed on his knees, and then pleaded with folded hands. "Please don't cry; my sweetheart. I cannot bear to see you in tears. Punish me, if you like, but do not hurt yourself. I know, I'm the one to blame, I deserve punishment," admitted Tatya; he managed to squeeze out some tears.

The sight of her lover on his knees appeared more than intoxicating for any woman. For a mistress it created multiple impacts. It looked exactly like what the doctor had ordered. She hunched over, grabbed Tatya's shoulders, pulled him to his feet and hugged him hard. "Don't do that; I love you. Oh! How much I missed you?" Kanta wept.

Tatya embraced her, kissed her on her head and gently wiped the tears, rolling down her cheeks. "I've left my home," he whispered into her ears.

Kanta could not believe her luck. All the love that she craved for happened to pour down now, as if a cloud bursted over her head, and the water seeped through her skin and gushed through her blood.

"Really," she said, and then beamed.

"Yeah," nodded Tatya, with a smile so broad that it almost ripped the corners of his lips. "From now on it will remain just you and me," he pointed, juggling his finger between him and her. "To hell with politics, I can't sacrifice you for anything in the world," he revealed, stroking her head.

The mistress surrendered. "I love you. You are the world to me. How much I longed to have you in my arms?" she declared and kissed Tatya.

It seemed the estranged lovers rediscovered their love for each other. Suddenly, the woman in Kanta showed up abruptly. "What about Abba?" she asked, nervously. The insecurity resurfaced.

"I left my family for you. Abba kicked me out of the house, but I don't care for anyone more than you," assured Tatya; he held Kanta's hand and kissed it. "All this while, Abba stopped me from visiting you, but not anymore. We'll run away into the world of our dreams, marry and raise a family."

Kanta blinked and shook her head. She could not believe her luck. "When do we go?" she asked, impatiently.

Tatya kissed her on her cheek, and whispered into her ear.

"Hmm, yeah, hmm, hmm, yeah," Kanta nodded her head, smiling. "How romantic it sounds?" Kanta drooled, looking into his eyes.

"It's all planned," Tatya concluded.

Kanta hugged him tight and wept with joy. Her dream, finally, had appeared on the threshold.

CHAPTER 39

▼

The LOFA revolutionaries succeeded in creating an impression on the people of Tendukheda. Ten youth volunteered to join the LOFA. Comrade Sameer took the responsibility of killing the man-eater of Tendukheda. The plan appeared to lay a trap near a water hole that the tiger visited. Comrade Sameer, Pandu and Munda would go and lay the trap. Comrade Munda belonged to a hunting tribe and possessed knowledge about tigers and their behavioural traits. He would guide the expedition. Comrade Ramesh, who suffered from a headache rested in Tendukheda. He would give preliminary instructions to the ten new recruits, who volunteered to join the LOFA.

Early next morning, the trio set off towards the water hole that lay on the other side of the plateau near the hillock, where the tiger killed Bandu. The sun ascended the beautiful hills that surrounded Tendukheda, and the air smelled pristine. The forest gradually warmed up to the morning; the birds on the trees twittered, while a flock of crows soared over the track and vanished behind the hills. Mountain eagles and hawks stretched their wings, and glided over the valley in search of prey. A thin veil of mist, which covered the valley slowly lifted, like the curtains in a theatre, exhibiting the lush green mountains.

The trio trudged along the steep mountain path, winding through the hills for over an hour. They witnessed toddy tappers, gliding up toddy trees to tap toddy. Farmers, who watched over their fields all night to protect their crops from wild pigs and bears, bounded down the road to the village. They headed bamboo baskets filled with fresh fruits and vegetables, which their women would then carry to the weekly hatts (bazaars) and exchange them for salt, tobacco and clothes; items that the Gonds usually purchased from the markets.

Comrade Munda hunkered down on his hams; he scouted the track for pugmarks, when they reached the foot of the plateau. "I don't see any pugmarks," he lamented.

"We'll lay the trap near the water hole and come back tomorrow," said Comrade Sameer; he squatted on the road and motioned Pandu to rest. "Sit down to regain your breath," he gasped.

Pandu sat down; he opened his backpack and pulled out a water bottle.

Munda hunkered down between Pandu and Comrade Sameer. "Give me some water," he requested Pandu.

Sameer frisked his pockets. "Do you have a pack of bidis?" he asked. He stretched his legs out, and then stuffed his hands in his pockets. "I'm not carrying any."

"Yeah," replied Pandu. He yanked out a pack of bidis from his breast pocket and offered them to Sameer, who picked one and lit it.

Pandu offered Munda. "No I don't want to smoke. Give me the water," insisted Munda. Pandu took a swig of the bottle, and then handed over the water bottle to Munda.

"I'm tired to the bone. I wonder why those kids came this far?" asked Sameer; he took a puff and exhaled.

"They looked mischievous and full of adventure. Especially that kid, who demanded his chocolates," added Pandu; he lit his bidi.

"He's the one the tiger killed. Bandu," divulged Munda; he flashed the water bottle at Sameer.

"No," replied Sameer.

Munda corked the bottle and placed it on the ground. "I feel better," admitted Munda; he cast a glance at Pandu, who overlooked the hills. "What are you looking for?" questioned Munda.

Pandu seemed to explore the hills. "This place looks blessed with beauty and water running down the hills. Back home, Ramwadi appears a desert. Is there a way out to carry this water to my village?" asked Pandu, taking a puff and looking at Sameer.

Sameer cocked a wry smile. "It's all possible, but the bloody netas appear interested in making money. They will not think constructively," replied Sameer, winking at Munda. "Don't waste time thinking over it unless you wish to become a Minister and face us," joked Sameer.

Munda laughed. "Hey. If you become a mantri, how will you face us?"

Pandu laughed at the proposal. "First thing I'll transport this water to Ramwadi," answered Pandu; he remembered his family and sounded nostalgic. "Back home, the cotton must be ripe and ready for harvest. I miss my home."

Sameer patted Pandu on his shoulder. "We all have something at the back of our minds. But remember we fight for a better system that's the reason you joined us," reminded Sameer.

Pandu turned emotional; his eyes turned moist. "I don't think the farmers in these hills kill themselves. They look self-sufficient and happy," said Pandu.

Sameer smiled. "They remain happy, because they stay untouched. The moment their needs change to greed, they will start killing themselves. Nature will retaliate, if you do not respect her."

Pandu mulled over what Sameer said.

Comrade Sameer pulled out a piece of paper from his pocket and unfolded it.

"What's that?" inquired Munda.

"It's a part of my father's collection of essays and stories. When I was a child, he used to read out stories and essays to me. This remains one of my favourite essays and explains the value of nature. When the white man wished to buy the Red Indians land, in eighteen hundred and fifty four, the white man asked the Red Indian chief to quote a price for his land," Sameer explained, waving the paper. "This is what the Red Indian Chief quoted. The mining Companies and Government make similar offers to our people—compensation and rehabilitation. Would you like to hear what the Red Indian Chief said?"

"Yeah," replied Pandu and Munda.

Sameer threw away the bidi butt and read out. "How can you buy or sell the sky, the warmth of the land? The idea is strange to us. If we do not own the freshness of the air and the sparkle of the water, how can you buy them? Every part of the earth is sacred to my people. Every shining pine needle, every sandy shore, every mist in the dark woods, every clearing and humming insect is holy in memory and experience of my people. The sap, which courses through the trees, carries the memories of the Red man. The white man's dead forget the country of their birth when they go to walk among the stars. Our dead never forget this beautiful earth, for it is the mother of the Red man. We are part of the earth and it is part of us. The perfumed flowers are our sisters; the horse, the great eagle these are our brothers. The rocky crests, the juices in the meadows, the body heat of the pony and man- all belong to the same family.

'So, when the Great Chief in Washington sends word that he wishes to buy our land, he asks much of us. The Great Chief sends word that he will reserve us a place so that we can live comfortably to ourselves. He will be our father and we will be his children. So we will consider your offer to buy our land. But it will not be easy because this land is sacred to us. This shining water that moves in the streams and rivers are not just water but blood of our ancestors. If we sell you land, you must remember, that it is sacred and you must teach your children that it is sacred and that each ghostly reflection in the clear water of the lakes tells of events and memories in the life of my people. The water's murmur is the voice of my father's father.

'The rivers are our brothers they quench our thirst. The rivers carry our canoes, and feed our children. If we sell you our land, you must remember, and teach your children, that the rivers are our brothers, and yours and you must henceforth give the kindness you would give any brother. We know that the white man does not understand our ways. One portion of the land is same to him as the next, for he is a stranger who comes in the night and takes from the land whatever he needs. The earth is not his brother but his enemy, and when he has conquered it, he moves on. He leaves his father's grave behind, and he does not care.

'He kidnaps the earth from his children. His father's grave and his children's birthright are forgotten. He treats his mother, the earth, and his brother, the sky, as things he bought, plundered, sold like sheep or bright beads. His appetite will devour the earth and leave behind only a desert. I do not know. Our ways are different from your ways. The sight of your cities pains the eyes of the Red man. But perhaps it is because the Red man is a savage and does not understand.

'There is no quite place in the white man's cities. No place to hear the unfurling of leaves in spring, or the rustle of an insect's wing. But perhaps it is because I am a savage and do not understand. The clatter only seems to insult the ears. And what is there if a man cannot hear the lonely cry of a whippoorwill or the arguments of the frogs around a pond at night? I am a Red man and do not understand. The Indian prefers the soft sound of the wind darting to the face of a pond, and the smell of the wind itself, cleansed by a mid-day rain, or scented with the pinion pine.

'The air is precious to the Red man, for all things share the same breadth. The white man does not seem to notice the air he breathes. Like a man dying for many days, he is numb to the stench. But if we sell our land, you must remember that the air is precious to us, which shares its spirit with all the life it supports. The wind that gave our grandfather his first breath also receives the last sigh. And if we sell you our land, you must keep it apart and sacred as a place where even the white man can go to taste the wind that is sweetened by the meadows flowers.

'So we will consider your offer to buy our land. If we decide to accept, I will make one condition. The white man must treat the beasts of this land as his brothers. I am a savage and I do not understand any other way. I have seen a thousand rotting buffaloes on the prairie, left by the white man who shot them from a passing train. I am a savage and I do not understand how the smoking iron horse can be more important than the buffalo that we kill only to stay alive.

'What is man without the beasts? If all the beasts were gone, man would die from a great loneliness of spirit. For whatever happens to the beast soon happens to man. All things are connected.

'You must teach your children that the ground beneath their feet is the ash of your grandfathers, so that they will respect the land. Tell your children that the earth is rich with the lives of our kin. Teach your children what we have taught our children that the earth is our mother. Whatever befalls the earth befalls the sons of the earth. If men spit upon the ground they spit upon themselves.

'This we know: the earth does not belong to man; man belongs to earth. This we know. All things are connected like the blood, which unites one family. All things are connected. Whatever befalls the earth befalls the sons of the earth. Man did not weave the web of life; he is merely a strand in it. Whatever he does to the web he does to himself. Even the white man, whose God walks and talks with him as friend to friend cannot be exempt from the common destiny. We may be brothers after all. We shall see. One thing we know, which the white man will one day discover. Our God is the same God. You may think now that you own him as you wish to own our land: but you cannot. He is the God of man and his compassion is equal for the Red man and the white. This earth is precious to him, and to harm the earth is to heap contempt on its creator. The while too shall pass; perhaps sooner than all other tribes contaminate your bed and you will one night suffocate in your own waste.

'But in your perishing you will shine brightly, fired by the strength of the God who brought you to this land and for some special purpose gave you dominion over this land and over the Red man. That destiny is a mystery to us, for we do not understand when all the buffalo are slaughtered, the wild horses are all tamed, the secret corners of the forest heavy with scent of many men and the view of the ripe hills blotted by talking wires. Where is the thicket? Gone. Where is the eagle? Gone. The end of living and the beginning of survival," concluded Comrade Sameer; he folded the piece of paper and tucked it in his pocket. He pointed to the valley below. "Imagine if all this turns into a coal dump. What will happen to this beautiful landscape? Gone and the people here will fight for survival. They will walk around like the Living-dead; the end of living and beginning of survival."

"Let's go. We need to lay the trap," reminded Munda.

Comrade Sameer nodded, and then motioned Pandu to rise. The trio walked silently for another two kilometers; they reached a riverbed. A small stream flowed into the river; huge dung heaps littered the sand and led to a waterhole surrounded by trees. A few wild buffaloes lay submerged in the water hole; muggers and otters moved around the sandy banks of the riverine hidden by huge moss coated boulders perched on the edges of the riverbed.

Munda halted abruptly. He hunched over, looked down and pointed his finger. "This is tiger scat," he discerned. His colleagues observed what he showed. Munda scouted the surrounding. "This must lead us somewhere. Step carefully," warned Munda, jumping over the scat.

The soft sand appeared trampled and disturbed by buffaloe hoofs. Munda followed the trail. Suddenly, his eyes twinkled. He pointed ahead. "There appears a pugmark!" said Munda; he raced ahead, halted and bent over to scrutinise it.

Sameer and Pandu followed him.

"It's a strong male tiger," Munda deciphered, beaming at the sight.

Sameer and Pandu followed him and nodded.

Pandu looked ahead. "The tiger must take this route to drink water," guessed Pandu.

Sameer unstrapped his gun, and then surveyed the area, while Munda proceeded along the trail. He treaded carefully, moved his eyes about and pointed ahead. "Look more pugmarks and then they disappear behind those boulders into the jungle," he disclosed, pointing at the boulders, which separated the water hole from the jungle.

Sameer and Pandu followed him, with their eyes scouting the surrounding.

Munda pointed at the small opening between the boulders. "We'll lay the trap somewhere there. The buffaloes can't take this root so the tiger must be coming from there."

"Go ahead and lay the clasp," said Comrade Sameer.

Munda followed the trail, reached the rocks and crossed over, while Pandu and Sameer followed him to the opening and watched him lay the trap.

"It's a good trap littered with lots of leaves. We can bury the trap here," said Munda; he crashed on his knees, swept the foliage aside, laid down the iron and steel clasp and covered it with leaves. "It's done."

"Come over," ordered Sameer.

Munda crossed over and joined his colleagues.

"We'll come back in the morning and check. I'm sure the tiger takes this route," said Munda.

"Yeah," agreed Sameer.

The afternoon sun moved overhead, when the three men strutted back to Tendukheda.

A dark moonless night loomed over the dry patta and a faint breeze fanned the hard soil, rustling the sparse vegetation on the rocky terrain. The vast expanse of land lay empty in the December cold, except, a man, who seemed busy in the middle of the night. He wrapped a black scarf over his face, and wore a pair of black shorts, which made him invisible in the moonless night. He would have remained unnoticed, but for the clutter of the shovel, which scooped out the mud from the ditch. The man worked with haste, gasping as he dug the shovel in the mud, and then hauled the mud over the edges of the ditch. He threw down the shovel, straightened up, swiped the beads of sweat trickling down his forehead against the ends of his scarf, spat on the flat of his palms, rubbed them hard, hunched over and picked up the pickaxe. He gasped, while he rolled his eyes around and surveyed the terrain; it looked deserted. He took a deep breath, heaved the pickaxe over his head and bludgeoned the earth. The blade pierced the earth; the man pushed against the handle and uprooted the rocky soil.

He panted as he hammered repeatedly, and then looked around furtively, after every blow. It appeared he feared company. A bundle of clothes wrapped in a tattered blanket rested between the ditch and an abandoned rusted tin board, which fluttered against the breeze. The clutter of the pounding, breathing and fluttering infected the calm of the errie night.

The man paused for a breather; it appeared the exertion had drained him. He surveyed his effort; the ditch sunk two feet below the ground. He gasped and estimated. "Another two feet and the work will finish," he thought to himself, raised his head and overlooked the terrain, which remained desolate. He gasped and wondered. "When will they arrive? I need some rest."

He clamoured out of the hole to the bundle of clothes, pulled out a tattered towel and wiped the sweat that trickled down his body. He sprawled, with his back to the ground, shut his eyes and prayed. "God forgive me. I'm doing it for a living," he murmured to himself. He wrinkled his face, nodded his head, clasped his hands together and entreated the heavens for mercy. His heart melted and he cried.

Suddenly, something stung him on his back. "Ouch!" he blurted, opened his eyes, sat up, curled his hands and scratched his back. A black ant hopped on the back of his palm and scurried across. He straightened his arms, grabbed the ant and flung it away. He then reached for the bundle, yanked out a pouch of tobacco, prepared his stimulant, tossed a pellet into his mouth, dusted his palms and sat with his arms piniced to the ground. He tossed his head upwards, shut his eyes and rested for a while.

"I must get over with it," he reckoned with himself, jumped to his feet, descended into the ditch and continued pounding the earth. He hammered with all his might, as if, venting the anger gripping him and cried. This time he rarely waited for a breather, as if, the anger gave him the added energy to pelt the earth. In quick time, he scooped out the earth, hammered again, until he sank another two feet below the earth and stopped. He studied the excavation and appeared satisfied with his labour. "This must suffice," he said to himself, hauled his equipment out of the hole, clambered out and scouted the landscape. He stared at the road that slithered through the terrain. "They will come, when they have to. I've done my job," he mused, laying down his tired body and shut his eyes.

After about an hour, the sound of an engine disturbed the ambience of the errie night. The man appeared lost in sleep, while dust spirals tailed the jeep, hurtling down the the road, with headlights beaming. The jeep reached the pit and screeched to a halt. A man alighted and raced towards the pit.

"Get up we've arrived!" he said, shaking the man out of his slumber.

The man sat up disturbed, rubbed his eyes and jumped to his feet.

"Come along!" said the other man, hurrying back to the jeep.

The driver shot him a tensed look. "What's the matter Hira? I hope all is fine," he questioned.

"Yeah, he was asleep," replied Hira, hunching over the window of the jeep.

The driver heaved a sigh of relief, opened the door and hopped out. "Hey Vasu! Have you dug the pit?" he asked.

Vasu nodded his head and hobbled towards the jeep. "Tatya, it's four feet deep," he replied.

"Good job," commented Tatya. He hunched over, scrambled inside the jeep and shut the engine. The lights died down and silence engulfed the terrain. Tatya pointed to the jeep. "Go and get it!" he ordered the two men.

Vasu and Hira walked to the rear of the jeep. Vasu appeared worried; he nudged Hira and whispered. "I don't feel good."

"We have no choice. Just don't give it much thought," consoled Hira, opening the rear door. "I'll go inside and haul it. You stand with your back to the door and load it on your shoulders," explained Hira; he stashed his foot on the footrest, and then clambered inside the jeep.

"Hurry up," shouted Tatya; he yanked out a torch from the socket in the dashboard and flashed it.

Kanta lay cuddled on the rear seat. Her throat strangled, with the ends of her sari wrapped around her neck. Vasu went dizzy in the head; his heart churned with guilt and he trembled at the sight. He whirled around; Hira hauled the body on Vasu's back.

"I hope you're fine," asked Hira.

Vasu's eyes turned moist and his legs quivered, while he hauled the body, and staggered to the pit.

"Throw it in!" ordered Tatya; he flashed the torchlight at the pit.

Vasu lowered down and dropped the body near the pit. Hira joined him and the two men laid it at the bottom of the pit.

Tatya cocked a wry smile. "Good! The bitch thought she got the better of me! Bury the bitch!" he ordered.

Vasu picked up the shovel, and then gently pushed the soil over her body.

Tatya raged. "Hurry up! We don't have the whole night!" he chided Vasu.

Vasu fumbled. "Yeah," he hesitated, and then hurried the shoving.

Hira and Tatya looked on, while he completed the task.

"It's done," said Vasu.

"Follow me!" Tatya waved to the two men.

Vasu and Hira followed Tatya to the jeep. Tatya climbed in the driver's seat, opened the glove compartment and yanked out a wad of currency.

"Take it," he said, flinging the bundle at Vasu.

Vasu picked up the bundle that fell on the ground, and then bowed before Tatya. "Thank you," he said, touching the bundle to his forehead.

Hira nodded at Vasu, climbed into the jeep and the machine blazed away in the moonless night.

Vasu looked up to the sky and clasped his hands. "Vithal forgive me," he begged, crying. He then dressed up; wrapped the blanket around his shoulders; gathered his tools and walked away in the darkness of the errie night.

CHAPTER 40

▼

The next two days seemed agonizing for the revolutionaries. They patrolled the water hole and adjoining areas, but the tiger remained elusive. The tiger hunt proved difficult but hopes soared, when a group of honey collectors informed the guerrillas that they spotted the tiger, near the water hole. It had attacked the group, but they successfully chased it away. Munda stayed determined to give it a last shot, because he believed that the tiger would hang around the water hole to avenge his defeat. This inference forced the guerrillas to take to the mountains and track the tiger.

They set off early morning and reached the spot, where the honey collectors encountered the tiger. It appeared a ten minutes walk from the water hole. They clambered up the dense terrain, and progressed slowly, hacking the branches and bamboos scattered on the track. Munda and Pandu chopped and cleared, while Comrade Sameer gave them cover.

"I can't see a thing through this bamboo cluster," complained Comrade Sameer; he looked around furtively, with gun in hand. "I doubt the tiger can see us."

"Hold tight and don't loose guard. This beast appears devious," warned Munda, shoving aside a branch, lying on the path. He pointed to his right. "Pay more attention on this side. The wind blows in this direction."

Comrade Sameer looked up at the trees for an omen; the shrill cry of a langoor or the nervous flutter of birds. He craned his neck to catch the sharp bark of a mousedeer or the bellow of a sambhar.

"Move on," said Pandu, who stood between the two. The trio continued their journey to the water hole.

"Keep looking around," reminded Munda.

"Crunch! Crunch! Crunch!" the dry leaves crackled, and the twigs cringed, while the three men treaded cautiously through the foliage.

"Damn these leaves! It's difficult to move stealthily!" grumbled Pandu.

"Ssh," Munda stabbed his finger on his lips. "Don't speak loudly. Keep a good eye on the bamboo clumps," he whispered.

The trio reached the water hole and overviewed it. There seemed no signs of a tiger here.

Munda frowned. "What do we do now?" he asked, frustrated with the effort; he mopped the sweat off his forehead. It stayed moist and humid in the forest.

"Do we hang around for more time?" asked Pandu.

"It's pointless hanging around here. Munda go down and retrieve the trap or it'll trap another animal," commanded Comrade Sameer, slinging his gun around his shoulder.

Munda extricated the gun slung around his shoulder, dropped it on the ground and removed his backpack. "I need a splash. It's hot and humid here," he said, descending to the water hole.

"I'll join you," added Pandu; he too placed his gun and backpack on the ground, yanked out a pack of bidis from his pocket and lit one of them. "Take one and relax," he suggested to Sameer, offering him the pack.

Sameer pulled one bidi out of the pack. "This tiger appears a moody animal, which makes it difficult to predict movements," opined Comrade Sameer; he lit his bidi and puffed at it.

Pandu shrugged his shoulders. "I have no idea," he admitted, casting his sight about. "Let's go down to the water hole."

Sameer nodded his head; the two men descended the mound. When they reached the water hole, Munda had finished cleaning his face. "I'll go and fetch the trap," he stated, heading for the boulders that lay between the water hole and the jungle.

"Yeah, we'll wash ourselves," replied Sameer, puffing out smoke.

Pandu stepped inside the pool, bent down, scooped out water and splashed it across his face. "Oooh," he sighed, scrubbing his face.

Comrade Sameer enjoyed his smoke and waited for Pandu to finish. Pandu stepped out and wiped his face dry. Sameer threw away the bidi butt, handed over his gun and backpack to Pandu, and stepped inside the pool. "Keep guard," cautioned Sameer.

Pandu held the gun, while he watched over the surroundings. "What's the plan for tomorrow?" he asked.

Sameer hunched over, and then scooped out water. "We'll leave for the coal fields in the morning. We can't wait any longer," he replied, splashing the water across his face. "We have many more villages to cover."

"I think we should have left two days earlier. We're wasting our time on this tiger expedition," protested Pandu.

"It's not a waste of time. It's a part of our duty," said Sameer; he wiped his face with a scarf.

"We're not here to hunt down a man-eater. It's not easy," complained Pandu; he handed over the gun to Sameer.

"I understand, but the gesture is important. We have to empathize with the people of Tendukheda in order to win them over; otherwise, we appear no different from the Government. It is important to share their grief and show some concern. The gesture is important not the result," reasoned Sameer; he slung the gun over his shoulder.

"Comrade Dinesh never functioned in the same way. He threw his weight around and threatened the people. But, I see you have a different approach to convince the people," revealed Pandu.

"The main problem with our organization in Gadchiroli appears lack of quality cadres. We suffered many reverses, because a few traitors betrayed LOFA, and the police arrested many of our fighters. It's not easy to train new recruits and immediately hand them the command of a dalam, because the sudden aura of power makes them tizzy and they get tempted to misuse it," explained Sameer, pulling his gun over. "This machine has tremendous power, and the one, who holds it wields complete power over another. If the wielder stays irresponsible, he will abuse it. It happened with Dinesh. He misused power to make money and then quit the LOFA. I wish to make many changes in the organization, but it will take time. My recruitment drive strives to create a well-knit and disciplined group of fighters that believe in the LOFA ideals. First; we need to get our captured committed leaders released from prison," stated Sameer; he then looked at the boulders and recalled. "I wonder why Munda takes so long."

Munda reached the spot, where he had laid the trap. He sat on his hams, swept aside the carpet of dry leaves that covered the iron clasp. His face contorted. "Where is the trap?" he wondered, with his hands groping around in the litter. "Damn it!" he exclaimed in frustration; he dropped his hands, crawled around the foliage and groped about. Suddenly, something flashed in his mind and he whirled about to watch the trail, which led into the jungle. He noticed footprints. "The forest guards must have taken it," he thought, jumping to his feet.

He heard Sameer call out to him. "Munda! Munda! What's the matter?"

Munda turned around to face the water hole, and then shouted back. "The forest guards have taken the trap. I fear someone has informed them."

"Come over we must leave," shouted Sameer.

"Yeah," yelled Munda; he stepped forward and scanned the ground, while he trudged along. He halted and mulled over the place, where he placed the trap.

A pair of eyes watched Munda from behind the bamboo clump that led into the jungle. The cluster lay at a distance of twenty metres from where Munda stood and pondered. The eyes had watched the three men descend to the water hole and two of them drop their weapons on the mound. Munda now stood with his back to the bamboo cluster empty handed behind the boulders that lined the water hole. The eyes watched the events patiently as if waiting for an opportunity. The time had arrived.

The bamboo cluster released its missile, which raced towards Munda. Munda clambered up the rocks strewn on the path leading to the opening, which led to the water hole. He sauntered along oblivious of the missile that tracked him and waved out to Pandu and Sameer. The missile covered ground and reached ten metres from Munda. This appeared the perfect lanch pad for an aerial assault. The hinds propelled the body into the air as if a propellant, launching a rocket against the force of gravity. It exhibited aero-dyanamics at its best; mid-air the body flattened, shifted strength to the anterior and dipped down for the assault. The blitz hung at the peak of ferocity ready to take on Munda. The lightning ambush shattered the forest calm. Munda sensed the danger and whirled around to examine the commotion. He gawked at the spectacle that stared him down and froze, as if he surrendered before a firing squad.

Pandu and Sameer saw the tiger poised over Munda. Sameer positioned his gun and fired, "bang," at the tiger. The bullet whizzed through the air, but missed the tiger that landed on Munda.

"Bang, bang, bang," three more bullets billowed through the wind but missed.

"Ouch, help, help," Munda screamed for help.

The big cat seized Munda's neck, and then cracked the windpipe. Munda wriggled like a fish scooped out of water then lay immobile. The tiger stared at Pandu and Sameer, and then charged towards them.

"Shoot, shoot," yelled Pandu, quivering at the sight.

Sameer straightened his weapon and then triggered another round of bullets. "Bang, bang, bang," fired the muzzle of the gun. The bullets hit the rocks, but the tiger appeared undettered. He jumped the rocks, crossed over and plodded through the sand. Pandu fled the scene to collect his gun; he hit a rock and tumbled down the mound. He gathered himself, his body shaking with fear as he trudged through the sand. Sameer stood his ground and continued to pump bullets.

"Bang, bang, bang, bang," he fired his Kalishnikov, at the tiger. The tiger roared, charging at him. Sameer fixed his eyes on the tiger and pulled the trigger. "Bang," the bullet ripped the air; the tiger staggered and then collapsed ten metres from Sameer.

"Ooh," Sameer heaved a sigh of relief, and then whirled around to see Pandu.

Pandu panted, clamouring up the mound; he turned around to measure his chances. The sight relieved him; the danger had vanished. "Huh, huh," he panted, soaked in sweat. He saw Sameer dropping on his knees in the sand, and looking up to the sky, as if thanking his stars for saving his life.

Suddenly, the two men gathered themselves and ran towards Munda. "Munda, Munda," they shouted. They reached the dead body, lying in a pool of blood, which spluttered out of the neck.

The two men dropped on their knees. "Munda get up," Pandu shook him, while Sameer examined his pulse. Pandu looked at Sameer and jigged his head. Sameer nodded his head in despair. Pandu turned hysterical, the bloody sight disturbed his senses and he lost control.

"Get up Munda. We've killed the tiger," he screamed into Munda's ears, with tears rolling down his cheeks.

"We failed him," moaned Sameer; he flung the gun on the ground, and then buried his head in the ground in remorse.

"That coward attacked Munda from behind!" shrieked Pandu, pointing at the dead tiger. "Come and face me. You bloody beast," Pandu screamed with rage; his eyes reddened and he shook violently. He looked around and saw the gun lying next to Sameer. He prostrated, seized the gun, jumped to his feet, and then bolted towards the dead tiger. "Come and kill me!" he howled, brandishing the gun. He reached the dead tiger and then halted. His face stiffened and nostrils flared at the sight. "Kill me!" he fumed, pumping bullets into the tiger.

Sameer raised his head at the commotion and then charged towards Pandu. "Control your anger Pandu. Give me the gun," shouted Sameer; he grabbed Pandu from behind and tried to wrest the gun.

"Leave me alone," Pandu yelled, resisting Sameer. It appeared the anger had overwhelmed him and he forgot decorum. "I'll kill all the tigers in this jungle!"

Comrade Sameer succeeded in wresting the gun from him. "Control your anger," he warned Pandu, who dropped on his knees sobbing.

Sameer hunkered down next to him, and then patted him on his back. "Control, control," he entreated Pandu, shaking his shoulders. Pandu dropped his forehead on the ground and wept. Sameer slung the gun around his shoulder, pulled up Pandu and hugged him hard. "Be brave, remember you are a revolutionary," said Sameer, with tears in his eyes.

The revolutionaries broke down oblivious to the surroundings and mourned the death of their Comrade.

All of a sudden, the sound of a gunshot resonated in the air, followed by an announcement over a speaker. "Troops have surrounded you, surrender yourselves to the law. Don't attempt to escape."

Pandu pointed to the mound of rocks, while Sameer whirled around to see the wildlife warden and four forest guards standing on the mound pointing their guns at them.

"What do we do?" asked Pandu.

"We'll see what happens," replied Sameer.

Four forest guards charged towards the dead tiger and examined it. "It's dead!" declared one of the guards.

Michael Strosberg and Linda Kohl, dressed in khakhi shorts, T-shirts, sued leather shoes, with cameras dangling from their necks, emerged on the mound and darted towards the dead tiger. They pointed their handy cameras at the dead tiger and took photos from different angles. The pot bellied wildlife warden lumbered upto the tiger, with sweat trickling down his forehead.

Michael frowned, slamming his fist on the flat of his palm. "Mr Warden!" he raged, pointing at the two revolutionaries. "The two of them have killed a harmless tiger in cold blood. You must arrest them and put them behind bars. They have violated the wildlife protection act. Let them rot in jail for seven long years, otherwise, I'm reporting this killing to the press," he threatened, pointing his lens at the two men and clicking their photos.

Linda sat on her hams, examined the cat and caressed the fur coat of the tiger. "He's a strong male and they have killed him," she lamented, with tears in her eyes.

Michael Strosberg gently pressed her shoulders to console her. "How can we preserve the rich bo-diversity of our forests, when you have such brutal poachers prowling in the jungle?" questioned Michael in contempt, with his eyes fixed on Sameer. "The reason why the tiger count diminishes each year. In nineteen eighty-nine, India reported a population of almost four thousand tigers, but this figure has dropped to below two thousand. It means India looses close to hundred tigers each decade. Add one more to that figure now," stated Michael, pointing at the dead tiger. He shrugged his shoulders. "How much more do we do?"

The wildlife warden moved his eyes around in guilt. He walked to Michael. "We're doing our best, but these tribes, living in the jungles kill at will. They kill all the animals for food and sport," he alleged, staring down at Pandu.

Michael nodded his head and then frowned. "These lame excuses will not work, if you wish to save the tigers from extinction. You know that the High Court appointed our committee to minitor the progress made with respect to wildlife protection and submit a report. Do you expect us to submit death certificates, on behalf of the committee? Is this the reward we get in return for sacrifices made to save the tiger?" he sneered, casting a glance at the dead tiger. The sight of the dead tiger irritated him again and forced him to turn around. "This can't go on. I want you to do something serious. It happened before my eyes."

"There's not much the warden can do. It's the LOFA, which remain the biggest threat to the jungles and incite the tribes to kill tigers," said a man, stomping towards the group, and accompanied by another man, who carried a tiger trap in his hands.

"It's pointless arresting them and taking them to the police station. Kill these revolutionaries here," suggested the man, with the tiger trap. He held the tiger trap before the entourage. "See this warden."

The warden shook his head. "Dinesh, did you find the other revolutionary? We received information that there were four of them," he asked.

"We scanned the entire area, but failed to locate him. Pandu will tell us about his whereabouts," replied Dinesh; he cocked a wry smile at Pandu, and then walked up to face him. "I thought you surrendered to go back, marry and settle down."

"Damn you traitor! You betrayed us to the police!" yelled Pandu; he dashed towards the two men. The guards dropped their guns and followed Pandu, who pushed Dinesh to the ground. They grabbed him before he lunged on Dinesh.

"Stop him," yelled Linda. "What's going on here?"

"Hold him tight," ordered the warden, running up to Pandu.

The chaos gave Comrade Sameer the opportunity, because all the men gathered around Pandu and turned their backs on him. He quickly removed the gun slung around his shoulder, raced to the spot and then pointed the gun to the back of the warden's head.

"If you move; I'll shoot your head," warned Comrade Sameer. He cast his eyes about the other men. "Leave Pandu alone or I'll blow your warden's brains off," he threatened, and then fired a bullet in the air.

The gathering looked stunned at the sudden reversal of fortune. The shot unnerved them and they looked at each other wondering how to react.

"Everyone raise your hands and back off!" ordered Sameer; he dug the barrel into the warden's head and his eyes flashed. "Or I'll blow his brains off! Order your men!"

The warden signaled his men to follow the instructions. They raised their hands and stepped back. Pandu gathered himself, and then ran towards Sameer, while the warden stood helplessly, with his hands raised to the skies.

"That's Dinesh and Tikre," said Pandu, pointing at the two men.

"Yeah," replied Sameer.

One of the guards raced to fetch his gun.

"Bang," fired Sameer. The bullet hit the man's head and he slumped on the ground. "If you value your lives then do as I say or you'll meet the same fate!" yelled Sameer. "Pandu go and collect all the guns."

Pandu shuffled about gathering the guns. He piled up the guns at Sameer's feet, and then held one in his hand.

"Frisk Dinesh and Tikre," ordered Sameer.

Pandu frisked them. "They're clean," he said.

"On your knees in a single file and face me," ordered Sameer.

The hostages followed the instructions. Linda and Michael quivered at the sight.

"Give me the cameras. Pandu collect them." shouted Sameer.

Michael and Linda surrendered their photo-equipment to Pandu, who delivered it to Sameer. Sameer took the cameras from Pandu, and then hurled them back over his head. "Look around and take a good look at this forest for the last time," said Sameer.

The scene looked scary, with the two revolutionaries, pointing their guns at the hostages and one forest guard, lying in a pool of blood.

"These jungles belong to us and we own this land. You have trespassed into our territory and violated the law. Your forest act may claim dominion over the forests, but we do not recognize your laws. Our customs and conventions protect the forests and we do not need your conservation laws to tell us about the importance of preserving the forests. If your government thinks, it can bribe a few of our men and take away our forests you are mistaken. Traitors like Dinesh and Tikre will pay for treachery, because I will prove my words. They cannot escape the wrath of the LOFA. Pandu bring them here," ordered Sameer.

Pandu dashed to them and then pushed them. "Go," he demanded.

The two men crawled on their knees, and joined the warden. They knelt with their back towards Sameer.

"Raise your hands," ordered Sameer.

The two men obeyed. Sameer shifted the gun and pointed it at the back of Dinesh's head.

"You two have betrayed the cause of our revolution and forfeited your right to live," said Sameer; his face stiffened, he took a deep breath and pulled the trigger of the gun. "Bang," the gun shifted, and then fired again, "bang." The bullets sliced through the heads and the two men crashed on the ground.

The sight of the cold-blooded executions unnerved Michael and Linda, who had never witnessed such ruthless killings.

"This is insane! You can't kill people like that," stuttered Michael Strosberg; he quivered and gulped the lump in his throat. Linda broke down with fear.

Sameer stared at the two tiger conservationists. "Thirty minutes, since you arrived; yet, all you talked about was a dead tiger. All you mourned for was a man-eater, who feasted on the blood of our people," he shouted, and then paused; his face wrinkled. "Not once did you turn and inquire about Munda. I put it to you: are we not human?" he sneered, stabbing his finger in his chest. He cocked a wry smile. "The brutal killing of Munda by the tiger never bothered your conscience. All the while, you ranted Tiger! Tiger! Tiger! If by chance, one of you had suffered the same fate, you would have shot the tiger dead and defended your action, as a right to self-defence. If any one of our people take something from the forests. These forest officials call them thieves and punish them mercilessly," fumed Sameer; he pointed his gun at the forest guards. "The indiscriminate killings of our people by forest guards go unrecorded as if they don't exist. Why? They presume our people criminals. That coal field over there," ranted Sameer, pointing in the direction, "has destroyed the forests and threatened the livelihoods of our people, who have lived off the forests for generations. But your government calls it development and has deployed para-military forces to protect the coal fields that feed the thermal power plants, which generate electricity for your people. That coalfield remains the biggest threat to the environment and the root cause of the Tiger-Tribe conflict and you have the gall to call us criminals and push us out of our natural habitat. It's your development that has killed the lung sacks of the planet and your people need to stand trial not we."

Michael interrupted. "We understand your grievance, because we have studied tiger-human conflict for months. We can negotiate a settlement, if you allow us to talk," quavered Michael. He wrinkled his face as if begging for a chance. "I mean discuss."

Sameer laughed. "Yeah let's talk," he agreed.

Michael heaved a sigh of relief. He dropped his hands and crashed on his ankles.

"Put your hands up and talk!" warned Sameer; he jigged his head and motioned Michael to lift his hands.

Michael raised his hands. "Fine," he murmured.

"Good, now make it quick. I don't have the entire day," quipped Sameer.

Michael rolled his eyes around and pursed his lips. "We accept you as humans, but you must join civilization. I mean join the mainstream . . . ," he hesitated, gulping the saliva down his throat.

Sameer narrowed his eyes, tilted his head and curled his lips in contempt. "So what happens, if we join civilization? Go ahead," he sneered.

Michael's face dropped. He feared he annoyed Sameer; he shot a look at Linda.

Linda saw his predicament and interjected. "He means development like good roads, clean drinking water, schools and jobs with a steady income for the people in the jungles," her voice tapered down, at the sight of Sameer's face, which appeared unimpressed with the argument. "Hmm . . . Talk right . . . I'm talking . . . ," she stuttered, jigging her head.

Sameer stared her in the eyes. "Jobs which will vanish after the mining companies have exhausted the mineral resources, damaged the environment and disappeared. Education, schooling, clean drinking water and healthcare for the adivasis should have happened long ago. Why this sudden concern for the adivasis after the Government discovered that the adivasis sit on mineral resources?" taunted Sameer; he twisted his lips. "Huh!"

Linda's face dropped. "I understand your concerns, but the point remains that the tribes must join the mainstream and shed isolation. In a democracy, they possess the power to facilitate change and regulate government inaction. Look where civilization heads and where the tribes stand . . . ," her voice died down, because Sameer waved at her and interjected.

"Your civilization bulldozes this world towards extinction," he pointed at her, and then stubbed his finger on his chest. "Including us and we stand on the verge of extinction, because of your civilization," he fumed.

"Both share the responsibility to save this world from extinction so why not join hands," Michael appealed to Sameer.

Comrade Sameer nodded his head in disapproval.

Michael's face frowned. "Why do you refuse us?"

"If we join you; this world will not exist for long."

"I fail to understand you," admitted Michael; he looked perplexed.

"You will never understand us, because you think too highly of your civilization. For us to understand each other either you join us or we join you."

"Why don't you join us?"

"You have no heart. You think profits over people."

"Intelligence spurs innovation and progress. Change leads to evolution."

"Change also leads to devolution, when it spurs greed and a ceaseless desire to satiate depravities."

"You cannot generalize exceptions. Progress aspires to give humans the opportunity to express themselves. Do you insist that civilization give up thousands of years of progress and regress to the Stone Age?"

Sameer laughed. "Progress must offer all humans, an opportunity to prosper: not a few at the cost of the others. When you need natural resources for the development of the mainstream population you cannot uproot the lives of other people," he stated, with a tinge of sarcasm. He pointed at Michael and continued. "You misconstrue the word progress, and use it for your convenience," he dropped his hand and then went on. "Progress must lead us to greater co-existence, understanding and compassion for all. It must instill trust not spur fear. It must lead us to believe that all remain equal. Your civilization made boundaries, piled up weapons of mass destruction, created a war mongering ideology—nationalism to protect these boundaries, which symbolize a will to dominate and instill fear in other nationalities. Progress resembles a cyanide pill coated with sugar, a polite word that glorifies greed and consumerism, and camouflages a drive to subjugate smaller cultures in order to control and exploit their natural resources. You package this as national interest; raise an army on a diet of patriotic fervour, make them believe in martyrdom and wage war for natural resources. The same forces, you unleash upon us, because you want the natural resources in the jungles. Your civilization hinges on the bedrock of greed and reckless consumerism, which remains a euphemism for progress. However, greed as a word does not exist in our vocabulary. We take what we need, because we respect our forests—the trees, animals, air and water. Our basic philosophy remains—live and let live. How do we gel with your model of progress, which heads towards extinction?" narrated Sameer.

Michael mulled over and questioned. "What do you wish?"

Sameer curled his lips in contempt. "Admit you want the resources, stop using euphemisms like democracy, progress, development and higher standard of living. It stinks of hypocrisy. We will resist," he declared.

Michael creased his forehead. "Why fight over perception? Where will this gun lead you?"

Sameer stroked his gun. "Perception backed by power makes history. It symbolizes resistance to injustice. If you give us life, we will join you. If you give us survival, we will fight you. We do not wish to walk around like the living dead. We do not wish to sacrifice our self-respect and dignity on the altar of your development," he asserted, brandishing his gun. "We possess the right to determine our destinies, to retain our culture and live the life we choose. We will not part with our freedom. What kind of freedom does your democracy offer, if it snatches our freedom to give economic prosperity to others? I call it a conflict of interest, rife with logical inconsistencies, better understood as exploitation," he mocked.

Michael nodded his head and pressed his lips. "It sounds romantic, life with a backpack, gun in hand, mission to overhaul a system and create a world bereft of injustice. What makes you confident that you have a panacea for the imperfections of human systems?" he doubted.

"History—the story of successful and unsuccessful gambles. This gamble may pay, may not, but the gamble remains. We will take our chance, because we believe we will succeed. Ideologies will come and go, but resistance will remain. Presently, we represent resistance beyond the territories we wrested from the bourgeoise State. Those we command, we will defend. We have succeeded partly; we will strive to succeed fully."

Linda interjected. "What about the tigers and the jungles?"

Sameer took a deep breath and then exhaled slowly. "Mr Conservationist we need a heart to save the world and not intelligence. Were you born in a forest, near a stream, under a tree, in the open meadows? Have you lived your life in the midst of a forest? If you live off the forest, you will not destroy the forest, because your spirit remains entwined with it. We do not need wildlife wardens and forest officials, who never saw a jungle all their lives; yet, took up this job after they cleared an exam to support a family to preach the sanctity of forests to us. We will take care of the forests. The forests and wildlife stay threatened by poachers, poltical mafias and wildlife officials, who plunder the resources to make money. Why make tribal people scapegoats? Look at these beautiful hills," Sameer pointed to the hills around the jungle; he whirled around with his hands to the sky. "Imagine a world without these jungles."

All of a sudden, Pandu shouted. "Comrade the rangers are fleeing!" he alerted Sameer.

Sameer spun on his heels and watched the three rangers run in three different directions. "Damn it! Stop or I'll shoot!" he warned the fugitives, and then gnashed his teeth.

The rangers had seized the opportunity, and appeared in no mood to heed the warning.

Pandu looked worried. "What do we do?"

Sameer said nothing; he positioned his gun and fired at one ranger. "Bang," the barrel of his gun billowed. The bullet hit a guard on his back, and he crashed on the ground.

"Please stop!" begged Linda, crying.

"Kill!" answered Sameer; his face raged. He directed his gun at another ranger and fired. "Bang, bang," the bullets hit the ranger on his back; he staggered and crashed on the ground.

"Don't kill, please," Linda continued to beg.

The gun tilted to hit the last target. "Bang," Sameer pulled the trigger, but the bullet missed the target. Sameer clicked the trigger again. "Bang, bang, bang," exploded the barrel; the bullets rammed into the target, knocking it down.

Linda and Michael stared dumbfounded.

Sameer cast his sight on Pandu. "When in doubt-shoot!" he shouted and then stared down at Michael and Linda, who trembled.

"Don't play smart! I presume you designed this conversation to digress my attention. Civilizational Intelligence!" he mocked, booting the warden.

"Ouch!" moaned the warden.

Michael's voice jammed in his throat; his face dropped and he nodded his head in fear. "No . . . no . . . ," he hesitated, gulping the saliva down his throat.

Sameer kissed his gun and then laughed.

Linda and Michael watched in horror. They now feared for their lives. Linda had cried and then plugged her ears and shut her eyes, at the sight of the killings, while Michael grew anxious, thinking of the fate that awaited them.

The warden shivered, when he saw the forest guards shot in cold blood; he held his ribs and hunched over in pain. He turned around and fell at Sameer's feet. "Have mercy," he begged, weeping, "I have a family . . . ," he stuttered, quivering with fear. "I only work for the Government and follow orders. Spare my life," he groveled before Sameer.

Sameer wore a grim look. The renegades disturbed his poise and he wished to get over with the ordeal. He pointed the gun at the forehead of the warden. "I hate this uniform. It stinks!" he ranted.

Linda screamed, "don't kill please," she slammed her eyes shut, and plugged her ears.

Michael stared at the ground and Pandu looked away.

"Bang," Sameer fired from point blank range. The bullet ripped through the forehead, spluttering blood in all directions. The warden collapsed on the ground like a sack of poatatoes. The gun took another toll and appeared on a killing spree.

Pandu turned his head, and then wrinkled his face. Linda looked up to the heavens; tears streaming down her eyes and muttered between her lips. "Holy Christ, please save us," she prayed.

Sameer grinned, walking towards the conservationists. He watched their crumpled faces, begging for life. It appeared as if death approached them closer, and closer, and closer, and closer, and halted before Linda. It appeared a matter of time.

Pandu's eyes turned moist; his heart melted; he pursed his lips and shook his head. "Where did fate bring me?" he thought to himself. He wished to appeal to Sameer, but protocol prohibited him. He stood there anxiously.

351

Linda shut her eyes and drew the cross over her heart. "Christ, please save us," she prayed, quivering, with tears in her eyes. She turned to Michael, as if watching him for the last time.

Michael looked at her, with tears streaming down his eyes. He folded his hands and begged Sameer. "Kill me, but spare her. Let her go," he pleaded.

Sameer stood with a stiff face; his eyes fixed on Linda. He waved his hand at Michael, as if ignoring his plea. "Do you believe in God?" he asked Linda in a soft voice.

"Yeah . . . ," stuttered Linda.

"I want you to ask your God a few questions," said Sameer, pointing the gun at Linda. "Will you ask him on my behalf?"

"Hmm," murmured Linda; her voice stuck in her throat; she pressed her lips and nodded her head.

"Ask your God: why he created such an imperfect rotten world? Why he created violence? Where did he disappear, when the police shot my father, while he led a peaceful protest, against a steel company? Why does poverty and misery exist? Why he appears so helpless against evil? Why he turns his back on good? Why he protects the robber barons that ruin his creation? Why he favours the corrupt bourgeoise politicians that rule the world? Why he accepts money and offerings in temples to answer prayers? How much money will he take to save our tribe from extinction?"

Linda's heart pounded at the sight of the gun. She felt the pressure seethe through her body. It would end in seconds she thought and burst out. "God wants peace," she shouted; her face crumpled as she wept.

Michael folded his hands and bowed down before Sameer. "Stop this and let her go. Kill me if you want," he begged, with tears in his eyes.

"Ha! Ha! Ha!" chuckled, Sameer. "Thu!" he spat on the ground, and then stared at Linda.

"Do you wish to hear, what Roger. Waters has to say about: what God wants?"

Linda nodded her head in fear.

"What God wants God gets God help us all
What God wants God gets
The kid in the corner looked at the priest
And fingered his pale blue Japanese guitar

The priest said
God wants goodness, God wants light
God wants mayhem, God wants a clean fight
What God wants God gets
Don't look so surprised
It's only dogma
The alien prophet cried
The beetle and the springbok
Took the bible from its hook
The monkey in the corner
Wrote the lesson in his book
What God wants God gets God help us all
God wants peace God wants war
God wants famine God wants chain stores
What God wants God gets
God wants sedition God wants sex
God wants freedom God wants semtex
What God wants God gets
Don't look so surprised
I'm only joking
The alien comic cried
The jackass and hyena
Took the feather from its book
The monkey in the corner
Wrote the joke down his book
What God wants God gets
God wants borders
God wants cracks God wants rainfall
God wants wetbacks
What God wants God gets
God wants voodoo, God wants shrines
God wants law, God wants organized crime
God wants crusade, God wants jihad
God wants good, God wants bad
What God wants God gets," narrated Sameer.

Linda cracked under the gun. It appeared too much to take. "If God wants us dead, shoot us and finish the ordeal," bursted Linda. She could not bear the torture anymore.

Sameer held the gun to her forehead, and then moved his finger over the trigger. Linda breathed heavily; she shut her eyes. Sameer shot a glance at Michael, who quivered and pleaded again. "Kill me. Let her go," he entreated.

Sameer looked at Linda. "I don't know what your God wants, but the LOFA doesn't permit killing civilians. The others died, because they wore uniforms; symbols of the State. I will take you hostage and interrogate you. The decision lies with the Supreme Council. Get up," ordered the commander.

Linda continued to tremble with her eyes shut. Michael shook her hard. She opened her eyes and saw the gun had disappeared and Michael beaming. He hugged her hard and kissed her forehead.

"What happened?" she inquired, as if dazed at the happenings. "I'm alive," she wondered, grabbing her arms.

"Yeah," nodded Michael; he repeated what Sameer said. Linda hugged him hard.

Sameer took a few steps backward, and then motioned Pandu to come closer. The conservationists stood up; their faces looked relieved. The agonizing moments had passed.

Sameer whispered into Pandu's ears, and then pointed at the conservationists. "The rules remain simple to follow," Sameer thumbed his fist. "First, don't play smart, any attempt to flee may cost you your life, second." He flashed his index finger, "don't attempt an assault on either of us, otherwise, we will not consider you civilians anymore and you meet the same fate like these forest officials and third," he flicked open his middle finger. "Just follow us and obey our commands," he dropped his fist, and then raised his eyebrows anticipating consent.

"Yeah," nodded Linda and Michael. They appeared too scared to try anything foolish.

Michael suddenly felt his neck. "My camera," he said, and then dabbed his chest. He realized something missing.

"You can take it," replied Sameer.

"What about the tiger?" Pandu inquired.

"Burn it. I don't want anyone making money from it," ordered Sameer; he shot a glance at Linda, who beamed at the suggestion.

Sameer yanked out a piece of paper and a pen from his pocket, scribbled a few words on the paper, hunched over, and tucked the message under the collar of the dead warden.

Linda and Michael hurried to the water hole and retrieved one camera that Sameer flung away.

"Where's the other camera?" asked Linda.

Michael shrugged his shoulders. "Look around the rocks," he pointed out, moving his eyes about.

Linda searched the rocks that lined the water hole.

"Hurry up, we don't have the time in the world," pestered Sameer.

"I can't find the other camera," replied Linda.

"Leave it and come along," said Sameer.

Linda and Michael gave up the hunt and followed Sameer and Pandu into the jungles. The tiger's body burnt in the backdrop of the setting sun.

CHAPTER 41

▼

Kanta's burial continued to haunt Abba. He soon realized that he deceived himself into believing that Kanta vanished from his sight and retrieved his political fortunes. The Dalit Human Rights Organisation protested more aggressively, because his rival Dada knew that Abba had played foul, but Dada suffered from limitations; he could not go beyond a point. The most he could do appeared to lend tacit support to the organization to keep the issue burning. The sudden disappearance of Kanta came as a rude shock to the people of Ramwadi and tongues started wagging.

Dada hated the Chief Minister, because the Chief Minister denied him a Cabinet berth. This appeared Dada's opportunity to even it out with Abba and his mentor the Chief Minister. Egged by his colleagues in the rival camp, Dada backed to the hilt the Dalit Human Rights Organisation's demand with the hope that the high command will demand the Chief Minister's resignation. The stage looked set to unfold the political drama.

In the midst of this political tug-of-war, Abba cringed under the pressure of a CBI investigation, which the Dalit Human Rights Organization demanded. So far, Abba played his cards well to save Tatya, but there appeared a danger that lurked in the background: Vasu. Abba promised to give back three acres of land to Vasu in lieu for the cover up, but failed to return it. He feared the prospects of Vasu turning hostile, so he tricked Vasu into waiting until the matter subsided and ended.

The hostage crisis; an aftermath of the water hole massacre came as a rude shock to Pandu's family. Pandu and Sameer found their photos flashed across the cover pages and screens of all newspapers and television channels. They made headlines and gained notoriety for the hostage crisis they precipated. The police force swooped down on Pandu's family to interrogate them. "Tell us about your involvement in the water hole massacre?" demanded the police from Vasu and his family, who pleaded innocence with the police, but the cops appeared dissatisfied, arrested the family, put them behind bars and charged them with abetting terrorism, though, the police never showed the same zeal in investigating the disappearance of Kanta.

Vasu and Pandu's families spent four days in police custody before Abba intervened and requested the police to release them. The police demanded money and Vasu shelled out all the money he received from Tatya. Vasu's financial condition worsened; he forfeited his investment in the Rabi crop. To make matters worse, the sucker pest disease (lalya) devoured all the cotton in his farm. Vasu, now, gave up all hope he harboured about Pandu returning to Ramwadi in the aftermath of the water hole massacre. All his efforts to save Pandu had washed down the drain.

Abba took full advantage of the crisis. He summoned Vasu after his release from police custody and demanded a share of water in Vasu's tube well. Vasu stayed forced to divert water to Abba's sugarcane plantation. In short, Vasu's situation deteriorated to irretrievable levels and his moral plummeted. So far, it appeared Vasu had failed his daughter, now the fear of failing his son haunted him and made him anxious. Abba showed no intention of returning Vasu's land; Vasu needed to act, because it seemed he lost all. What will Vasu do to get back the land he forfeited to Abba?

The hostage crisis took its toll on Michael Strosberg, who grappled with the tough jungle life. The guerrillas moved from place to place to avoid the para-military forces, which searched the forests for the revolutionaries. The government reeled under severe international pressure to rescue the foreign hostages. The Supreme Council of the LOFA ordered Sameer to take the hostages to the Kolamarkha camp. The journey proved a nightmare for Linda and Michael, who remained unaccustomed to jungle life under stress. Mosquitoes swamped them in the nights and despite rubbing mosquito repellant creams over their bodies, the menace continued. Within a week, Michael Strosberg suffered from Malaria; his health deteriorated rapidly and troubled Comrade Sameer. Linda pleaded with Sameer to release Michael for medical treatment, but Sameer could not do much because the negogiations between the Supreme Council of the LOFA and Government failed to cut ice. This forced the LOFA to remain adamant and hold back Michael and Linda.

The mediator, Krisnaswamy, appeared a deputy editor of the, "Lok Andolan Samachar," a newspaper based in Nagpur. The LOFA demanded the release of their twenty-five hardcore guerillas imprisoned in Nagpur awaiting trial. The Government refused to submit to their demand, because it would lower the morale of the para-military forces and police, who protested. The Director General of Police expressed his displeasure to the Home Minister. He argued against the swap, because the twenty-five revolutionaries captured with tremendous effort at the cost of the lives of police officers, remained important members of the LOFA, with vast experience in guerilla warfare. Besides, five of these appeared ideologues, representing the think tank of the organization. Their arrests had weakened the movement of the LOFA in Gadchiroli and adjoining areas and their release would give a fillip to the movement.

Comrade Sameer and Pandu saw their stock rise within the LOFA, which appeared thrilled with their achievement. Pandu, though, appeared fatigued and wished to return to Ramwadi, but the situation seemed dangerous and more complicated for him. He remained on the hit list of the security forces of the State.

Developments in America hastened. Monty Agarwal sat in a board meeting in New York, when he received the news of the hostage crisis. Sam Strosberg remained tensed at the fate of his son and dispatched Monty to India to tackle the hostage crisis. Sam spoke to the Secetary of State of America and the US Ambassador to India, who took up the matter with the Indian Government in Delhi. However, despite these backroom manouvres, the negotiations failed to yield concrete results. The biggest worry remained Michael's health, which became so critical in a fortnight that the LOFA permitted a private doctor to examine and treat Michael. The Doctor declared Michael critical and recommended the Supreme Council to admit him in a hospital. The Supreme Council appeared in a catch twenty-two situation, because the Government failed to concede to their demands in the belief that the American angle will force the LOFA to submit. Majority of the members of the Supreme Council refused to yield, irrespective of the status of the hostages.

Krishnaswamy's endeavours to persuade the LOFA to release Michael bore no fruit. The LOFA refused and insisted that Monty pressurize the Indian Government. Monty appeared worried because of the fate of Coal Asia Private limited, which might suffer if the LOFA felt slighted. The matter appeared delicate and Monty suggested to Sam that he pull strings to force the Indian Government to yield. The Secretary of State made it clear that the matter remained internal and India must find a way out, but American lives stayed precious and America remained concerned about Michael's health.

India feared the internationalization of the issue and undue advantage the LOFA might derive from the publicity. The trick appeared in settling the issue backdoors, without drawing dissension from the Indian media. India understood that Michael Strosberg remained the son of an influential Senator in America, who might contest the next US Presidential election. Further, India appeared reluctant to disharmonize the Indo-US relationship, which stabilized after the cold war and needed American aid to ward of a potential Sino-Pakistani threat in the sub-continent. The challenge lay in an honorable exit to deflect adverse media publicity.

In Kolamarkha: Linda and Pandu sat by Michael and nursed him. Pandu developed a good relationship with the conservationist and narrated his story to them. He talked at length about Ramwadi and a farmer's life. Linda told him stories about the project she handled. They understood each other better and realized that they aspired for the goodness of life. The health of Michael troubled them and Pandu wished that LOFA released Michael.

This morning looked a little dull, as the clouds covered the sun, and the gloom of a monsoon day swept across the forest. The LOFA waited for Krishnaswamy's proposal, while Michael lay on a carpet in his tarpaulin tent, with Linda and Pandu sitting on either side. Michael felt weak and he spoke in measured words with great effort.

"Linda," he quivered, under a pile of rugs. "I don't think I'll live long. I can see it coming . . . ," he stuttered.

Linda dropped the book, "The One-straw revolution," by Masanobu Fukuoka, which she read, and then tucked her hand under the rugs and held his hand, which scorched. "Don't give up," she boosted him, with tears in her eyes. "You're a fighter and we have a mission to save the tigers," she said; she gently rolled her palm over his forehead.

Pandu, who cleaned his gun, felt uneasy and looked up. His eyes turned moist at the sight of Linda. "I'm confident that the LOFA will release Michael this afternoon. He will recover," he stated, with a heavy heart. He appeared displeased with the rigid stand taken by LOFA, but he remained powerless and tried to infuse hope into Michael.

"What's taking them so long?" asked Michael, his voice barely audible.

"Sssh," Pandu stabbed his lips. "You must rest. All is well. Don't worry," said Pandu; he stood up.

"Where are you going?" asked Linda.

"To find out," replied Pandu; he slung his gun around his shoulder and walked out.

Linda stroked Michael's forehead. "I gather it's the last round of negogiations today. As Pandu said, we will be released soon," replied Linda, with tears in her eyes. She could not bear to see Michael suffer anymore.

Michael smiled. "It's an irony of life; an American counting his last days in a jungle in India. Yet, I feel good that it happened on duty, for a cause I believed in. I have no regrets in life," he philosophized.

"Please don't talk. You must conserve your energy. Please rest," said Linda; she gently placed her finger on his lips. "You're not dying. You'll live to save the tigers," she said, kissing Michael on his forehead.

Michael went on. "People with millions of dollars sometimes appear far removed from reality, they ignore what happens around them. They seem too comfortable to realize that many do not have the luxuries, but stay more contended. I discovered a world beyond billions of dollars; it makes me happy. I am not sure, how dad will take it. He appears too concerned of business and political interests. Yet, I know that he loves me and I love him too. Tell him that his son died a happy man," said Michael; he smiled again and held Linda's hand. "Tell dad to withdraw his mining interests. He made his fortune; now he must payback. If he cannot give away what he made then tell him to invest in restoring the environment. The suggestion might shock him, because I know he sent me here to manage the mining business and not pursue my tiger interest. However, I forgive him for that. Tell my family that I really loved them," Michael expressed his wishes slowly.

Linda cried and hugged him. Her voice appeared stuck in her throat, because a strange feeling overwhelmed her. It seemed to sap her faith though she tried to fight it from within.

Comrade Sameer stepped inside the tent with Pandu. Sameer wore a solemn face and cast his eyes over Michael. The sight worried him and a feeling of guilt overwhelmed him. "I'm sorry for the inconvenience caused to you, but I'm doing my best. The Supreme Council will take a call on this matter. But, from what I've gathered; Krishnaswamy should come here any moment and we'll move you to a hospital," he stated; his eyes turned moist and he looked away.

"What's the hitch?" asked Linda.

Sameer nodded his head. "Some members of the politburo demand a ransom, but the Government refuses to accept all demands. Some want the mining to stop. It appears a hotch-potch situation," replied Comrade Sameer.

"Damn the money! The Government must pay it and let us go. Can't they see Michael dying," riled Linda.

"I agree with you, but we can only cross our fingers and wait for the deal to unfold. I spoke to a few seniors they appear angry with the government's crack down on the people of Tendukheda," explained Sameer.

"We understand your predicament," said Linda.

The news sent a chill down Pandu's spine. "I worry for my folks back home. The police must have picked them up. I'll need to go home and check," he worried.

Sameer turned his eyes on him. "You can't go till this matter settles. Hang on till the crisis ends," advised Sameer.

A small boy burst inside the tent with a gun slung around his shoulder. "Lal Salaam Comrade," he saluted Sameer, panting.

"What's the message?" asked Sameer.

"The mediator has arrived," he gasped.

"Hmm," murmured Sameer, motioning the boy to leave. "I will come."

"Lal Salaam," the kid saluted Sameer, slammed his foot on the ground, whirled around and raced away.

Comrade Sameer squatted on his hams and felt Michael's forehead. "The temperatures running high," he worried, turning his sight at Linda. "I'll do my best. We will move Michael," he assured Linda, stood up and walked out of the camp with Pandu.

Six men sat huddled under a tree, along the rim of the training camp. Krisnaswamy, a short and dark man, with a receding hairline sat in the middle of the group. A group of fighters cordoned the group, with their backs to the men, standing with guns in hand and overlooking the jungle. They stood at fifty metres from the men, who confabulated. Sameer and Pandu hurried to the meeting. Sameer motioned Pandu to stand next to a sentry, who kept guard. Pandu joined the security cordon, while Sameer walked over to the group.

Krisnaswamy lit his bidi, and then broached the discourse. "The Government says that it will accept your demands," he exhaled slowly. "The LOFA will choose the place for handover of prisoners. The money you demand will be delivered on the release of hostages," explained Krishnaswamy; he paused and cast a glance over his shoulders.

The members nodded their heads.

Krishnaswamy took a puff and then waved his bidi. "But they have one condition."

A member of the council interjected, with a frown on his face. "What condition?" he inquired; his eyebrows bumped together in a scowl.

Krishnaswamy fixed his eyes on him and puffed. "This deal will not be released to the press," he stated.

The ruffled member interjected again. "Rubbish."

Krishnaswamy flashed his bidi, motioning him to listen. "Please let me finish," he pleaded and then paused.

The member nodded his head in disdain.

Krishnaswamy continued. "The Government will declare that it exchanged ten prisoners for two foreign hostages, but will not mention the ransom," he concluded, taking a puff.

"Damn the condition!" fumed the anxious member; he rammed his fist on the ground. "We want the people to know the truth; it will raise our goodwill amongst the adivasis."

The other members nodded their head in agreement.

Krishnaswamy lifted his shoulders in a shrug. "The Government wants to save its image and not annoy the police and para-military forces. Otherwise the media will tear into the government," he opined.

The angry member shook his head. "What about the morale of our cadres? We want the police and para-military forces to know that we will resist. We want publicity," he demanded.

"Yeah," nodded the other members of the council.

Krishnaswamy tossed the bidi butt away. "Do you imply you don't accept the offer?" he asked the members.

The members looked at each other.

Krishnaswamy went on. "Remember your gesture will have international ramifications. The American leadership will not take it lightly and the media will blame you for the intransigence. I feel that you accept the offer, because of the hostage's health," suggested Krishnaswamy, motioning Sameer to come closer.

Sameer walked upto the group and then saluted. "Lal Salaam," he slammed his foot on the ground.

"What about the hostage?" questioned Krishnaswamy.

Sameer sat down. "I fear he may die. I felt him a few minutes ago; he burns like a furnace on fire. We must not let him die here; it will complicate things. The State will unleash its forces against us. Frankly, I need time to rebuild the organization in Gadchiroli. I'm not in a position to fight an all out war," pleaded Sameer.

"He has a point," pointed Krishnaswamy. "Why bother about media publicity? The image of the Government has damaged beyond repair. Even the American media questioned the security arrangements for the hostages. I don't think the cover up will help the government better its image," he reasoned; he rummaged through his shoulder bag, yanked out a newspaper and spread it on the ground.

The cover page of the Lok Andolan Samachar carried the pictures of Pandu and Sameer standing next to the dead tiger.

Sameer's blood boiled at the sight. His face stiffened and he exploded. "We hate this media bias. Comrade Munda killed by the tiger figures nowhere in this paper," fumed Sameer; he flicked the pages and then slammed his fist on the newspaper.

Krishnaswamy raised his hand. "Please listen to me. We received a few pictures from the Government, which claimed that the investigating team retrieved a camera from the water hole, which revealed the pictures. I chose the best out of the lot, which I printed on this cover page," he submitted, pointing at the picture on the cover page. He tapped Sameer's fist. "Please allow me," he requested, with raised eyebrows.

Sameer stared at Krishnaswamy, and then pulled his fist away in a huff.

"Thank-you," said Krishnaswamy; he folded the newspaper and tucked it in his shoulder bag. "This, for your kind information, appears the best of the pictures the Government released to the press. If you see the others, you will shoot me," sneered Krishnaswamy.

A member of the council stared down at Sameer. "You should have picked the camera and left the scene of killings," he advised.

Sameer's jaws dropped; a lump appeared in his throat. However, his heart raged at the reprimand. "Damn these idelogues; they know nothing about fieldwork," he thought to himself.

"We want an explanation," demanded another member of the council.

Sameer took a deep breath. "Comrade I apologize for the mistake. However, you must believe that at the spur of the moment, we wished to get away with the hostages, because we feared that reinforcements might arrive. The cameras belonged to the hostages and they dropped them by the waterhole, although, we managed to locate one. We searched for the other, but failed to find it, so we hurried away," explained Sameer.

"Where is the other camera?" asked the member.

"With the hostages," replied Sameer.

"Damn the hostages!" riled the member.

"But the role appears damaged," Sameer stuttered.

"How do you know? Did you check it?" parried the member.

"The hostage confessed. She will not lie to me," replied Sameer.

The Council laughed. "Ha! Ha! Ha!"

"Are you some kind of a God? You must never believe their words. Check it yourself," ordered the member.

Krishnaswamy's face lit up; he interrupted. "If I get the authentic photos printed with the hostage's exclusive interview; it will help my career. I will have pulled out a coup of scoops."

The member gestured to Sameer. "Send someone to fetch it."

"Yeah," murmured Sameer; he stood up, raced towards Pandu, conveyed the errand and darted back to the conference.

"Let us put this proposal to vote," said one of the members. "Those for the proposal raise your hands," he announced.

Sameer's heart froze; he bit his lips.

All the five members raised their hands.

Sameer beamed at the sight. His heart lightened as if a ton of weight vanished. He took a deep breath and then exhaled.

Krishnaswamy heaved a sigh of relief, applauding the vote. "A good decision and don't bother about the publicity. I promise to carry a full-page interview of the hostages. The people will get to know the true story from the horse's mouth. Where's the sick hostage?" asked Krishnaswamy.

Sameer pointed to the tent. "Over there."

Krishnaswamy looked in the direction. "A hired air ambulance of Coal Asia Private Limited will carry him to Nagpur," he stated, and then turned his gaze back at the members. "The Government conceded to your demands, because of American intervention, otherwise, the police force refused to budge; the reason the Government wants to mislead the media. It'll lead to all kinds of inferences," said the mediator; he stood up along with the members. "Go and collect the hostages," he directed Sameer.

Sameer raced to the tent to reveal the good news. Inside, Pandu and Linda wept. Sameer exploded inside excited. "You're free," he yelled; suddenly the sight frightened him. His excitement vanished; his face dropped. He fixed his eyes on Michael then turned to Pandu, who looked away and cried. Pandu shook his head, walked to Sameer and embraced him.

"It's too late," Pandu whispered in Sameer's ears.

CHAPTER 42

▼

The Dalit Human Rights Organisation succeeded in moving the Court, which ordered a CBI investigation into Kanta's disappearance from Ramwadi. Abba's worst fears came alive. Meanwhile, Vasu grew impatient as the days passed on; now, with the CBI investigation bound to happen, Abba held back his promise. Vasu knew that Abba reeled under immense pressure; he feared Abba's intentions and decided to approach the police station at Vithalwadi.

He entered the police chowki at Ramwadi and saw Kendre busy, scribbling something in the register on the desk. Vasu walked upto him and then halted at the desk.

"Huh," Vasu cleared his throat to make his presence felt.

Kendre looked up and scrunched his face. "What do you want?" he asked, with contempt.

"I wish to register a complaint," replied Vasu.

Kendre reclined in his chair and crossed his ankle over his knee. "I see," he yawned, tucking his palms under his head against the backrest. "Against whom do you wish to register the complaint?" he questioned derisively.

Vasu cleared his throat, and then took a deep breath. "Abba Deshmukh," he answered.

Kendre wriggled in his chair, dropped his ankle and hunched over. "Abba you mean," he stuttered, pointing in the direction of Ramwadi.

"Abba Deshmukh, the sarpanch of Ramwadi," Vasu reieterated loud and clear.

Kendre waved his hand and shook his head in disbelief. "Do you mean what you say?" he asked, elbowing the table.

Vasu fixed his eyes on Kendre. "Yeah."

Kendre grabbed the glass paperweight, and then spun it on the table. "Do you know the consequences of this?" inquired Kendre, slamming his palm on the paperweight and staring at Vasu.

Vasu nodded his head.

"What's your complaint?" sneered Kendre.

Vasu narrated his story.

Kendre laughed at Vasu. "We can't register your complaint," he declared haughtily.

Vasu remained unfazed. "Why?"

Kendre reclined in his chair, pointing at Vasu. "An ignorant discredited idiot," he alleged in a gruff voice, dropped his hand and continued, "making allegations against a respected person in Ramwadi, expects me to believe him. I don't believe what you say," jeered Kendre. He knuckled the table, stiffened his face, straightened himself and assumed a regal poise. "Now let me explain the law. The discretion whether to investigate a complaint or not rests with the police and in your case the police finds your allegations not reasonable enough to investigate."

Vasu gripped the edges of the desk, and stood his ground. "What is reasonable enough?" demanded Vasu; he appeared determined to fight like a cornered tiger.

Kendre rammed his fist on the table. The doggedness irritated his nerves, but the audacity worried him. "I'll put it more directly. The Chief Minister's secretariat instructed us not to register a complaint against Abba Deshmukh. If you wish to change the instructions, then go to the mantrayalaya in Mumbai and bring it in writing to us. Remember, these influential people belong to the Deshmukh clan and they run the state," explained Kendre.

Vasu's heart congealed; tears rolled down his eyes and he raged. "Influential thieves," he sneered, shaking his head. "He grabbed my land," cried Vasu. "I have nothing to offer my son. I swear he will pay for it. I curse him, because he trampled my stomach," yelled Vasu; he shook violently and the anger in his eyes reflected the intensity of his pain.

Kendre dropped back on his chair at the sight. A chill went up his spine, when he felt the vibes tug his heart. He raised his hands. "Listen and try to understand me," he reasoned, trying to calm down Vasu. "I'm here to take orders from my seniors. I can't go against the orders of the Chief secretariat," he wrinkled his face to express his helplessness; he looked around, elbowed the table and whispered. "I suggest you settle the matter with Abba."

Vasu slapped the table. "I'm tired of visiting him. He will not listen to me. He gives false promises," complained Vasu.

Kendre motioned Vasu to sit down; he picked up the telephone. "I'll ask Abba, if I can register a complaint against him," he said, dialling Abba's number.

"Namaskar Abbasaheb. I'm Kendre," he introduced himself, and then explained the situation in brief. "Yeah Saheb, hmm, hmm," he palmed the receiver, and then addressed Vasu. "Sit out. I'll call you over."

Vasu stood up and then hobbled outside the hall.

Kendre watched him go, and then resumed the dialogue in a low voice. "Yeah Abbasaheb I made him wait outside. He seems disturbed and angry. Hmm, hmm, hmm, hmm, hmm. I fear he may visit the headquarters. Hmm, hmm, O.K.," he slammed the receiver, and then called out. "Come in."

Vasu walked back to the desk.

Kendre smiled. "I talked to Abba and he says that he wants to talk to you. He will return your land, when you meet him. Go back and meet him," suggested Kendre.

"What if he fails to listen?" inquired Vasu.

Kendre frowned at the nagging. "Listen, you go and meet him. He will deal with you. Go," he snapped his fingers.

Vasu stood up dejected, walked out of the chowki and headed for Ramwadi.

The incident shook Abba off his senses. If Vasu dared to go to the police station, and register a complaint against him, he could very well spill the beans to the CBI. The politician foresaw the tactics that Vasu employed, but he remained apprehensive about the prospects of his rivals backing Vasu. Abba appeared cornered and beaten at his own game. He sat in his chamber, with all kinds of thoughts criss-crossing his mind. He cracked his knuckles and shook his head. "Damn the politics! It worries me all the time," he thought to himself. He tapped the floor with his feet, bit his lips, stood up and paced the hall up and down. He appeared restless, while he thought, as if he wished to execute all he conjured within minutes and reach a conclusion.

The door leading to his home creaked. His wife stepped inside the chamber. "Lunch is ready," she stated.

Abba waved at her. "I'm not hungry," he declared.

His wife noticed his anxiety. "What's the matter? You need to eat," she insisted, in a soft voice.

Abba halted and stared at her. "Damn the hunger! It's all because of your son," he fumed, hurling his hands over his hips. "Go and feed your son!"

His wife twisted her lips. "Stop blaming me. He's your son too; you should have disciplined him," she retorted, in a defiant manner.

"I'm sick of this politics. It drains me."

"Why don't you quit?"

Abba raised his hands. "I have blood on my hands," he admitted, and then dropped his hands and looked away. "If I quit; I'll be hanged."

"Things will work out, but why stay hungry."

"Things work out, if you're clean; if you're dirty, you have to keep scheming to get out of the murk," said Abba; he waved at his wife. "Leave me alone. Go."

His wife shook her head, and then walked out in a huff. Abba sat down on his chair, and then gazed at the tiles. The CBI investigation crept back into his head; he wrinkled his face and knuckled his forehead. An hour past by, but he continued to sit and think.

Somebody knuckled the door. Abba looked up to find Vasu at the door. Abba's blood boiled at the sight; he grabbed the arms of his chair to control his anger.

"Come in," he said.

Vasu walked in, with a stiff face and stood before Abba.

Abba slapped the arms of his chair. "I told you I'll give back your land. Why are you running to the police chowki and complicating matters?" asked Abba.

Vasu maintained the stiffness in his face, as if he preplanned the manner to approach Abba. "I have nothing, but the land to bequeath to my son," he answered.

Abba pointed at him. "Are you blackmailing me?" asked Abba.

Vasu nodded his head. "No. I haven't said a word," he replied, fixing his gaze on Abba. "I'm only interested in my land."

Abba stood up in a huff, walked out of the hall into his house and returned with a piece of paper in his hand. "This is your sale deed," he said, showing the paper to Vasu.

Vasu took it from Abba's hand, and then perused the document.

"Tear it apart," ordered Abba.

Vasu tore it to pieces.

"I hope you're satisfied," asked Abba.

"Yeah," said Vasu.

The two men watched each other silently. It appeared an uneasy moment, the kind that appears, when a relationship sours. Abba shook his head, and then motioned him to leave. Vasu walked out.

For the moment it appeared, as if Vasu's efforts paid, though he remained wary of Abba. Besides, Shoba's future stared him in the face, because she appeared as good as widowed. Pandu had damaged things beyond repair. His chances of returning to Ramwadi remained bleak. Vasu would have to slog it out to repay the loan and interest. His gamble had complicated things for him. The road ahead appeared bumpy and treacherous.

Sam Strosberg looked shattered. The ocean waves lashed at the sand on the beach that rolled down his mansion. Sam stared poignantly at the expanse of water, tossing about in the Caribbean Sea. He elbowed the railings of his balcony, pondering over the death of Michael. He noticed the lighted yatchs and liners anchored on the shores, tossing about on the dark waters. The wily and tough Senator resembled a rudderless ship floating in an ocean. The death of his only son made him directionless. The heir to Strosberg Incorporation vanished; no matter how hard he tried, Sam could not come to terms with Michael's death.

Suddenly, the billionaire businessperson pipped to run for Presidency appeared clueless about his purpose in life. The death halted him in his tracks, and forced him to rethink. The ceaseless running around with ambition stopped. He never expected it to come so early, but it came like a bolt in the blue and bared his emptiness. All this while, he appeared a man on a mission, with no time for his family.

Now, he seemed a living-dead, with all the luxuries that life offered, but without a son. He could go on and on, running around until he dropped dead, talk big about life, its struggles, bouncing back and moving ahead, but he remained an embodiment of emptiness.

The sheer hollowness of his existence haunted him for the first time. His money, his power and influence failed to dodge fortunes treacherous turn. He stared into the darkness, gripped the railing, tightened the muscles on his face, shut his eyes, pursed his lips and cried. The strong wind blew away the tears rolling down his cheeks, as if cleaning his sorrows buried in his heart. He opened his eyes, and watched the sky dotted with millions of stars.

"What am I compared to those stars?" he philosophized; his ego cracked. "Do I really count in this Universe? How much do I measure in the Cosmos?" he thought to himself, nodding his head and answered. "Not a speck."

A hand dropped over his shoulder. Sam turned to see Monty patting him. "Sam, I feel your sorrows," Monty emphatized, with a grim face. Sam took a deep breath, and then exhaled. "It's a matter of time. Time will heal your wounds; you'll get over it and move on."

Sam cocked a wry smile. "Get over and move on," he jeered, looking down and shaking his head. "Nah Monty, things have changed. As I reflect over my purpose in life, I realize that I headed in the wrong direction. Money, power and influence appeared my goals. I seemed vain in believing that I remained the best and most competitive man to run America and the world. Suddenly, I feel jolted to my senses. I have realized that I don't deserve to run this country," he submitted, with a sigh of relief.

Monty laughed. "Come on Sam, don't blow things out of proportion," Monty remarked, gently fisting Sam's shoulders. "America needs a tough guy like you to run the show. Take some time out. You need a break, till things fall in place," suggested Monty, in a bid to console Sam.

Sam disagreed; he shook his head. "Not anymore. I plan to retire and seek quality time for myself. This reckless running around and pretending must stop," confessed Sam.

Monty's face dropped; he dropped his hands and leaned against the railing. "What do you mean to say?" he asked, shocked at the way Sam talked.

Sam crossed his hands over his chest, whirled around and stood with his back against the railing. "I will not run for US Presidency," he admitted.

Monty straightened up; his face wrinkled as he interrupted. "What?" he questioned, in disbelief, twisting about and facing Sam.

Sam's eyes widened; he raised his eyebrows and nodded. "I said I will not run for US Presidency. I sincerely feel like giving away my wealth in charity, becoming a yogi and retiring to the mountains in search of peace and truth," Sam expressed his desire, and then smiled.

Monty stared in disbelief. "Stop joking. You'll forget it and move ahead," he insisted, hoping the renunciation appeared a fad.

Sam lifted his shoulders in a shrug and pressed his lips. "You may choose to think as you will, but I must admit the truth. This Presidency stuff appears a means to satisfy an ego. Presently, it sounds hollow and hypocritical to me, because I know I lack the moral stature to run the world."

"You know nothing," fumed Monty, taken aback by Sam's thoughts.

Sam inhaled a deep breath, and then exhaled. He spun around and watched the ocean. "American politics looks morally bankrupt, and we thrive on this bankruptcy. Do you recall what Lincoln said, 'you can please some of the people some of the time, but not all the people all the time.' What have successive Presidents done to the American people?" he questioned, tilting his head to face Monty and hunching over the railing.

Monty looked on without a word.

Sam turned his sight at the waters. "They fooled some of the people, all the time, won elections, and then forgot conveniently that they mislead the people, who reposed their faith and trust in them. We, politicians call it political acumen, statecraft, Machiavellism, or whatever, but the truth stays that we failed to deliver to the American people what we promised. We made false promises and lied," he confessed, and then paused for a breather.

Monty lifted his shoulders in a shrug. He appeared surprised with Sam's way of thinking.

Sam crossed his hands over his chest. "We possess the power, which envies many in the world; yet, do we exercise this power responsibly to run America and the world? Just look at the Middle

East. Our policies have forced the people to hate us. Our foreign policy, which pursues our national interest backed by huge firepower and millions of dollars, has invited the wrath of millions of people over the world. Where do you think we lead the world as leaders?" he questioned.

Monty raised his hands. "Freedom and Democracy," he answered.

Sam nodded his head. "We appear headed for a glorified apocalypse and ignore the truth that this world needs a leader with impeccable moral values. This world needs a political leader, who strives to take decisions that will benefit generations. What are we? Petty politicians bothered of winning the next election. How long will we continue to mislead the American electorate and deceive ourselves? It looks hunky-dorry to put on crocodile hide, flash our toughness and glorify chauvinism, but we cannot run away from our conscience," Sam alleged; he dropped his hands and jabbed his finger on his chest.

Monty wriggled with unrest. He failed to fathom Sam's sudden idealistic rhetoric. He stared at Sam without saying a word.

Sam pointed to the skies. "The Bible talks about judgement day. How do we propose to face judgement day?" he inquired, hurling his hands over his hips.

Monty interjected. "We live in a real world, which runs differently. Don't sound biblical," he rebutted, with a frown on his face.

Sam nodded his head. "The truth remains that most American politicians appear so damn arrogant that they will not hesitate to bribe and get around judgement day, because they have this tremendous self-belief in their material strengths: money and power. The truth remains that we have ruined America, and destroyed the world," alleged Sam; his face reddened and eyes widened. He took a deep breath and exhaled.

Monty patted Sam on his shoulder. "Calm down," he requested him.

Sam shrugged his shoulder and twisted his lips. He pointed to himself. "I have witnessed American politics closely, in fact; I live and breathe it and believe me it stinks of decadence," he stated, wrinkling his nose and dropping his hands on his hip. "Our foreign policy based on Morgantheau's, 'realism,' provokes destruction and mayhem. We deceive ourselves, when we coat a cyanide pill with sugar and declare our selfish interests—a fight for freedom and democracy. What about the altruism Christianity preaches? Its plain self-interest glorified as national interest and run on a war raking ideology called nationalism," Sam fumed.

Monty shook his head. "What do you suggest?" he questioned.

Sam looked him in the eyes. "Power carries responsibilities and the world looks at America as a role model. We set the benchmark for others to emulate, and look at what we manifest, a cowboy brandishing a gun, riding on the priaries, and shooting helpless wild buffaloes for sport. Exactly the opposite of what the world needs. The world needs a morally upright leader to emulate," he answered, slapping the railing.

Monty's eyebrows bumped together in a scowl, and he wondered how to handle Sam.

Sam laughed. "Just scour the American poltical landscape, and you will notice the good leaders pushed to the wall, and their voices gagged. What does it take to run for American Presidency?" he asked with contempt, and then paused and continued. "Loads of money called fund raising capacity. Bullshit!"

Monty countered. "Money is needed," he snapped.

Sam smiled wryly. "What happens when you enter the White House? You spend the next four years, paying back all you raised. In reality, the American President stays forced to dole out favours to big fat American MNC's and arms manufacturers to clear his debts. This, we call American investments that promise jobs to create incomes. The American President appears more of a salesperson of the highest order, who straddles the globe for markets, and for the companies that funded his election campaign. He poses like a roadside bully, with a carrot and stick in each hand. He dangles the World Bank and IMF economic policies, and brandishes his military firepower at those who refuse to conform. All this for the democracy he claims to defend," explained Sam, in a derisive manner.

Monty remained stunned to silence. He looked away in anger.

Sam went on. "We lost the moral sature that Abraham Lincoln created. Presently, if we wish to salvage it, it appears like searching for a needle in a haystack. The Great American people deserve a better leadership. Fellow Americans criss-crossing the globe feel the hate our leadership has generated. I admit I do not qualify to run America and the world, a truth, which Michael's death enlightened me about. I remain proud of Michael and love him even more. I lost him, the greatest loss of my life. Businesses may crash, but I can put them back in order as I did all my life, I can vouch that it looks easier. But to loose a son like Michael means loosing my soul," moaned Sam Strosberg.

Monty gently placed his hands over Sam's shoulders to console him. "I can see and feel the loss you suffered," he spoke, in a low voice and dropped his hands.

Sam's eyes filled with tears that streamed down his cheeks. His words blurred as he poured out his grief. "Michael warned me to go slow, he reminded me more than once to think beyond power and money," stuttered Sam. He brushed aside the tears, which rolled down his cheeks with his hand. "I mocked him and called him idealistic. Today, the same words haunt me. It appears that he won and I lost," Sam admitted, with a heavy heart, pointing to himself and lamented. "Today, I realize that I lived in a world of delusion," he looked at the star-studded sky. "If you look at the sky; you see a million stars staring down at you, with contempt, as if mocking your insignificance. I wonder now: Where is Sam Strosberg the billionaire in this Cosmos?" he questioned, in a melancholic tone and then answered. "A speck in this universe; for all the toil, cunning, and influence I wasted to reach this far, I see the stars mocking me, because I traded my conscience and peace of mind very cheaply. I appear the worst businessperson in this Cosmos, because I sold my peace and happiness for a few billions to live a life of greed and material pleasures. I appear the biggest failure on earth," wept Sam, burying his hands in his palms.

Monty's eyes turned moist, as the words tugged at his conscience. A sense of fear gripped him, when he saw the sky. It appeared he never philosophized so far, but now Sam's words made sense. He turned his eyes on Sam, and patted him on his back, but Sam remained inconsolable. It looked like he wished to pour out all the guilt buried deep down in his heart. He seemed lost in penance.

"What do you propose to do with all the money?" asked Monty; he wished to get rid of the fear, which gripped him.

Sam looked up; he appeared calm and his eyes sparkled as he spoke with abandon. "I'll spend it as Michael wished to restore the environment. Rockfeller and many other billionaires charitised their wealth, now, I gather why they did it. Carnegie killed himself I often wondered why, but now I understand how wealth kills. I propose to invest money in developing non-conventional forms of energy sources, finance rainwater-harvesting programmes in poorer countries, create greener belts around the world to protect forests and wildlife, spend on recycling waste materials, finance the research of a viable eco-friendly substitutes for plastic and so much more," he beamed full of enthusiasm. "It'll help Michael's soul rest in peace. Suddenly, I feel as if I can do more constructive work than the American President can. I never thought like that before, because my mind remained clogged with selfish thoughts."

A chill went down Monty's spine. His heart churned out the sediments of guilt buried deep down and made him uneasy. He spoke to please himself. "Your renunciation will not save America, because American politics will continue down the same path. It seems that you're running away from reality," Monty defied Sam's renunciation of realism.

Sam took a deep breath and then exhaled; his heart felt lighter. "I run away from lies and deceit, which you call reality. Why do we deceive ourselves, by sounding diplomatic? My renunciation will make a difference, because at least it will save America from one thug. It may seem a drop in the ocean, but each drop makes an ocean. At least, I have the gall to see through myself and accept the bitter truth. The bare truth and not the reality that you politely allure to," replied Sam, with conviction.

The conviction stumped Monty, who suffered a dilemma; he creased his forehead and looked tensed. He wished to test the waters. "Sam, we have investments in India, Latin America, Africa and other parts of the world. You cannot walk off and leave me in the dark. You have a responsibility towards me," he argued.

Sam waved off his concern. "I've a greater responsibility towards the environment. If you cannot see beyond yourself, then at least think of your children and their children as a part of you and ask yourself, 'where do I lead them?' This world belongs to all that inhabit the planet and we do not have the right to damage the environment to hoard wealth. I'm pulling out my investments that ruin the environment and using the money I made to restore it," revealed Sam.

Monty's heart felt heavy. He sweated despite the ocean wind that swept the balcony. He came to console Sam, but it appeared he needed consolation. "I understand what you imply and it makes sense, but I fear you more than ever, because you enlightened me. I reveled in ignorance, which insulated me from introspection. However, your introspection has forced me to reflect," divulged Monty.

Sam put his hands over Monty's shoulders and tried to reason with him. "The truth remains that you stayed unhappy, because your actions contradicted peace. Greed devoured your peace of mind, like a voracious caterpillar which feeds on leaves and never tires," explained Sam; he looked at Monty who appeared troubled. "I suggest you take some time out and think over your life. Only when you sit alone and reflect, will you discover your happiness. Step out of this rat race for survival; keep myself busy buzz, which strangles truth and living. Stop living to survive like the living-dead and live to live life," advised Sam.

"Hmm," murmured Monty; the soul in him appeared stirred.

"Let us eat. I'm hungry," said Sam.

The two men walked inside the banquet hall and sat down for dinner.

CHAPTER 43

▼

It appeared many nights, since, Vasu last slept at his farm. The erratic load-shedding schedule, now, shifted to the early morning hours, besides Vasu stayed forced to channel his water to Abba's sugarcane plot. He accepted the deal, because Abba bore the cultivation expenses for the Rabi crop. Tonight, he decided to go and sleep in his farm. He thought he succeeded in wresting his three acres of land from Abba and felt relieved. He took pride in his land, but all these days he felt as if the land never belonged to him. It robbed him off his peace of mind and sleep. Besides the village ridiculed him and looked down upon him. Now, the tide changed and he could walk with his head held high.

He dined, sauntered off to the dry patta and then stretched down on his back at a distance from the neem tree. He watched the beautiful star-studded sky, hanging overhead and reflected upon his life. He dreamt of living a modest life of dignity, but fortune killed his dream. He endured all the rough and tumble that life offered, but when he thought of his daughter his face wrinkled. So far he accepted Pandu, despite what happened, but the aftermath of the waterhole massacre changed his thinking. He regretted his decision and felt he betrayed his daughter. He tossed about at the thought of her fate.

"What would become of her?" a thought flashed across his mind. "What will happen to Pandu?" he wondered, staring at a shooting star, whizzing past the sky; a chill raced down his spine. "Can Pandu come back to Ramwadi?" he asked himself, ruminating and shaking his head. "Shoba's in-laws appeared nice people, but how long can

Shoba continue to stay at Pandu's place," it occurred to him; his heart felt heavy and tugged his conscience. "I need to do something," he told himself; a lump appeared in his throat at the thought of another responsibility. "Bring her home," his conscience whispered. He turned it over in his mind. "What will the village say?" he weighed the possibilities, tucking his hands under his head. "How will it matter? The village never says well about me either," he envisaged, frowning at the conclusion. "Will Mangala agree?" he questioned his decision; his blood boiled. "She will toe the line. I will not listen to her this time," he formulated, gnashing his teeth. "She forced me into this situation. I should not have listened to her that night," he reviewed what happened and sat up in anger.

He pointed to the mound of earth. "On that fateful night over there it happened, when she sneaked in and broke the news. The curse," he riled, picking up a stone and flinging it in the direction of the mound. "Thu," he spat on the ground; his heart congealed, as he recalled the fateful moments and he wept. He buried his hands in his palms and whined. "How much more to endure?" he wondered, clenching his fists and ramming them on the ground. He gasped and kicked his feet about as if the thoughts and anger strangled him. He wished to vent out his rage against God, people and the system, which betrayed him.

He looked at the sky in anger, with tears streaming down his cheeks and raised his hands. "Vithal, where are you? Why don't you help me?" he questioned, and then wept. Suddenly, his heart froze; he dropped his hands, lowered his head and shook it vigorously. "He doesn't exist," he conjured, dropping his palms on his head and shutting his eyes. The wind whistled as it blew over the deserted land. Vasu dropped his hands; his shoulders sagged as he stared at the land. He dug his hand in the soil, scooped out a handful and lifted it above his shoulders. He released it slowly against the wind, which carried it along. "How much more blood will it gulp?" he wondered, looking at the soil flitting in the air.

Suddenly, he heard the rumble of an engine in the air. He strained his ears to discern the noise, which grew louder. He twisted around and watched two headlights darting along the dusty road. His heart pounded at the sight, and anxiety overwhelmed him. His instincts goaded him to to run and hide. However, he argued that the jeep would swap tracks and take the road to the taanda. He stood up and watched, as the jeep rattled down the bumpy road. It reached the point, where the two roads intercepted. Vasu held his breath. "Go, go, go," his instincts pleaded, heart beckoned and legs itched. Vasu's mind grappled with his instincts and he stayed confused. The jeep roared as it hurtled towards him; the lights pierced his eyes; he raised his hands to screen the beams. The jeep screeched to a halt ten metres from Vasu, and then the lights died down. Vasu blinked and lowered his hands. Four men disembarked and then raced towards Vasu. Vasu sensed danger, when he saw the men.

"You swine," shouted Tatya, pushing Vasu, who stumbled and crashed on his butt. Tatya kicked Vasu in the ribs.

"Ouch," shrieked Vasu, reeling on the ground.

Kendre hunched over, caught Vasu by the scruff of his collar and hauled him to his feet. "You've grown too big for your boots. How dare you complain against Abba?" he threatened, slapping Vasu across his face.

The sudden events unnerved Vasu and he appeared terrified at the sight that greeted him. "Tatya please," he folded his hands, begging for mercy.

"You think you can get the better of us by running to the police station, yeah," Tatya howled, kicking Vasu on his butt.

"Ouch," Vasu screamed in pain.

The four men beat Vasu mercilessly until he staggered and collapsed on the ground. They then dug their boots into his body. Vasu cuddled to ward off the blows that rained on him from all directions.

"Enough," shouted Tatya, motioning the cops to stop the pounding.

The men withdrew, while Vasu groaned in pain. Tatya sat on his hams and looked at Vasu's bloodied face that appeared cut and bruised. "What did you say to the police?" Tatya questioned, with contempt.

Vasu continued to groan in pain. He appeared dizzy and weak and could barely move his swollen and cut lips.

Tatya looked down on him with a cocky smile. "I heard you complained that we stole your land. This filthy land," Tatya mocked, kicking the soil. He twisted his nose and spat on the land in contempt. "Thu," he quivered, with rage. "We stole your land," Tatya taunted, with a gruff voice, and then stared at the cops. "You see this patch of infertile land," he pointed out the land, addressing the cops. "Will anyone take it for free?" he asked with scorn. He directed his finger at

Vasu and laughed. "He says that we stole his land. He forgot to tell you that he borrowed money for his daughter's wedding to that terrorist hiding in the jungles," he jeered, spitting on Vasu. "Thu! He takes money, fails to return it and then complains that we stole his land. You swine," yelled Tatya, kicking Vasu.

Vasu groaned in agony and gasped for breath.

Tatya lowered down on his hams. "Show me the light," he ordered, snapping his finger.

Kulkarni and Bhosale lit their torches and directed the beams against Vasu's battered face. Tatya grabbed Vasu's collars, pulled him up and looked at him. Vasu appeared limp, with his face swollen and nose bleeding. Tatya pushed Vasu away and then stood up. "Beat him to death and bury him here," he directed the cops.

"I have a better idea," stated Bhosale. "Make him run and shoot him dead. A man abetting terrorism, when confronted by the police refused to surrender and attempted to flee. The police shot him dead. It will make fantastic news," suggested Bhosale.

Tatya flashed his hands. "Do what you want, but kill him before the CBI arrives," he declared; he shot a glance at Vasu.

The cops nodded their heads.

"The CBI will arrive and he will live to talk," a voice asserted in the darkness.

The men appeared shocked and looked around furtively.

"Torchlight," said Kendre.

Bhosale and Kulkarni beamed their torches around.

"Who is it? Come out," stuttered Kulkarni, beaming his torch about. Suddenly, he quivered at the sight on the ground. A man wrapped in a blanket, with a scarf around his face, lay on his stomach, with a gun in his hand. The beam shivered in the darkness.

"Drop your torches or I'll shoot," threatened the man.

The torches crashed on the ground. The man jumped to his feet and then raced thirty metres through the darkness. The cops quivered as the sound of shuffling feet approached and, finally, halted before them.

"Who are you?" Kendre stuttered, swallowing the lump in his throat.

"I am witness to the murder of Tillya and Sushma," replied the man. He pointed his gun at Tatya, who shivered with fear. "He murdered them," stated the man.

"It's Pandu," Tatya's voice quivered; he looked sideways at the cops as if seeking help.

The man loosened the knot that bound the scarf around his face. The scarf dropped down. "Yeah, I'm Pandu," he showed his face.

The cops trembled at the sight of Pandu, with gun in hand. They recalled his photo in the newspapers; the waterhole massacre lingered in their minds.

"What are you waiting for? Go and get him," Tatya ordered the cops half-heartedly. He tried to scare Pandu.

The cops looked at each other wondering, who will bell the cat.

Pandu smiled wryly. "Come and get me. Do you hear what the scum says? How dare you disobey him?" taunted Pandu; he looked at Tatya. "The one who moves will face a bullet. Stay where you are and go on your knees."

The potbellied cops and Tatya dropped on their knees.

"Raise your hands," ordered Pandu.

The men obeyed. Pandu walked up to Tatya and kicked him in the stomach.

"Ouch!" screamed Tatya, hunching over and grabbing his stomach.

Pandu kicked him again.

"Ouch! Don't hit!" pleaded Tatya, falling on the ground and then curling his body.

Pandu put his foot on Tatya's neck and pressed it.

"Ouch! Don't," gasped Tatya; his eyes reddened and he squirmed for breath.

"Damn you thug!" shouted Pandu, pressing him hard. "Bloodsucking leech!" fumed Pandu.

"Huh, huh, huh," Tatya wriggled for breath.

"How do you feel? Good, eh," Pandu teased, shifting his gaze to the cops. "I can see your army of Gangsters and hired thugs, who help you rape helpless women and grab land," he alleged, spitting on Tatya, "thu!" He released his foot.

Tatya gulped the air hungrily, blinked and folded his hands. "Leave me, please. I'll give you what you ask for," he offered, begging for mercy, with tears in his eyes. He looked terrified.

"Damn your money! Thu!" Pandu raged, spitting on Tatya. The mention of money maddened him; a sense of vengeance gripped him; his eyes flashed and he looked at the cops. "It's always the money that you splash to get away from the law and cops like these oblige," ranted Pandu. He stiffened his face, gnashed his teeth and moved his gun about. "How much did he offer you thugs to cover up the deaths of Tillya and Sushma?"

The cops wriggled in fear and remained dumbfounded.

Pandu's eyes settled on Kendre; he called to mind what Kendre did and shook violently. "Kendre you piece of shit! I am asking you how much you took. Are you deaf, you swine," howled Pandu.

Kendre wriggled in fear; his voice choked and he sweated.

Pandu slammed his foot on the ground to vent his seething anger. He looked vulnerable, gnashing his teeth. "Speak up you swine!" screamed Pandu, stashing his finger on the trigger of his gun.

"No, no," Kendre's voice quivered, at the sight of Pandu loosing control. He cracked under pressure and pissed in his pants. "I'm under pressure. You want to go; you go. I will not do anything. I will let you go," he spoke incoherently, as if, he lost his mind and cried.

Bhosale saw him and trembled. "He lost his mind. Let us go, you kill Tatya if you want," he stuttered, with sweat dripping down his forehead.

Pandu lost his patience; his nostrils flared. "He lost his mind, eh. Then let him die!" he retorted, firing at Kendre. "Bang!" exploded the gun, tearing the silence of the night. The bullet raced through Kendre's forehead, and he crashed on the ground, with his eyes wide open.

The cops squirmed with fear. Kulkarni went dizzy at the sight; his vision blurred, head reeled and he collapsed on the ground.

Pandu pointed his gun at Kulkarni and fired. "Bang," the bullet ripped Kulkarni's chest; he lay still. "Bastards on the payroll of this swine!" ranted Pandu, kicking Tatya in the ribs.

"Ouch!" squeaked Tatya.

"Come here," Pandu ordered Bhosale.

Bhosale wrinkled his face and cried. "Spare me, please," he begged, prostrating with folded hands on the ground. "Please, please, spare me," he insisted.

"Come here or I'll shoot," Pandu reiterated.

"No, no. I'll come," Bhosale's voice quivered; he hauled himself and crawled up to Pandu.

Pandu put the gun to his forehead.

"I swear I didn't see a thing," Bhosale entreated, trembling with fear; his face soaked in sweat.

"Liar!" remarked Pandu.

"I will not tell anyone," Bhosale cried.

Pandu pulled the trigger. "Bang," the bullet sliced through Bhosale's forehead. The blood spluttered and splashed on Pandu's face. He grabbed the ends of his blanket and wiped his face. "Thu! Filthy scums!" he spat in disgust.

Pandu looked down on Tatya, who lay curled on the ground, with his head buried in his palms. He quivered like a sick man, suffering from fever. Pandu stashed his foot on Tatya's arm. "Get up, you coward," he demanded.

Tatya continued to squirm in fear. He appeared too terrified to look up.

"Get up or I'll shoot!" warned Pandu.

Tatya wept with fear. He pushed himself up slowly; his body aching from the blows he suffered.

"Don't kill me, please," his voice trembled, while he stood on his knees.

Pandu kicked Tatya in his crotches.

"Ouch," Tatya squirmed in agony; his eyes almost popped out of the sockets, and he felt his head burst. He tumbled over and reeled in agony.

"How does it feel to rape?" Pandu asked with contempt and then sat on his hams.

Tatya screamed and wriggled on the ground. Pandu shoved the barrel of the gun in Tatya's mouth. Tatya cringed, gasping for breath. He folded his hands and begged for mercy. Pandu looked him in the eyes and beamed at the sight. "Die!" he mocked Tatya, pulling the trigger. "Bang!"

"Long live the revolution!" Pandu shouted, brandishing his gun and jumping to his feet. He raced towards Vasu.

"Vasu, Vasu," he called out as he ran. He reached Vasu, who lay on one side on the ground, as if unconscious. Pandu hunched over, and then shook Vasu's shoulder. "Get up!" he said to Vasu.

Vasu dropped on his back, with his eyes shut. Pandu's face dropped at the sight. He shook him again, but Vasu failed to respond. Pandu's heart missed a beat; he trembled as he examined Vasu's pulse. Pandu slammed his eyes shut, looked up with a scrunched face and shook his head. He opened his eyes, crashed on his butt and wept. "Forgive me," Pandu clasped his hands, begging forgiveness.

He sat next to Vasu for a few minutes in remorse and recalled the last time he met Vasu. He looked at the empty cotton field; his heart melted. "My cotton will see me through. Wait and watch," he remembered Vasu's last words to him, when Vasu channeled water to the crops.

Pandu cried as the words came back and tugged his heart. "Cotton killed Vasu! Bloody Sahukar!" he concluded in his mind. He stared at the empty field, and remembered the days, when he toiled the land with hope and fervour. He watched the neem tree and pondered over the fond memories it brought back to mind. "Family lunches, gossip, arguments and love," he recollected, and then smiled. His eyes fell on the sugarcane plot; his smile vanished; he frowned and felt his anger returning. "He forced me out of my land, village, family and home. It started there," he fumed, breathing heavily. "It must end!" he shouted out in anger. "He will not let my family live. What will happen to them?" he questioned, ruminating; a fear creeped into his mind. He stood up in rage and then charged towards Ramwadi. Later, that night gunshots rattled the silence, hovering over Ramwadi.

In the morning, when the village awoke the people found two bodies, lying in a pool of blood. Ramwadi had changed.